"*To Catch a Coronet* by Grace Hitchcock is ous novel has it all: sparkling dialogue, a chant for baking, and a dreamy hero who l I loved it and highly recommend it!"
—Colleen Coble, *USA Today* best-selling author of *Fragile Designs*

"A fast-paced tale that sees a privateer and lady baker engage in all manner of Regency exploits as they attempt to unmask a Napoleonic spy. This sweet confection is sure to appeal!"
—Carolyn Miller, award-winning author of the Regency Brides and Regency Wallflowers series

"What a fun story that's filled with sweet romance and tinged with adventure. An unexpected heroine and a dashing hero take the strangers-to-friends-to-more trope in a delightful direction, complete with some near-death experiences, friendly banter, embarrassing escapades, and a teensy bit of piracy . . . of the heart and otherwise. A romantic romp for Regency and historical romance readers alike."
—Pepper Basham, award-winning author of *Authentically, Izzy* and the Freddie & Grace Mysteries

"An endearingly unorthodox heroine and a dashingly secretive hero provide the perfect recipe for a delicious romance seasoned with smart wit, swoony kisses, and surprising twists. Muriel and Erik had my heart and my allegiance from their adorable meet-cute to the sweet epilogue—and all the intrigue in between. Grace Hitchcock's first foray into the Regency era is a smashing success, and I look forward to what the rest of the series has to offer!"
—Carrie Schmidt, ReadingIsMySuperPower.org

"With ingredients of charm, romance, danger, and her signature humor, Grace Hitchcock has baked up a delectable treat with her debut Regency novel. Long-time Regency fans will devour this fresh take on ballroom romance as eagerly as Captain Draycott did Muriel's creations. Picking this up won't add to your waistline, but it will leave you pleasantly satisfied and craving the next Hitchcock Regency romance."
—Crystal Caudill, Carol Award finalist and author of *Counterfeit Love*

Best Laid Plans
To Catch a Coronet
To Kiss a Knight
To Win a Wager

A NOVEL OF BEST LAID PLANS
— ONE —

To CATCH a CORONET

GRACE HITCHCOCK

KREGEL
PUBLICATIONS

To Catch a Coronet
© 2024 by Grace Hitchcock

Published by Kregel Publications, a division of Kregel Inc., 2450 Oak Industrial Dr. NE, Grand Rapids, MI 49505. www.kregel.com.

Grace Hitchcock is represented by and *To Catch a Coronet* is published in association with The Steve Laube Agency, LLC www.stevelaube.com.

The persons and events portrayed in this work are the creations of the author, and any resemblance to persons living or dead is purely coincidental.

Scripture quotations are from the King James Version.

Cover design by Faceout Studio.

Library of Congress Cataloging-in-Publication Data
Name: Hitchcock, Grace, author.
Title: To catch a coronet / Grace Hitchcock.
Description: First edition. | Grand Rapids, MI: Kregel Publications, 2024. | Series: Best Laid Plans; book 1
Identifiers: LCCN 2023043381 (print) | LCCN 2023043382 (ebook)
Subjects: LCGFT: Christian fiction. | Novels.
Classification: LCC PS3608.I834 T6 2024 (print) | LCC PS3608.I834 (ebook) | DDC 813/.6—dc23/eng/20231004
LC record available at https://lccn.loc.gov/2023043381
LC ebook record available at https://lccn.loc.gov/2023043382

ISBN 978-0-8254-4809-6, print
ISBN 978-0-8254-7086-8, epub
ISBN 978-0-8254-6987-9, Kindle

Printed in the United States of America
24 25 26 27 28 29 30 31 32 33 / 5 4 3 2 1

For Charlie, Sammy, and Eli.
Having a sister who writes romance is a dangerous thing—
a dedication to you was bound to happen. Love you!

Bless the Lord, O my soul: and all that is within me,
bless his holy name. . . .
Who redeemeth thy life from destruction; who crowneth
thee with lovingkindness and tender mercies.
PSALM 103:1, 4

Chapter One

Chilham, April 1813

"Tonight is the night!" Muriel Beau held up the gold band, admiring the ring in the flickering candelabras of the powder room just off the assembly hall's ballroom. The piece was simple, but her dear Baron Deverell would appreciate that she had chosen to present him with her family's one and only heirloom. He would treasure it as much as she had.

"Muriel, this is mad—even for you. You cannot seriously be considering going through with this?" Vivienne Poppy pressed a gloved hand on either side of the threshold to block the doorway that led to Muriel's happily ever after.

Muriel slipped her father's ring onto her gloved thumb. "After having two fiancés arranged for me by my well-meaning parents, each of whom I unfortunately had to release from his promise due to our lack of affection for one another, among other things, I finally have the courage I need to rise to the occasion. I will have no more of this endless cycle of waiting and hoping, followed by nearly unbearable disappointment."

Vivienne sagged against the doorframe. "I know you were disheartened in your previous matches—"

"Disheartened? One gentleman was in love with another lady, and I overheard the other tell his friends he was embarrassed to have me by his side, but my dowry was so significant that he would overlook his discomfiture. So, yes, I'd say I was disappointed, at the least." As always,

Muriel shielded herself from the memories and instead focused on the ring and all the joy it promised.

"I know, but please stop and think. Even though you were not born into your position, you know as well as I that this is not how it is done in polite society. What if Baron Deverell rejects your proposal? What then? How will you salvage your pride? Your reputation?"

Muriel twirled in the mottled looking glass, admiring her empire-waist gown that complimented her petite and full figure, pausing only to adjust her short pink slashed sleeves with their tufts of white crepe and silver bands. "He won't. My Deverell hasn't spoken of marriage yet because he is only wishing to make certain of my feelings, what with me practically jilting two of his acquaintances. What man would want to propose to a woman who might cry off the wedding? Well, I *am* certain about him, and Baron Osmund Deverell will know my true feelings before this evening's end."

Vivienne pinched the bridge of her nose and closed her eyes. "Which are?"

"That I love him, and I would *never* jilt him. We are meant to be together, and it is time I take control of my future and cease this ever-pressing need to please the beast that is society." Her pulse raced with the awareness that all the dreams she had long held dear—of being loved and accepted by a handsome gentleman despite her rough tendencies—were only a proposal away if only she had the courage to act.

Vivienne released a weighted sigh and grasped Muriel's hand in her own. "While I appreciate your quoting my own novel to me, it does not mean I agree with you in this instance. This is not one of my works of fiction, wherein grand gestures always result in a favorable outcome. If you *must* ask the baron to marry you, at least ask him in private. If it is a chaperone you are needing, I humbly offer my services in place of the ballroom full of witnesses."

She threw her arms around her dear friend, giggling. "Cease your worrying. He won't reject me! And a departure from the rules requires a grand gesture for all to accept it. Trust me, Vivienne, this will be so romantic, you'll be writing your next novel based on our love story."

Vivienne groaned and stepped aside. "I certainly hope so and pray the baron answers favorably, for your sake as well as your family's."

"If I wasn't certain of his affections, I would not ask." Muriel twisted the ring around her thumb, her heart hammering. Good thing she was wearing gloves. Her hands were sweating profusely. But she supposed any lady would be perspiring when the gentleman of her dreams was about to kiss her for the first time. In all these months of courting, she thought Baron Deverell would at least *attempt* to kiss her cheek. Well, after the romantic proposal she had planned for tonight, he would be so moved and convinced of her affections he would no longer be so reserved. He would kiss her in front of all, effectively silencing the disapproving society matrons with his devotion.

She swept into the assembly ballroom that smelled heavily of tallow candles that alighted the wall sconces and wooden chandelier overhead. Baron Deverell was not difficult to find among the milling crowd, all dressed in their finest evening wear, with his broad shoulders clothed in the latest of London's fashions and his shock of golden curls that never could be trained into a pompadour. She rested her hand over her chest at the sight of him, this gentleman who was about to be *her* dear Baron Deverell. She wove through the crowded room, laughing as she was jostled by the merrymaking. She could hardly wait to claim her promised Scottish reel with him and sweep him away from that horridly lovely raven-haired Miss Fox, who seemed to be ever near these days. If Muriel weren't so certain of his partiality for caramel locks and chocolate eyes, she would have been tempted to give in to her jealousy. But soon she would never have need to fear any other woman attempting to abscond with his hand. She waited for his easy smile to spread at the sight of her and was rewarded with a flash of the darling set of dimples that proclaimed his echoed delight.

"Miss Beau, is it already time for our dance?" His rich, cultured timbre enveloped her as he extended his hand, nodded to Miss Fox, and led Muriel onto the parquet dance floor.

The music swelled and she whirled to and fro, admiring his performance of the reel and basking in the fact that he was about to promise himself to her forever. When their hands met once more under the center chandelier surrounded by the fresco of two lovers encircled by cherubs, lending to the romance of it all, Muriel tugged him to a halt while the other couples continued to swirl about them in perfect time. His eyes widened, and he at once attempted to recommence the reel with her. She shook her head, beaming up at him, confidence brimming. "Baron Deverell, I—"

"Miss Beau? Are you ill?" He moved to assist her from the parquet dance floor, his cheeks reddening as the whirling and thudding of feet about them lessened and the chamber orchestra came to a grating cessation. "Is it your ankle again?"

His heightened color gave her pause, and in that moment she realized he might not appreciate such a public display of affection. But she was committed now, as all were staring at them, some even subtly pointing, most likely thinking she had stumbled and missed a step and yet again upset a perfectly good reel. Before she dwelt more on what she was about to do, Muriel grasped his hand, holding it firmly, though he was making it difficult with his unrelenting tugging. She gripped it more securely and sank onto one knee, mindful to keep her hem over her ankles. "Baron Deverell, from the first moment I beheld you across the room of my parents' parlor last Christmas, I knew you were the only one for me."

Murmurs filled the ballroom, the fluttering fans ceasing their wafting as even the merchant gentlemen's rumbustious merriment fell silent. She smiled to the crowd encircling them as he tugged again. He was causing this to be far less romantic. "Everyone in this room well knows of my decision not to marry until I have found love. Well, I am proud to say my heart has indeed been taken." Muriel lifted the precious ring from her thumb. "It has been taken by you. Baron Deverell, will you do me the great honor of marrying me?"

He blinked at her for several moments, his silence roaring in her ears, but she kept her gaze fixed on him and stayed her nerves, waiting for the rest of her life to begin.

Baron Deverell clutched her by the elbows and forcibly lifted her to her feet. "Miss Beau, whatever do you think you are doing?" he hissed into her ear. Smiling and nodding to the other guests, he fled with her toward the rear of the room and the doors that led to the stairs.

Her reply wilted in her throat, along with her hope. She pressed the heel of her hand over her heart, kneading at the knot of pain there. She attempted not to grimace as her gaze darted about the room, confirming the sneers were all too real as gossip spread, the matrons condemning her for her rash act, the maidens staring openly. Miss Fox cast her a piteous frown as, heaven help her, Elena Whelan elbowed through the crowd, the songbird of Kent already wearing a smug smile at Muriel's mortification. An involuntary whimper slipped past her lips, eliciting laughter from Elena, whose dowdy companion scowled and elbowed her into silence, offering Muriel a smile drenched in sympathy.

Had she come this far only to fail? *He must not have heard me in all the commotion.* She cringed. Even in her crazed state, she could see that reasoning was weak, as it would mean everyone in the room understood her meaning while Baron Deverell somehow did not. She dug her heels down, preventing him from fleeing, and again lifted the ring to him. "Baron Deverell—Osmund—will you marry me?"

He grunted, released her, and pushed the door open, motioning for her to go through. This time, she complied and preceded him on the stairs as the chatter began to rise. The ground floor, while less populated than the ballroom, unfortunately still held an audience of those wishing to escape the heat of many bodies in one hall. Vivienne had been right. Even if Baron Deverell was about to agree to marry her, the proposal had been an unmitigated disaster. "Say something, Osmund."

"Confound it." Baron Deverell raked his fingers through his hair, sighing. "*Miss Beau.* Why on earth did you think I'd say yes to such an unprecedented proposal?"

"You mean besides your courting me? I thought you'd think it was romantic." Her account sounded pathetic to her own ears.

"Calling—not courting." He corrected as a couple filed down the stairs. He guided her into the sitting room and to a vacant corner, where he paused beside an open window, whispering, "I was going to tell you tonight I have already decided to end our time together and *court* Miss Fox."

"Miss Fox." She gasped, her stomach tightening. "You were calling on Miss Fox too? Even though you have been court—calling on me since Christmas?" She corrected herself, the drastically less romantic word catching in her throat. The room seemed to close in, squeezing the air from her lungs, as it spun in her vision. She flapped her hand at her scooped neckline, attempting to cool her flushed cheeks, but her darling Calypso turban allowed for precious little draft. "And what about our weekly drives to and from Dover?"

"To be fair, I was calling on your stepfather in the beginning in an attempt to sell Mr. Fletcher my tea selections for his stores across England. And you were acting as your father's emissary for personally inspecting my tea warehouse, as he was feeling under the weather on those occasions."

Of course, it had started as her acting as emissary. But what of the trip to his late grandmother's cottage in Dover to ask Muriel's opinion on whether he should sell the newly inherited property? Wasn't that a hint of his wish to marry her? To show her that he could put a roof over her head? Well, that *was* before she'd learned of his holdings in London and his family's estate in the country, but it was difficult *not* to read into his asking her opinion. She lifted a single brow. "You spoke of courtship only last month."

"Once and very briefly. I apologize you had to find out this way. I had to diversify the risk." He pressed his lips into a thin line, crossing his arms over his broad chest and leaning down to her to add, "After all, you said it yourself. You have jilted two others. I did not wish to be the third and ruin my chances of happiness this season, which is why I began to see Miss Fox. And I must say, after two weeks at her side—"

"*Two* weeks?" Her voice squeaked in her attempt to keep her mien clear of tears. *A gentleman of honor would never do such a thing as court multiple women . . . unless there is some sort of rule I missed in that etiquette book I skimmed.* Even after being adopted into society upon her mother's marriage to a well-born investor, Muriel still found herself lost in this world of stolen moments and veiled meanings, so different from their cozy bakery, where all she'd had to worry about was having enough sticky buns for the morning orders and bread to last the day. But, even so, surely a gentleman did not call upon two ladies at the same time? "How could you call on us both for two weeks?"

He shrugged, picking at the window frame and creating a mar in the paint where there hadn't been any before. She resisted the urge to ask him to cease.

"How could I not, Miss Beau? You have been distant for a fortnight. I thought you were about to release me."

"I was not being distant. I was planning tonight, trying to make it special for you." Those blasted tears cracked her voice, betraying her confidence. Her fingers sought the comfort of her father's ring, twisting it again and again, until it warmed her thumb.

Sympathy flashed through his hazel eyes as he ran his hand down her elbow to her wrist. He wrapped her gloved fingers between his strong hands, calloused from years aboard his merchant ship. "My dear Miss Beau, while I am flattered to be the first man in society to receive such a public proposal from a lady, I'm afraid I have already informed Miss Fox of my intentions, and it would be impossible to retrench now, even after your beguiling declaration. I will treasure tonight, even if I am unable to provide you the answer you desire."

Impossible? No, he was only being kind as he always was in saying so. She swayed, pressing her hand to her cheek.

"Miss Beau?" He grasped her by the sleeves, crushing her sweet new gown of pink and white that had given her a bridal air.

Against her will, her face smashed against his crisp waistcoat, his cologne filling her senses, making her heart sore and limbs weak, which caused Baron Deverell's solid arms to encompass her. If she closed her eyes, she could still envision the dream she had longed for, where Baron Deverell accepted her hand, kissed her in front of all, and swept her away to his family estate to wed her. She felt her lips pucker and her chin lift. She was at once shifted in his arms.

"As tempting as it may be to kiss you, I have no right now, Miss Beau," he whispered, slowly putting her at arm's length even as he kept a firm hold on her waist to keep her upright.

"Oh no." Vivienne's voice broke through the haze, drawing Muriel back to the ghastly present to find her two dearest friends weaving through the curious onlookers to their side.

"Thank you for your assistance, Baron Deverell. I shall attend to her now." Tess Hale's arm wrapped about Muriel's waist and pulled her into the safe circle of her closest friends.

"I—I must excuse myself to explain things to Miss Fox." Baron Deverell bowed to them, his gaze meeting hers one last time. "I hope you realize I am truly sorry for the embarrassment I've caused you tonight, and should I hear anything less than the best of things being spoken about you—" He fiddled at the knot of his silk neckcloth and swallowed. "I apologize most profusely."

"Thank you. Please attend to Miss Fox. I am well," Muriel managed to squeeze out, along with a smile to demonstrate to him that she was not at all crushed, though she felt her chin tremble, which spoiled the attempt to appear strong. From his pained expression, she knew that he knew that she was not at all fine.

The room began to spin again. *Please, Lord, my humiliation knows no end tonight. Do not let me faint too.* Her friends each gripped an elbow and steered her through the crowd and straight out the door, the chilling air making it difficult to draw a full breath. They ducked against the assembly hall's stone wall to keep from being spotted by the late-night pedestrians about the lane who had not secured a ticket for this evening's ball, craning their necks to get a better look at what was occurring in the ballroom on the second level. Muriel chanced a stride away from the wall to glance to a floor-length window above them and groaned when she found it was positively buzzing with partygoers. At one woman's frantic gesticulation with her fan, the entire room seemed to turn as one to the windows facing the torch-lit lane, peering at her, Vivienne, and Tess out of doors, effectively confirming all rumors that she, Muriel Beau, had been rejected.

Muriel pressed a hand to her mouth. Her accounts would not be long in making their appearance. Fully roused, she cried, "We've got to move!" She tugged her friends down the lane a couple of houses, halting only when they were safely out of sight of the ballroom.

"W–we need to fetch our cloaks." Vivienne shivered as mist dusted their turbans and shoulders. "My stepbrother would not approve of us being out of doors without him—"

"Her reputation is already damaged, so what is one more departure from society this night? Besides, we both know she'd rather be soaked and frostbitten than go back." Tess's cold fingers dug into the gaps of Muriel's stays as she rubbed her other hand up and down Muriel's already-crushed sleeve. All three of them shivered in their thin gowns. Tess nodded to the row of carriages lining the street in front of the assembly hall. "Since Muriel and I arrived on foot, we need to hail the hackney coach."

Vivienne broke away and secured the only hackney in the village, waving the coachman forward. Numbly, Muriel settled into the worn coach with her friends on either side as they tucked her under the hack's musty navy blanket. She turned her nose into her sleeve, fighting a gag from the blanket and was instead greeted with Baron Deverell's enchanting cologne. Her eyes stung.

Such a harsh awakening from the spell he had cast over her. Had he ever cared for her? Or was he like all the others, merely attracted to the prospect of her stepfather's business, connections, and substantial dowry to bestow on his only daughter? *But Miss Fox's dowry is several thousand less than mine.* In her heart, she knew the true reason why Miss Fox was preferable over her. Everyone did. She rubbed her temples and groaned. "Why did you let me propose marriage to him in front of everyone?" She rested her head on Vivienne's shoulder and focused on her familiar scent of lavender instead of the baron's cologne to keep the tears in check.

Tess rubbed her hands, leaning into Muriel for warmth, her red curls trembling from her suppressed shivers. "From what Vivienne says, you were determined, and we all know how you are when you set your mind on something."

"I couldn't have stopped her even if I were wielding a mace and a box of pastries from Gunter's." Vivienne crossed her arms and lifted a brow to Muriel as if waiting for an apology.

She ignored their retorts, knowing they were right. This situation had been entirely her idea. She was the one who had ignored sage counsel and run straight into a scandal that would live beyond her years. Ton mothers across the country would point to her as an example of what not to do, trotting out Muriel's shame every time their high-born daughters dared to bend polite society's ridged rules, warning all debutantes of the consequences of departing from the safe arms of etiquette, no matter how romantic it might seem at the time. "Where are we going, anyway?" she murmured, partly to distract them.

"Fletcher Manor. And along the way we will figure out what to do before your parents hear of the news," Vivienne replied, relaxing her posture once more and batting the trio of overlarge egret feathers adorning her headpiece out of her eyes.

"Do?" Muriel snorted, knotting the worn fringe of the blanket. "There is nothing to do now. There is nothing left for me here."

"That is a touch dramatic." Tess looked like she was about to roll her eyes before she recalled the gravity of the situation and instead ran her finger under her lower lashes to disguise her misstep.

Muriel buried her face in her hands. "I am never going to be able to show my face in polite society again."

"Well, that much is true." Tess tugged the blanket to cover her legs. "By morning, everyone will have read about it in the papers across the county."

Vivienne leaned across Muriel and batted Tess's knee. "Not helpful, Tess."

Muriel fought to straighten her shoulders. She was stronger and more resilient than most wallflowers from her years as a baker's daughter keeping early and long hours, but this humiliation scorched her far worse than any mishaps with the oven. "I must keep running is all. How far do you think the coachman is willing to take me?"

"In this ancient hackney? We'll be fortunate to make it to your stepfather's estate before the wheels fall off. Besides, your family and whole life are here." Tess tapped her bottom lip with her forefinger. "We simply must find something so wonderful for you to accomplish that it covers tonight's scandal once and for all, allowing you to re-claim your place in the elite set."

Muriel kneaded her fist over the knot in her stomach. "The only way that will happen is if I make an advantageous match, which I never will now, as I have isolated myself from every eligible gentleman in Chil-ham through my rash behavior."

Vivienne gasped, clapping her hands. "That's it!"

"What's it? Do you have a gentleman hidden in some country estate we don't know about and who would not have heard about tonight's events?" Tess teased.

"Of course not. I overheard Mrs. Gordon tonight, talking about her plans for her daughter."

"Her three-year-old?" Muriel lifted her brows. "I do not see how that could possibly help me, unless you think I should become a gov-erness."

Vivienne waved her off. "She was speaking of the future, of course. Mrs. Gordon said that she wants more for her daughter—"

"She is from one of the wealthiest families in the county," Tess inter-jected. "What could her little darling possibly obtain that she doesn't already possess?"

Vivienne waggled her brows. "What is the one thing the Gordons cannot achieve in Chilham society?"

Muriel's eyes widened, hope flooding her being. "A title," she breathed. "Mrs. Gordon wishes for her daughter to eclipse the gentry and become part of the aristocracy."

"That's brilliant, Vivienne." Tess clapped. "And with her vast dowry, Muriel should have her pick of suitors . . . as long as her past stays in Chilham. But, if she makes haste, she may have a proposal from a destitute London lord before the gossips do their worst."

Vivienne dipped her head in a bow, her wiry golden curls bobbing. "And there you have it. The perfect means of getting you out of this little predicament—marry an English nobleman and all will be forgotten."

With this plan on her heart, she had the hackney drop her at her family's manor and, without speaking to anyone, rushed upstairs to her chambers on the second floor and rang for her fleet of trunks to be lined along her bedroom wall. Yanking off a glove, she paused to slide off her father's wedding band before removing the other. She swallowed back the pain of rejection. While it was not customary for men to wear wedding bands, her first memories of her father had been his large, calloused hand wrapping around hers, the gold ring on his little finger flashing in the morning light on their walks to the bakery.

She swiped away her tears and returned the ring to its place on a simple gold necklace that she always had about her neck. While Mr. Fletcher had welcomed Muriel into his home upon his marriage to Mother and even invited her to call him Father, she knew she was a burden to him. A cherished burden, perhaps, but still a burden. One day, she hoped to have that feeling of complete belonging again. After tonight, she doubted it would be possible in Chilham.

Setting her jaw, she began pulling her gowns from the closet and laying them on her bed. She had just removed a third gown to pack when her mother's lady's maid appeared to summon her to her mother's chambers.

"And Miss Muriel," Mrs. Lyon whispered, clasping her hands before her pristine black uniform as they made haste down the long burgundy rug of the second-floor hall, the floors of the ancient hall creaking underfoot, "I must warn you that a note arrived a moment before she sent me to fetch you."

They know. Anger flared toward the yet-to-be-named busybody who deemed it necessary to bear tales to her mother and stepfather. "Thank you for the forewarning, Mrs. Lyon." Muriel placed her hand on the doorknob, drew a bracing breath, and stepped into her mother's cozy private parlor with the fireplace flickering along with the candelabras and gold sconces.

"Oh Muriel," her mother whispered from the chaise lounge in the bow window, burying her face into her infant's dark hair, inhaling his sweet scent as if to calm herself. "Whatever were you thinking?"

Her stepfather shook his head, his hand resting on Mother's shoulders. His height and portly stomach seemed out of place against the delicate pink walls of her mother's bedroom and parlor. "The Widow Whelan has penned us the most dreadful account, but I am certain she did not present the most accurate view. Would you care to explain what happened, dear?"

Perhaps she should hold little Declan and take a sniff of his fluffy hair herself to calm her racing heart. But, with the full story yet to be disclosed, Mother would need him. She straightened her shoulders and launched into her horrid tale while her stepfather paced the length of the parlor to the bedroom threshold and back, his hands folded behind him. Muriel at last collapsed onto the foot of the chaise lounge beside her mother and drew the baby into her arms, snuggling him close. The steady rise and fall of his tummy soothed her, his sweet, perfectly round cheeks making it impossible not to press a gentle kiss on them.

Muriel's stepfather paused at the coffee tray before the fireplace, pouring himself a cup before answering. "A title is a lofty goal . . . though not a wholly unattainable one. I believe you may be correct that the only means of repair is to outstride society's expectations for your status. As you know, my old schoolmate Sir Alexander Ingram and his wife have a residence in London—though I believe in Sir Alexander's most recent letter, he mentioned his wife's traveling to see a sick distant relative. If she has returned, I am certain they would be delighted to act as your chaperone, as they have no daughters of their own to usher into society."

Relieved, Muriel nodded. As usual, her stepfather had understood her desires perfectly and sought to meet her needs as he would his own children's. "Excellent. I was hoping you could contact them. You've spoken so fondly of the captain and his wife over the years that I knew they would be my best option if I were to attempt this rather dramatic move."

Mother's lips trembled. "But, if you marry a lord, you will leave us—not just this house, but this county."

Father grasped Mother's hand in his. "Which is the worst of it. We would be loath to part from you, Muriel, especially your little brothers. But, if we agree to this plan and it ends with a marriage, you must promise to visit your mother and our family every Christmas and we to visit you in the summers." He swallowed, emotion clouding his words. "The pain of your absence would be too much to bear otherwise, my sweet daughter, and because of that, I plead with you to choose wisely. Do not allow a title to mar your judgment in the man's character, which should be far superior to his title if a marriage is to work."

She would miss her parents and her three sweet brothers dearly, but what other choice did she have? She looked to little Declan, with his darling full lips parted in sleep, his warm breath against her cheek filling her heart with longing. If she were to have any hope for children of her own one day, she needed to leave her small village to meet her husband. "If I can find a gentleman half as kind as you, Father, I will be rich indeed. And you all know I would come home often even without a promise to do so."

Mother dabbed at her eyes with her lace cuff. "Then we will do our best to support you in your undertaking and have a new wardrobe made up to greet you at the Ingrams' residence. Our girl shall only be seen in the best."

Muriel grinned with more daring than she possessed. "Let the hunt for an English lord commence."

Chapter Two

London

MURIEL HAD TWO MONTHS TO find an English lord before Parliament recessed along with the season, and after her first morning's extensive calling with Lady Ingram, she had already committed more faux pas than she could count. Apparently, for every rule she didn't know in Kent society, there were two more to take its place in London.

It had taken an agonizing two weeks to arrange her travel from Chilham to London what with securing an invitation from the Ingrams and having a fleet of new dresses ordered and altered. During that time, the village had treated her as a pariah. The censure against her had grown so palpable she even deemed it necessary to neglect Sunday service, after which the vicar called upon her to offer her his advice and pass her a sealed letter. He said it contained a psalm he thought she would find useful. But, in truth, she had been so mortified by his calling to offer advice she scarcely recalled what he had said and had tucked the note away in her reticule to avoid being reminded of the encounter and her lack of decorum.

But after the last residence where Muriel had accidentally dropped an iced sponge on the settee, her shortcomings were growing more and more evident despite Lady Ingram's assurance that Muriel's vast dowry would go a long way in smoothing out any inadequacies. Even so, as there was no time to prepare before the marquess's dinner party tonight, where the Prince Regent would be in attendance, she was beginning to wonder if she had sprung out of the baking tin and into the oven with her scheme for redemption.

Muriel ran the soles of her shoes over the decorative foot scraper in the recess by the Ingrams' front door in Grosvenor Square and followed the elegant Lady Ingram into their opulent yet cozy London house. Fighting against the urge to slouch against the closed door at her overwhelming failure, Muriel surrendered her bonnet to the Ingrams' butler, Clayton, mortified after the events of the morning and exhausted at the prospect of the chase before her.

"I know this morning was rather difficult for you, my dear." Lady Ingram patted Muriel on the arm, her gray eyes sympathetic as she paused in the foyer. She whispered something to the butler before turning to Muriel. "Why don't you find your way to the kitchen and bake us something delightful? Clayton is having the staff vacate it now. Your father mentioned it always calms you, and I've already forewarned the staff to accommodate you. We can discuss circulating amongst the nobility more in depth after tonight. I want to see you in action before I attempt to help mold you."

Hadn't her mishaps today been evidence enough that Muriel desperately needed instruction? But she smiled her thanks to her hostess and started for the kitchen. She crossed through the grand dining room to the impressive courtyard gardens, lingering on the gravel path through the luscious flower garden that led to the detached kitchen. She plucked a blossom and inhaled, closing her eyes against all distractions. *Lord, you know the desires of my heart. I've waited so long for a family of my own—for a gentleman who saw beyond my lack of rank. How much longer do I need to wait?* Her stomach rumbled. She needed to bake. Perhaps she would hear the Lord amidst flour, sugar, and yeast.

She tucked the flower into her coiffure and tentatively opened the door only to find that the cook and staff had already quit the area, leaving their preparations for the next meal on the corner of the far counter and the cast iron open range hot for her use. Humming, she tied on the clean apron she found laid out for her on the long pine table that was scrubbed pale from years of use, the scarring in the wood sanded down but still visible. Measuring, sifting, mixing, and rolling, she sorted through her mistakes and brought them to the Lord, hoping for a solution to save her reputation in London before she had truly even begun her search for her titled lord at tonight's grand ball.

By the time her apple pie was ready to come out of the oven and her second batch of vanilla scones was ready to go in, she had a comforting sheen of sweat on her brow and her prayers had turned into singing—or rather bellowing—her favorite hymns. Wiping her hands on her apron, she worked out a recipe that she thought would be a match for the sponge she had tasted and promptly dropped during her calls this morning. She rose on her tiptoes to reach the tin marked Flour on the third shelf in the dry larder, which was acceptable if one was of an average height, but Muriel, being only an inch over five feet, could only scrape the bottom of the ten-pound tin with her fingertips. She snatched her wooden rolling pin from the table and used the tip to scoot the tin to the edge of the shelf, intending to catch it as it fell.

A man's large, calloused hand shot above her head and seized the tin. "Allow me to assist you."

Her song strangled itself in a gasp. Whirling, she rammed into his arm, causing the tin to slip from his grasp and the heavy pin from her hand. Both knocked him on the head, loosening the lid and showering them with flour as he fell to his knees with a grunt and then collapsed face flat onto the brick pavers.

"Lord, have mercy." Muriel clutched her hand to her throat and sank to her knees beside the crumpled giant. Grabbing his muscular right shoulder with all her strength, she flipped the man onto his back and saw at once that his left arm was in a sling. His large, Grecian nose trickled blood from his fall to the bricks. Other than that and the lump already forming just below his thick chocolate hairline, he was in marvelous physical condition. With his impeccable jawline and the sun-kissed skin that she glimpsed beneath the flour, she knew he had enjoyed fine health before waltzing into her kitchen. She leapt to her feet and ran for the pitcher of water on the counter. Pitcher wrapped in her arm, she dipped her fingers inside and flicked water onto his flour-covered face as if he were a pie crust, continuing the practice until a fine paste had formed on his forehead and a moan escaped his full lips.

"Oh, thank God. I haven't killed him," she whispered, sinking onto her heels and wiping her forehead, feeling the grit of flour roll across her skin. She leaned over him, her dark hair spilling free from her coiffure over her shoulder, flowing down to his chest. "Sir? Are you hurt badly? Sir? Can you hear me?"

As he was once again lying too still for comfort, she dared to rest her hand gently on his chest, feeling beneath his waistcoat hardened muscles that spoke of years of hard labor. She patted the magnificent man's cheek with her left hand, hoping to wake him. "Sir?"

His strong hand grazed over his brass waistcoat buttons until it rested atop hers, tightening as he coughed from the bits of flour he'd no doubt inhaled. His thick, paste-covered lashes flickered and, focusing on her, his dark eyes widened at the sight of her. He lurched upward, wincing.

She pressed her hand to his chest, forcing him to stay seated. "Sir? Are you hurt?" She repeated.

"Nothing that time won't heal." He ran his finger over the lump with a grunt, his words slurring, "I apologize for alarming you, miss." He motioned to a crate sitting at the open back door. "I was delivering a package for his lordship."

She sank back on her heels. *With an injured arm? He must need the money, and here I've potentially injured him further!* "My apologies, sir. I didn't hear you knock or enter the kitchen . . . or dry larder." Her gaze ran over his coat. Though covered in flour, it was well tailored for a deliveryman who was desperate enough to work through an injury. *Perhaps he has fallen on hard times and has mouths to feed at home?*

"With your singing, I imagine not." His molasses eyes sparkled at her.

Her cheeks warmed at being caught. Hopefully he would think it from the heat of the oven. "So are you going to tell me your name? Or did I knock that directly from your head?"

"Erik." He extended his hand to her, his delicious, deep voice commanding the room, even if it was only her and the baked goods.

He was most certainly a deliveryman. In her brief time in London, she had learned the nobility always expected one to know their titles and would only introduce themselves with the fullest extent of their names. But she would not be snobbish with a man who would have been a match for her only a decade ago by reciting her full name. She accepted his hand, shaking it as she had in the old days and enjoying the freedom of informality. "Pleasure to meet you, Erik. I'm Muriel."

"Ariel? What a lovely name."

"Thank you." She swallowed back the need to correct him. What did it matter? He would only ever see her again on the off chance she was in a baking storm and he was delivering something to the kitchen.

He hoisted himself up and extended his hand to help her stand even as he swayed on his feet.

She scrambled to her feet and wrapped her arms around him at once, steadying him as she craned her neck to assess his coloring. His lips quirked into a surprised half smile at her actions, as if he was not accustomed to females throwing their arms about his waist. Her cheeks heated once again at her forwardness. Even if he was a deliveryman and unavailable, he was still a man and she a supposed lady, and here she was with her arms about him. She pushed him toward a stool alongside the counter where she had been working. "Perhaps you should have a seat? Are you hungry?" Without waiting for an answer, she snatched a vanilla scone with bits of melted chocolate inside and handed it to him.

He nodded his thanks and took a bite, his eyes widening. "This is divine, Miss Ariel. I have not tasted such a delightful treat in months."

"My secret ingredient is soured cream." She couldn't keep herself from querying, "Do you have a gaggle of children? You must take some with you to your family. It's the least I can do. I have a dozen I can spare." She piled the warm scones into a cloth along with a few pastries, tying the corners into a knot and pushing away the old ache of wishing she were baking for her own little ones and husband.

"That is entirely unnecessary, but I can't seem to find a way to say no." Erik grinned and accepted the makeshift sack. "And as I have no family or children, I know I will be feasting on your baking for my dinner."

Oddly pleased with this striking man's lack of a wife and that he enjoyed her baking, she tested the tin that held the apple pie and, satisfied it would not burn him, covered it with a cloth and slid it over to him, making a mental note to replace the items from her pin money. "Please, take the pie as well."

He looked as if he were about to protest, but then he inhaled the delightful aroma of cinnamon and grinned. "I thank you, Miss Ariel, for your kindness."

She smiled up at him—he was still taller than her even while seated—and nodded toward the small crate, partly to get her mind away from his arresting eyes that made her wish to bake a chocolate confection in the same hue. "So, what's inside the crate? It must be important for you to risk your life by entering my kitchen unannounced."

"Well, usually a domestic delivery does not entail such risks." He winked at her, finishing off his scone. "I'm delivering exotic tea. His lordship has quite the taste for it."

"Ah, do you work for a tea merchant?" she interjected as she rested her hip against the counter and crossed her arms, unable to keep herself from attempting to piece together this handsome man's story.

"I'm a sailor, which led to this." He gestured to his arm. "So I am anchored until my arm heals, which hopefully won't take too long, as there is much for me to do at sea."

"I'm so sorry for your injury. You must have been doing something exciting to receive it. I've only sailed the River Thames once when I came here with my parents years ago. I never tossed my accounts once, which the captain said is a trait needed at sea."

His lips parted. "You spoke with the captain about tossing your accounts?"

She checked the clock atop the cook's desk, peeked into the oven, and retrieved the scones, a burst of vanilla filling the air. "It came up because Vivienne, my dearest friend, was ill, and I wished to provide a remedy. I asked the staff to prepare some ginger tea for her. While I waited for them to ready the brew, I snuck to the bowels of the vessel to explore and was found out by none other than the captain—"

He hid his chuckle behind his hand.

"Did I say something diverting? I'm always saying something odd when I get too comfortable around someone," she muttered, raking her fingers down her cheeks and shaking her head. "I suppose I must simply remain uncomfortable for my time here in order not to shame myself."

"Not at all . . . I've simply been aboard a ship for a long while and haven't had such delightful conversation in quite some time."

Her brow lifted at his turn of phrase, which seemed rather polished for the crewmen she had encountered. Perhaps it was his deep voice that made every word seem elegant. His gaze held hers in a most disconcerting manner, as if he found her captivating, and the spark in her belly echoed his interest. *No. No! You had your chance to find any man of any status you desired in the whole county of Kent, and you ruined it. A title or nothing, Muriel Beau.* She dropped her gaze and bent to retrieve the flour tin and save the remaining flour. "Be that as it may, I don't think very many London girls are like me."

He claimed the tin at once and set it on the counter for her. "No, I think not, but I must say again that these scones are the best I've ever had. Where did you train?"

Relieved at the change in topic, she measured away for her sponge and, without telling him of her mother's marriage to a gentleman, spoke to him of her happiest days in her little bakery in the village of Chilham.

The Earl of Draycott held the pie to his chest with his injured hand as he closed the kitchen door behind him and took the side door that led out toward Brook Street, still smiling from the gentle baker's behavior toward him. It had been nice to be seen for a few moments as a fellow servant and not a captain, or an earl—even if it had resulted in a ruined suit and a lump on his forehead. The pretty country baker had made it worth the pain with her attention, the mound of scones, and the tantalizing pie.

Children darted around him from behind, thin and bedraggled, their eyes lingering on the pie in his hands. Though wrapped with a cloth, the sweet aroma wafting out called to all nearby. He sighed. If the pie were half as tasty as it smelled, he would have been in for a treat. He handed it, along with a coin, to the eldest in the group, a scrawny girl of mayhap seven years or so in a gown that was more tatters than fabric. The trio scampered off with whispers of thanks. He grinned at their enthusiasm and for the excuse it lent him to return to Ariel's kitchen all the sooner, under the guise of needing another baked good in compensation for his head wound and bloodied nose.

It had been quite nice to have a pretty girl smile at him without guile or farce. The thought of her bright eyes made him hesitate, though. It was not prudent to flirt with any woman with whom he could not possibly have a future, no matter how excellent a baker she was . . . not with the clause in his uncle's will about his state of matrimony and his need for an heiress to sustain the Draycott estate for future generations. Apparently his prize money from the war against Napoleon was insufficient. Further, he hoped to hire this unusual baker when he at last retired from chasing smugglers and French ships across the high seas, even if it required him to poach her from his old friend and captain, Sir Alexander. No, it would not do to think on the maid beyond her baked goods.

As no hackney would wish him in his coach with the flour coating him, he trotted down to a less populated street toward his London residence in Berkeley Square when a shadow caught his eye. He fought to maintain his easy gait. Ears attuned to the boots clicking a steady pace behind him, he cautiously reached into his coat, wincing against the pull on his shoulder wound. He gripped his gun and, in a single motion, whirled around, planting the barrel of his pistol into the chest of the man. "Why are you following me?"

The man lifted his hands, a knife gripped between his middle fingers. "I don't want no trouble."

"Then you shouldn't have come looking for it. Did Requin send you?"

His gaze clouded. "Don't know no Requin. You gave money to my litter."

"And you wished to thank me with a knife between my shoulder blades and pilfer the remainder of my funds?" Erik challenged, his jaw clenching.

The man's eyes flicked over Erik's shoulder. Keeping his gun trained on the man, Erik risked a glance to ensure it wasn't Requin's man creeping up on him. Two women on the front step of a row house skittered to a halt at the sight of his gun before dashing inside, which gave the pickpocket a chance to bolt. Erik didn't wish to risk firing at a man in the row of houses, where families might exit at any moment. If the man were in Requin's pocket, he would be dealt a far less generous hand for his failure. Likely, though, he was naught but a common thief.

Erik returned his pistol to its holster under his jacket and chastised himself for the close encounter. He paused at the edge of Berkeley Square's gardens, frowning as he gazed up at his building. Though he had not seen the place in the nearly three years since signing his last contract with the crown, he'd sent more than enough funds for his estate's care. Yet not a single curtain was drawn. Thoughts of the pickpocket faded as he trotted to the front door and tapped the wrought iron knocker. He hadn't let the staff know he'd returned, but that was the nature of being wounded. It left little time for warning. Even so, someone should have been at the door to welcome him or anyone who might approach the house. He pulled the bell, the strident ringing sounding through the carved front door.

When no answer came, he patted his pockets, found the skeleton key, and unlocked the door. His jaw slacked at the dust covering every surface, the cobwebs expertly woven between the chandelier's crystals, and the gilded looking glass covered in a gray cloth that might have been white at some point. As he strode farther into the foyer, he noticed dust did not lift from the marble floors, as if they, at least, had been swept recently. He scowled.

"Mrs. Hodge?" He called up the stairs for the housekeeper, leaning over the gold leaf stair rail that left his palms covered in dust. In all his years staying with Uncle over his winter breaks from sailing, Erik had never seen this house in such disrepair, with cracks in the front windows, dingy drop cloths over every piece, and even the gilded sconces caked in dust.

"Mrs. Hodge?" He strode down the hall toward the basement kitchen, his footsteps echoing the pounding in his chest. Had his nemesis discovered his true identity and followed him home at last? He ran his hand over his freshly shaven jaw. It wasn't the best of disguises, but at sea he had worn a full beard, only ever shaving when he returned home. The only ones who had ever seen him without a beard were the skeleton crew he trusted to see to the ship while others took in the delights of London. Surely, he would have been notified if Requin had attacked his residence and staff in revenge for Erik's capturing a high-ranking smuggler in his ring? But what else could he think when his well-paid staff was nowhere to be found?

If there had been an attack, you and all of London would have been notified. He exhaled and took account of the ground floor. If his modest four-storied home was this deviant, how much worse off was his castle in Draybridge? He searched the length of the house for the housekeeper, or anyone at all. The place was all but abandoned. At a thumping at the rear servant's entrance, Erik ducked into the shadows and watched as the doorknob turned and his retired butler, Trumbull, ambled inside, a basket over one arm and a cane clutched in the other. His clothes were clean, albeit in desperate need of replacing.

"Trumbull?" Erik strode out of the shadows.

"Erik Draycott?" His wrinkled lips parted and slowly spread into a smile, revealing his yellowed teeth. He swung open the back door. "This explains your two trunks on the back stoop, my lord. You are home at last. It's been, what? Three years?"

Erik nodded and fetched the luggage himself, hefting one end of his largest trunk first, the effort straining the stitches of his once-fine suitcoat as he dragged the trunk inside. "An injury forced me to return unexpectedly." Wincing, he readjusted his black cloth sling and nodded to their surroundings. "Where is everyone? And why on earth is this place in such disrepair?"

"I thought you knew, your lordship. Your steward closed up this house, save for me to keep it from being robbed."

Erik eyed the bent man. If Mr. Trumbull was all that stood between this place and danger, it was a wonder the house had not been emptied by burglars. "That is preposterous. I have been sending more than enough funds to see to its upkeep." *Either Guy Mayfield is being overly zealous in his attempt to save the estate, which I highly doubt, or the payments are being intercepted.* He clenched his fists. He trusted his steward unreservedly, and Requin's reach had proven to be further than he had thought possible in the past. He could not afford to underestimate him again. If Requin was behind the missing funds, more than just his London house was at risk.

"I do not know the reason, my lord. Mr. Mayfield said you wrote to him and asked him to redirect the funds for this house to some bank in London."

Requin knew. Erik's neck prickled. He didn't know how the smuggler had discovered his identity . . . and why had Requin stopped his attack with the funds of the London residence? Which bank was funneling money into his enemy's pocket? He swallowed, attempting to keep his expression and voice clear of emotions. "I shall remedy that at once. The place looks dreadful."

Trumbull set his basket atop the surprisingly clean kitchen table. "It's all I can do to climb the levels each night to draw the curtains and light and unlight the lamps to keep people from thinking the townhouse is completely vacant and unguarded. My knees wouldn't allow the climb today. Besides that, I try to thoroughly clean a room a week."

At a room a week, no wonder the house looked as it did. "Which one is clean now?"

"I set up my room in the butler's pantry, so it is clean as well as the kitchen." His cheeks reddened. "Now I am wishing I didn't just clean my rooms this week. However, the rotation—"

"Please. Do not fret on my account." Erik unbuttoned his coat with his good arm, grimacing as he slipped the ruined piece from his shoulders and off his injured arm, at once returning his left arm into the sling, the strain leaving a sheen of sweat on his brow as his shoulder and wrist throbbed. His hand slipped to the pain medication in his pocket.

His London doctor, who had been Erik's first call upon disembarking this morning, had insisted on supplying him with it the moment Erik admitted to the pain keeping him from sleeping for the past two weeks. After ensuring that the rapier wound to his shoulder was clean and on the mend, the doctor insisted on immobilizing Erik's wrist and shoulder with a wrap and sling for the remainder of the week. At Erik's protest, the doctor reminded him that he was fortunate to have only a sprained wrist and a clean shoulder wound. He'd narrowly missed damage to his ligaments that would have rendered his arm fairly useless. Not to mention that the cut could have easily festered. Erik had to swallow back his retort on having an efficient ship's doctor, lest he elongate the conversation.

For the pain, the doctor assured Erik that opium was quite effective. Still. Erik withdrew it from his pocket and bit the cork, tugging it free from the neck as he thrust the bottle out of the back window, turning it upside down. The contents splattered on the cobblestones as they drained away. He'd rather never sleep than rely on that devil's brew. He'd seen firsthand what it could do when his uncle was lost in grief over his wife's death. Trumbull made no comment as Erik tossed the empty bottle into the rubbish bin.

"I will be bunking with you until I can acquire new staff and get to the bottom of the redirection of the funds. Until then, I need to ready myself for a ball tonight in Kensington Gore. The Prince Regent will be there, and I need to make his acquaintance at last, considering my newly inherited title." He regarded his trunks and ran his hand over his left shoulder, grunting. "I am loath to ask it of you, but would you mind acting as my valet?"

"Of course, my lord." The butler beamed. "To feel useful again is a wonderful thing."

Erik adjusted the strap anchoring him to the land when his soul longed to be at sea making a difference in the war against Napoleon. "Yes, I understand how you feel." He cleared his throat and shook off his self-pity. If he must be grounded, he would at least lobby for one more contract from the Prince Regent's advisor, giving him another year to capture the greatest smuggler of his time. And with Sir Alexander acting as advisor, he would be setting sail with his new letter of marque within a fortnight.

Chapter Three

MURIEL'S KNEES WOULD NOT CEASE their jumping as she stood in the reception line in the Hughlots' grand foyer on Kensington Gore with Sir Alexander and Lady Ingram. The thought of meeting the Prince Regent of England was all too much. *Don't think about how many failed seasons you have behind you, and you will do just fine.* She scowled at her step-grandmother's words, which were always there, ready to cut her down if Muriel ever gained a dash of confidence outside of the kitchen. She shook the thought from her mind and whispered to Lady Ingram, "How ever did you manage to get us an invitation to a marquess's dinner party hosting the prince?"

Lady Ingram's lips twitched. She flipped open her painted silk fan, hiding their whispers from view. "We are courtiers of the king, my dear. I've known the Prince Regent since my marriage to the captain, the date of which event I will not confess, lest I reveal my age."

Muriel swallowed. She would be quite the outsider.

Sensing her discomfort, Lady Ingram patted her arm. "Don't fret. Sir Alexander has long been a favorite of the Prince Regent, even before Alexander was knighted, and we know him to be quite kind. I know you are nervous but remember your goal. In order for you to put the messy business behind you and your family, you at the very least need a subsidiary title. Aim for a duke, of course, but that is a rather lofty ambition with there being a limited number of dukes. You may settle for a viscount, although I would rather your children, besides the firstborn son, to be given more than just the courtesy of being called 'honorable.' I suppose the goal here is, of course, for you to secure a title."

Muriel's head spun as the music grew with each step forward in the line. It was one thing to plan such a daring venture with her bosom friends and quite another to attempt to do so . . . especially without them at her side and in the unfamiliar ballrooms of London. She should have accepted their help. However, she had gotten herself into this mess alone, and it was her responsibility to fix it alone. At least, that is what Grandmother Fletcher had said when she strictly forbade Muriel from bringing such pretty, eligible friends. Doing so would greatly increase the competition and narrow her options for a good match. Of course Father at once stood against his mother with a ready defense of his adopted daughter, and he again assured Muriel that she didn't need to leave Kent. However, it was because of her love for her new family that Muriel had to prove she was more than what everyone in society saw—a baker out of her kitchen and out of her element.

She knew Kent society had blamed her lack of decorum and abiding by societal norms on her common upbringing. Muriel had been born in a clean, albeit small flat above the bakery where she and her mother worked until just before Muriel turned seventeen. That was when Mother and her new investor, Mr. Fletcher, met and fell in love over baked goods. Much to the chagrin of Kent's polite society, they married, and Mr. Fletcher moved mother and daughter to his freshly updated country estate, Fletcher Manor. All of which allowed Muriel a debut in polite society's ballrooms. After only a year of etiquette lessons and training, she had been an unmitigated disaster.

Despite her stepfather's sweet reassurances, Kent society would always view her not by her stepfather's heritage but as a parvenue, courtesy of her mother's marriage to the wealthiest untitled gentleman in the county. Father's position was not enough to smooth over the apparent flaws in his choice of a wife and stepdaughter. But now that she was in London, where nearly no one knew of her beginnings, Muriel knew she could at last hide behind her stepfather's fortune long enough to interest a respectable titled suitor . . . that is, if she managed to follow society's guide. She was nearing five and twenty, and she well knew a wallflower did not propose to a gentleman. Her only excuse was temporary madness brought on by Vivienne's well-penned romance novels, published under her nom de plume. Those tomes would forever skew Muriel's outlook on love and marriage. *So I might argue this is all Vivienne's fault.*

"You have been trained to be a lady from the moment you were seventeen. You will not shame yourself in the royal court if you only remember your etiquette." Lady Ingram continued her encouragement as the line before them shortened, and they approached the marquess and marchioness of the four-storied residence, the aloof Hughlots.

Muriel fluffed the sapphire tulle at her shoulders, knowing the pearls sewn into the tulle and sprinkled across her bust were perfection. To complement them, along with the graceful trio of ivory egret feathers in her high, loose bun, Muriel's maid, Charlotte, had sewn pearls into her coiffure that would take an hour to remove. Staying close to Lady Ingram's elbow, she found they were next, her palms instantly growing clammy. She brushed her fingers against her father's ring on the delicate gold necklace and drew a deep breath. She greeted the hosts with her most brilliant yet demure smile, gathered her glimmering skirts of sapphire, and curtsied in a cloud of perfection.

With her greetings exchanged without tragedy and a compliment directed toward her ensemble from Lady Hughlot, she released her train to fall behind her and was ushered into the grand salon. In the corner, a quartet was assembled beneath a succession of paintings depicting the generations of the marquess, each one taller than she. The lively quartet was already enticing guests onto the hardwood dance floor. Muriel looked around as surreptitiously as she could manage. Though older than her stepfather's manor, this house bore its age with a level of opulence that every society lady in the county would envy. The platinum silk wall coverings shimmered in the flickering candlelight of the gold chandeliers, which also illuminated the gold leaf moldings and fine artwork around the room that was obviously created by the masters. She studied the nearest cluster of paintings by Hogarth, Gainsborough, and Reynolds. She pressed her hand to her chest at the elegance surrounding her, then, feeling her lips part, quickly remembered herself. "Where is the Prince Regent, Lady Ingram?"

"He appears two hours into the party, just before dinner is served," the portly Sir Alexander interjected as he joined them, kissing his wife's cheek and bowing to Muriel. "I believe the food to be his favorite event of any evening."

"Mine too," Muriel whispered, her stomach already rumbling.

"That and the music. He has a fondness for it. Do you sing, Miss Beau?" Lady Ingram inquired.

"Miss Beau!"

Muriel's heart plummeted at the sight of the dowager viscountess of the last noble family they had called on that morning. She doubted Viscountess Traneford had forgiven her for damaging the settee and costly rug by dropping her iced sponge. Behind her stood a gentleman, stunning in his own right, who winked . . . at *her*?

Muriel glanced over her shoulder and found only a gangly hobble-dehoy sipping his punch. This Corinthian was indeed smiling at her. She straightened, her pulse hammering. This was it. She well recognized the signs of an eligible, advantageous match being proposed, but never had it happened to her. With her two fiancés, it had been all arranged contracts with no wooing, yet this man appeared as if he was actually eager to make her acquaintance. He could be just the nobleman to take her mind off the dashing Baron Osmund Deverell for good.

"Miss Beau, may I present to you my son, Lord Tristian Traneford, Viscount of Traneford."

Muriel dipped her head and curtsied, her practiced conversational tidbits nowhere to be found.

Lady Ingram clasped his hand in both of her own. "My dear, Tristian.

So good to see you again. Your days at the university kept you away from us for too long."

He grinned, his tanned cheeks stark against his bright smile and ebony hair. "When I was offered the fellowship to travel and study in Cairo, I couldn't pass it up, even if it meant keeping myself from attending lovely gatherings such as this." His gaze lingered on Muriel. "And now, it seems that my waiting has rewarded me with being present for this beautiful country rose's first ball with us."

Well, that did it. Any thought she had composed flew from her head again.

"Would you do me the honor of a dance?" He bowed to her, extending his hand.

Did he sway just slightly? She managed a demure nod and allowed him to sweep her onto the dance floor, where the back and forth of the reel permitted her a moment to gather herself. He had been quite animated over the mention of his studies, so she cleared her throat and ventured, "What did you study in Egypt? I'm imagining it had to do with the pyramids?"

His grin flashed, momentarily blinding her senses to all else in the room. "The lady speaks! I am an entomologist and was studying beetles." He shrugged. "It may not have been the lordliest way of spending my time, but I am hopeful the book I am composing about my discoveries will turn a tidy little profit to help support my family and enable me to return to the site." He cleared his throat. "Speaking of which, I'm certain you were made aware of the Traneford family's situation."

The hopping motion of the dance required them to part. When they met again, she queried, "Situation?"

"No need to be coy, Miss Beau." He whirled them about the perimeter of the floor. "I've heard all about how forward you country girls can be, and I hear you take the cake."

She stiffened, her blood pounding in her ears. "And what exactly did you hear about me?" She kept herself from searching the crowded room for someone she recognized who could possibly have borne the dreaded tale all the way from Chilham.

He leaned down to whisper in her ear, the liquor on his breath making her fight a gag. "That if I pause with you under the chandelier, you will be unable to keep yourself from proposing, saving me the trouble of offering you a jewel to tempt you into an engagement with me."

Her jaw dropped. Here she had been feeling inferior due to her lack of station, when this man was nothing but a self-absorbed blackguard. At her frown and no doubt scalding cheeks, he had the nerve to laugh and direct them toward the center of the room, where he paused under the chandelier with an impish grin.

"I'm waiting." He laughed again, lifting his eyes to the chandelier surrounded by a fresco imitation of the discoveries at Herculaneum.

"This is not amusing in the least," she hissed, tugging against his hand, which held hers in a vice. He was too strong for her. The memory of Baron Deverell under the chandelier was crushing her lungs. Her proposal was supposed to have been glorious, treasured forever, and now it was tainted by the mocking of all who heard of it. No one viewed it as she had in the powder room that evening—a moment of precious hope and true love taking wing. "Please," she whimpered, tears of frustration threatening at her lashes. "You will ruin everything."

He leaned down to her once more. "I have the title you want, and you have the funds I need to continue my lifestyle. Shall you get on one knee, or shall I?"

"Cease this at once." She attempted to tug free once more, smiling through clenched teeth for the benefit of the curious onlookers and blinking furiously to keep her tears in check. Her reputation would not be ruined because of one inebriated, entitled man who wished to make sport of her for his own entertainment.

A giant of a man stepped between them with his back to her. He gripped the viscount's shoulder, his fingers discreetly cinching on his collarbone and forcing the cad to release his grip on her wrist with a grunt of pain. The mysterious gentleman enveloped Muriel in his arm, drawing her away from the horrid viscount and into the reel once more. She looked up to thank her rescuer and gasped. In the dazzling splendor of the court with the candlelight blurring as they whirled, she would have thought she imagined him if not for the obvious sling and the lump still visible beneath a dark curl on his forehead. "Erik?"

"Ariel?" he breathed, holding her upper waist with one arm while her free hand rested on his shoulder as his other was in the sling. "What are you doing here?" His mind churned through their earlier encounter. She had been wearing an overlarge apron, and, while he had gotten a good view of her delicate train before he darted over to help her in the pantry, women's fashion always eluded him. Certainly, he chased down spies and smugglers on the high seas, capturing them in traitorous acts, but the thought that a certain fabric might be too fine for a baker had never entered his head.

And besides, once they'd been dusted with flour and he'd had his senses knocked from him, all he noticed were her pretty eyes and her delightfully winning manner. She had been beautiful coated in flour, and now she was stunning, with dark chestnut curls framing her face and one spilling over her creamy, almost-bared shoulder. There was no mistaking her status in tonight's finery.

"Actually, my name is *Muriel*. You misheard me earlier. And I am not the Ingrams' cook. I am their guest, Miss Beau." She worried her full bottom lip, remorse flooding her features. "But please know I wasn't having a lark with you. Everything else I divulged was true. And in my defense, you assumed my role as much as I did yours, and I didn't wish to be rude by correcting you on my station."

"Indeed—"

"Wait a moment." Her eyes narrowed. "If you are a gentleman attending a ball, what were you doing in the kitchen with a delivery? Was that a falsehood as well? Are you some criminal nobleman who uses the ruse of delivering crates to fool unsuspecting staff into allowing you into homes of elite members of society to spy on them?"

Criminal nobleman? He fought to keep his grin steady as the dance drew them apart.

When she reached his side once more, she lowered her voice. "I do not wish to leap to conclusions. Sir Alexander was a captain, and he's told me tales of his time in the war and of finding traitors where you least expected them."

"I never claimed I was a deliveryman. As you said, you assumed . . . like I assumed you were the baker since our clothes were covered in flour when we met. However, I truly was delivering a gift to Sir Alexander, who happens to have been *my* first captain. He has a fondness for exotic tea." *Which I intercepted from Requin on its way from Burma.*

Her brows lifted as suspicion fled her features. He lifted his good arm and she twirled beneath it. "Your captain? Well, you must be of a high rank now, given you are at a nobleman's ball, and yet, I do not even know what to call you. Using your Christian name at this point would be unforgivably forward."

"Would it?" he teased, thoroughly enjoying her unbridled conversation.

"You know of my former life, and I don't even know your surname. That is hardly fair." She laughed and leaned toward him, whispering, "We should do as polite society insists and have a proper introduction lest rumors begin to swirl about the ballroom after your gallant rescue. Maybe you should fetch Sir Alexander to introduce us and forget our little encounter in the kitchen."

Forget the beauty covered in flour who had rendered him unconscious when no man had ever accomplished that feat? *Never.* He bowed his head to her as they continued their dance. "True, but as we have already been seen dancing, we cannot allow anyone to witness an introduction as it would be out of order. I'm Captain Erik Draycott, Earl of Draycott."

Her eyes widened at his title. "So, not only are you *not* a delivery-man, but you are a captain and an earl?"

"Would you rather I were a deliveryman?"

Her lips quirked. "Mayhap. Well, when I curtsy at the end of the dance, know it is in conclusion but also in greeting. It is a pleasure to meet you, sir—I mean, my lord. Honestly, in Chilham we only ever had gentry to address, other than visiting noblemen, so I didn't study the proper addresses as I should have."

He chuckled at her stumbling over his title. "Please, call me Captain Draycott."

"Very well, Captain Draycott. I'm Miss Beau, Baker of Chilham."

He swallowed his laughter at her introduction and shifted his hold on her slender waist. One-armed dancing was more difficult than he had anticipated, but to have her near made it worth the stares they were receiving. "It is an honor, Miss Beau, Baker of Chilham. Do you answer to Lady Baker?"

"Apparently, as well as Ariel. Alas, I am afraid you must address me as Miss Beau, lest people think I am giving myself a title or knowledge of my former occupation circulate." Her lips quirked in mirth once more. "Shall you keep my scandalous beginnings a secret?"

"You will be pleased to learn that I'm rather adept at keeping secrets."

"Thank goodness." She cleared her throat and asked more seriously, "How could you tell I was in trouble with the viscount? While it felt like an eternity that I was held captive by him under the chandelier, I know it was only a few bars of music."

"I knew the viscount when we were lads in school. He was a rascal then and grew up to be even more of a rake." He frowned. "And when I saw a lady attempting to tug free of him, I knew I had to aid said lady before he caused further damage."

"I thank you for your service, my lord." She smiled up at him, her chocolate eyes sparkling in the candlelight. "Two gallant acts in a single day with an injured arm, which I am guessing has a much more exciting tale behind it than you disclosed, with you being a captain and all."

"Mayhap." He laughed and skirted the topic. "I hope you will not judge all English noblemen by your experience with Tristian Traneford."

"How could I when I have such a chivalrous knight before me now?" She smiled up at him.

"Say much more and you shall have me blushing, my lady baker." While her words would have seemed coquettish coming from any other lady tonight, Erik's chest swelled with the sincerity of her praise. As the dance ended, he bowed to her and escorted her off the dance floor as guests cast him curious glances.

Long before Erik had discovered he was to inherit his uncle's lands, he had dreamt of working aboard a ship, and had done so for nearly twenty years in total under Alexander Ingram. After his aunt died and he was told he was to inherit, he had studied for years to prepare himself for the task, both on land and while at sea. By the time his uncle died, Erik had reached a position of authority, had already signed his second contract to work on behalf of the Crown, and was actually making a difference in the war against Napoleon.

His continuation of work after his uncle's death led his neighbors to believe that he did not possess the funds to attend the season or even host at home . . . a story that was no doubt perpetuated by the dilapidation of his London residence. However, Erik had allowed the rumors of his dwindling wealth to circulate unchecked, for it kept the English ladies far from his castle's doorstep. He had no time for a relationship and had little desire to take a wife, considering the secrets there would be between them. His second identity had nearly overtaken him when his uncle died. Erik had returned only long enough to install a steward he trusted before returning to his call of duty. At sea, the Earl of Draycott was no more, as he chased French smugglers and seized their ships as the infamous privateer Captain Warrick, a nom de guerre whose reputation had been built by a succession of men.

He cast a glance down at the inimitable lady beside him and felt the smallest fissure in his resolve to keep himself apart from all single, unattached females during his time on land in his desire to better acquaint himself with Miss Beau. Unlike the ladies who had attempted to lure him into matrimony before, Miss Beau possessed a strength of character that could only have been brought about by hardship. And such a lady a gentleman did not meet every day, especially one who baked with such skill.

Before he could properly request to escort her to tonight's dinner, gentlemen he had known since he was a young shaver swarmed her. At once, he observed her draw herself into the prim lady she thought society wished her to be—demanded she be—and Erik couldn't help but grin that he alone knew the real woman behind her mask . . . at least, for now.

Chapter Four

THE CHAMBER FELL SILENT AS the Prince Regent strode into the ball-room in all his finery. George IV's closest companions, along with the host and hostess, flanked him, but Muriel couldn't help but glance over her shoulder to where Erik stood with Sir Alexander, a broad smile softening his chiseled features. Ladies cast Lord Draycott coquettish smiles, fluttering their fans and inviting the handsome lord to speak with them even when there was a regent in the chamber. *An earl who pretends to be a deliveryman?* She understood their fascination. *How on earth has this man, glorious in character and countenance, remained without a wife for so long?*

The music turned to a lively reel, transforming the atmosphere at once from awe into vivacity as couples returned to the floor. The merriment about them was nothing like she had imagined of stiff nobility. Certainly the company was more reserved than that at a country dance, but she felt the thrill radiating from those about her as they thoroughly enjoyed the evening and the novelty of having the Prince Regent in the same room—a novelty that she would write home about at once. Though, to truly do the letter justice, she would need a better look at the royal.

She rose on her tiptoes to peer over the shoulders around her, hoping to catch a glimpse of the portly gentleman. In the light of the flickering sconces lining the room, she caught Lord Traneford staring at her. His inebriated grin chilled her as he sloshed his half-empty glass into the chest of a nearby footman and loped toward her, apparently ready to complete her humiliation now that she was away from her hero. She whirled around to seek sanctuary with the Ingrams, but they were lost to her in the mass of guests. Jostled by those attempting to get closer to the Prince Regent, the press of people warmed the chamber to the point of drawing perspiration from her brow, even though she had spent years baking with sweltering ovens. As she weaved through the crowds as best she might, aiming for the perimeter of the room, a whimper escaped her for fear of having lost her party for the entirety of the evening when she felt her wrist seized. Turning, she released a sigh of relief. "Lady Ingram! Thank goodness you found me. I lost sight of you."

"My apologies, dear. Sometimes the crowd has a way of separating parties, but someone has requested to make your acquaintance." Lady Ingram's eyes sparkled.

"Hopefully he possesses better manners than Lord Traneford," Muriel muttered under her breath.

Lady Ingram didn't seem to hear her as she expertly maneuvered through the crowd to the front of the grand salon, pausing at a knot of nobility, who, upon seeing them, parted. Muriel was met face-to-face with the Prince Regent. Her heart dipped, and she felt in danger of fainting. She plastered on the pretty smile she had been trained to deliver, expertly curtsied with Lady Ingram, and demurely folded her hands around her fan, waiting for him to address her first.

"I hear from my dear Lady Ingram that you are from the county of Kent." His gaze roved over her, not in an unseemly fashion but rather as if he were appraising her as a lady. "I have a great fondness for music. Do you sing, Miss Beau?"

"Often and quite poorly. The servants are kind enough to keep their complaints to a minimum."

The Prince Regent threw back his head and laughed. "I do love a country lady's honesty." He patted her arm. "Well, musical or not, I find you quite a charming young lady, and I would love to see a coronet atop those curls someday if you should wed well. Enjoy your evening and time in London, Miss Beau." He nodded to Lady Ingram, effectively ending her introduction.

Muriel's hand shook as she rested it atop Lady Ingram's, and another young lady stepped up to meet the future king. Muriel blinked at the familiar bright, dimpled smile of Elena Whelan. The songbird of Kent had followed her across the countryside.

⚜

"All I require is one more contract, Captain Ingram, and I'll have him. I know it. If you'd only give me a year, I could at last bring Requin before a judge." Erik resisted the urge to ram his fist into the library bookcase. Ingram was now one of the Prince Regent's closest advisors in regard to chartering privateers, yet he would not listen to reason. *Why is he so against my having a third contract when so much is at stake?*

"It's *Sir* Alexander now. And why should I award another letter of the marque to someone who is bent on destroying the legacy of the great Warrick, when I might assign it to another who would bring in Requin the way I wish him to be—dead?" He lifted his glass of flip in salute.

"Because most privateers average two or three ships captured a year. I bring in four prizes for the Crown per annum as Warrick."

Ingram snorted. "I brought in six under the same name."

"Which is the only reason you are in this court instead of on the deck of the *Twilight Treader* at this very moment."

"Careful, boy. You may have been born to be a lord, but I was born with a sword in hand. I can still gut you as easily as gulp flip with nobility." Ingram's eyes flashed, his fist clenching around his glass of brandy and sugar. "I know you are passionate about your position, which is why I awarded you my legacy in carrying on the name of Warrick, the most feared pirate of our time. Yet what have you done?"

Erik pressed his lips into a firm line. He would not apologize for the way he had chosen to captain. Even though his time on land had been short after his aunt's passing, that was when he had met his greatest friend, who later became his second-in-command, and now served as his steward, Guy Mayfield, and had been led to kneel before Christ. It was because of Guy that Erik had never spilled a drop of blood in service to Ingram's thirst for prize money, and it was Christ who had called Erik to fight for the Crown—without deaths. "I've chosen to rule the seas my way. I do not condone needless bloodshed."

"And by avoiding bloodshed at all costs, you are, in fact, costing my legacy everything." Ingram growled. "I didn't make the name of Warrick to mean a peaceful seizure of a ship. I meant the name and flag to strike *fear* into the hearts of all sailors."

"It is because of that fear I am able to take ships peacefully."

"Not for long." Ingram lifted his glass to two gentlemen entering the darkened library. "It's time for the next Warrick to take over. One that is not afraid of spilling blood. It's a shame Guy Mayfield retired."

Erik did not bother correcting him on that score. "Sir Alexander—"

"However, your current second-in-command, Adams, will do for the position just as well." He slapped Erik on the shoulder, shifting into a display of comradery for the newcomers. "Eight more weeks and then you can finally enjoy this role you have so graciously reminded me that you inherited, *my lord*. Now, if you'll excuse me, I must find Lady Ingram."

Erik trailed after Ingram and sank into the shadows of the hall just outside the ballroom to collect his temper. Every time he brought in an enemy's merchant ship, it helped in ending the war with Napoleon that much sooner and, therefore, sparing precious lives. Why would Ingram refuse to bring his request to the Prince Regent when Erik had brought into port four prize ships in a single year?

His fingernails dug into his palms, Ingram's taunt burning in his lungs. Certainly Ingram's prize average had been higher when he held the identity of Captain Warrick, and, despite years of chasing Requin, Erik had yet to catch the elusive smuggler. But that wasn't what had his stomach in knots. It was Ingram's statement that another should be awarded the contract *and* the famed nom de guerre in Erik's stead . . . his second-in-command. Blast whoever had discovered his identity and requested his funds to be transferred.

Erik was on the verge of collapsing Requin's gunpowder-smuggling empire. They could not afford to allow the brigand to remain on the sea, aiding France, only because Ingram coveted a bigger yield in prizes won by his ship, *Twilight Treader*. But, if Ingram persisted in his insinuation that it was time Erik retire from the privateering life and see to his estates, Erik would have to go about his work by another means. He would not be forced out of his position only to have another capture the smuggling ring and thus reap the rewards of his years of labor. If Ingram required the ship, Erik would purchase another. Unfortunately, he could not buy the fear that the name *Warrick* had given him.

Recently, signs of Requin's reach had bled into the London grocers' guild, if the messages hidden in various dry goods Erik had managed to intercept were any indication—something Ingram knew nothing about, as he wouldn't even linger long enough to hear of Erik's findings. Erik simply had to discover how far, or rather to whom, the smuggler's reach extended. The problem was the sheer number of nabobs and upstarts who could be involved. If only the search would follow the cadence of sensational stories, he might start with the most villainous working gentleman or nobleman in the room and find Requin within the fortnight. His glance skittered to a cluster of gentlemen and rested on Traneford, who was so deep in his cups that he should be removed from the premises. No, Requin would never allow his men to lose themselves while on a mission. *Lord, show me what to do. I cannot do this on my own.*

He felt a bump from behind him and turned to discover Miss Beau, her eyes widening as if just as startled to find herself with company as he. "Miss Beau?"

"Erik! I mean, Captain Draycott." She ran her fingers around and around the ivory neck of her fan. "I was momentarily overwhelmed and needed a minute away from the crowd to gather myself. I thought I was alone at last. I'm so sorry to have disturbed you."

"It isn't Lord Traneford again, is it?" He straightened, glaring at the man still standing by a potted palm, downing another glass.

"It's nothing to worry you, truly," she replied, her gaze appraising him. "But it seems that you may be in need of my help? What has you so down in the mouth?"

His lips quirked at her directness when a thought occurred to him. "Perhaps you can help me. I would be honored if you would attend my garden party next Friday."

"A garden party? In London?" Her brows rose. "I haven't seen much in the way of private gardens, but my time here has only begun."

"At my castle in Draybridge." He chuckled, praying that his castle was in better standing than his London residence.

Her lips parted. "At your *castle*?" She pressed her hand to her throat. "Goodness gracious me, yes. This will be the first castle I've ever been invited to step foot inside. I've visited mansions before, of course, though only barely. As for Chilham Castle, even with my stepfather's connections and—" She cut herself short as his grin broadened.

"I take it you are comfortable in my presence?" he teased, even though it heartened him greatly to be her anchor in London.

She leaned forward and whispered, "As I was the one who revived you from being knocked senseless, I'd say so . . . even if it was my fault and a most horrible way to make your acquaintance." She slapped her hand over her mouth. "But again, we were supposed to forget that beginning." She straightened her shoulders and shook her head as if to return to the stiff lady he had witnessed her become before. "I will *not* shame my family."

It would not do for her to become formal with him, not after he had met the genuine lady baker. Erik captured her hand in his. "From what you have told me of them, I think they are proud of you, my lady. And I dare say you will prove invaluable to me in your presence at my garden party."

"But how does my attending a party help you?"

"By improving my mood, of course." He grinned. A new plan to capture Requin's inside man formulated even as he spoke. He had only eight weeks until his contract was up, and, according to the doctor, it would take at least three weeks for his shoulder to fully heal, during which time he needed to be near the doctor, lest his arm fester or take a turn and he lose the full use of it. If he was to be land bound, he would make the most of every opportunity to mingle with the wealthy merchants of dry goods to ferret out Requin's informant, starting with an irresistible invitation to a garden party at Draycott Castle.

Chapter Five

As HIS CARRIAGE ROUNDED THE corner, Erik gritted his teeth, preparing himself for the prospect of the castle's neglect after the way Requin's villainy had extended to his townhouse. The wheel hit a rut and sent the wicker basket on the opposite bench sliding toward a quick end. He snatched it up and inhaled the sweet aroma of the pastries within. He had finished the last of Muriel's scones along the two-hour ride. The few pastries that remained were being rationed in the event there was no cook to be found at the castle. At another jolt, Erik groaned. If it hadn't been for his arm, he would have ridden and cut his travel time. Of course, if it hadn't been for his arm, he wouldn't be coming home at all.

He hadn't returned to the village of Draybridge since his uncle's untimely death, but the instant the carriage wheels thumped over the old arching stone bridge, a sense of home flowed over him. He craned his neck to peer through the window at the quaint village with its flower gardens at the side door of every townhouse, its tiny shops, bakery, school, chapel, and businesses. It had been his aunt's doing in having all the flower gardens added. He gripped the sill with his good hand, his knuckles whitening at every passing face. He had inherited the castle and, along with it, the responsibility of this village. It was his duty to see it and its people continue to thrive.

As his carriage passed, villagers paused along the pathway to stare at the crimson and white crest of two rearing horses on the carriage door, a clear declaration of who was the occupant. He waved to those he recognized and nodded to the few new faces in his town. He would have to attend services on Sunday and greet all there. However, he doubted he would be staying long enough to pay and receive calls. When he completed his mission, he would have plenty of time for being the lord of the land. Until then, he trusted Guy Mayfield implicitly to guide the village in his stead.

The carriage rolled past the last house at the edge of the village. Once he drove through the trees, he would see Draycott Castle rising above the lake surrounding it. While traveling the few miles between the village and his castle, Erik compared the land to the estate of his childhood. Apart from a few overgrown spots, it seemed as if time had passed it by. Cresting the hill, just beyond the tree line and hilltops, he spied the beautiful gritstone and limestone work of his castle that had withstood the test of time. Stonework layered by generations of earls adding to the legacy created the sprawling castle it was today, with its hundred rooms, chapel, courtyards, and terraced garden beyond the lake, which gracefully transitioned to the forest beyond it.

The carriage rattled over the drawbridge, the wheels jolting over the boards and sending the basket tottering again. He threaded his arm through the handle and, supporting his left arm to keep it from jarring, he waited for the carriage to halt and hopped down into the sprawling courtyard. Craning his neck, he stared up at the four-storied entrance tower with its impressive arched threshold. *All seems well.*

"My lord?" a gardener called, pausing in his work of trimming spent blooms from the pristine vine that climbed the walls surrounding the castle's main entrance and that greatly softened the ashen gray and brown stones of the ancient building. The gardener bowed and jogged inside, no doubt alerting all to the lord's presence.

Erik thanked the hired coachman that Trumbull had recommended and strode about the courtyard, taking account. It was scrubbed clean, the windows glistening in the morning light. A pair of children chased each other in the sunshine. He offered a smile to the children, who at once dashed into a darkened doorway leading to the servants' kitchen.

"Lord Draycott." His steward and former first mate, Guy Mayfield, trotted out of the house, grinning as he shrugged on his coat. "What a marvelous surprise."

Erik set down the basket and clapped him on the shoulder and pulled the man he had known since boyhood into a fierce embrace. "It has been too long."

Guy grinned. "Too long? It's been an age. I was beginning to think you were never returning to dry land."

Erik held the elbow of his bad arm and leaned back to take in the building. "Well, I greatly appreciate your stewardship. Everything looks well in order here."

Guy Mayfield nodded, his eyes shadowing for a moment as he caught Erik's calculated tone. "Unlike the London house. I take it you have been there?"

Erik nodded, thankful Guy had been the one to bring up its derelict state. "Yes, I was going to ask you about that."

Guy frowned. "I take it you did not receive my letter?"

"What letter? The last time I received anything from you was six months ago."

He grasped the basket's handle and motioned Erik inside. "That is what I thought. Perhaps it is something best discussed within the library to keep any pickthanks from rattling on about things that are best kept quiet."

His senses on alert, Erik nodded to each servant in passing, greeting those he remembered from years spent at the castle. Striding through the second courtyard and entering the library, he found tea had already been set for them beside the crackling fireplace. Guy rested Muriel's basket of pastries beside the teapot as Erik ran his fingers along the familiar spines of books, remembering the fun he'd had as a lad swinging from wall to wall on the library's four ladders while imagining that he was swinging from the rigging of a ship. He had cracked his head a time or two, but it had taught him balance.

His steward poured them each a cup and handed one to Erik. "Shall we get down to business, my lord?"

Erik accepted it and waited, running his finger along the rim of the cup as his steward leaned against the fireplace mantel, poking the fire within.

Guy set his cup on the mantel, keeping his gaze on the flames. "There was a series of burglaries, my lord, where nothing of value was taken . . . a warning, I believe. I wrote to you, and now that I have confirmed you did not receive my letter, I fear there is something far more dangerous lurking in the waters." He met Erik's gaze. "From my time as your second-in-command, I learned to follow the signs when it came to Requin. I believe he was the one who had a letter sent to me requesting the redirection of funds from your London house to a bank in London. I did it once."

"What?" Erik shot to his feet. "Do you have the letter?"

His steward nodded. "The second time I received the request for an even greater sum, I grew suspicious. I traveled to London to look into the matter and, upon my arrival, found that the bank closed the account where I directed the funds." Guy crossed the room to the heavy desk in the corner and removed a key from around his neck, fitting it to the lock. "I decided that for the safety of the staff, I needed to vacate the London premises. I wrote to you, in our code, of my decision to withdraw the funds in full from your accounts lest Requin attempt to forge a letter to the bank itself. After that withdrawal, I secured half of your funds in coffers here, locked for good measure in the hidden room."

"And the other half?"

"Dispersed in six banks across England. I did not wish to send any more money than necessary to your London residence, lest Requin discover the source and attempt withdrawal of your funds once more. I send a rider every month with minimum funds for the London house."

Erik released a low whistle. "And what about Trumbull? Didn't you tell the butler of the danger?"

"I've told him multiple times. He has been losing patches of his memory, my lord, and has no recollection of the burglaries. I felt rotten leaving him there, but he was adamant that his remaining was what you would have wanted. I had to think of the safety of the rest of the staff, and he needed a position and shelter. I have a nephew who comes by every week to ensure the man has everything he needs."

"You mentioned nothing of consequence was stolen. What exactly was taken?"

"That was the disconcerting part, my lord. They never filched anything, but rather mussed up the rooms they entered, and the final time..." He swallowed.

"Yes?"

"On the final burglary, they left a flag atop your bed." From the desk he withdrew the letters and a thick folded black cloth, unfurling the flag to reveal a pirate's bleeding heart. "I believe it means 'death awaits.'"

"Actually 'a long, painful death awaits.'" Erik ran his hand over his jaw. If his uncle hadn't been ill for years and nursing opium in his crippling grief, Erik would have suspected foul play in his uncle's demise with such threats being left in his very home. "And the letters?"

Guy handed them to him. "After the second request, I studied the letters. If I hadn't been so busy with the estate, I would have discovered it at once. I felt quite the gull. The man's hubris forced him to leave a clue behind to display his cleverness."

Erik skimmed the letter for any sign of Requin. "Where?"

"To be fair, you have always been consistently inconsistent with your signature. He pressed the nib into the paper so that the *r* in *Erik* and *Draycott* would resemble what?"

"Shark fins." Erik frowned. To anyone else, it would seem a mistake—as if the writer were in a rush. Requin did not make mistakes. "I can see why you removed the staff."

Guy ran his hand on the stone wall. "This place was built to withstand war. I figured it was the safest of places for them and your funds."

"War? Have you armed the footmen, Mayfield?" He chuckled.

"Only with the cutlery. I pity the man who broke into Cook's kitchen with her cleavers lying about the butcher block." He sighed. "I would have written you a second time. However, I feared Requin was intercepting anything I sent, and he might piece together our code. I made the choice to simply await your return and took a risk writing to the man posing as you to say that you lacked funds to run the London house. There was no way I was going to allow a farthing more to drop into that smuggler's hands."

Erik sipped his tea. "I would have done the same in your place. Now I have made a plan to draw Requin's English counterpart out, and it starts with a garden party here."

Guy's brows lifted as he grinned. "I suppose we have fought our enemy with a show of canons and guns to no avail. We might as well try fighting the man with tea and cakes. What's the plan?"

♛

Muriel barely kept her mouth from watering as she stood in Gunter's Tea Shop studying the confections lining the shelves behind the counter. She had heard about the famed shop. Her stepfather had even ordered a cake brought by carriage to surprise her on her twenty-first birthday, but never had she beheld such magnificence all in one room before. It was little wonder the room veritably brimmed with fine ladies and gentlemen waiting to place their orders, even with a line of carriages beside the shop's iron railings bearing more patrons eager to order sweets from the shop's sidewalk waiter. Muriel stood mesmerized as her mind whirled with possibilities for her little bakery in Chilham. Perhaps she might find security there if she didn't procure a title. That way she could at least follow her passion of baking and attempt to gain the fame of this shop.

"Anything else, Miss?" The young baker's assistant asked, pencil poised to add to her shamefully long list of baked goods.

"Do you have anything else that doesn't possess a hint of strawberry, dried, jammed, or infused? Not that I wouldn't love it, I'm certain . . . It is only, strawberry does not agree with me."

"There are a few fresh pear—"

A strident giggle behind her drowned out the assistant's reply.

"How lovely to see you, Miss Beau."

Muriel stiffened at the too-sweet voice of Elena Whelan.

"And the humorous thing is that I saw this shop and thought of you. I had this inexplicable intuition that if I entered, I would find you just where you would be in Chilham. And here you are."

After years spent avoiding her barbs in a tiny village, how on earth had the girl managed to find her in a shop in Berkeley Square with all of London at her fingertips? "Miss Whelan." Muriel curtsied, resentment making the action arduous. "Lovely to see you as well." She cleared her throat. "I was, however, very surprised to find you so far from Kent."

Elena shrugged. "When my mother caught wind of your little scheme, she decided I should attempt it as well. I meant to greet you at the Hughlots' ball, but with the Prince Regent waiting for my curtsy and then proceeding to have a delightful tête-à-tête with me that ended with a request to hear me sing, I know we both understood what etiquette dictated." She batted her lashes innocently. "Unless you've skipped that part in your training as well."

Muriel gritted her teeth. She deserved that one.

"I've been wishing to express my regrets over my dear cousin's horrid rejection of you." She sucked in a breath through her teeth. "Such a frightful moment for you and witnessed by so many too. It was good of you to depart within a fortnight. It would have made things awkward for Osmund in his courtship with the lovely Miss Fox."

The assistant impatiently tapped his pencil against the pad and cleared his throat.

Muriel smiled at him. "My apologies for keeping you. I think if you add that pear-something to the list, I shall have all I need for now." She reached into her purse for the amount, her cheeks tinting at being caught purchasing so much . . . even if it was for research for her own business, and she *was* intending on sharing her treats with the Ingrams and kitchen staff.

"Best be careful. All the fine fare available in London threatens the waistline." Elena's lips quirked as the assistant held out two large boxes over the counter to Muriel.

Muriel snorted and expertly balanced the boxes in one hand. "If I can grow up in a bakery without having my waistline affected, I'm certain one trip to Gunter's will not prove a burden."

"Quite true. Of course, all the dancing helps as well. I saw you with that handsome captain the other night." Elena sidled up next to her, keeping her eyes on the goods before them.

Of course Elena had seen them. And, having discovered he was an earl, she most likely wished for an introduction. Would Muriel never be free from her tormentor? While they had debuted the same season, there was one distinct difference between them that prevented Miss Whelan being labeled a wallflower such as Muriel had been—Elena had received and rejected at least three eligible proposals a season, marking her as the most desired heiress in the county. For unlike Muriel, she was born into polite society, was an accomplished lady, and did not have several little siblings to share her father's wealth. She was positively dripping money. Elena could afford to wait for a gentleman with something more to offer than good looks and a bit of prestige, unlike her mother, the Widow Whelan, who had forfeited any chance of a title upon her hasty marriage to a handsome, wealthy merchant gentleman.

"I heard he was titled," Elena prompted, pointing out a knotted biscuit to the assistant and laying her coin atop the counter as he boxed it up.

Muriel sighed. "His name is Erik Draycott."

"And?" Elena clicked her tongue, taking the box. "You are the most infuriating girl. What's his title?"

"He is the Earl of Draycott, and he possesses a castle in Draybridge."

"My, that is quite the improvement over a lowly baron. Though I'd caution you to guard your heart, as I heard he is a man focused on his career with no intention of taking a bride."

Muriel glanced sideways at her. "And you know this how?"

Elena released her trilling laugh again. "I just do. But I think a pretty face will be just the thing to convince him otherwise. Along with the right dowry, of course." She leaned closer and went on in a stage whisper, "I heard his London house is all but in shambles. And what earl would earn his living at sea when he could wed and spend the rest of his days as a handsome lord should? In wealth and with a handsome wife at his side holding his bouncing baby."

In her brief time with Erik, she could not imagine him lounging about in a great London house. She *could* see him in the House of Lords, though. He was certainly passionate enough, but she gathered it would take an act of God to get that man to leave the sea . . . and a heaven-sent wife could be just that. She shook her head and sighed. She had to get the man from her thoughts, for she would not make the same mistake twice. She would wait for a gentleman to approach her with courtship.

"Muriel? Muriel, are you listening to me?"

"Yes?" She blinked and shifted the boxes in her arms. "I mean, no. My apologies. What did you say?"

"I asked if you were going to the earl's garden party in Draybridge?"

Muriel pressed her lips into a firm line to keep herself from rolling her eyes. "If you are attending his garden party, didn't you already know his name?"

Elena laughed. "I can tell a lot about where a woman's affections lie from how little she describes the bachelor in question to another eligible lady."

"See you Friday." With a nod to Elena, Muriel hurried out to the sidewalk. She needed to get taste testing and baking straightaway, before her imagination led her astray again.

Chapter Six

MURIEL GRIPPED THE LEATHER STRAP of the carriage as she was jostled on the country road leading from the lovely village of Draybridge to Draycott Castle. Despite the discomfort that came with such journeys, she was thankful to relax on the twenty-mile trip. She was still quite unused to London's frenetic pace. In Chilham there was hardly a social season, rather a smattering of parties as the occasion arose—the only constants being the holidays. But in the City, there were at least two events and a party to choose from every day and evening, and the selection was not only political, but required vigilant planning of how one dressed so as not to wear one's nicest of gowns twice in a row, but also not offend the hostess by dressing down. Thankfully, with her new wardrobe she possessed dresses enough for every outing.

With all the events, Muriel had scarcely had time to escape to the kitchen in the days leading up to this party, though she had to admit she was thankful for the constant flow of outings, as it allowed the week to pass quickly. The anticipation of Lord Draycott's garden party was driving her to distraction. She gripped the wicker basket with her free arm, inhaling the scents of the baked goods inspired by Gunter's, which she had stayed up until midnight preparing to bring Erik today. Lady Ingram had attempted to gently dissuade her, yet Muriel knew he would enjoy them as he had on their first secret introduction that she would keep close to her heart.

"We are nearing the castle now, if you'd care to look," Sir Alexander called from atop his steed through their carriage window.

Muriel all but flung herself through the open window, gasping at the sight of the expansive castle hedged by a lake. A calming meadow of what had to be bluebells rose from the left curve of the shining waters. The most brilliant terraced gardens she had ever beheld rose from the right of the lake, with lush tree-covered hills beyond. She didn't know castles could have such gardens. It was little wonder he wished to host a garden party with grounds such as these at his disposal. As the carriage neared, she spied a series of brilliant white tents set up for the day's events in the expansive gardens. Her heart raced at what wonders they might contain.

Instead of directing them over the drawbridge into the castle, a footman pointed the coachman to the path on the right. The wheels crunched on the gravel as they rolled to a stop, merely paces away from the gardens. Muriel fairly danced in her seat as she waited for Sir Alexander to dismount and open the door, holding his hand to Lady Ingram. Muriel almost forgot her basket in her haste. She snatched it at the last moment, though she now understood why Lady Ingram hadn't wished her to bring it. This was no intimate Chilham garden party—the grounds were already swarming with well over a hundred nobility, all dressed in their finest attire befitting the occasion. Footmen circulated with silver trays filled with delightful treats that appeared to be from the hand of a master pastry chef. Her trifling basket of goods paled in comparison. *When will I ever learn to follow advice?*

At the front of the gardens, under an arch woven in thick vines and deep purple wisteria clusters, stood Erik in well-tailored pantaloons and polished Hessian boots, with a dashing black frock coat over a burgundy vest and a matching neckcloth. She liked that his collar was not as stiff as some of the dandies' nearby, which were so high they hindered the men's ability to turn their heads without shifting their shoulders.

Upon seeing her, Erik's grin flashed.

Lady Ingram whispered over her shoulder. "I see you have already made quite the favorable impression on our dear earl, but keep in mind that he is determined to return to sea."

"Of course, my lady." Muriel couldn't keep the heat from rising at her neck. She regarded her white muslin gown trimmed in gold lace. She didn't often wear white anymore, as it was more of a debutante's color, but for the garden party, she thought it suited her and secretly hoped the earl thought so too.

Erik clasped his old captain's arm. "Good to see you again, Sir Alexander. Lady Ingram, welcome." He motioned the Ingrams farther into the castle gardens, his gaze resting on Muriel.

Sir Alexander and Lady Ingram continued inside without her, and Muriel curtsied at his bow. When Muriel lingered with the earl, her chaperones cast her curious glances over their shoulders, but they were soon greeted by another guest and drawn away, leaving Muriel and Erik with a modicum of privacy.

Erik folded his hands behind his back, rolling to his heels and back. "Miss Beau, I spy a basket. Dare I hope there are baked goods within? Perhaps another pie?"

She shifted it in her arms, allowing him to take it from her, his grin setting her at ease. She had guessed correctly that he would appreciate her efforts and not think her an odd country maid for bringing a basket to a party. "Pastries abound, along with the scones you liked and a pear tart as well as another pie. You did enjoy the pie, yes? With the excitement at the Hughlots' ball, it slipped my mind to ask your opinion on it."

He sighed. "I am afraid I was not able to taste it. I met some children who were far more in need of it than I." He lifted the lid of the basket and exclaimed over the bounty, slapping a hand to his waistcoat. "If I am not careful, I will lose whatever muscle I possess before I return aboard ship. You shall ruin me, for if I lose my reflexes, I will be no good to anyone."

"Oh, I doubt you could lose all that hard-earned brawn with a single basket. I think it would take a bakery full of goods to so much as leave a mark." She admired his broad shoulders and his strong, clean-shaven jawline before finding said jawline dropping in . . . shock? She straightened, realizing her mistake in an instant. "What I meant to say was, um, enjoy."

He snapped his lips shut with a laugh, his shoulders shaking as he squelched it. "I shall trust your judgment that my physique is safe." He drew out the pear tart and took a bite, closing his eyes in delight. "I do not know how you held off from eating this on the journey."

She gritted her teeth, clasping her hands behind her. "Would it be horribly unladylike of me to admit that there may have been six tarts more prior to our carriage ride? Though I did share them."

He handed the basket to a nearby footman as a chaise approached. "It seems you will have to bring me another basket in reparation for the theft of my gift then." He touched her elbow, and she felt such a spark she almost jerked her arm out of his reach. "Please, enjoy yourself at the party, Miss Beau, and I will find you later to discuss the punishment for the theft of baked goods."

Warmed by the promise of later, she almost didn't see the lady stepping down from the open traveling carriage—almost. *Elena Whelan.* She turned on her heel and melted behind the topiaries as Miss Whelan commented on the unfinished pastry in Erik's hand.

"It is from the delicate hand of the delightful Miss Beau." His deep voice filtered through the crowd to where she stood behind the evergreens, nonchalantly plucking a flower from the bed and inhaling the blossom's scent.

"There is nothing delicate about her hands, Lord Draycott." Miss Whelan released a trilling laugh that Muriel recognized well from her years in the same ballroom.

She grimaced and refrained from ripping the yellow tulip to shreds. Yes, her hands were scarred and tough. She took great pains to keep her nails neat and tidy and make use of all the hand cream the shop in the village ordered for her. Naught disguised their years of labor.

"How kind it is of you to humor her when you have such a feast in store for your guests in the gardens that I can spy from here." Elena examined the tart with a smirk.

Muriel's cheeks heated as she located the tables Elena mentioned. She was right—again. Disgusted with herself for eavesdropping and allowing Elena to have any sort of influence over her temper, Muriel spun on her heel and forced herself to maintain a graceful pace. She would distract herself by riddling out the recipes of the tent's selection of baked goodies. Standing before the display of pink and white confections, spun-sugar delights, biscuits, and cakes, she appreciated the bounty with a professional's eye. At a cheer from the guests, she turned to find footmen carrying in a masterfully molded vanilla ice in the shape of a swan. Her mouth watered even as she hesitated, remembering Elena's comment on her waistline. *Nonsense. Elena shall not spoil my day with her vindictive taunts.* Muriel stepped in line to await her goblet of ice and had selected a petite iced almond sponge and a tart when a throat cleared at her side.

She nearly choked on a bite of tart at the sight of Viscount Traneford in a rifle green coat and striped waistcoat lifting the brim of his hat in greeting, his dark hair glistening with sweat. She shielded her mouth as she returned his bow with a shallow curtsy. No matter how he had treated her, she was determined to be the lady everyone doubted her to be.

"Miss Beau, I wish to apologize most profusely over my gross misconduct the other night. My mother warned me of the strength of the host's flip. I paid little heed." His neck reddened to his ears as he ran his fingers over the carved head of his stylish walking stick. "I am afraid my time abroad has greatly lowered my tolerance, and I made rather a cake of myself—no, a complete fool. I beg of you to forgive me."

Muriel set aside her plate, dusted her fingers free from crumbs, and tugged her glove on once more, studying the man before her, who bore little resemblance to the inebriated rake of a few days ago. "I must admit, my lord, that I was greatly offended and thought very ill of you."

His eyes widened at her honesty. "My actions warranted that opinion. But if you allow me a second chance, I shall spend the rest of the day attempting to make amends. I promise you, Miss Beau, I am not typically so cavalier in my treatment of ladies such as yourself."

Cavalier? You attempted to humiliate me in front of all of London by reminding me of my worst moment. Well, worst caught moment. There was still that once when she tore her gown, exposing her crimson buntlings. "And why should I believe you?" she snapped, knowing her cheeks were already becoming the color of her former underthings. Lord Traneford should be the one who was discomfited. "You were determined to make light of my pain."

He removed his tall beaver hat, running his fingers about the perimeter, true remorse shining in his eyes. "I reunited with some old friends of mine that night, and, while it is no excuse, I allowed them to sway me into drinking more than I should have. They goaded me into acting as I did before Cairo." He shook his head. "Believe me, I never would have acted so if they had not plied me with such strong drink, and I intend on making it up to you."

Erik's warning against the man's character flitted through her mind. "What happened in Cairo?"

"While I was there, my father died and left the family with precious little to carry us through. I left behind my boyish gambling and became the man my family needed." He sighed. "My moment of weakness upon my return resulted in my abhorrent behavior toward you." He slapped his hat against his knee.

It wouldn't do to reject his apology, even if she would most certainly guard herself against this man's promises in the future. "You are forgiven."

"Miss Beau, you are a saint. If you will give me a second chance, I would dearly love to call upon you next week."

She frowned. "You wish to see me?"

He gritted his teeth. "My family's circumstances have not changed, and any woman who is willing to forgive a drunken outburst is one with whom I wish to become better acquainted."

"I'm not certain that is such a good idea."

"If you still find me wanting after I have sworn off all strong drink, I will owe you a forfeit. Mayhap introduce you to a nobleman or two who might be more to your liking?"

While she doubted she would find any sort of true connection with Lord Traneford, the broader opportunity for introduction to other eligible noblemen was too good to neglect. "You would do that for me?"

"If such a promise is what it takes for you to accredit my sincerity, yes." He grasped her hand and gave a small bow over it. "Do you agree to these terms?"

She would rather not. But wasn't the whole point of coming to London to find an eligible suitor? And a viscount was certainly not one she should spurn. *Forgive, but verify his change of heart.* She nodded even as the handsome face of Erik Draycott swept through her heart. *A viscount in hand is worth more than a handsome earl in the bush, I suppose.* "If you wish to call, which I admit to doubting that you actually will, I will not refuse you."

Erik surveyed the party with pride. Perhaps a garden party wasn't the best means of keeping his wealth a secret and keeping potential brides at bay, but if he were to out the smuggling ring before his contract with the Crown was complete, he had to have all the merchants in one place. The first part of his strategy had been a smashing success. Now he needed to discern which merchant was responsible for the products he had seized and discovered hidden messages in over the past year—hollowed out sugar cane, bricks of tea, and molded chocolate. Then he'd piece together any sort of pattern between his interaction with Requin and shipments that the Crown had intercepted.

Unfortunately, in the week leading up to the party, he had done precious little toward that goal, besides inviting nearly all the wealthiest members of the grocers' guild. He'd been beset with his duty to set the castle and London house in order, but until the issue of Requin was resolved, his duty to the London house would have to wait. His first concern was for the safety of the staff. Trumbull had been reluctant to abandon his post in London, but at Erik's insistence that he was needed for the garden party, the elderly butler at last acquiesced.

Erik wove about the grounds, greeting lords and ladies and merchants alike, when he spied Miss Beau and Lord Traneford together. His pulse pounded in his ears as she gave the viscount an aloof smile.

Erik tilted his neck, cracking it as he pasted on a smile and strode toward them. "Lord Traneford, I thought I told you to leave the lady be," Erik said, keeping his voice low and tone threatening.

Muriel stepped forward. "It is well, my lord. He was begging my pardon."

"And securing her approval to call upon her," Lord Traneford added, a glimmer of triumph in his eyes.

Erik narrowed his gaze at the man. While it spoke well of her character to forgive Traneford, he did not believe the viscount for a second, no matter this act he was putting on for Muriel. Did she actually believe him? Perhaps ladies were more trusting in the country. He would not stand for her good nature to be humiliated a second time.

"Why, Miss Beau." Miss Whelan joined them, twirling her parasol. "It has been some time since we had a decent talk."

"We had quite the tête-à-tête at Gunter's Tea Shop only this week." Muriel's gaze returned to her goblet of ice and plate of barely touched sweets.

"Yes, but our time was cut short before we discussed your dance with Baron Deverell. I did so wish to speak with you about it." Miss Whelan's eyes sparkled.

Erik did not understand what ball the lady was referring to, but then, he'd been at sea until lately. Whatever it was caused Muriel's confidence to vanish, along with her color. He wished to take Muriel's hand to offer her support, even though such a thing was never done.

"Perhaps another time, when we are alone. Pray, excuse me. I quite overlooked that I was supposed to speak with Lady Ingram about a matter." She nodded to the group and departed in Lady Ingram's direction, only to bypass her at the last moment, exiting the terraced gardens at the back, taking the path leading to the woods.

Miss Whelan hid her smug smile behind her fan and turned her bright eyes to Erik. He was supposed to mingle and gather information from all present. The point of this affair, after all, was to sift through anything and everything the guests presented regarding their shipping interests. But at the sight of his confident Muriel's retreat, his gut twisted. The mission could wait for a moment.

"Excuse me, Miss Whelan, Lord Traneford." He gave them a stiff bow and stalked after Muriel, down the gravel path, past the stone walls that melted into rolling hills, and toward the tree line. She was surprisingly fleet of foot for such a petite maiden, and he was forced to trot to reach her before she disappeared into the woods. "Miss Beau!" he called, refraining from clutching his wounded arm, which had taken to throbbing in his attempt to keep up with her.

She halted and swiped her fingertips under her long lashes, sniffing in rapid succession as she averted her blotchy face. He retrieved his handkerchief from his coat pocket and held it out to her. Keeping her back to him, she released a blow that resembled the call of the swans swimming in his lake. He nearly laughed aloud. However, the thought of such a kind soul in distress wiped any mirth from the situation.

He was at a loss as to what exactly Miss Whelan had said to cause such a reaction from such a sensible woman. But there was no doubt more than just the dance was on Miss Whelan's mind. He nearly rolled his eyes at his puerile deduction. *No, truly? A child could have surmised as much from the context.* He really needed to get to the sea again, where his mind was clearer, sharper. The blowing of her nose brought him to the present once more.

"My apologies, my lord." She dabbed her red nose, his initials the only adornment at the corner draped over her hand. "I must look a sight. Honestly, that woman causes such a rise in me—always has since the day we debuted together. She has made it her undertaking in life to put me in my place. She punishes me for my mother's marriage to Mr. Fletcher."

His brow furrowed. He had not been expecting that. A feud over a suitor while at a ball, yes, but a feud over their mothers? "And why is that?"

"The Widow Whelan wished for my stepfather's hand. He preferred my mother."

If Muriel's mother was anything like her daughter, he understood why Mr. Fletcher preferred her. "I see." What he saw was that she avoided mentioning the ball and whatever had happened there to shake her confidence. If she wasn't ready to divulge the details, he would not press. He glanced back at the party, knowing where his duty lay, yet everything in him ached to comfort her.

"You must think me a weak woman to cry so many tears over bruised feelings. It's rather pitiful, and I do not wish to be pitied." She straightened her shoulders and stuffed the fine handkerchief in her reticule with a grimace. "I am certain you do not wish for this to be returned until I have had it laundered."

"I appreciate your thoughtfulness." He offered her his good arm and decided that all else could wait until he had made her laugh. "Perhaps a change of scenery might be beneficial. Just beyond the tree line, there are ruins of an ancient abbey built nearly eight hundred years ago."

Her eyes widened. "Truly? I've read ever so many stories about ruins of centuries past and the lost loves that roam amongst the fallen stones. I'd dearly love to see it if you do not think your guests will miss you."

"Love to see what?" Miss Whelan approached from behind, parasol still twirling as she joined them.

He kept a pleasant enough smile in place, even though she was the reason they needed to take a turn away from the party. "The ruins of Draybridge Abbey."

"How fascinating." She placed her hand on his injured arm. "Shall we?"

Pain radiated through his shoulder, and he gritted his teeth. "Of course." He had meant the ruins as a means of distracting Miss Beau, but as he could not politely refuse, he motioned the pair down the path.

Muriel's brow lifted at Miss Whelan's arm atop his injury, recognizing the insensitivity. "Elena—"

Miss Whelan tripped over a root and stumbled forward with a little cry. Erik at once released Muriel and wrapped his good arm around the other woman's waist to spare her a fall.

Miss Whelan gasped and rested her head against his shoulder. "Thank you, Lord Draycott. You do not mind escorting me the rest of excursion to the abbey, do you? Muriel is much more sure-footed than I."

Muriel smiled her consent, but from the annoyance edging her eyes, he recognized she was as dissatisfied with the arrangement as he. She strode before them and plucked a handful of yellow wildflowers as Miss Whelan secured his good arm. The lady did not cease her chattering of the day's events ahead of them nor her incessant twirling of her parasol as they strode beneath the canopy of beech leaves. "And did I hear correctly you hired an opera singer for the end of the day?"

He nodded. "My uncle was a great patron, and I had a mind to continue the tradition."

His comment was at once swept up in Miss Whelan's line of questioning, which left precious little time for thinking of one response before she required another of him.

The stroll to the woods would have been more pleasant with only Miss Beau, yet as the gravel path turned to dirt, the impropriety of being alone with Muriel occurred to him for the first time. Despite Miss Whelan's trying nature, he was thankful to have another present to save Miss Beau from further scrutiny. Following the path the groundskeeper kept clear, he stole a glance toward Muriel as they rounded the bend to the sounds of the spring flowing behind the moss-covered stones of the once-glorious abbey.

Chapter Seven

MURIEL TRACED THE STONES WITH her fingertips, imagining the time when these ancient walls stood strong and tall, filling the forest with praises to the Lord from those within. Her arms prickled as she ambled along the hard-packed earth where the church floor had once been. Now it was littered with leaves and boasted of a few trees springing up in the glade, offering splayed sunlight upon the abbey's congregants below. Ferns sprouted in the cracks between the moss-covered stones of what remained of the walls.

"How beautiful to dedicate one's life to God in such a manner." Muriel closed her eyes, basking in the reverence.

"You still could join a convent if you are in need of a sanctuary," Miss Whelan interjected, shattering the moment with her strident laughter.

"My bakery is . . . well, was my sanctuary before I came here."

Erik tilted his head. "I've never heard of such a thing. What do you mean?"

"Our vicar once told me any place can be a sanctuary if we dedicate it to God and work diligently unto Him. For instance, your ship could be your sanctuary if that is where you feel closest to the Lord."

"It sounds rather like heresy to me," Elena returned, rolling her eyes. "A sanctuary is a place of worship, not a bakery."

"Exactly! Anywhere you worship the Lord can be a sanctuary—from abandoned ancient ruins to my little shop in Chilham."

A distant rumble brought her attention to the darkening sky. Clouds swept across the gray dome, harassed by the same wind that whipped the leaves at her feet. Muriel shivered, her thin muslin doing little to shield her.

"Ladies, I am afraid I have been remiss." Erik raised his voice above the wind. "I should have tasted the storm approaching in the air. We best make haste back to the castle before the heavens open." The wind whipped his hat from his head, sending it tumbling down the path.

Elena stood on the edge of the furthest wall that dropped about six feet to the spring. She spread her arms and tottered on the ledge, grinning at the earl. He was too focused on chasing down his hat to notice her foolishness.

Muriel snagged Elena's hem and snatched her back. "Take heed, or you shall fall into the spring."

"Maybe I desire to do so in order to gain his attention," she hissed, jerking her skirt away. "And if I happened to fall in and become distressed, he'd have to carry me all the way to the house."

"Carry you with his injured shoulder and wrist?" Muriel crossed her arms as Erik dusted off his hat. "I think your scheme may be flawed."

Elena dabbed at the drizzle upon her cheek with her sleeve. "Yes, you may be right." She leapt from the wall with little care and slipped on the now wet stones, crying out as she landed on her derriere.

"Miss Whelan?" Erik darted to her side, kneeling before her in a manner that had Muriel wishing it was she who sat in the dirt.

The little minx . . .

Elena groaned, clutching at her boot. "My ankle."

Lightning blazed overhead, illuminating Elena's tears and very real pain, shooting a pang of guilt through Muriel's heart. She knelt beside them and discreetly lifted Elena's hem to prod the ankle.

Elena released a wail and swatted her hem out of Muriel's hand. "Whatever are you doing?"

"Seeing if it was truly hurt or simply a momentary pain."

"I think I can ascertain that without you causing further injury." Elena frowned.

"Can you lean on me and put a little pressure on it?" Erik wrapped her arm about his neck and slowly rose. The moment she put weight on her foot, she sank to her knees with a cry.

"I can't carry her. The pressure of holding her in my good arm is straining the injury in my shoulder," Erik murmured to Muriel as lightning crackled overhead, sending Elena into a fit of tears. "And I am loath to leave you both out here unprotected."

"Unprotected?" Elena's voice rose. "Unprotected from what? You do not have wild animals about, do you?"

"It's a forest, Miss Whelan," replied Muriel patiently. "Yes. I am certain there are wild animals about. However, I believe Lord Draycott was thinking more along the lines of the two-legged variety."

"Lord Draycott, I implore you not to abandon me!" Elena reached out to him, panic flashing in her eyes.

A crack of lightning had Muriel clutching Erik's arm for half a second before she recalled herself. "I don't think it is safe for you to be running across the exposed path to the castle at the moment, my lord. Her injuries are far from mortal. The abbey offers a bit of shelter in the corner turret."

"It will topple on us if the bats do not end us first." Elena's tears turned into a whine.

Muriel rolled her eyes as she bent to take Elena's arm, moving them to the shelter without Erik's aid. "I cannot speak to the bats, but take comfort in the fact that, as the abbey hasn't crumbled in centuries, I doubt it will decide to tumble tonight."

♕

The lightning crackled overhead, and Erik winced as Miss Whelan's screams matched the thunder in intensity. The frantic sound sent dozens upon dozens of bats flooding through the arched doorway. Her shrieks could have woken those lying in the cemetery beyond. However, Muriel barely seemed to notice the bedlam as she gathered the dry twigs and branches that had collected over time along the edges of the wall from the rise and fall of the nearby spring. She arranged them with such expertise in the center of the ancient room that he couldn't help but be impressed. He gathered the remaining sticks and set them beside her as she sank onto her knees, finishing the arrangement without any care for her pretty gown.

She rummaged along the perimeter of the turret before selecting two stones, which she struck together thrice until a spark shot onto the crinkled leaves. She bent and blew upon them until the ember blazed to life.

"Huzzah!" She rocked back on her heels, dusting off her hands in victory.

"How on earth do you know how to do that?" Erik laughed in amazement.

She gave him a grin and shrugged. "My grandfather raises black-faced sheep in Dover. Before my mother's marriage, I used to spend a few weeks of the year with them at the tail end of lambing season. My grandfather believed in my being useful, and oftentimes, when a mother would begin birthing, we'd be in the far meadows. When the weather turned, my grandfather taught me how to build and tend a fire so he might finish the lambing."

Miss Whelan's fingers reached toward the blaze, and for the moment her complaints and hysteria-induced hiccups ceased in the flickering warmth.

Erik's stomach gave a mournful growl, and his cheeks heated. "Now, if you manage to provide sustenance, I shall truly be impressed."

She laughed, the melodic nature of it making his heart light. Color sprang to her cheeks, and she reached into her reticule and lifted out a napkin, a sealed letter falling to the ground as she did so. She unfolded the napkin to reveal four baked goods. After stuffing the letter back into her bag, she handed a baked good to each of them and returned the remaining one to her purse. "I was saving them for tonight when I could go home and attempt to recreate them, but if we need to eat the last one, I shall consider it a worthwhile sacrifice."

Erik laughed and split his plum cake with her. To his delight, she did the same with her chocolate biscuit, never feigning a lack of appetite as she bit into the cake as heartily as he, closing her eyes as she savored the burst of flavor. "Why not simply ask my chefs for the recipe? I'm certain they would happily oblige you."

She shrugged as she finished off his offering and took a bite from her own biscuit. "I enjoy the challenge of figuring it out for myself now that I am no longer in my bakery every day to keep myself sharp."

"One would think you'd cease bringing up such an ungentrified topic," Miss Whelan commented without guile, nibbling at her confection. "If I were in your shoes, I'd never set foot in a kitchen again to keep anyone from remembering my past."

"I'm afraid it goes against my very nature to cease baking. In fact, it is my sincerest hope to return to running a bakery one day, even after I wed. However, if I return to Chilham a spinster, you will certainly see me on my promenades to the manor every day after an early morning at the bakery helping my assistant."

"Is that what you do every morning, *unescorted*? I thought you were taking your daily constitutional. I cannot believe Mr. Fletcher still allows you to walk unattended all the way to the village at such an hour."

"My father's most trusted footman escorts me in the early hours and returns to the manor after I am safely delivered, as I insist on walking alone on my way home each morning," Muriel explained as she held her fingers toward the flames, warming them.

Elena's eyes widened. "I assumed you sold the shop long ago, upon your mother's marriage. Was that birthday cake I had made in the village bakery from you?"

"Indeed." Muriel cast another fistful of leaves into the fire, watching them blaze to life before they disintegrated into ash. "We discussed selling the bakery after Mother's marriage, but my stepfather is a perceptive man and knew that too much change might make it difficult for me to adjust to our new life. So Father encouraged me to hire a baker to take up the extra work, allowing me to work only part of the day and Mother to retire to the manor."

Elena snorted, adjusting her position on the packed earth. "How untoward. It is little wonder you suffered from two broken engagements and found it necessary to propose to Baron Deverell. Any man who caught wind of such shockingly independent behavior would be loath to take you on."

Erik turned to Muriel, unable to conceal his astonishment. *She is so independent and yet, she proposed to a baron?*

Muriel seemed momentarily frozen in the act of poking the fire with a stick. Then she scowled and tossed it into the blaze. Avoiding his gaze, she dipped her head under the guise of riffling through her reticule for the last pastry, which she split into three portions. "That was unkind, Elena."

Elena accepted the treat and popped it into her mouth. "Well, you must have had a very good reason to propose in the middle of the dance at the assembly hall then."

He couldn't help but ask, "Is that correct, Miss Beau? Did you propose to a baron?"

At the shattered look on Muriel's face, he knew it was true, and Miss Whelan's barb had found its mark in Muriel's heart. The strong woman he thought he had found in Miss Beau vanished as yet another desperate husband hunter took her place. The biscuit turned to dust in his mouth.

Chapter Eight

"I WAS FOOLISH AND HAVE learned since then." Muriel focused on stoking the fire with another stick, but she knew she had lost Erik's respect as she had that of so many others. She was an opportunist of the worst degree in his eyes. *As well I should be, with the way I behaved. Foolish. Foolish girl!*

"So you were a debutante when this happened?" Erik prompted as he cautiously leaned against the wall, testing his weight gradually with one shoulder.

Elena laughed. "She proposed three weeks ago—hardly enough time for all that learning from her mistakes nonsense."

Tears stung Muriel's eyes along with the wafting smoke. Why had she thought she could outstride her problems before word spread from Kent? Elena was right, again. Muriel had done little to learn from her error. She had only attempted to outrun her colossal blunder. The thought of the vicar's sealed letter in her reticule flitted to mind. She had carried it with her as she promised him but had yet to summon the courage to read it. Perhaps if she had read it, she actually would have learned a lesson instead of simply running from her problems.

"So, tell us, what exactly did you learn?" Elena pressed, her smile too sweet.

Muriel dropped the stick into the fire and rose, dusting off her hands and shaking out the leaves clinging to her filthy hem. "It's only drizzling now. I will go for help."

Erik pushed off from the wall. "Miss Beau, you cannot possibly go out in this. You must allow me—"

She didn't linger to hear the rest of his plea and ducked out of their shelter, Elena's cruel giggles following. Erik may think her a vain, goosecap girl, but there was so much more to her than that one moment. In her desperation to start her family, had she sacrificed any chance of possessing one? *Lord, help me. If this is my path, let me forget my dream of a husband and a family of my own.* Her tears mingled with the rain as she gathered her skirts and hurried down the path, slipping here and there on a muddy patch. She steadied herself before she tumbled. She ran her hands over her face, plastering her hair out of her eyes and deciding to focus on the task at hand rather than the painful past.

"Miss Beau!" Erik called from too close behind.

Picking up her pace, she ducked under a branch to cut through the woods and broke into a run, the stretching of her muscles lessening her pain. She was from the country. She would be fine.

"There are bogs not far from the path! Muriel, do not stray."

Grunting, she lessened her stride and pressed her hand to her waist, gasping for air. She had traveled over sixty miles to leave the past behind, yet here was Elena, ready to present it on a silver platter to anyone with a willing ear. The rain began again in earnest, and she wrapped her arms about herself, wishing she had her spencer jacket as Erik jogged up beside her, cradling his splint. Remorse flooded her. She hadn't thought of his arm. She blinked away the raindrops, hoping he would mistake her tears for the rain. "Forgive me, Lord Draycott. I could not stand to be by her side another moment."

"She was rather pointed in her attack," he admitted and glanced over his shoulder toward the clearing. "And she was not pleased I left her behind. Perhaps that will teach her a lesson in refraining from being brazen-faced in the future so as not to drive away with her sharp tongue the people who would rescue her."

Relief filled Muriel that he had not fallen under the spell of the heiress's fair face and fortune. "Be that as it may, what she said is shamefully true." She pushed back her bangs with both hands once more to better see him and assess his disappointment, shivering in her dread. "I made a horrid mistake before I came to London, and if I could take back that moment, I would."

As the rain increased, he removed his sling and fine coat and draped it around her shoulders despite her protests. He slipped his arm back into the sling and used his good hand on her upper back to guide her under a massive ash tree. "Why did you do it?"

"I think I lost my senses." She laughed, the weight of his coat comforting her. "I should have known better than to follow her advice." She shook her head. "No. I cannot blame it on listening to bad counsel. I *knew* what I was doing was not acceptable. She merely pushed me over the edge of sanity."

"Whose advice?"

She sighed as the rain coaxed the last tendril from her coiffure and her hair tumbled to her waist. "I will appear even more foolish to you if I admit to it. It was Elena who set the idea into motion. She mentioned that her cousin, Baron Deverell, did not have the courage to commit to me because he believed I was uncertain of my feelings and would jilt him as I had cried off his two acquaintances."

"You jilted two other gentlemen?" His voice rose, confusion clouding his handsome features.

She waved him off. "It was not quite so dramatic as it sounds, and they were well compensated for my breech in promise—that is to say, my stepfather's promise. Dear Mr. Fletcher arranged the marriages for me. There was no genuine warmth between us, as one gentleman was in love with another woman who lacked wealth, and the second, well, he had a certain taste for—" She looked away. She would not admit to her horrifying discovery that he frequented his mistress in Dover thrice a month. She was certain if her stepfather had been aware of Sir Josiah Montgomery's well-kept secret ladybird, he would have never initiated the match in the first place. It was only by the grace of the Lord that her grandfather had discovered the cad with his doxy and wrote to her. "It was actually the baron who discovered me in tears after I followed my second fiancé, Sir Josiah Montgomery, to Dover on a suspicion that turned out to be true. Baron Deverell set aside all his business in Dover to drive me home as I was too watery-headed to drive the curricle myself." She shivered despite the coat. "It was his kindness in that horrible moment that first drew my heart to him."

Erik's lips pressed into a deep line as he rested his good shoulder against the tree, cradling his injured arm. "I see. If I ever encounter this Sir Josiah Montgomery, I will have a difficult time not thrashing the man."

"My stepfather saw to that already." She dipped her head, determined to finish the tale. "Elena caught me on one of my walks back from the village and made a very compelling case for the baron. And I, who fancied myself very much in love with the baron, agreed with her and ignored my dearest friends. I do not know how Tess and Vivienne put up with me after that one. I am a pariah in my own village." She rested the back of her head against the rough bark. "I don't know why I am confessing the most humiliating part of my life to you instead of allowing us to simply part ways after Elena's attempt to crush my spirit." She sighed. "My birth will earn you no friends and neither will this tale once it circulates in London."

He grasped her slender hand in his and threaded it around his soaked sleeve. "Thank you for trusting me with the whole truth. Now that we have that sorted, we best fetch help for our friend in the woods, lest she begin screaming again. The woman's tongue can cut glass."

She laughed, smothering it at once with her hand. "That is unkind of us, Erik." She fought back a grimace at her lapse in etiquette. "I mean, Lord Draycott."

"With the secrets shared between us, I'm just Erik when it is the two of us, *Ariel*." He winked at the first name he had called her. "I fear I shall have a difficult time thinking of your name correctly after our memorable encounter."

"As you should only be calling me Miss Beau in public, I don't mind Ariel when we are alone." Truly, the sobriquet warmed her soul.

He pushed himself off the trunk. "Are you ready to astonish my guests by our appearance? I hope the ruins were worth the gossip this little adventure will raise."

"They are beautiful." She sighed, looking back to where the ruins lay. "If it weren't for Elena's presence, I'd wish your party to be a house party so I might explore the grounds further."

"As would I."

♔

They returned to find the servants had moved the garden party inside to the castle's great hall. The walls were now lined with the tables from the gardens, the food seeming to have been spared the downpour. The pair of them stood dripping on the marble stones of the threshold where Erik directed four footmen to take a sedan chair to fetch Miss Whelan and sent another footman for the village doctor.

Someone caught sight of them, and word spread among the guests of the past two hours' events, which explained the absence of the earl and the two ladies. The Widow Whelan at once required smelling salts, quickly supplied by Erik's neighbor and member of the grocers' guild, Viscount Sullivan. Muriel moved to the viscount's side. As she whispered something to him, his eyes widened. Erik frowned. The viscount was a handsome fellow, but rather on the roguish side for Muriel. *What does she want with the man?*

The viscount moved to the widow's side and grasped her hand. "If it will bring you comfort, Widow Whelan, I will join the footmen in the fetching of Miss Whelan."

"You are a true nobleman," she cried from behind the lace kerchief she pressed to her forehead, flicking narrowed eyes to Erik as if she blamed him for her daughter's plight.

Erik bowed his head to Sullivan. "I thank you, Viscount. I would attend her, but my injury makes the trek difficult, and I would hate to slow the footmen in the rescue of Miss Whelan."

"It is my honor, my lord." Viscount Sullivan darted out the door, earning approving nods from the guests.

Erik felt a pang that it should have been him to follow the footmen. However, his arm was throbbing, and he had spent too much time away from the party as it was. He needed to mingle if he was to have a hope of catching a hint of any nefarious activity among the grocers' guild. He joined the party in the great hall as Lady Ingram draped a shawl over Muriel's shoulders and directed her to stand before the grand stone fireplace that was large enough to fit his bed within.

Guy Mayfield joined him, handing him a cup of tea. "Should I ask the doctor to see to your arm after he sees to the young lady, my lord?"

He rubbed his aching shoulder, angry he was healing so slowly. "Unless the stitches have torn, I should be well."

Guy lifted his brows but did not press him. "I haven't heard of anything suspicious from the merchants using the docks along the Thames nor around the dates we discussed."

"And how, may I ask, did you weave such questions seamlessly into your conversations?"

He shrugged. "It was easier than you would think. I complimented the food and asked which dry goods they imported, as you likely had purchased their fine products, and I simply had to praise them properly for their part in today's success. You would be surprised how much information one can obtain from flummery."

"Brilliant."

Guy grinned. "I thought so. Now, what's this about you being caught in the rain with that pretty Miss Beau?"

Chapter Nine

MURIEL CERTAINLY HAD LITTLE WISH to pay a morning call to Elena Whelan after yesterday's long journey home, but as they had gone through what Lady Ingram dubbed "the great ordeal" together, it couldn't be avoided. And since Lady Ingram had a call to pay a few doors down in the same square as the Whelans' current Berkeley residence, the task fell to Muriel alone.

She pulled the bell and waited, folding her gloved hands before her pretty primrose skirts as her lace-trimmed ethereal cloak fluttered in the wind. When the butler pulled open the door, she presented her card to him without waiting for his greeting. He accepted it with a nod and showed her to the lavish drawing room with a decorated plaster ceiling and paneled walls painted a delicate rose that invited guests in despite the ornate gilded sconces and gold-leaf looking glasses. Elena reclined on a mint brocade chaise lounge, her foot propped up on a matching pillow trimmed with gold tassels, her nose buried in a book until the butler cleared his throat.

"Miss Whelan—"

"Muriel!" She dropped her book atop her lap and reached out both her hands in greeting, her smile bright. "I told the butler to show you in directly should you come today, and here you are. How lovely of you to call on me!"

Is she actually being nice to me, or did the apothecary mix her some heavy medicine to induce such behavior? She cautiously returned the smile and tentatively grasped Elena's hands.

Elena swung her foot down, tossed aside the pillow, and patted the seat beside her. "I hear I have you to thank for sending the dashing Viscount Sullivan to my aid yesterday, transforming what had been an unmitigated disaster into a turn of fate." She gestured to the flowers atop the mahogany side table. "He has been most attentive, sending me all sorts of confections and flowers and this novel." She lifted it to Muriel, displaying the rich leather cover with a gold scrolling revealing it to be one of Vivienne's most popular titles. "I thought he didn't even notice me at the garden party, and when he burst through the woods and into the ruins of the abbey with rain dripping down his dark locks and greatcoat, he looked quite gallant. It was as if I had been transported back in time and my medieval knight was coming to my rescue."

"Which is why he selected a copy of *A Knight and His Lady*?"

"Mayhap it is a secret message of his intentions." Elena's cheeks heated as she leaned forward and whispered, "After all, he even took a moment to examine my *bare* ankle for any breaks."

"He what?" Muriel gasped.

"He was a naval doctor before he was given a title for services rendered to the Crown and took over his father's merchant business. To have such a famed surgeon attend me, who is now a viscount and wealthy merchant?" She reached for her silk fan beside her on the chaise and flapped it wildly. "It was all so romantical, and I have *you* to thank for being the architect behind it all, my dear, dear Muriel."

Muriel smiled, vigilant yet that the hullabaloo was a trap. "Well, while I was at the dessert table, I noticed you were speaking to him and seemed most interested, though I assure you no one else would know such a thing," she rushed to soothe Elena, lest her sweet mood turn sour. "I only did because I know you."

"A fact that is all-too shocking, especially after the way I've treated you for the entirety of our acquaintance." She dipped her head, her cheeks warming. "I'm ashamed of bringing up your proposal to my cousin with the earl. Though, I suppose it is better he discovered that bit of your sordid past from you rather than any gossip. One could almost say I did you a favor."

It was rather a convoluted apology, but it was the closest Elena had ever come. Muriel patted her arm. "At least the worst is over. He knows of my baking and of my proposal, so I suppose you *did* do me a favor." *If by "favor," one means ripping off the bandage before the wound has a chance to heal, then yes.*

"Mother is most pleased with you."

"Truly?" Muriel was unable to mask her surprise. The Widow Whelan had held a grudge against her and her mother for years after Mother's marriage to the most eligible bachelor in the village.

Elena nodded, running her fingers about the rim of the book before clutching it to her chest. "And because of your kindness, I've quite decided we need not let the past dictate our future. We needn't be on opposite sides. We are both heiresses. We should aid one another in our search for a husband."

Muriel blinked. This was all too sudden, wasn't it? Though she had seen love soften even the hardest of hearts, the last time she had taken Elena's so-called offer of friendship, no matter how short, she had ended up proposing to Baron Deverell on the dance floor. *But to refuse and make Elena an enemy?* She suppressed a shiver, remembering poor Miss Jennings. After Elena's sharp tongue shredded her reputation over an innocent moonlight garden stroll with the gentleman of Elena's flighty attention, the woman had been forced to leave not only Kent but the country, setting sail to the Americas. "I would enjoy that." Muriel was pleasantly surprised her voice did not betray her hesitancy.

Elena's eyes sparkled. "Wonderful. Now, at the Merrions' party tonight, anyone who is anyone will be there, and I was thinking—"

"Party? But won't your ankle keep you at home?"

She stood, strolling about the room without a limp. "The viscount said it should be all but healed as it was more than likely a light twist and nothing more. However, he commanded me to keep my foot elevated until the party." She bent and sniffed one of the delightful orchids he had sent to remind her of him. "If you mention my extensive dowry to the viscount, I'll be most grateful. The hostess requested I sing tonight, so with my talent and his knowledge of my dowry, he will be unable to resist my hand."

"Of course." Who could refuse Elena when one knew what she was capable of?

She clutched Muriel's hands. "You are such a dear. Now, let us converse over the list of gentlemen you have already met so I can formulate a plan that sees both of us happily wed by the end of the season." She lifted the silver bell on the side table and rang it until the butler appeared. "Please send in the tea cart and pastries from Gunter's."

"You have pastries from Gunter's?"

Elena smiled. "I know how fond you are of their shop, so I had the footman retrieve a basket for when you called as Lady Ingram promised you would. I ordered a veritable feast of sugar, so I insist you take home whatever we don't eat for your taste-testing baking."

After a half hour of the most confusing conversation she had ever had with a Whelan, Muriel was grateful to step outside. She lifted her face to the sun and drew three deep breaths, an act Mother had taught her long ago to clear and focus her mind. The rattle of wheels broke her concentration, and she found the tiger hopping down from Lady Ingram's carriage to hold open the door to the barouche.

"That was a much longer call than I anticipated. I would have wagered you'd rush out at the civil quarter-hour mark. I have been kept waiting in the hot sun and had to instruct the coachman to turn about the square several times to simply endure the tedium."

"My apologies." She settled herself beside Lady Ingram as the barouche pulled toward Grosvenor Square and set the basket from Gunter's on her lap. "Might we stop at the shops? I sorely need new trimmings for my bonnets."

"I didn't know you enjoyed trimming." She blinked.

Muriel shrugged. "I don't. Elena will be joining us tomorrow in the parlor to pass the time, and she thinks I could learn a few things from her."

Lady Ingram pinched the bridge of her nose and sighed. "I do not understand you young ladies. First you state that you cannot stand to call upon her, and now you are having her over to trim bonnets as if you were cater-cousins."

"It is difficult to explain. I suppose the great ordeal did indeed bond us in a fashion. Would you care to join me in shopping, Lady Ingram?"

"I'm afraid I have a meeting today. But if you wish to go shopping, you need a companion as well as a footman to carry your packages."

"I've never required a companion before. I do not wish to put anyone out."

"And now you are living with me," Lady Ingram chided gently as the carriage rolled the short distance to their townhouse. "Your maid shall attend you."

"Charlotte?"

"Yes, take her."

"I'm not certain if she is available."

"It is not her choice, my dear. Your stepfather pays her a fair wage to attend you." She grasped the groomsman's hand and descended as the butler opened the door for them, two footmen filing out to see to any needs.

Muriel disliked putting out her maid but called up the steps. "Clayton, would you mind asking Charlotte to fetch a silk shawl from my room, along with her own hat?"

The butler bowed and sent a footman away to do her bidding.

"Be certain to return before the afternoon ride I arranged for you." Lady Ingram lowered her voice so as not to have the servants overhear. "You've kept Lord Traneford waiting longer than I like. He's an old family friend, and I would not like him, or his mother, to think you were giving them the cut indirect."

"I fear I've never been much of a horsewoman." Muriel detested sounding so petulant, but truly, spending the afternoon with a fellow who had attempted to publicly embarrass her was not her idea of an entertaining pastime. *But he did ask for forgiveness, and you agreed to give him a second chance.*

"The groom and I will look after you. Enjoy your shopping, dear." Lady Ingram pecked her on the cheek and slipped inside as Charlotte ducked out, shutting the door behind her.

"Miss Beau?" Charlotte held up the shawl and gripped her bonnet in her other hand.

"I hope you are willing to do a bit of shopping?" Muriel motioned her inside the barouche and handed the emerald silk shawl back to Charlotte. "This will brighten your ensemble, and we shall appear as two ladies about the shops."

"I couldn't, miss." Charlotte shook her head, folding the shawl as if to set it aside. "In the country, where we are tucked away, it's fine to converse as we do behind closed doors. If all of London sees you treating me as a companion . . ." She shook her head again in rapid succession, as if the very thought was too wicked to whisper. "They will soon catch wind of your habit of disregarding etiquette."

"Nonsense. Shopping by oneself is half as enjoyable as doing so with a friend." She rested her hand on her maid's arm. "Please, do say you will oblige me? You know I do not have a friend as of yet in the City."

"Besides the handsome captain?" Charlotte wiggled her brows, referring to their countless conversations about the earl while dressing Muriel's hair.

"Yes, though I doubt he'd find ribbons and lace as fascinating as you do." She giggled as they alighted the carriage at the shops on Oxford Street. "Besides, what other chance are we going to have to explore such marvelous shops as there are offered here in London?"

"I thought you were attempting to find a husband here and thereby secure free access to these shops?" Charlotte teased and drew the shawl over her severe uniform, the emerald piece and its brilliant golden embroidery bringing a new radiance to her eyes.

"Yes, well, that has yet to be determined. But, hopefully, with the plethora of invitations awaiting me on the foyer table, I will find a gentleman willing to overlook my background."

Charlotte shook her head. "You always speak as if your upbringing was a fault, miss, when I think a gentleman of true character would admire you for it."

Muriel swiveled to her friend. "That bit of nonsense sounds as if you have been reading Vivienne's latest work, *Hearts of Gold*."

Charlotte giggled. "You know that I cannot resist reading whatever you leave on your bedside table. It's your own fault for being away for most hours of the day and possessing so many gowns that I don't have to remake them every day."

After shopping for an hour and gathering a stack of bits and bobs to restyle a remarkably hideous bonnet that Muriel had found for a mere sixpence, she was at last feeling the tension leave her shoulders as they strolled down Oxford Street. Finding herself before her stepfather's original tea shop, she paused. "I know we have tea aplenty at the Ingrams'. Nonetheless, we cannot possibly leave the shops on Oxford Street without visiting Father's tea shop. It will be interesting to see his shop after all these years. He mentioned several times that I should visit it before I depart London."

Pushing the door open, she breathed in deeply, the scent of teas filling her being. The clerk smiled and greeted them before turning back to the short line of customers waiting to place their order.

Muriel took care to keep her elbows at her sides, as the tea shop was filled with displays of the finest tea sets. Along the walls were tins upon tins of the exquisite tea that had set her stepfather apart from his competitors and resulted in the need for more shops to open in Brighton, Bath, Chilham, and Dover. With each new shop, his name grew, along with his wealth. This shop was tidy, albeit overcrowded with tea sets. The shop would do better to cull the selection. She would mention it in her letter to Father.

Her gaze fell on a pretty blue pattern that looked familiar. Where had she seen it before? She traced the gold rim, a memory surfacing. She had caught sight of it through the window of Baron Deverell's inherited cottage by the sea. He had mentioned wishing to begin supplying Father with fine china as well as tea. Surely this was one of Baron Deverell's selections for her father's shop. She waited for the familiar pang to fill her heart—to steal her breath. But it did not come.

"How lovely. Are you considering this for Lady Ingram?" Charlotte asked. "I know you mentioned purchasing her something nice for her troubles." Her stomach growled, and she pressed her hand to her stays.

Muriel turned away from the set. "Charlotte, please tell me I did not interrupt your repast?"

Charlotte's cheeks tinted. "I neglected breaking my fast because I became lost in Miss Poppy's novel after I readied you. There is no need to rush. I can wait until we return to the Ingrams'."

Muriel regarded the now even longer line. The tea set for Lady Ingram would have to wait. She grasped Charlotte's hand and steered her out of the shop and back to the carriage. "There is no need to wait. I have a basket from Gunter's." She climbed inside without waiting for the groomsman and flipped open the hamper to the wealth of delights inside.

Charlotte grinned. "I knew when you said shopping, we would no doubt end up with confectionaries."

"Then aren't you glad you accompanied me?" Muriel winked and held up two filled pastries.

"Why do you think I was ready so quickly?" Charlotte teased and bit into one, closing her eyes against the loveliness.

After consuming their sweets and enjoying one more shopping excursion, Muriel begrudgingly returned home to change for her ride in the park. She quickly concluded she should not have consumed so many sweets, especially with the stays under her new riding habit having to be tugged even tighter to fit properly. Apparently, the seamstress had thought Muriel's bust a good three inches smaller. She felt near to bursting perched atop a flighty horse as she and Lady Ingram rode into Hyde Park for her meeting with Lord Traneford.

"Normally, I would not attend such a meeting, as you would have arranged it 'by chance' without my knowledge. However, as you have yet to learn the ways of London, I thought it best to attend to protect your reputation." Lady Ingram flicked her reins, encouraging her mount around a puddle as the groomsman followed a dutiful distance behind them.

"Arranged by chance?" Muriel swiveled in her saddle as she took in the sights of the park with its graceful lawns, manicured gardens, and vast, curving lake with ducks and swans swimming about. The whole tableau lent a peaceful air to the otherwise hectic city.

"I had many such chance meetings near the Serpentine when Sir

Alexander was courting me." Lady Ingram smiled to herself. "As a mere sailor, he was below my other suitors' stations and therefore not as desirable a match for me. But we were in love, and love finds a way of convincing even the severest of fathers to part with their daughters. Soon my father relented and came to love Ingram. Father even passed Ingram his ship." Something flashed in her eyes . . . a memory perhaps. It did not seem a happy one. However, at the sight of Viscount Traneford on his dappled gray, her expression melted into a smile as they reined in their mounts and waited for the striking lord's approach.

"Now, I know he was rather a cad at your first meeting," Lady Ingram whispered. "But I knew him as a boy. While not the most amiable of fellows, he can be pleasant enough when he makes his mind up, and I do believe he has determined to be quite kind to you. Keep in mind he is a viscount, and it doesn't hurt that he is roguishly handsome. Your oldest son would retain the title while the rest would be deemed only as 'honorables.' It is a travesty to be sure, but his title would more than redeem your little country indiscretion."

"It's the 'roguish' part I have trouble with." Muriel fumbled in her seat as her mount danced to the side. As Traneford approached in a well-tailored riding jacket, her father's warning about seeking character above a title flitted through her heart. *Well, Traneford has asked for a second chance, and isn't that exactly why I am here? For another chance at a good match? He deserves the same courtesy, and it does show strength of character to admit erroneous behavior.* She smiled, playing along with the odd, unspoken London rule of clandestine non-meetings.

"Lady Ingram and Miss Beau, what a pleasure to happen upon you both." Lord Traneford greeted them loudly enough for a passing couple on horseback to overhear. "May I join you ladies in your outing?"

At Lady Ingram's nod, Muriel shifted her horse to the front of the group and sent it into a trot. The groomsman followed suit, allowing the viscount to join Muriel's side.

"Miss Beau, you are quite the picture of an accomplished horsewoman."

"I thank you, my lord." At least she appeared the part in her new crimson riding habit. When it came to horses, she preferred to be in a curricle, coach, or anything that did not require her to handle the beast alone. Following her stepfather's instruction, she kept her back as straight as possible and maintained her weight on her right leg that was wrapped about the horn. *Lord, please do not let me fall.* Squeezing her left leg to the horse's side as she pressed her riding crop to its right side, she clicked her tongue and managed to get the beast to maintain its steady walk. "So tell me what first drew you to entomology, Lord Traneford."

During their ride, she found Traneford pleasant enough. While she feared building trust would prove a difficult task, she wasn't bored in his company, nor so exhausted from his chosen topic of conversation that it turned her cross-eyed like some of the country gentry candidates she had endured in the past. Still something felt off. *Why would a viscount be so concerned with my bruised feelings? And such a handsome viscount at that? Certainly, his title alone is enough to attract eligible heiresses throughout the country. Why is he interested in me?*

"What say you, Miss Beau?"

She gritted her teeth. Once again, her mind had wandered too far. "Pardon?"

"Would you allow me the honor of escorting you with the Ingrams to Vauxhall Gardens tomorrow evening? I haven't been in years. It was most diverting last I attended. There are apt to be several musicians playing throughout the gardens."

"I have heard wonderful things as well—" Her stomach tumbled over itself in a familiar, terrible way. She paled. Was that extra-sweet raspberry pastry in Elena's basket in actuality . . . strawberry? If so, she had very little time.

Erik directed his horse through the park, tugging on his hat as the wind picked up. Returning to London to attend the gentlemen's fencing club this morning to converse with the local merchant gentlemen had been a colossal waste of time. As per the doctor's orders after the strain of being caught in the rain and Miss Whelan's fall, Erik still wore the sling and would do so for yet another week. Unable to practice fencing himself, he had been forced to make the excuse that he wished to study the art. Consequently, he had been shunted to the retired gentlemen of the grocers' guild, who were there more to observe the sport than to pick up a rapier. It was their merchant sons he needed to be questioning, but they were too busy on the piste to converse.

He was finding nothing. After nearly ten days landbound with naught to show for his efforts, he was growing desperate . . . a trait that would do him less than any good. But he supposed it took time to gather information without resources from the Crown, and Requin was not a mastermind for being careless. Running down enemy ships on known trade routes was child's play compared to this.

Erik sighed, praying his meeting with Sir Alexander would prove more favorable than the last one. Though, with his lack of new information, he doubted the captain would recant in his determination to set Erik aside in favor of his second-in-command, Adams. If only Ingram would allow Erik to use his contacts about London. With those, he might have a chance to gather enough information to lead to the capture of the criminal who had put his career in jeopardy.

At the sight of a brilliantly dressed woman atop a fine mount, his heart skipped. Muriel. He nudged his horse toward hers. "Good afternoon, Miss Beau."

"Lord Draycott." She gave him a strained smile, her cheeks pale as she reined in her mount. "What a surprise."

Is she not pleased to see me? He filtered through their farewell at his party, recalling nothing that would broach such a reaction. "I was on my way to see Sir Alexander."

"Is it really a surprise?" Traneford mumbled half under his breath as his horse shifted beneath him, pawing the ground. "How many gentlemen did you expect to have an unexpected encounter with today, Miss Beau? In the future you might wish to keep a diary to spare us embarrassment."

She twisted in her saddle to scowl at him. "I am not like the London ladies, Viscount Traneford. I am not playing coy."

"Not yet, at least." He pressed his lips into a firm line.

"Miss Beau would be happy to accept your invitation, Viscount," Lady Ingram said as she inserted her mare into their circle. "Erik? How fortuitous. We were planning a trip to the Vauxhall Gardens, and I remember how much you enjoyed them as a boy. You simply must attend with us to see if they are still as delightful as they once were."

"I'm afraid I must return home," Muriel interjected, her voice sharp.

Lady Ingram scowled. "But you've only just happened upon Lord Traneford, and it is such a lovely day."

She pressed her hand to her waist for only a moment, which was all it took for Erik to understand the situation.

"I fear Miss Beau is not well."

Her widened eyes expressed shock at being found out. She slowly nodded. "I feel rather lightheaded."

"Oh dear. That will not do." Lady Ingram peered closely at Muriel's face. "You do look pale, my dear. You cannot possibly make it to our appointment with Lady Sutton on the other end of Hyde Park in your condition. Only, she will be most offended if I do not appear for our appointment."

"There is no need for you to miss your call, Lady Ingram," Erik said. "I shall escort Miss Beau, as I was traveling to your home to see Sir Alexander. The groomsman may follow us while Lord Traneford escorts you. Once we are at your home, I'll send the groomsman to the Suttons' to follow you home."

"That would be most agreeable. Thank you." She eyed Muriel. "If you feel the least bit faint, dismount. I do not wish to write your family about a mishap involving your plunging headlong off one of my horses."

Bidding all farewell, Erik's pulse quickened. He was nearly as alone with Muriel as he had been the morning they met. His draw to her was undeniable, but he must remember his calling. The Lord had set him to be a captain not only to end the violence of Warrick's reign, but to save the lives of men on both sides. By reducing the gunpowder being smuggled to France, Erik could give England the advantage it needed. Just because Sir Alexander was attempting to remove him from his position was no reason to surrender the fight now. As much as he wished to pursue the lovely Miss Beau, he had no right to when he was otherwise engaged in service to the Crown and God.

"I'm afraid we may need to make a dash for it, Erik." She pressed her hand to her mouth.

At her calling him by his name, he sat up straighter and drew his mount nearer. "Are you about to faint?"

"No. I'm afraid a lady does not speak of these things . . . but I fear I have no choice in the matter. Excuse me." She jerked the reins of her horse to guide him behind a group of trees. The sounds of retching prevented Erik from following.

He backed his horse away to afford her some privacy . . . or at least the semblance of privacy.

When she reappeared, her cheeks were as crimson as her gown. "And now, I fear I have lost all mystery." She chuckled, keeping her mount away from him.

He handed her his handkerchief, casting about for something to discharge her discomfiture, but could think of nothing to say.

She wiped her lips, then tucked the cloth up her sleeve. "I'm afraid that makes two handkerchiefs I owe you."

"I'd rather payment in scones."

She laughed. "Then you are in luck, as I made a fresh batch last night after a particularly trying drive."

"A trying drive from my castle? But it is merely two hours from your residence."

"During which time I was lectured by Lady Ingram. She disliked my being with you and Elena in the abbey instead of paying attention to a certain eligible viscount, which led her to press me to visit Elena this morning and the plan for Vauxhall with Lord Traneford."

"My condolences."

She patted her horse's mane. "It might surprise you to know that Elena has embraced me as her friend and wishes to see me wed by the end of the season."

His jaw dropped, not only from Elena's abrupt change of mind, but Muriel's admission of wishing to marry so quickly. No lady would ever say such a thing to a man she thought was interested in her. But, if even Lady Ingram was encouraging Muriel to seek the attentions of others to secure a match this season, why would Muriel think he was free? He snapped his mouth closed. After all, she mayhap did not even have the time to wait to marry him even if he were open to courtship. Why did he care? Lady Ingram was correct in assuming that his heart was at sea.

"I'm afraid that if we are to remain friends, there is something else you should know about me."

"Yes?" he asked hesitantly. "You've already admitted to jilting two gentlemen, though for good reason, and proposing to a baron. Please tell me it is not as shocking as all that."

"Almost, as witnessed just now. I am averse to strawberries. Thankfully, I did not ingest a crippling dose. Usually I can tell when something tastes off, but this time I was in such a hurry I mistook some of the filling in a pastry from Gunter's for extra sweetened jammed raspberries. In my defense, I have hardly ever eaten strawberries due to my reaction to them as a child."

"Well, I daresay that is as shocking as the rest." He winked, at once realizing his mistake, but she didn't seem to notice. He reached into his pocket and withdrew another handkerchief, unfolding it to display peppermint drops. "I've found peppermint is quite useful in settling one's stomach."

She popped a candy in her mouth. "I'm glad this did not ruin our friendship."

Friendship. He frowned as he halted his horse before the Ingrams' residence and dismounted. Did she see past his elegant title to the man beneath and find him lacking in the traits she desired in a match? There was a reason he kept his privateer life a secret, as the occupation had certain connotations. He reached for Muriel, his good hand wrapping about her petite waist as she placed her hand on his shoulder and slid from the saddle, stumbling into his chest.

Her long lashes lifted as she met his gaze for half a moment in which the busy square faded from view before she pushed herself upright and preceded him up the steps to the stucco-covered brick building. The butler opened the door and narrowed his eyes at Erik as if he had witnessed their moment from the sidelights.

She handed her riding crop and hat to the butler and paused with Erik in the marble foyer. "I wish I might visit, but I need to take some ginger tea and rest."

He bowed to her. "Your secrets are safe with me, my lady. I have been aboard many a vessel with a seasick sailor and still respected him by the end of it."

Her eyes sparkled. "Very good, my lord. I thank you." She hurried up the stairs, waving to him at the first-floor landing before continuing to the second floor where the bedrooms were.

The butler escorted him through the hall to the library with French doors that opened out to the small courtyard garden. Sir Alexander reclined in a wingback chair reading the news sheets before the crackling fire. The fireplace boasted two caryatids holding up the marble mantel, which had a decorative plaque in the center depicting a Roman chariot drawn by two horses.

"Lord Draycott. What kept you?" He folded his copy of *The Morning Post* and called to the butler in the doorway. "Clayton, fetch us a tray of new refreshments."

"I apologize for my tardiness. I came across Lady Ingram in the park."

"Ah, yes. That would explain your quarter of an hour delay." He motioned Erik to take a seat on the upholstered settee opposite his chair. "Forgive me for not rising, Erik. My leg is acting up again. Let's hope your wound will heal fully and not forever warn you of impending weather."

Erik waited for the butler to close the door. "Have you heard any news?"

"If I had, I would be telling your second-in-command, as Adams is currently in charge of the *Twilight Treader*. It was quite the bold move asking me to approve another contract at a ball where anyone might have overheard us." Ingram pressed his lips into a firm line.

"We were alone. Besides, my request matches my narrative—a captain returning from an extended campaign. They simply do not know that I am serving them as a privateer. And I believe it was you who brought up the name Warrick."

Ingram huffed. "Next time, send an encoded message to my residence and wait for my answer. Do not break protocol again, Draycott."

"Yes, Capt—*Sir Alexander*." Erik ground out as the door opened. He rose to admire the gardens as he waited for Clayton to set the service neatly on the side table and exit before continuing. "Have you given any more thought to my request?"

Ingram snatched up a plate of sandwiches. "The Prince Regent and his advisors, including myself, believe that with Napoleon's retreat from Moscow in October, the war is turning in our favor and should be ending this year. Therefore, I am reluctant to renew the contracts of privateers."

"Even of the famed Captain Warrick, terror of the seas? Surely, your reluctance does not extend to your own ship."

"As I said before, I did not bequeath my title to you for you to weaken my legacy." Ingram reached for the pot of chocolate and poured himself a cup. "While I did not condone unnecessary violence in my time as Warrick, I did set an example of my prowess by burning a ship or two a year, leaving the captain to fend for himself on the wreckage. The sharks did the rest for me."

Which is, by definition, unnecessary violence. "I promised you when I took over the title I would keep the legacy alive. To this day, sailors across the seas still fear Captain Warrick, as I secure four prizes per annum when the average is—"

"Have you not listened to anything I have said? Everything you have accomplished is done without violence except that one time on your last voyage when you boarded Requin's very ship and still allowed him to get away because he knew you would not fight him to the death."

"Requin needs to be charged for his crimes and pressed for any information. He is too important to simply kill—"

"You have gained a reputation for becoming soft in your thirst for more prize money. He took advantage of your weakness."

"Perhaps. Less violence means less damage to the ship and goods and therefore, higher prize money for me and you and subsequently taxes for the Crown," he retorted, selecting a sandwich from the tray. "A fact of which you are well aware, *Captain Warrick*. The act of burning a ship for instilling fear alone . . ." He shook his head. "It seems wasteful."

"Indeed, it is wasteful." Sir Alexander leaned forward and swept a few iced cakes onto his plate. "Nonetheless, if the name is to continue to bear the full weight of my legacy, a ship must be sunk on occasion. For posterity of the name of Warrick if nothing else." At Erik's stalwart silence, Ingram popped a cake into his mouth, his jowls jiggling with each chew as he smacked his lips over the icing on his fingers. "Now, what can I help you with today, as I am not renewing your contract?"

Erik swallowed back his retorts regarding the cruelty of unnecessarily sacrificing captains' lives for the sake of a reputation. While he had been captain of the *Twilight Treader,* no deaths had occurred, and he took great pride in the fact. "I still have almost two months as a privateer before my contract is complete. Since I am without a ship and unable to track smugglers leaving or arriving at port, I will chase the smugglers on land. However, as I am without a crew of men at my call, I need your contacts in London."

"I refuse your contract, and you still wish to aid the Crown?" Ingram chuckled. "You are an earl, boy. Enjoy it. Do you know how difficult it has been for me to get in with this crowd? People have often wondered how I, a sailor not even from the gentry set, landed in their high-society world. Imagine if they knew how I earned my knighthood? You do not know how fortunate you have it."

Erik shrugged. "I took the risk of Warrick's mantle as well. You will recall I did not always know I would be given an earldom."

"You knew at sixteen—well before I offered you the title of Warrick."

"I do not regret my choices to fight for king and country. It is because I am a lord that it is my duty to serve the Crown in any way that I can. As Warrick, I can make a much greater difference than as Lord Draycott."

Ingram chuckled again. "So righteous. Be that as it may, my contacts have all but disappeared as of late." He frowned as he gazed out to the courtyard, where the gardener was pruning a tree that was draping over the brick wall. "If you keep nosing around, it is only a matter of time until Requin discovers your identity. Best you retire Captain Warrick to Adams and throw Requin off the trail. Become the man you were always meant to be—the Earl of Draycott. Perhaps, even take a wife? My wife and I are attending Vauxhall Gardens on the morrow. You should join our party. Surely, there will be a pretty lady there to catch your eye. Might I suggest our little baker from Chilham? Lady Ingram did not enjoy the idea of you two courting for some reason, and was most intent on inviting Lord Traneford, but Miss Beau's dowry is too substantial to ignore."

"There is too much left to accomplish before marrying. And Adams is barely one and twenty! I only appointed him to the position after Mayfield's retirement to show my deference to your opinion in the first place." He should have refused. He should have known Ingram was positioning to replace Erik after ignoring Ingram's first demand he burn a perfectly good prize ship. *Such hubris to think Ingram would allow me to appoint the next Warrick.*

"And I stand by that decision. The lad showed promise at nineteen, and he has proven himself fearless. I heard how he defended your life after Requin winged you. It was providential that he was there. I was not so fortunate." Something akin to fear flashed in the man's eyes.

"I am not afraid of Requin," Erik scoffed.

"After the gruesome fates he left my friends to endure"—Ingram shook his head—"you should be."

Chapter Ten

MURIEL DUCKED INTO THE MERRIONS' conservatory, filling her senses with a deep breath of the rich greenery and aromatic blooms surrounding her. Having Elena Whelan as a friend was exhausting. Muriel's feet had not departed the dance floor since she arrived. Lord Traneford had claimed more than his fair share of dances, which left her only two choices—hide away for the remainder of the ball or allow society to consider her matched with Lord Traneford. If it hadn't been for Elena's timely performance, she might never have escaped the determined lord.

She ran her finger over a delicate blossom and sank down on the marble bench beneath the potted palm's branches. Lord Traneford was certainly proving himself to be kind and thoughtful. No matter how easy his company became, her mind always drifted to a handsome captain earl.

"Miss Beau?" Erik's deep voice warmed her, the sight of his broad shoulders bringing a skip to her heart. "What brings you here? I thought you had suitors aplenty and had no need to hide yourself away like a wallflower."

"Wallflowers are not the only ones who need to catch their breath or find it necessary to hide away." She peeked around the overly large potted palm, whose fronds reached the glass dome above them that allowed starlight to spill upon Erik's dark hair.

He chuckled. "So you *are* hiding. From whom?"

"Well, Elena for one. She has made it her task to see me married not before the season is over, but before the night is over."

"Was that not your task in coming to London? To find yourself a husband?"

She swiveled away from him, his teasing cutting her. Out of all her new acquaintances in London, he was the only one she thought would understand her heart. As much as Lady Ingram would wish Muriel to redirect the conversation, she could not let this comment rest. "Haven't you ever had a dream that was so dear it made your heart ache?"

He blinked, clearly taken aback at her reply. "I suppose everyone has."

"But was it so dear that it hurt at the thought, and people did not understand your pain? Maybe even mocked you for it?"

He slowly nodded and settled on the bench beside her. "Why do you wish for this dream, Muriel? You own a bakery. You have a family and yet, you dream as if you are all alone in the world."

"For more years than not, I was alone, Erik. My mother worked diligently to see me clothed and fed. She would tell me of times when my father was still alive, and her tone fairly bled with longing. I suppose, over the years, her longing for family became my own. When she married Mr. Fletcher, I thought that ache would disappear, and it did for a time, when my brothers were born. It did not help matters that my stepfather's mother dislikes me and treats me as an unwanted guest at Fletcher Manor. She tried to see me wed countless times, only to see me fail due to my inferior birth. With each failure, the ache became more pronounced. I know my mother loves me, as well as my stepfather. Despite their best efforts, I still feel like an outsider in my own home. Therefore, I dream. I wish others would not judge me too harshly for it."

"I do not."

She swiped away the unbidden tears with her fingertips as Erik's hand found hers, the pressure assuring her that he understood. "What are your dreams, Erik?"

His gaze swept up to the starlit dome, pausing as if to collect his answer. "My dreams have always been at sea. There is something about the open water that calls to me, the way the waft of the salty air and the constant sun on my face strip away the pomp and circumstance of a title. Aboard, we are simply captain and sailors. There is order. There is a steady cadence that I did not have as a child. When my parents died, I felt uprooted, and I too longed for a place that was truly mine. I did not realize at the time I would inherit Draycott Castle. My aunt, though sickly, was still young at that time. When she died, there was another uprooting in knowing there would be no other heir but me. I was adrift for those two years studying on land, preparing for my new position. I eventually convinced my uncle to allow me to return to sea. Even until I received word of my uncle's death, I believed I would live most of my life aboard deck."

"Was that difficult for you? Losing the last father figure you possessed?"

"I loved my uncle, but Sir Alexander was the closest man I had to a father after my own had passed. I was loath to part from the life I had built to embrace a life I had never thought to desire, as Earl of Draycott Castle." He jerked a leaf free from a rosebush. "And now Sir Alexander is encouraging me to retire my life on the sea, even though he knows how much the sea is part of me. How much I need it."

"Does he simply wish for you to do your duty by your village in Draybridge?"

"Yes." He rolled and unrolled the leaf between his fingers. "And no."

"Meaning?"

"Meaning that I have not performed as well as he would have liked. When he was captain of my vessel, he managed to secure twice as many enemy ships as myself."

"But I heard from the ladies in attendance that you manage to capture more enemy ships than most other naval officers *without* bloodshed, which is a greater triumph, I believe." She placed her hand on his arm. "With this news, what are you going to do? Are you truly considering resigning your commission and returning to Draycott Castle permanently?"

He flicked the leaf to the ground. "My whole life is the sea. I do not know how to anchor myself to land when my heart longs for the open water."

A wife would be an excellent start.

"There you are, Miss Beau." Lady Ingram swept into the conservatory, startling the pair of them to their feet. "Lord Traneford approached me when he was unable to find you after Miss Whelan's aria." Lady Ingram frowned upon seeing she was not alone in the darkened conservatory.

"Is that who you were hiding from?" Erik whispered, grimacing at Muriel. "Do you need my protection?"

"Mayhap."

With a nod to Erik, Lady Ingram drew Muriel away. Muriel cast a glance back to Erik, disliking prematurely ending their quiet conversation.

"Now, what's this about you not meeting Lord Traneford for the minuet? He was quite surprised by your absence. I assured him that you must have had a good reason for missing the dance."

"We have already danced a scandalous three times together. I tried to tell him that I cannot afford to be seen dancing with him again." *Especially when I need to find a way to admit to Lord Traneford that I do not wish to be courted by him.*

"You have no other serious prospects," Lady Ingram whispered. "You need to entertain him, or you will be seen as a flirt *and* a jilt. I suspected you did not wish to dance, so I've sent Lord Traneford to join a game of whist in the card room. You will be his partner."

"But—"

Her lips pinched. "Miss Beau. You are my charge, and as such, I will have no argument from you over what *is* and isn't proper."

"But Miss Beau has already promised to be my partner for the card game, Lady Ingram," Erik interjected from behind them. "Isn't that correct, Miss Beau?"

She couldn't rightly agree without directly lying, so she simply accepted his arm and gave Lady Ingram a remorseful smile. "We shall join Lord Traneford's table."

Lady Ingram frowned. "Very well, but, Lord Draycott, do make it clear you have no interest in my charge other than friendship. We both know you have a love only for the sea. I do not wish for Miss Beau's chances to be ruined if it appears an earl is interested in her when he is merely passing the time until his wrist heals."

Muriel winced at her bluntness. *Heaven forbid anyone think that.* She knew she could not afford to create an attachment that was single sided. As of yet, the earl had shown her only kindness. Never anything more . . . not like Baron Osmund Deverell and his tendency to touch her arm or brush the back of his hand against hers. The memories still brought a twinge in her heart.

Erik guided her to the card room, which was bursting with tables of four players each, seated with cards in hand. The candlelight flickered in the girandole's convex mirror, magnifying the glow enough for the players to read their cards. Lord Traneford spotted them from across the room and motioned them to the back. Footmen and their trays stood aside as Erik wove through the tables to one where the players were rising, having completed their game.

Erik held the back of her chair as Lord Traneford grinned down at her.

"Lady Ingram informed me that we were to partner for whist. I haven't played in an age, so I may be a liability as a partner."

"Actually, she spoke out of turn, as Miss Beau promised the privilege to me," Lord Draycott replied.

Lord Traneford frowned as Muriel spotted Elena along the perimeter of the room, observing the games. "Never fear, gentlemen, I believe we have found our fourth!" Muriel summoned their footman, and he at once approached Elena on Muriel's behalf.

Elena bent down beside Muriel as Lord Traneford dealt the cards. She flipped her fan open to hide behind and whispered to Muriel. "I haven't seen Viscount Sullivan in a quarter of an hour. Have you seen him?"

"Not since the quadrille."

Elena frowned, the effect making the beauty's plump lips even fuller. "Perhaps I should check the library. He did mention a great love of books."

"Allow him to seek you out," Muriel whispered and patted the back of the vacant chair. "Won't you join us? We need a fourth to begin."

Elena looked to Lord Traneford and to the earl and back to Muriel, her eyes sparkling. "Two after your hand? My, my."

Muriel felt her cheeks heat at Elena's assumption. Traneford directed a scowl toward Erik.

"Very well. I know Mama would not approve of me chasing any man—title or no. Besides, I did promise to help you, did I not?" Elena whispered and took her seat, which sent the gentlemen scrambling to their feet to bow. She acknowledged them with a brilliant smile and a nod, gathering her cards. "I do enjoy a good game of whist, and I am quite in the mood to take a pound per point when I win."

Lord Traneford cleared his throat. "I am loath to disclose this, but if we could not play for money, I would be much obliged. After losing a ghastly sum before I left for Egypt, I vowed never to gamble again."

"How very respectable." Muriel appreciated his wish to abstain from a practice that was considered customary in his circle.

"What? Not even for a measly pound a point?" Elena complained. "The most you might lose is hardly worth all this fuss."

"We shall do what we did at the bakery," Muriel interjected, sending Lord Traneford a smile. "We will play for biscuits! Each player will have a different type to make it a bit more fun in winning. But the trick is not to eat them all while playing. I claim Shrewsbury cake!"

"How perfectly charming." Lord Traneford signaled the footman. "Bring us four dozen of four different varieties of your finest biscuits, including Shrewsbury cakes and sugar biscuits."

※

As Erik dealt thirteen cards to each player for their fifth round of whist, he could not help but admire the noble heart of his partner seated across from him. Even though Traneford had sought to humiliate her in front of all of London society upon their first meeting, when given the opportunity to return the slight, Muriel chose instead to shield him from ridicule. Not only that, but she had shared a piece of herself that might have been jeered as well. As it was, their playing for biscuits took flight, and a half hour into their game, the lady of the house, Lady Merrion, approached their table, eyes sparkling.

"What a novel idea, Miss Beau. The rest of the guests have begun requesting biscuits for play as well. I simply had to thank you for transforming my little card room into the talk of the party! Everyone is attempting to gain a table now to play for cookies."

"I hope I did not put your cook out by instigating this run on biscuits?"

Lady Merrion laughed, fluttering her egret-feather fan. "She has sent every biscuit in the house upstairs, and I just sent a footman to have Gunter's open for us to raid their supply for the morrow. We cannot have our guests departing unhappy because we ran out." She patted Muriel on the shoulder. "It has been a delight to have you, my dear, and I hope you will call upon me this week."

"It would be my pleasure, my lady." Muriel smiled up to the hostess before Lady Merrion sauntered off to attend her other guests.

Muriel won trick after trick, finally bringing their score to five points, winning the game at last. She piled her mound of biscuits and slid them over to Erik. "You need these more than I. I heard your London house does not yet employ a cook?"

"Where on earth did you hear that?"

"The maids talk." She grinned.

"But I only just hired them." Erik mumbled around a Shrewsbury cake.

"Be careful or all of London will know your secrets before the week is out," Muriel teased, sending his heart to stammering even as she and their party rose. Lord Traneford claimed her arm once more, leading her away into the crowd.

To his pleasure, she looked over her shoulder and smiled at him.

Chapter Eleven

"WHERE ARE YOU TAKING US?" Charlotte gripped the side of the curricle, bracing herself for Muriel's wild turn.

"St. James Street!" Muriel called, gritting her teeth and fighting the urge to close her eyes at the terror of driving a pair of horses through London. There were far too many obstacles for comfort, and some of them weren't even stationary. But after yesterday's party at the Merrions' where Lord Traneford played her doting escort, Muriel set aside her fears of driving the curricle and took Charlotte with her to end her suspicions of Lord Traneford once and for all.

She could not trust Lady Ingram's generous assessment of the man's intentions, not after his horrendous first introduction to her. She had forgiven him, but she doubted his change of heart, especially after Erik's declaration that the man had been a trial as a boy and at university. However, working in Egypt did put him in a more favorable light, as surely it took some amount of character to relinquish one's comfortable lifestyle in pursuit of passion and bugs.

"Pardon me, Miss Muriel. Did you say you were directing us toward the *male* precinct after the morning hours?" Charlotte's voice rose as they narrowly avoided a potato vendor and his cart. "You told Lady Ingram we were just going for a leisurely drive, and I daresay, this is neither leisurely nor just a drive. The acceptable hours for shopping in the precinct have already passed and—"

"We *are* going for a drive." Muriel lifted the reins to demonstrate.

"It just happens to be by route of St. James Street. I need to know if Lord Traneford is a changed gentleman who had a bad night, or if he really is a rogue with a plan for my fortune. I do not wish to repeat my past by allowing myself to hold a gentleman in affection who does not deserve it. As for the time, we had to wait after the morning hours to ensure he had departed his residence for the club."

Charlotte gripped her bonnet as the curricle ran over a sack that had fallen off the wagon in front of them. "And this doesn't repeat your past actions? You know St. James Street is all but forbidden to ladies."

"Don't be so humdrum, Charlotte. It's not as if I am going to halt the carriage and propose to a stranger in the middle of the busy road." She snapped the ribbons, following the street signs she had studied this morning on the City map hanging in Sir Alexander's library. "Lord Traneford has rooms in this precinct, and I wish to ascertain from his kitchen staff if he *entertains* as my previous fiancé, Sir Josiah Montgomery. I cannot suffer a third jilting."

Charlotte pressed her lips into a firm line, knowing exactly what Muriel was referring to. "Couldn't you just send someone else to inquire on your behalf, miss? Perhaps the Ingrams' footman?"

"I do not know the Ingrams' staff well enough. What if one of them mentions it about town that I was looking into Lord Traneford's past? It would seem as if I had set my cap for the viscount when I most certainly have not. I am aware this plan is fraught with potential scandal if we are caught, but I have no other recourse. My father instructed me to verify a gentleman's character before accepting his suit, and that is exactly what I am about." She directed the curricle to the back entrance of his St. James residence, carefully fixing the horses to the post. She righted the odious bonnet she had spent all morning trimming with Elena and stepped up to the door and knocked. Charlotte scrambled down and stood beside her, nervously folding and unfolding her hands before her skirt.

A footman opened the door, his eyes widening at the sight of two women on his back step. He met Charlotte's gaze for a moment before returning to Muriel. Though dressed in her plainest driving gown, Muriel's station was clear. "Miss?"

"Hello, I was wondering if I might speak with the housekeeper?"

"Lord Traneford doesn't employ one here—just me and my sister who is the maid and also does the cooking. His housekeeper sees after his and his mother's country estate during the season when his lordship is in London."

"May I speak with the maid of the house?"

Confusion flitted through his expression. He slowly nodded and waved them inside. "May I ask your name first?"

Now came the difficult part. *How to remain anonymous when I don't wish to seem in need of a madhouse or as if I am planning a robbery.*

Charlotte stepped forward. "We wish to inquire after Lord Traneford's character. How long have you known him?"

His eyes widened. "I—I don't think I can discuss such things with two women I have only just met and whose names I don't even know."

Charlotte smiled at him, even going as far as fluttering her thick lashes. "As you can to see, this fine lady is no servant. She is an acquaintance of his and wishes to see if he is a worthy match for a friend." She leaned forward. "A *very* wealthy friend, so she must be certain of his character before she recommends him."

"I see." He stuffed his hands into his pockets.

"Who is at the door, William?" A pretty girl with riotous brown curls joined him, casting curious glances to the women. William informed her of their request as rain broke through the dark clouds. She motioned them further inside. "Lord Traneford is a good man to work for and has been nothing but respectful to me and my brother. He does have a tendency to get buried in his work, though, and creates the most frightful messes with all his bugs and wings spread over his desk."

"And for pleasure? What does he pursue?" Muriel dared to ask.

"He enjoys racing in his curricle, hunting, and cards," the footman interjected. "Though, I should mention that he no longer plays freely with his money. He is determined to keep the family name honorable after the actions of his youth." William cleared his throat and rested his hand on the maid's shoulder. "We've most likely said too much, so if you'll excuse us."

Charlotte nodded her thanks. "Very good. Well then, he may do quite nicely for your friend, eh miss?"

"And who is your friend, may I ask?" the maid said, brows lifted.

Muriel retreated to the door. "As you said, we should be on our way."

A bell rang in the kitchen and William turned to see which bell was summoning him. "Looks like the viscount has returned early and is ready for his nuncheon in the library. If you will follow me, ladies, I am certain the viscount will wish to see who is inquiring after him."

♛

With his latest guest enjoying his cup of tea, Erik held back a sigh as he poured himself a seventh cup. He could hardly bear to look at it, much less drink it, after spending the past two hours in the gentlemen's club sifting through stories. Even though he was under strict advice to let the case of Requin lie and hand over the title of Warrick to his second-in-command, he did not wish for three years of work to grow cold by giving in to fear.

However, his plan to converse with the gentlemen from the grocers' guild that he suspected were involved with Requin and who frequented the clubs had been excruciating. The task required him to question every merchant without their suspecting him, which resulted in his now knowing more than he ever wished to about silks and satins and the latest of fashions brought over from the war. Perhaps many years ago, when he'd considered becoming captain of his own merchant vessel, the news would have interested him. He was a different man now with a new destiny. He had no desire for the peaceful life of a simple merchant.

One last gentleman merchant, Draycott. "I heard tell you and your brothers inherited your father's fleet of merchant vessels?" He forced enthusiasm into his tone. "How does your business fare?"

"Indeed, we did. My father had us take over the family business more than three years ago. We ship dry goods mostly—some high-quality tea too. Got us a goldfinch who pays a cod of money for us to stand in for his usual supplier if needed."

He stiffened at the mention of tea . . . that had been the conduit of his latest interception. "A goldfinch, you say?" Erik handed him a plateful of pastries.

Mr. Coates nodded and selected a tart. "You might know his business—Fletcher's Tea Shop? He has shops all over England."

Fletcher? Erik nearly spilled his cup of tea. Was Muriel's father involved with the smuggler? Surely not. He swallowed and set aside his cup. "Do you run ships for him regularly?"

"Like I said, only when his other supplier falls through. It's only happened a handful of times over the years. When it does—" He released a low whistle. "We are flushed in the pockets."

"Thank you, Mr. Coates." Erik rose. "I must be away. Do enjoy the plate of pastries with my compliments." Erik slammed on his beaver hat as he strode out of the gentlemen's club. He reached for his horse's reins with his good hand, vaulted into the saddle, and nudged his horse into a walk. It was still a little painful to manage with one arm in a sling, but it was better than having to take a hired coach about the City. He had turned onto St. James Street toward his London house when he spied two women in a curricle careening around one of the apartments. He frowned. Judging by their mode of transportation alone, he knew a fine lady was present.

He squinted. *Is that Muriel? What on earth is she doing down here at this hour?* His latest conversation pressing on him, Erik urged his horse into a trot and caught up with the rushing vehicle. Gentlemen passing on the sidewalks cheered and called out to Muriel in the most untoward manner. If his arm would allow, he would halt his horse and box their ears. *I could still take any of these young bucks with one arm.* He gritted his teeth against one comment in particular and rode up beside the curricle. "Miss Beau!"

Her face paled. "Erik? What on earth are you doing here?"

"I was going to ask you the same question, Miss B—"

She shook her head so violently her overlarge and quite hideous bonnet was in danger of toppling from her head. "I would prefer it if you would *not* shout my name in the middle of St. James Street. It hardly bodes well for anonymity."

He frowned. "And with such a request, you seem to be well aware you should not be here at this hour. This is the men's precinct and—"

"I know. I had my reasons." She snapped the reins at the call of another youth and directed the horses as quickly as possible to another, safer street.

Erik sent the dandy a scowl and easily overtook her as she exited the precinct. "As a close family friend of the Ingrams, I must insist you tell me what you were about."

Muriel frowned at him, pulling back on the reins to stop the horses as her maid fiddled with the tassels on a silk shawl that, given the quality, was undoubtedly Muriel's. "It is hardly your business, and I do not answer to you."

"And here I thought we were friends," he prompted, shifting his fistful of reins to rest on his cinnamon-colored pantaloons.

Her pressed lips softened. "We are."

"Then, please set my mind at ease and tell me why I saw you exiting the rear of the apartments."

"Fine. I was checking to see if a gentleman of my acquaintance truly is a gentleman."

"I'm guessing you are speaking of Lord Traneford?" Erik frowned. "That does little to still my fears."

"I wanted to ask the housemaid her opinion on the viscount. I came at this hour because I thought he would not be at home."

"You thought?"

She shrugged, but from the bloom of adventure in her cheeks, Erik knew she was not as nonplussed as she was attempting to appear. "He arrived shortly after we did. We only just managed to slip away when his footman went to fetch him to force us to face the man we had been inquiring about."

Erik ran a hand over the back of his neck. "Do you know the risk you took in calling on a gentleman's home without your guardian?"

"I had Charlotte." She leaned toward him, pushing the repugnant snuff-colored bonnet out of her face to stare fully at him. "But even so, you must vow never to tell a soul—especially the Ingrams. They have already approved of Lord Traneford and have arranged for me to see him at Vauxhall Gardens this very night. It will seem as if I do not trust their judgment."

"You might have saved yourself the risk of scandal and asked me," he replied, though he admired the fact that she wished to discern the man's character for herself without relying on the Ingrams.

"You departed the Merrions' party so early last night that I was unable to seek your opinion. I would think with you being a captain that you would understand the pressing need to take action."

He stifled a chuckle and shifted in his saddle. "Fair enough. And what did you ascertain of the man's character?"

She sighed. "The maid admitted to him being a decent sort these days. I was not wrong in my forgiving him."

He pressed his lips together, not at all liking the idea of her traipsing down to St. James with only an abigail to accompany her to the viscount's bachelor residence. Something could have easily befallen them both. "You should have sent someone to inquire on your behalf."

"And risk word getting out that I was so interested in him?" She snorted. "But now, thanks to you, I'm certain someone overheard you call me by name, and now my secret trip will come to light anyway, and it will be worse than before."

"I apologize for my lack of perspicacity, Miss Beau. I was merely shocked to see you." His horse pranced to the side, eager to be off. "So I take it from your investigation that you decided you enjoy Lord Traneford's company after all?"

She cleared her throat, cheeks blossoming once more. "This is hardly a topic that I should be discussing in the street with you. But, after my findings today, I cannot rightly refuse to see him when he calls, as it seems he has indeed turned over a new leaf. I have no excuse left at my disposal."

"I see." *Not exactly a glowing response to a gentleman caller.* He suppressed his smile. "I shall have to become better acquainted with him. I only knew him long ago before he departed for his fellowship in Egypt. It seems he has changed. Forgive me for interrupting your drive." He tipped his hat and turned his mount.

"Erik, wait." She bit her lip. "I mean, Lord Draycott. Will you be attending the gardens with us this evening? You never sent your reply to Lady Ingram."

Erik knew he should keep himself apart from Muriel after last night, yet the idea of spending the evening with her in the glamorous gardens under the moonlight was all too tempting . . . a scenario a former cad like Lord Traneford might attempt to exploit. *I should go if only to protect her from him . . . and to learn more about her stepfather's business.* "What time shall I meet you in Grosvenor Square for our trip to Vauxhall Gardens?"

She grinned and, in her glee, inadvertently flicked the ribbons, sending her horses careening down the street once more. "Arrive at seven!" she called over her shoulder, laughing.

He shook his head. He would have to take care with Muriel Beau. The once firm lines of the stars directing his life's ship were growing blurry.

Chapter Twelve

MURIEL FLUFFED HER EMERALD SLEEVES, admiring how the rich color complimented her chocolate eyes and hoping that a certain captain would take notice of them under the starlight in Vauxhall Gardens. *Stop this at once, Muriel Beau. You well know the consequences of fantasizing affections where there are none on his part.* She straightened her shoulders. She should be thinking of the viscount, a highly eligible match beyond her imaginings. She supposed given Lord Traneford's line of work, his remaining single was preferred, as surely a gentleman did not wish a wife to join him on his research trips that would undoubtedly bring him in contact with all sorts of danger. She was fortunate enough that Lord Traneford had become available during her season in London. At the sound of the front door shutting, all thoughts of Traneford vanished. Erik was here! She sped to the gilded looking glass to place the finishing touches on her dark locks and tug the curls framing her face and the nape of her neck into place.

"He will fall in love with you before the evening is out, Muriel," Charlotte encouraged her, adjusting the strand of beads woven into Muriel's high coiffure. "And by 'he,' I mean the man who has truly caught your attention."

Muriel felt her cheeks warm. "Erik Draycott may have caught my attention, but he is still heavily focused on the sea. He has no desire for a wife as far as I can tell, and as Lady Ingram said, I do not have time to wait for him to notice me." *No matter how much I wish he would.*

She made haste down the stairs, her slightly more sensible evening slippers for the gardens sounding her arrival before she appeared in the parlor where Erik stood, hat in hand, looking magnificent in his biscuit-colored knee breeches and navy long-tailed coat that were well tailored, leaving no doubt of the powerful man sporting them. She skidded her gaze to his strong jawline and met his smile with her own. Goodness, it was going to be difficult not to allow herself to fall completely in love with a man who had come to know her so well and still did not judge her harshly, especially an honorable Corinthian that cut such a fine figure.

"Where are Sir Alexander and Lady Ingram?" She glanced to the clock on the mantel. Surely, she had not lingered so long before the looking glass?

"They were departing as I arrived. I believe Lord Traneford sent a note asking for them to pick up him *and* his mother." He cleared his throat. "There was not room for me in the coach with the addition, and as they did not wish me to travel alone to our destination, Sir Alexander suggested I attend with you. Lady Ingram was rather put out with the suggestion, but in the end, acquiesced. Do you mind?"

Mind? I daresay I prefer it. She shook her head, proud of herself for keeping such a thought to herself. "They said it was proper?"

"They trust me as a son."

She followed him to the door, ignoring Charlotte's wide, knowing smile as she placed Muriel's wrap about her shoulders. Muriel prayed he did not notice as she rested her hand in his and allowed him to help her inside the awaiting hackney.

"My apologies. I did not plan on having my own coach for tonight."

"Please, my lord, think nothing of it. So the Ingrams trust you like a son? When did you serve with Sir Alexander?"

"I was actually the cabin boy on his merchant ship."

"Oh? Being a fellow merchant is how Sir Alexander knows my father so well—though I believe they also were schoolmates." By his knitting brows, she knew she was rambling again. She rushed to explain, "My stepfather made his fortune in the tea trade." *Steer the conversation back to Erik!* "So tell me, what sort of man of war do you captain?"

He cleared his throat. "You don't really wish to know all that, do you?"

"I do. I wouldn't have asked otherwise."

"Most women tend to avoid the topic."

"I am not most women." He certainly did not seem like a patronizing sort of man. *Why is he being so guarded over such a simple question?* The coach jolted her against the walls, and she reached for the leather strap hanging from the roof to steady herself, scowling at his evasiveness. The drive was far too short for her to inquire further at the moment. She would learn more about the man. She only needed the right baked good to break down his defenses.

The coach halted and he unlatched the door and hopped out, extending his gloved hand to her. She placed her hand in his, her heart beating wildly within her breast at his touch. He threaded her hand through his arm, and she nearly sighed from the comfort of being near him—her only true friend in London besides Charlotte. She lifted her gaze and blinked, finding herself not in gardens of any sort. They were at the edge of the Thames, where a row of gondolas bobbed in the current. If she were with any other gentleman, she would be alarmed. "Why aren't we taking the bridge?"

"It was my understanding that you've never been to Vauxhall before. Is that correct?"

"Yes, but—"

"There is no better way to see it for the first time than the famed water entrance of old." He nodded to the vessels at the dock, leading her to the first available gondola.

Her pulse hummed. She had dreamed of a gondola ride alongside her dearest one ever since she read about it in Vivienne's debut novel three years ago. She bit her lip. This was going to be difficult. It was as if he were trying to make her fall in love with him.

He leapt into the gondola, landing with such ease it barely swayed under his weight. "Are you coming, my lady baker?"

She grinned. Gripping her silk shawl tight against her, she leapt as well. The little boat careened to the side and his arm slid around her waist as she flung her arms about his neck, praying she did not fall into the river and ruin the night. Anchored to him in a forbidden embrace, she lifted her face to his and her breath left her at the closeness of his full lips to hers.

※

With her arms about his neck, arms that possessed a silkiness to them despite years of working in her bakery, it was all Erik could do not to shift forward those few inches and kiss her. He cleared his throat and slowly released her. He grasped her hand instead as he assisted her to the velvet-covered seat at the end of the gondola before sitting across from her on the seat reserved for companions.

"Sir? Why would you sit there with such a lovely lady present?" The gondolier motioned with his hand. "Please join the lady. The view is much better when you enter the gardens."

He gritted his teeth. He did not have time to indulge in this passing fancy of love and marriage. He was a privateer. His calling was to the seas . . . was it not? He had just enough time to take one last voyage against Requin once he was well enough to leave. It was necessary that he stay focused—nevertheless, he found himself saying, "Is that agreeable with you, Muriel?"

"I'm certain it has been years since you've seen the gardens yourself. I'd be loath for you to miss the view." She scooted to the far end of the seat, leaving ample room for him to join her.

He settled beside her, knowing that anyone in passing would assume they were either married or courting. It wasn't fair to her. And yet the proximity was enough to make his blood hum. *Distract yourself.* "So the Ingrams have told me you have brothers."

She smiled up at him. "I have three. Frederick is five, Charles is three, and little Declan hasn't even reached half a year." Her eyes grew misty, and she pressed her hand to her lips. "Pardon me. It's rather difficult to be apart from them."

"I have no experience with siblings. I imagine it is painful to be away, especially with the wee one so young."

Muriel blinked the tears from her eyes. "Indeed. Do you have anyone you miss while at sea?"

He shook his head, gazing out on the Thames as the murky brown river lapped at the small vessel, sounds of merrymaking flowing from the gardens to the river. "I know I told you that my parents died when I was quite young, and I was sent to live with my uncle and aunt. However, I did not disclose the catalyst for my taking to the sea. After the same illness that took my mother and father seized hold of my aunt, my uncle spent a significant amount of his fortune on trips to the seaside and various treatments in hopes of her recovering. He eventually purchased an estate by the sea to accommodate her needs, which put the castle in dire straits. I volunteered to become a ship's boy to keep from further burdening my relatives."

"How old?"

"Eight years. I was rather old for beginning the position, but my uncle's childhood friend, Alexander Ingram, awarded me the opportunity. I took to the sea with a joy I had never known. Certainly, I had a happy childhood at Draycott Castle whenever Captain Ingram spent the winter season ashore, but the sea spoke to a side of me that I had not known existed. I worked as a cabin boy until my sixteenth year when my aunt died and my uncle requested I return to Draycott Castle to study to take over the earldom."

"And when the war began a decade ago? What happened then?"

He forced his limbs to relax. He disliked veiling the truth. *It is for her own safety. She cannot know this side of me.* "After two years of diligent study, I returned to sea under the command of Captain Ingram in the winter of 1803 at the age of eighteen."

While privateering was far from illegal if one followed the charter, it wasn't exactly a position the Ingrams or he wished to disclose to anyone. It was too gray of an area for the nobility to think acceptable in their polite society. When the war began, Ingram had turned from simple merchant shipping and reassumed his privateering identity for the Crown. For five years Erik sailed under his command—five hard years in which he struggled to balance obedience and his own conscience. He had never taken a life or drawn a drop of blood at the time. While some of the crew mocked him, Ingram protected him. Then Ingram was injured and passed the name of Warrick on to him. Under his control, Erik swore to himself to change the way the *Twilight Treader* was commanded. Thus far, he had never had to fire upon a single ship. Even without violence, *Warrick* struck terror into any sailor's heart— along with the flag the original privateer had created declaring it was he, black with crossbones over a sinking ship. Either was enough to inspire surrender.

"I stayed under Ingram's command for five years until his leg was injured. Then he was knighted for his services to the Crown and retired. At three and twenty, I was granted the position of captain and continue his legacy to this day." There. That was not a lie.

They arrived at the Water Gate entrance and, tossing two shillings to the proprietor, Erik helped her from the swaying gondola. "Close your eyes, Miss Beau."

Instead of viewing the entrance to the gardens, he kept his eyes on her as they stepped through the archways. "Open your eyes." He laughed in delight as her eyes widened and full lips parted in wonder. She clasped her hands at her slender throat at the sight of the lanterns hanging from the trees and minstrels playing their merry tunes as servants on their night off danced beneath the stars.

"Oh. Erik. It's splendid."

Did she know what she did to him when she called him by name? No one addressed him as Erik anymore. It was always *Captain* or *my lord* or *Draycott*. The tenderness she injected into his Christian name was enough to soften the hardest of privateers' hearts. What if Ingram's refusal to bestow a new contract was in reality a blessing from the Lord? What if God really was calling him to return home to care for the village of Draybridge? *Or is it simply the vivacity of Miss Beau that is muddling my brain?*

Chapter Thirteen

THE TREES SPARKLED AS WITH a thousand stars. She lifted her eyes to the branches. Lanterns shone overhead as if hung there by fairies to usher them into an enchanted spring party. Nearby, a band played a familiar country dance that had even the refined noblemen and ladies swaying to the jig as they traversed the grand walk.

She felt her hand guided into the crook of Erik's arm, and she smiled up at him. She longed to pull him into the dance and give in to the revelry, but that was what Muriel of old would have done. The new Muriel was too much of a lady to breach etiquette, and yet—she tugged his arm, dragging him down a bit to be heard over the music. "Before we join the others in the left colonnades of supper boxes, do you think we can explore some? I know they are expecting us. However, they might be late, and we might be waiting in the supper box for the rest of our party to arrive for ages yet."

For his answer, he pressed a hand to the small of her back and hustled them past the fountain in front of the semicircle where the diners looked out from their boxes to view the merriments. She laughed, knowing they were running to avoid being spotted by their party. Safely on the corner and out of sight, he slowed, leading her into the grove where a beautiful four-storied round orchestra box stood in the center. Beneath its domed roof and pointed turrets, dazzling lights lit an orchestra playing the most lively tune.

Erik chuckled.

"What?" She looked around for the source of his laughter.

He nodded to her slippers. "Your feet have not ceased tapping since coming ashore. Would you care to dance?"

Her brows lifted. "Do you know this dance? It is not one you would find in many London ballrooms."

He grinned and bowed, flipping his hand out to her. "We were not so refined aboard ship as you may imagine, Miss Beau. I can dance a country jig as well as any ballroom quadrille."

She rested hers atop his, a spark traveling up her arm as she gave in to the impulse for the country dance at last. The whirling, unrefined dance left her gasping in delight at Erik's adept dancing. He had not been exaggerating. She whirled in his arms, her shawl slipping from her shoulder and the lights blurring until all she beheld was Erik. For the first time since coming to London, she felt truly free.

The song concluded too quickly, and Erik led her from the circle of dancers, out to the pathway, past the second colonnade, and toward the entrance that would eventually lead them back to the supper boxes.

"What pulls you to Draybridge?"

"Pardon?" He tilted his head.

"Forgive my abrupt change in topic. Sometimes I forget to transition and ask what I am really thinking." She ran her fingers down the trim of her shawl. "Even at our first meeting, you confessed how your heart longs to be at sea, but lately I have sensed turmoil in this choice between remaining on land and returning to the sea. What makes you wish to stay? Do you have friends in Draybridge?"

He lifted his gaze to the lanterns hanging in the branches. "I suppose my hesitation is that after being in Draybridge for the garden party, I felt the need for my presence."

"Your steward does an admirable job, though."

"Indeed. In fact, my steward was my former second-in-command. Mr. Mayfield had some family obligations that called him to shore and required a steadier, less dangerous means of income. I needed a steward, so I offered him the position. I expect it would feel like old times should I return and we again worked side by side."

"Miss Beau, there you are!" Lord Traneford called, the rest of their party trailing behind him, including the Whelans and Viscount Sullivan. "I hope we did not keep you waiting at the entrance for long."

"Lord Traneford." She dipped her head. "We have been taking in the grounds for a half hour and have been well entertained by the delights of the gardens." She smiled and curtsied to the new guests, briefly clasping the Dowager Viscountess Traneford's hand with both of her own. "What a pleasant surprise. I did not know the Whelans or Lord Sullivan would be joining our party."

"Lord Traneford invited us over another game of whist last night, and, as Lord Sullivan was with us, he extended the invitation to him as well," Elena interjected, beaming as she embraced Muriel. "Quite the merry party we have become. Now, where are the supper boxes? I must admit that I am famished."

Within a quarter of an hour, all were seated in a supper box. Muriel found herself between Lord Traneford and Erik. Unlike formal dinners, the conversation did not follow turns, which led to the boxes surrounding them filling the colonnades with riotous conversation and bawdy laughter.

"What do you think of the supper boxes?" Erik called in her ear, just loud enough to be heard above the noise.

"Diverting, but not conducive for much else," she replied with a giggle. A deep laugh from a nearby box caught her ear, ripping her from the moment. She stiffened. *It couldn't be him.* She dared a glance, spying a familiar fleshy chin and painstakingly arranged windswept hair.

As if hearing her thoughts, Sir Josiah Montgomery lifted his attention from his mistress's neck to spot her across the way. He narrowed his eyes at her, leaving little doubt that he had yet to forgive her for tossing him to the side when she discovered his transgressions in Dover and, therefore, ending his trading business with her father . . . which would account for his dislike of her.

"Miss Beau?" Erik lightly touched her hand.

She looked at the tablecloth, her cheeks heating as her stomach turned. She swallowed. She must not allow seeing Montgomery with his tart to unhinge her. Daring to glance his way again, she found Montgomery still staring at her.

"I—I think I need some air." She stumbled to standing. Lord Traneford and Erik rose with her—concern in their countenances. She waved off everyone's inquiries with a forced laugh.

Lady Ingram grasped her arm as she tried to pass by, keeping her from leaving the box. "What's wrong?"

"I will be back momentarily, Lady Ingram. It's rather too warm."

Erik reached her side, but before he spoke, the Dowager Viscountess looked to her son. "Tristian, dear, will you escort Miss Beau?"

"It would be my honor." He bowed to Muriel and extended his arm. "Shall we?"

A moonlit amble with the man who thinks he is my beau? What could go wrong? She plastered on a smile and accepted his arm. Anything was better than having Montgomery and his mistress stare at her all evening.

"Well, I, for one, agree with my husband. I think it is time for you to retire, Lord Draycott, and enjoy all that London has to offer." Lady Ingram gestured to their surroundings.

"There is time for that yet after I finish serving the Crown," Erik replied, praying for a redirection in conversation. *Where is she?* He gripped his hand into a fist at the thought of Muriel with Lord Traneford out in the garden in the moonlight. This place did not have a promenade dubbed Lovers Walk for naught. He rose from the table as their order arrived. "If you'll excuse me, I believe I will take some air as well."

Captain Ingram's eyes gleamed. Of course the man recognized Erik's true mission.

Erik pushed past the crowds to the promenade lined with torches, which added an even more festive air to the thousands of lanterns dotting the trees. If this did not cause a couple to fall in love, he did not know what would. He broke into a trot, only skidding to a halt on the gravel when he spied a couple seated on a bench along the tree line.

"I believe we are well suited, Miss Beau." Lord Traneford grasped her hand in his.

Erik gritted his teeth. *Is he actually proposing already?*

"I have been engaged twice before, my lord. I do not intend on becoming engaged for a fourth time." Muriel straightened her shoulders.

Traneford laughed. "A fourth? Are you already planning on breaking my heart too, Miss Beau?"

"I am simply saying I have learned from painful experience that rushing into an engagement will gain us nothing but embarrassment and potentially heartache if a longer acquaintance discovers undesirable traits in one another before a wedding is discussed." Muriel dipped her head. "Not even a title can convince me to enter into an engagement lightly."

Erik's pulse slowed. The lady truly had learned from her past. If he had not already believed it, her declaration solidified it.

"My heart will not be easily swayed. If you honestly believe we would make a good match beyond the simple exchange of wealth for title, you must persuade me, sir."

Persuade her? What on earth does that mean? Surely she did not mean to insinuate that she wished for the man to kiss her?

"Then, convince you I shall." Lord Traneford leaned toward her, his lips pursing.

No! Erik burst from his hiding place, trying to keep his breathing tranquil.

Muriel shot to her feet, and Lord Traneford sent him a scowl.

"Sir Alexander and Lady Ingram were wondering what was keeping you both. Dinner has arrived."

"As much as I loathe the interruption during a most interesting tête-à-tête, I've been gutfoundered for an hour. Shall we, Miss Beau?" Lord Traneford extended his arm to her.

"I'm loath to keep you from your meal, Lord Traneford, but I fear I may faint if I must return to that crowded supper box at the moment." Muriel flicked her feathered fan.

"Even with it being open air?" Doubt tinged Traneford's query.

She offered a helpless shrug.

"No fear. I shall stay with her for a few moments yet." Erik strode to her side, aiding her to the bench seat once more. "Lord Traneford, would you tell the Ingrams we shall return in a quarter of an hour?"

Traneford scowled. Erik hid a smirk. He had played his cards well.

"Very well." Traneford slowly nodded, starting for the boxes. "If you haven't returned in that time, I shall come in search of you."

Muriel slumped back onto the bench with a groan.

"Muriel? Are you truly unwell?" He glanced down the path to Traneford's retreating figure.

"Do you recall my mentioning a fiancé with a mistress?"

He tensed. "How could I not?"

"I spotted Josiah Montgomery in the colonnade. It's the first time we've seen each other since my stepfather threw him out of our house after I revealed what I discovered in Dover."

Erik's fists clenched. "Did Montgomery say something to you?"

She shook her head. "He was too far away. But he gave me such a glare I thought he might burn me in my seat." She grasped Erik's hand. "I cannot return until I know he is gone. I cannot bear to see him with her. I thought I was beyond these feelings of mortification." She swallowed. "Did I tell you what he told me when I discovered them in a scandalously passionate embrace in a tearoom?"

Erik ran his thumb over her hand, waiting for her to continue even as a surge of protectiveness for this woman called him to leap into action. "I will not betray your confidence if you wish to disclose it to me."

"He told me I should be happy enough that he was marrying me, because I was only a tabby baker's daughter, and I should have expected him to have a mistress as I am not all that pretty, and most gentlemen have a ladybird on the side in any event."

"If you point him out to me, I will personally see to it that he departs at once." Erik growled, his fist curling even as his wrist protested the act.

She shook her head. "I want nothing more to do with him. I do not wish to see him, much less speak with him again."

"The man was a fool for what he did to you and in serious need of spectacles." Spying a tear glide down her cheek, he gently wiped it away with his thumb. *Such a kind, gentle spirit. That man did not deserve you.* "You are the most beautiful woman I have ever beheld."

Her long, tear-clumped lashes lifted and she studied him. "And you are the most handsome man I have ever beheld."

Erik's chest tightened. He could not allow himself the liberty of dreaming of a life with her when he was not free. He was not like Montgomery. He would not take advantage of her pure, trusting nature. He laughed and extended his arm to her. "On that note, shall we be getting back? And I promise if you see he is still there, I will find an excuse to sweep you away at once."

Muriel swiped at her cheeks. "He'd better be away, because I've heard the heart cake here is divine, and I have been longing to test it."

"In that case, I will find a reason to have Montgomery swept away at once instead." As he hoped, this brought a smile to her lips.

"That is exactly what my stepfather would say."

"Speaking of your stepfather, I met a gentleman at the club just this morning who works for Mr. Fletcher on occasion."

"Oh?" Her cheeks paled in the lantern light as her fingers resting on his arm trembled. "Wh–who was it?"

"A Mr. Coates from Coates and Sons Shipping." He wove them about the crowds surrounding the supper boxes, discreetly watching for her expression.

The apprehension fled her face, replaced with . . . relief? "Ah, Mr. Coates! I remember him well. How is he?"

Who was she expecting, to cause such a transformation? "He is well, albeit long-tongued."

She shook her head. "That is what I told my stepfather. However, he insisted on having someone ready should our first supplier fall through, and Mr. Coates was eager enough to accept Father's rate."

"According to Mr. Coates, it seems your first supplier has failed on multiple occasions. Why would your stepfather keep on someone so unreliable?"

She shrugged. "Father keeps me out of the business side and only calls upon me to aid him in selecting patterns for tea sets and occasionally act as his emissary to the tea warehouse when he is ill. The only reason I know so much about Mr. Coates is that he was quite talkative during one such inspection to the warehouse after he delivered a shipment." She rose on her tiptoes, craning to look over the crowd. "I cannot find Sir Josiah. I believe we are safe."

Lord Traneford spotted them from the box and waved, the rest of the party spying them at once. Knowing his questions would have to wait, Erik led her to the box. He would send a message to Ingram tonight and request he discreetly look into Mr. Fletcher's suppliers.

Chapter Fourteen

ERIK SPREAD HIS ARMS WIDE as he stepped out of the doctor's office on Welbeck Street, the steady rainfall making the street unusually empty. While his wrist remained wrapped to immobilize the sprain, his shoulder had healed nicely in the fortnight since his arrival in London. He rolled his shoulders gingerly, enjoying the freedom of unencumbered movement, even if the stiffness would take some time to work out. *What will Muriel have to say about my arm no longer being in the sling?* Seeing as he was only a half mile from Grosvenor Square, he decided to hike to Miss Beau's home, call, and find out. He swung his arm, testing it. Now that his arm was healed, he wouldn't have to take the coach to and from his castle. His horse could do the work in half the time.

By the time he trotted up the steps and lifted his fist, the rain had subsided to a gentle mist, but before he could knock, the door swung open. Clayton, the Ingrams' butler, stood on the threshold, a sealed letter in hand.

"Ah, my lord. I was watching for you. Sir Alexander thought you might call and said to tell you to meet him at Montagu House by four of the clock."

"The museum?"

"Yes, my lord." He blinked, offering no other insights, and handed him a ticket. "Sir Alexander secured your admission."

Erik pocketed the ticket. He suspected Sir Alexander only invited him everywhere either to display the life he could have as an earl or

131

to keep him so busy he could not pester for another contract. Sir Alexander must have forgotten it wasn't in Erik's nature to withdraw from a challenge.

"He also wished for me to hand this to you personally."

Erik accepted the sealed note, nodded his thanks, and waited for Clayton to shut the door before he tore it open, his heart pounding in anticipation of the contents. He had been waiting some days for Ingram to answer his encoded message.

Wrote to friend. Neither he nor first supplier a threat. Second supplier is a tax evader. A. I.

Tax evasion, eh? Not exactly the traitors he wished to capture, but perhaps Coates would yield some useful information one day. He grinned, tucking the missive into his waistcoat pocket. He could work with that. While Coates, the tax evader, may not respond to an honorable call to aid his country, he would likely respond to a threat. Erik lifted his hand and hailed a passing hackney coach. He had an hour before he needed to meet Sir Alexander. He would make use of it. "London Docks. Coates and Sons."

Settling onto the worn tufted-leather seat, Erik rolled his shoulder again, pausing as he realized his first thought regarding his arm had been about Muriel and not his mission. His gut twinged in guilt. Two weeks ago, he would have danced a jig to a sea shanty. Now his first thought was of how Muriel would enjoy seeing him better . . . and how he wished for her to see him as powerful as he had been before the injury.

Lord, what is happening? Why am I distracted from the calling You placed on my heart?

"Coates and Sons!" The hackney driver called, thumping his fist on the roof of the coach.

He grimaced. He had passed the entirety of the journey lost in thoughts of the lovely baker. *Concentrate, or you will get yourself killed.* Erik patted his greatcoat to ensure the pistols in his shoulder harness were not visible. When he had removed his coat in the doctor's office, his physician's eye had twitched over the weapons, but he had not betrayed his shock further. With Requin's men about the City, it would be foolish not to carry protection. He descended the coach before a shop with a wooden sign that hung lopsided from a broken chain. "Wait for me."

He shoved open the door, the copper bell jingling overhead. He squinted in the dark room. The only window was at the front of the building, and the room was lit only by a single taper.

"Lord Draycott?" The Mr. Coates he'd met at the club rose from behind his writing desk, the crumbs from his nuncheon dusting his waistcoat. He snatched up his cutaway coat from his chair and stuffed his arms through the sleeves before patting his greased hair that was combed over the thinning patch atop his head. He greeted Erik with a handshake, the grease coating his hair now on Erik's palm. "What can I do for you, my lord?"

"I don't have much time, so I'll get straight to it. Since our conversation at the club, I have discovered you owe a great deal of money to the Crown."

Coates's smiling visage vanished. "I don't know what you are implying. We are an honest business."

"Until you took it over." Erik examined the dusty shelves filled with ledgers and the massive map on the wall behind the man's desk.

"I don't know who you think you are, but you do not wish to get on my bad side."

"Same." Erik narrowed his gaze.

"If you are a lord, you are obviously well connected." Coates crossed his arms, studying Erik. "What do you want?"

"Information. Have you ever worked for a man called Requin?"

He snorted. "I work with a lot of people." He gestured to the wall of ledgers. "It's a shipping company, after all."

"Requin is . . . memorable." Erik ran his finger over the ledgers, marked by year. It would take weeks to go through them all. He removed a card from his waistcoat and extended it to Coates. "If you wish for your tax evasion to remain a secret, you will ask about him and send a note to my London residence the moment you hear of anything."

"No one comes into my family's shop and threatens us. If you know what's good for you, you will never come in here again." Coates jabbed his finger in Erik's shoulder, his eyes widening as he felt the pistol hidden beneath.

Erik ignored the throbbing in his shoulder from the man's jabbing and tugged his greatcoat so that both pistols' outlines were evident. "I will be expecting a note from you, or I will be reporting your theft." Erik strode from the building and into the hackney. "Montagu House."

After having to take an alternate route to avoid several carts that had overturned in the middle of the road, Erik was much later than he had hoped in arriving to the museum. Tossing his coin to the driver, he trotted up the steps as thunder cracked and handed his ticket to the attendant who stood just inside the front door. The man eyed Erik's dripping coat but waved him inside.

"Lord Draycott!" Sir Alexander summoned him from across the room in Montagu House, which housed the collection of the British Museum.

Muriel twisted her hands behind her back as she stood by the side of a tall, gangly gentleman donning a blond wig, a fashion that was still popular among the elderly set. When she spotted him, her expression melted into a genuine smile. "Your arm! The doctor released you from your sling at last!"

He grinned and rotated his shoulder to demonstrate his freedom. "Nearly good as new."

Her gaze fell on his wrist. "But your wrist is still wrapped?"

"I have nearly full range now, but my doctor is ever cautious."

Muriel slipped her hand through Erik's arm, guiding him away from her group and pointing to a rare coin collection as if she couldn't help but be drawn to it. "Thank goodness you have arrived."

"Oh?" He grinned down at her, quite getting used to the feel of her on his arm, despite his need to remind himself that friendship was all he was able to offer at this time. Though that argument had grown more and more difficult to remember. The past two weeks had been filled with invitations from the Ingrams that had brought him alongside Muriel daily, making his time in London a delight—something he never would have thought possible with attending teas, card parties, dinners, balls, operas, and the like every afternoon until he had met Muriel.

"Yes, Lady Ingram discovered my hesitancy to accept Lord Traneford, as I am sure you are aware since she has been inviting gentlemen out with us at every turn to further display Lord Traneford's desirability."

He chuckled. "I had suspected as much, but given your propensity to evade said gentlemen by engaging me in conversation whenever they are near, it seems Lady Ingram's efforts have proven fruitless."

"Unfortunately the current nobleman can't seem to be near me without touching me." She grunted, leaning forward to examine the chipped coins in the display case.

"He what?" he fairly growled—all thoughts of obtaining his next letter of marque vanishing.

Her eyes widened in alarm. "Oh! I do not think he is doing it purposefully. I believe he is rather unbalanced."

"I'm certain that's what he'd like you to believe," he mumbled. "Point him out, and I'll have a word with him that he will not soon forget."

She giggled. "If you do not believe me, stand beside him and see for yourself."

"I'm not going to stand close to a man I do not even know."

"I saw the judgment in your expression. He is a nice old gentleman and shouldn't be judged harshly simply because he is a bit unsteady on his feet." She wove them through the crowd toward the nobleman in question—the elderly fellow sporting the blond wig.

"You cannot be serious that Lady Ingram believes him to be a suitable match?" Erik whispered through the side of his mouth.

"He is extremely kind. Now, go stand by him." She released her hold on his arm and gave him a little nudge.

He stood beside the man, and as if drawn to Erik, the elderly fellow leaned toward him more and more closely in his commentary on the array of ancient medals before them. The man was still chattering when Erik slipped away to Muriel's side once more. "You are indeed correct. He is unstable. Why would they think he is a suitable candidate for you? He is well over seventy."

"Age shouldn't be an obstacle when it comes to true love."

He blinked. "What?"

"That's what I thought." She wrinkled her nose. "Lady Ingram told me that after I pointed out the gentleman in question is nearly fifty years my senior. A gentleman a decade, or even two, older than me might be an acceptable match. At his towering years, we would hardly have any time together before I was dressed in widow's weeds."

"With such arguments as that, I would suspect that Lady Ingram is tiring of hosting you," he teased.

The light in her eyes dimmed. "Do you truly think so? I've only been here a couple of weeks, and if she is tired of my company, I need to make arrangements—"

"My apologies, it was a poor jest."

They paused to peruse the rare manuscripts on display. "What about your prospects, Lord Draycott? Should I be baking a wedding cake for you in the near future? There is one I have been wishing to try that is four tiers high with the most elegant sugar flowers. It would take a full day to create."

Her tone was pleasant enough, but there was a brightness missing from her voice. He tugged the front of his greatcoat. He had attempted to keep her feelings untouched. Her tone hinted at something—something his heart was beginning to echo. "I believe I am preparing myself for a life alone, so I'm afraid your new cake will have to wait until your next friend weds. Perhaps Miss Whelan?"

Muriel smiled down at a pair of children weaving through the patrons, giggling as they chased one another, oblivious to the treasures surrounding them. If he wasn't mistaken, he spied a hint of longing in her gaze as the children disappeared into the crowd. "Don't be silly,

Erik. You are quite the catch, and as your dearest friend, I believe it is well within my rights to say such things."

Friend. He inwardly grimaced at the word's reappearance. "If a lady can catch me," he teased. The last couple of weeks of chance meetings and gatherings had shown her true nature to be as he had first guessed. She was kind, generous, and deserving. If he ever were to marry, it would be to someone like her . . . *or her.* The thought shook him to his core. He had not guarded himself as well as he had hoped.

"You must be fleet of foot, or else I think you shall be presenting some young lady a token of your love by the end of the season."

Someone bumped him from behind. He glanced over his shoulder, only seeing the milling crowd. He frowned. This was London, jostling was to be expected, especially in a crowded museum, but what was the point of written applications to acquire tickets if the museum was going to allow it to be overrun with visitors? "Are you thirsty, Miss Beau? I find myself in need of refreshment."

At her nod, he guided them to a table set up with refreshments. He ordered two lemonades and a pair of raspberry tarts and reached into his pocket for coin, only to have his fingertips brush . . . parchment? His senses on alert, he paid the fellow and handed Muriel her refreshments, then discreetly slipped his palm inside his pocket to withdraw a note. He turned them toward the corner of the gallery, and, keeping Muriel distracted with talking of her latest pastry attempt, he read the note.

Release me and the sea, or I will do more than pierce your shoulder. I shall pierce your heart. Miss Beau will pay for your persistence with her life. Requin.

He crumpled the threat in his fist, whipping about to search the room for anyone watching for his reaction. It was so crowded he doubted he would find the threat. He closed his eyes, focusing his senses. He opened his eyes and slowly turned, spotting a man darting out the door. His body tensed. He should run after him, but Requin hardly ever worked alone. Erik refused to leave Muriel unguarded with such a threat in the air.

"The lemonade is delicious. And that tart! Are you going to eat yours?" Muriel leaned toward him, batting her lashes. "Or are you feeling magnanimous?"

"Does that ever work?" He laughed to disguise his racing pulse, the threat burning in his pocket as he handed her the tart.

"I suppose it does." She unfurled her handkerchief and tucked the pastry away in her reticule, giving the bag a little shake to allow it to settle. "But, as your reward for your generosity, I shall have a dozen of these sent to your London residence."

"We should rejoin the others before we are considered in bad form for abandoning our party." He touched her elbow and, despite her protest, set down her half-finished glass of lemonade along with his and steered her through the crowd, careful to keep their distance from others, a difficult task given the unusually packed gallery. Every man they passed he examined, watching for Requin until they had safely reached the Ingrams' side.

She was at once joined by her latest suitor, who directed her to the nearest collection. She cast Erik a quizzical glance, but had little choice but to engage in the elder man's musings.

"Sir." Erik palmed the note to Sir Alexander in a handshake.

His brows rose over the unexpected parchment, and he coughed to cover his tell as he opened the note.

"The fiend has marked our Muriel?"

The old captain turned to his wife and whispered in her ear. She paled and whispered something back. Unlike most men, Ingram did not keep his wife in the dark concerning his recent retirement from chasing down enemy smugglers and spies and the dangers associated with the job. And because she knew of Ingram's past, she knew of Erik's position, earning Erik her gratitude for protecting her husband.

She seized Muriel's arm, drawing her away from the elderly suitor. "My dear, I fear I am growing faint. Will you see me home?"

Alarm flickered through Muriel's features as she wrapped her arm about the lady. "Of course! Erik, will you summon the Ingrams' carriage?"

He didn't dare leave their side, not with so many unknowns. He looked to Ingram, who nodded and slipped away. This threat changed everything. His gut wrenched. He would not take to the seas until he was certain Muriel was safe, and she wouldn't be safe until he caught the man who had evaded him these many years. The question was, how was he to protect her in the courts of London, where anyone could be a villain in disguise?

⚜

"We are going to stay at Lord Draycott's castle for a house party."

Lady Ingram seemed remarkably recovered after taking a few hours of rest. Now she blazed about Muriel's room, commanding Muriel's poor maid every which way, tossing Muriel's things in trunks as Charlotte trailed her, righting each item.

Muriel intervened as Lady Ingram was about to toss a porcelain figurine of a maiden and her beau that Muriel had just purchased into the trunk, and instead wrapped it delicately in a chemise before setting it among soft shawls and underthings. "This doesn't make any sense, Lady Ingram. I spoke with him at length at Montagu House, and he did not mention a word about hosting a house party in the country. The very action is not in season as Parliament won't be out until June. When could you have possibly spoken with him about a house party?"

"So many protests!" Lady Ingram scowled, rummaging through Muriel's top armoire drawer and lifting out the matching silk stocking to the one she held. "When you came upstairs to nap before tonight's ball, he followed us home and we arranged it all then. I know it is irregular, but weren't you telling me that you longed for him to host a house party, what with his beautiful castle and ancient abbey to explore?"

"Indeed, I would dearly love to go. What I want to know is, Why is there such an urgency to flee London? Why, we have a ball to attend at the Lucases' in an hour. It would be exceedingly rude of us not to—"

"It isn't important at the moment." She pinched the snuff-colored bonnet Muriel had found on sale and shivered, setting it back in the armoire on the top shelf far from view. "Why ever would you purchase such a piece?"

"I know it is hideous, but it was nearly free, and I remade it with Elena."

"And that was the result of your remaking it? The only way to save that bonnet is to burn it, my dear." She dusted off her hands and folded them before her skirts. "What is important is that you honor the earl's wish. Sir Alexander and I were discussing it and have decided that while Lord Draycott has yet to show you any interest beyond friendship, he is still quite eligible, and if he doesn't pursue you, Sir Alexander has secured invitations for the rest of our merry party, including Lord Traneford, Lord Sullivan, Miss Whelan, and the Widow Whelan."

Erik is more than eligible. But I will not make the same mistake twice in imagining a gentleman has romantic inclinations toward me and take myself to the brink of a proposal when he has none. No. If Lord Draycott wishes to be with me, he knows where to find me. She crossed her arms. "I do not wish to insult the Lucas family."

"Which is why I am attending the party and will make your excuses." Lady Ingram seized Muriel by the shoulders. "It will be quite the arduous night for Sir Alexander and me, as we will follow you to the castle three hours behind your coach. So, please, cease arguing and pack. You are in danger."

Muriel blinked. "Whatever do you mean? I'm a country baker. Why would I ever be in danger?"

"You are a baker turned heiress, which has placed you in the public eye, especially after your success here." She shook her head as Charlotte packed a turban, motioning her to pack it in another trunk. "I cannot say more."

"So it's a fortune hunter who is after me?" Muriel sank atop the bed, meeting Charlotte's wide eyes. She had heard of men capturing young heiresses and forcing them into a marriage in Gretna Green, as well as read about them in Vivienne's novels. Never once had she ever considered such a fate to be thrown in her path. The taint from her beginnings in society's eyes was usually protection enough.

"A fortune hunter?" Lady Ingram pressed her lips into a firm line. "Yes, you might say he is one of the greatest fortune hunters of our time. And therefore, Lord Draycott has sworn to protect you."

"Why would Eri—Lord Draycott—do that when I can simply return home to my stepfather's protection?"

"My dear, Lord Draycott owns a castle that was built to withstand assaults. A fortune hunter will not be able to easily abscond with you against such defenses and a moat, especially with a man straight from battle, such as Lord Draycott, manning her. You will be well protected."

"But surely you can see that I cannot go *alone* with him tonight, even with you following so closely behind. It will take the other guests time to arrive. I doubt society will approve of only our being there when we are calling it a house party."

Lady Ingram pinched the bridge of her nose and exhaled. "Which is why I have sent for your friends in Chilham to meet you there."

"You sent for Vivienne and Tess?"

"Of course. The missive should arrive tonight, and based on your testimony of their friendship, I fully expect them to be there by morning, before the others, and therefore able to assuage any gossip."

Muriel set out her favored traveling shoes and spread her ivory pelisse on the bed. "But that would still leave us unchaperoned for the trip there."

"Your maid will have to do." Lady Ingram snapped a gown and rolled it in her hands to prepare it for packing. "Please, set aside your fears and trust me. When a lady's very life is in danger, allowances must be made." She pursed her lips and gave a shake of her head as she handed the bundle to Charlotte. "Besides, you hardly arrived in London with a glowing reputation in the first place. I cannot be expected to work miracles." She clapped her hands. "Finish dressing in your burgundy pelisse, my dear, not the ivory. Jewel tones do marvels for your complexion. Now, if you'll excuse me, I must see to my own packing."

Charlotte lifted Muriel's emerald beaded reticule. "Do you wish for me to change this for your traveling reticule, Miss Beau?" At her nod, Charlotte dumped the contents onto the bed, the letter from the vicar fluttering atop the heap—still sealed. "Are you going to open this, miss, or shall I throw it out? I've packed it and unpacked it from your reticule every day since we arrived, and I daresay it will not last much longer with all the stains from pastries hidden in your bag, tears from being pushed about as you searched for coins, and—"

Muriel's gut twinged. "Pack it again, please."

Charlotte frowned. "Very well. Pardon me for saying this, but you shouldn't ignore the vicar's words to you much longer, miss."

"I'm not ready to hear them. I cannot bear to read of his disappointment in me."

Within an impossibly short amount of time, Muriel descended the staircase, clasping the handle of the satchel that held her recipes from her time in London. She was not going to risk having the bag tumble off the back of the carriage.

Erik stood at the threshold. The moonlight streaming through the sidelights into the foyer illuminated his broad form and chiseled features, as well as a pair of pistols tucked neatly on either side in his shoulder harness and a rapier sheathed at his waist. His wrist was free of any bandages. "Do you have everything you need for the journey, Miss Beau?"

"I do." Her gaze rested on his weapons, and even though she was hardly afraid, the presence of weapons on an honorable man who knew how to wield them was strangely comforting. "But where is your wrist wrap? Won't the doctor be angry with you?"

"I need to be able to use my weapons without it stifling my movement. I'm certain the doctor would understand if I had to choose between reinjuring my wrist or saving our lives." He winked, softening the gravity of his words.

"I appreciate your service in keeping me safe from the fortune hunter." She released a short laugh that sounded nervous to her ears. "I never thought what husband hunting might feel like on the other end, but surely this is rather more frightening. I could not rightly sweep a gentleman over my shoulder and abscond with him into the night."

Without seeming to hear her jest, he gestured toward the door. "I'm afraid we must be on our way."

Charlotte removed the satchel from Muriel's hands, silently squeezing her arm in assurance that she would see to it for the journey to the castle, and darted outside and into the awaiting carriage.

Bidding the Ingrams a swift farewell, Muriel allowed Erik to take her hand and lead her into the night. Waves of mist coated her pelisse as he held the door for her, ushering her inside, and she could almost imagine she was in one of Vivienne's novels, where the hero and heroine were whisking away into the night for Gretna Green. The illusion would be easy to believe if Erik would give her an adoring smile. However, the handsome fellow she had come to call friend offered her no reassuring smile. He assumed the seat across from her and Charlotte, who sat stiffly with the satchel on her lap. In a novel, he would have taken the seat beside Muriel. She sighed. Her imagination would not be allowed to take over.

The coach lurched over the cobblestones, and Muriel peeked through the tiniest crack in the drawn curtain to see London at night. As she expected, many of the grand houses shone from the merrymaking within, and the road teemed with awaiting coaches. Erik leaned forward and gently took her hand in one of his, shaking his head in admonishment and drawing the curtain completely closed. The rattle of the wheels on the cobblestones left precious little capacity for conversing without shouting. At last, the coach picked up speed as they left behind the City, the clattering dimming to a rumble as they traveled over the muddied earth.

"Is it safe to travel at night in the country? I've read many stories in the papers about highwaymen. There are accounts of one who dresses all in black, with hair as golden as the sun, who can leap from his horse to a carriage in a single bound, robbing all within," Charlotte whispered to her. For the first time, Muriel considered how frightening this was for her maid. Her stomach twisted in guilt.

"I have armed riders before and behind with torches, guiding and protecting us, Miss Charlotte. We are quite safe, I assure you," Erik interjected.

Muriel squeezed her friend's hand, turning her attention to Erik. "May I ask you something?"

"Have you ever allowed a negative response to that question to prevent you from querying?"

"Why did you offer to keep me safe?" She fiddled with her necklace. "I know you have business in London. Won't your being tucked away in your castle prevent you from accomplishing what you need to?"

He reached across the carriage and grasped her hand once more. "Muriel. Do you really imagine that I would place business over the safety of a dear friend?"

"I know you consider me your friend." Her ridiculous heart hammered so hard she feared he would hear it. She forced herself to add, "As I see you. A very good friend . . . who is sacrificing a great deal to come to my aid."

He pressed his lips into a firm line. "Indeed. But, you see, I do not like it when my friends are threatened. I take it quite personally."

"About that threat. Surely there is something else we can do to protect me from a fortune hunter than whisk me away to your castle in the country." It seemed such an action was highly improper. But if her guardians approved it, who was she to question the way of polite society?

His brows rose at that. "Do you not wish to return to the castle and explore it for yourself?"

"Of course, I do. You know I've been eager to ever since your garden party. But I do not wish to put you out in having you host me and my friends on such short notice simply to protect me from another."

"You could never put me out."

She cleared her throat. "Not even when my two dearest friends are about to descend upon your castle? Along with six others from London to make up the house party? What about your desire for solitude?"

"If it keeps you safe, not even then, my dear friend."

Friend. Well, I suppose that is better than him not thinking of me at all. The coach lurched, sending her tumbling forward from her seat. Erik grasped her by the waist as she fell atop him while Charlotte kept her seat by gripping the leather strap that Muriel had foolishly released in her worry over disrupting Erik's routine. *Lord, help me if his arms do not feel divine.*

"Are you hurt?" he mumbled against her hair. "Why aren't you moving?"

She shoved herself back. "My apologies. Exhaustion."

His lips quirked as she righted herself and gripped the leather strap with both hands. How was she not going to utterly fall in love with this man? She closed her eyes against the sight of his handsomeness. *If he wishes for friendship, I will be the best friend I can be, even if I never do get to love him in the way I desire.*

Chapter Fifteen

AFTER HAVING HER IN HIS arms for that one fleeting moment, Erik wished the coach to lurch again so he could easily catch her for another stolen moment of sweet nearness. He swallowed his sigh. However, she only wished to be friends, and despite the temptation to change her mind on that score, he had his calling on the high seas.

Unfortunately, even the Prince Regent had hinted that Erik's letter of marque would most likely not be renewed as the war was nearing a close, despite Erik's stellar reputation in bringing in enemy merchant ships full of cargo that would have aided Napoleon's troops and potentially elongate the war. He had pledged his heart and life to serve the Crown for honor's sake, not for reward. He shouldn't cease now. Not when he was so close to finding out who Requin was through the grocers' guild—something he never would have been able to do if he were at sea. Perhaps it was the Lord's way of telling him that his calling was changing with his new responsibilities to the village of Draybridge and its people. A castle needed an earl's leadership and protection. And so did Miss Beau . . . because of Requin.

He shifted in his seat, angling himself as if he were sleeping, and allowed himself to study Muriel's sleeping face. Her beauty had certainly captured his attention at first, along with her baking. But her spirit and strength of character were what drew him to her, and now that Erik knew her, he was unable to imagine spending his life with another.

Despite the serious nature of the threat, he couldn't help but be thankful she would be so near him in the weeks to come. If God was indeed calling him back to Draybridge, he was thankful she would be by his side. It was too bad Traneford would also be in attendance. If Erik lost her to Lord Traneford due to his confounded indecision regarding his pursuit of her . . . He grunted in frustration. *Such vacillation.*

While aboard his ship, he was used to thinking on his feet in the heat of the moment, determining in a breath the best way to take the enemy's ship without a drop of blood spilled. On land, everything seemed muddled until he paused and allowed the waters to clear. Now all he saw was Muriel and her sweet heart. He had been lying to himself. He could not stand idly by and watch Muriel fall in love with another . . . marry another—not when he had yet to speak his true feelings to her. Despite the circumstances, the proximity alone would present him with opportunities to woo her into becoming his countess if she did indeed feel more for him than friendship.

At last, the coach rolled over the familiar bridge leading toward his castle, the clatter of the wheels over cobblestones startling the two women awake. Muriel blinked her large eyes at him before turning away and discreetly wiping the corner of her mouth with her handkerchief.

"Are we near, my lord?"

"We are arriving now." Erik lifted the curtains to admire the moonlight on the lake, shimmering and reflecting upon his castle. With Muriel at his side in Draybridge, he no longer felt a rush to return to his mission at sea. However, now that Requin was threatening Muriel, it was time to end this pursuit and put the man before the king's justice, with or without the aid of the Crown.

The coach crossed the drawbridge and swayed to a halt in the first courtyard, and he hopped out, surveying the turrets for anything out of the ordinary before lifting a hand to Muriel and Charlotte as Guy Mayfield, Trumbull, and a handful of footmen stumbled out of the castle in their nightclothes.

"My lord?" Guy secured his banyan's ties more firmly at the sight of the women. "We had no word of your arrival, or we would have kept the staff awake."

"There wasn't time to send word." *And I didn't wish to chance the missive being intercepted.* He cleared his throat and nodded to the housekeeper, who appeared in a plain dressing gown and a mob cap. "Mrs. Hodge, I fear I must apologize. I know you will not be pleased with my announcement. I am hosting a house party here."

"What?" Her jaw dropped for a moment before she snapped it shut and inclined her head. "I mean, of course, my lord . . . When exactly are you planning on hosting this party?" She lifted her candle, shielding the flame from the breeze drifting through the drawbridge, her gaze resting on Muriel. "Why, is this a wedding party, my lord?"

"Miss Beau is the first of the guests, to be followed closely by her guardians, Sir Alexander and Lady Ingram, within a few hours." He looked to Guy. "Until the Ingrams arrive, I wish for you to draw the bridge. Lower it only for their arrival and that of any known guests and draw it again at once afterward. I will provide a list directly."

Guy's brows rose, and Erik knew there would be questions later. "Certainly. It will take some doing, as we haven't drawn it since testing and repairing it last summer."

"Whatever it takes, Mayfield. We shall draw it every evening at dusk for the duration of the house party." He lowered his voice so that only Guy might hear him. "Requin would not be so foolish to attack during daylight hours." He cleared his throat and turned to Mrs. Hodge. "Speaking of guests, after the Ingrams, I expect the next in our party to arrive at first light."

Mrs. Hodge pressed her hand to her chest, sending a wide-eyed glance to the butler. "Lord, have mercy. Mr. Trumbull, we will have to wake the village to order enough food to supply the castle for a breakfast, as well as wake the staff before dawn to ready the castle."

"I realize my timing is not ideal. Please send a few maids to make up two rooms for the Ingrams and Miss Beau. Oh, and her maid, Charlotte, will be acting as her chaperone and shall be staying with her in her chambers at all times."

Mrs. Hodge pressed her lips into a firm line and nodded. "Very good, sir. It will be a mighty busy night."

Erik gently grasped Muriel's elbow and guided her inside, loving the way her lips parted at the sight of his fine castle in the moonlight. *Step one, impress her with your castle. Step two, impress her with your nonexistent skills as a host.*

☙

The creaking of the ancient stairs was enough to make even the firmest nonbeliever in ghosts take a glance over her shoulder. With their candles casting long shadows against the time-glazed browns of the paneled walls, Muriel wished for Erik's presence on the chilly walk down the long gallery and up the second set of stairs to the bedrooms. Instead, she clung to Charlotte's trembling arm.

"This is most irregular," Mrs. Hodge tsked. "First, the earl is home after his uncle's death only long enough to assume the earldom and install his second-in-command from his ship as steward here. Then he disappears for nigh on three years. Now he's been home twice in such a short time? *And* hosting parties? Most unusual indeed." She opened a door, motioning them inside, where two maids rustled about making up the bed while a scullery maid readied the fire.

Muriel felt a twinge of remorse, knowing they had been roused from their beds to see to her needs after a long day's work already. She smiled to them and nodded to the scullery girl in thanks before taking in the pretty pink silk-covered walls. "How lovely."

Mrs. Hodge folded her hands at her waist. "Yes, the previous lord had this room done up for his future daughter. But, when one didn't arrive, it was given to female guests."

Muriel ran her fingers along the elegant, gilded furniture and moved to the window, gasping at the bright full moon outlining the vast upper garden across the lake. She could hardly wait until morning to fully bask in its blooms, for she hardly had time to appreciate it during the garden party.

"It's a lovely view in the morning light. The former Lady Draycott loved her gardens." Mrs. Hodge looked around to see all was in order, then nodded to the maids and ushered them out. "Now, is there anything else I can do for you?"

Muriel drew off her cloak but kept her reticule. "Would you show me where the kitchen is? I have some thinking to do."

Mrs. Hodge frowned. "The kitchen? If it is a respite you are seeking, the maids can wake the cook, Miss Beau."

Charlotte giggled. "I assure you, baking is her respite, Mrs. Hodge— one that Lord Draycott is well aware of. He would not mind."

"Well, if that is the case, of course," the housekeeper prattled, confusion mottling her tone. "Right this way, miss." She led Muriel out to the hall stairs down to the long gallery. "Now you can either take the steps to exit the gallery and run across the second courtyard or, as I prefer, take the route through the banqueting hall to the kitchen to avoid being outside at night. It's perfectly safe, mind you. I simply don't fancy it."

"Another courtyard? I was only here for a short time after his lordship's garden party moved inside. We had only just run inside from the abbey—"

"You are *Miss Muriel*? Of course! That makes much more sense why the earl has taken such a sudden interest in entertaining. I was so exhausted from planning the party on short notice that I fell asleep during the excitement and only heard of a lady called Muriel and never caught sight of you." Her eyes sparkled. "It is exciting that he brought you back. I wonder what he intends."

Uncertain how to interpret this, Muriel laughed as she strode out into the second courtyard, lifting her gaze to the stars. In their light, the chill of the castle being haunted faded. "One never knows what the Lord has in store, I suppose. Now, where is that kitchen?"

After insisting she preferred to be alone and the staff should return to their beds, Muriel baked a plate of Shrewsbury cakes and brewed a pot of ginger tea and took a seat, eyes on her reticule. After several bracing sips of tea to settle her stomach, she reached for the letter and turned it over in her hands, her heart aching in anticipation of the vicar's scolding. He had always been kind to her. It was going to be dreadful to read the evidence of how she had lost his respect after her social misstep. If she didn't read it, she could at least keep the illusion that the vicar still esteemed her. She also knew if she did not read it and returned home after her trip, he would ask about it, and she would be forced to say she didn't read it, which would be hurtful after the vicar had taken the time to copy a verse for her.

She broke the seal. As promised, the vicar had copied lines for her, from Psalm 103. She turned the sheet over, but there was nothing more, no note, no scathing advice. Thoroughly taken aback, she read,

> *"Bless the Lord, O my soul: and all that is within me, bless his*
> *holy name.*
> *Bless the Lord, O my soul, and forget not all his benefits:*
> *Who forgiveth all thine iniquities . . .*
> *Who redeemeth thy life from destruction; who crowneth thee*
> *with lovingkindness and tender mercies;*
> *Who satisfieth thy mouth with good things; so that thy youth is*
> *renewed like the eagle's."*

She pressed her hand to her lips, reading the words again—steeping her soul in them.

The vicar was not condemning her for her actions. The vicar was reminding her of the Lord's goodness, His forgiveness, and His promise to grant the deepest God-given desires of her heart. She lifted her face, a single tear sliding down her cheek. "Lord, redeem my destructive actions to see to my desires on my own—in my own timing—when I should have been trusting You to satisfy me with good things." She kneaded her hand over her heart that ached yet for a husband and children. "Renew my spirit, Lord, and help me to trust in You and Your timing for my future." She read the verses again and again, until the cakes were gone and her pot of tea grew cold.

Chapter Sixteen

"I COULD HARDLY BELIEVE IT when Lady Ingram's courier presented us with a letter in the middle of the night requesting we attend you at Draycott Castle." Vivienne strolled arm in arm with Muriel and Tess down a hill of daffodils toward the village of Draybridge. "If I hadn't been staying with Tess while my family was in Brighton, I never would have been allowed to travel to Essex, and I've always longed to visit an ancient castle in this part of the country. Such wonderful fodder for my stories." She drew a deep breath. "It seems the very air is charged with memories."

"I'm thankful you were not on a restrictive schedule with your publisher and were able to join me." Muriel leaned her head against her taller friend's shoulder with a contented sigh.

"However, Lady Ingram's logic is flawed. How is a party of three ladies less scandalous than a single lady under Lord Draycott's roof?" Tess snapped her fingers at her dog to follow more closely now that they had reached the bordering sheep pastures. Her mottled pointer complied at once, even as he cast longing glances at the black-faced sheep. "Don't even think about giving chase to them, Wolf."

Muriel scratched the dog behind his ear. Lady Ingram had been hesitant to agree to their morning walk unescorted, but at last agreed thanks to Tess's fearsome pet. "Your presence keeps all from assuming I am throwing myself at the earl until the rest of our party arrives. Besides the Ingrams, whom you met this morning, of course, Viscount Traneford and his friend Viscount Sullivan shall be arriving for dinner tonight, along with the Widow Whelan and Elena to make up the rest of the house party."

"Well, if a fortune hunter is after you, I must say that *I* am the only guest that it makes sense to have at your side. At least I can defend us." Tess lifted her skirts and withdrew the blade strapped to her calf, flipped it over in her hand in a practiced manner, and whipped her body around, flinging it at a tree, planting the knife deep within its bark. "All Elena Whelan can do is scream."

Vivienne shuddered as Tess retrieved the blade with a powerful yank. "While I'm grateful for your skills, I cannot help but question your father's judgment in teaching you such an odd means of defense for a lady."

"You carry a pocket pistol in the City," Tess reminded her, tossing the blade from one hand to the other, causing Vivienne to sidestep away from her.

"Yes. It's for use in only the direst of circumstances. Say, I'm researching for a story set in the slums, and I need to capture the essence of a hardened criminal."

Muriel gradually ceased listening, thankful for her friends' distraction to keep their line of questioning at bay. Now that the flight out of London was behind her and she awoke to her friends arriving, eyes bright with adventure, Muriel needed a moment to process everything—especially Erik's confusing desire to protect her. Until now, he had treated her only as a friend, but the way he cared for her in sweeping her away from danger . . . it left her carefully sealed emotions rising and threatening to burst the jar in her heart where she had hoped to keep them.

And then there was the viscount. She had not spoken to Lord Traneford more than a handful of times since she had stopped him from proposing that night in Vauxhall Gardens, and he was arriving in mere hours. She was fairly certain he would propose during the house party if she did not state her desire for friendship and nothing more . . . a conversation she wished to have over. Even though Lady Ingram insisted Muriel had given up the luxury of falling in love the moment she had made her abominable choice to propose to Lord Deverell, Muriel was not yet convinced.

She glanced over her shoulder to the sprawling castle rising from its island in the wide man-made lake, thinking of the earl who had sworn to protect her. Now, there was a man she could easily love if she were allowed—castle or no castle.

Wandering from the road, the girls sank down beside the creek for a reprieve, not bothering to cover their ankles in their solitary haven under a massive beech tree. Its twisted base provided a comfortable place to rest, while its branches dipped low enough for Muriel to climb up into it, her skirts draping on either side of the branch as she rested her legs on the massive limb, her back to the smooth gray trunk.

"What I don't understand is why a fortune hunter would come after you now." Tess dug an apple from her pocket and used her knife to cut it, tossing them each a slice. "You've had that fortune promised to you for years. It would have been easy for someone to snatch you away during your many walks to and from the bakery, even with your footman escorting you in the early mornings. Why now?"

"I have to agree with Tess. There is not much sense behind it." Vivienne wiped the apple slice on her sleeve as if the knife had somehow tainted it. "Unless sense has gone out the window in the earl's eyes where you are concerned. If that is the case, why has he extended Lord Traneford an invitation to the house party when the viscount clearly wishes to win your hand?" She shook her head. "I cannot make sense of it all."

Muriel shrugged, chewing her apple. "Mayhap there are fortune hunters now because London didn't know I existed before?"

"With the viscount attending you and an earl squiring you about town, I think you might be correct," Vivienne replied around her mouthful, reaching her hand back for Tess to hand her a second slice.

Muriel knew any young lady would be thrilled to have such a high-ranking nobleman calling upon her, and yet, whenever she thought of Erik, no other man seemed to measure up. "As for Lord Traneford . . . I think we may be better suited as friends."

"But isn't friendship a paramount foundation for marriage?" Tess tossed the apple core into the tall grass, then dusted off her hands and pushed herself to her feet.

"Unless Lord Draycott is the deciding factor," Vivienne interjected, astute as always.

Muriel sighed. "After all the trouble and expense I've caused my stepfather for a season in London, I may have to choose friendship over my hope of love after all. But not with Viscount Traneford . . . he is handsome, but we lack commonality."

"'*Hope of love*?' Not again." Tess moaned. "We cautioned you to guard your heart, Muriel. Please tell me that you have not gone and fallen for yet another man who will not have you?"

"I have done my best, but Erik understands me as no other man. He values me, even the traits the others would have wished for me to hide and amend." She glanced down at her hands, which bore the evidence of her years of labor—calluses and scars that no amount of fine creams or Gowland's lotion could heal. She sighed and slid off the branch, dropping to her feet.

Vivienne scrambled to her feet, extending her hands to each of her friends. "If you are determined to marry the earl, then it is up to the good Lord, Tess, and myself to see this match through."

"Pardon?" Muriel blinked.

Vivienne plunked her hands on her hips. "Never you mind. You are not to be involved in a courtship with the earl except by gently refusing the viscount's suit, frequent prayer, and keeping your wild ways in check, Miss Beau. We cannot have another debacle on our hands. If we are to evade your last fate, you must trust that we possess the talents it takes to see your dream of marrying a certain enigmatic earl through."

Muriel laughed, linking her arms through her friends' as they took to the road into Draybridge village in search of the bakery Erik had told her about.

A carriage rolled around the corner toward them, and, leaping to the side of the road, she spotted the Traneford family crest blazoned on its doors. Lord Traneford must have caught sight of her, for it slowed as soon as it passed and he hopped out, his cape billowing about him as his polished Hessian boots hit the packed earth. He lifted a hand in greeting. "Miss Beau!"

Vivienne's eyes widened. "You are certain you do not wish to wed him? He's stunning," she whispered as he trotted back down the road toward them.

"Stunning, but not for me. We would fulfill one another's requirements for marriage with my wealth and his title, but there is no passion betwixt us. He cares more for his bugs than me, and I do not fault him for it. And if I cannot bring myself to be jealous of his attention to beetles over me, entering into a marriage would be foolish." She greeted him with a smile and shallow curtsy before introducing her party.

He bowed to them after Muriel's introduction. "What a lovely surprise to happen upon you all. May I join you for the walk to the village? It seemed quite charming in passing."

"Certainly. It is too fine a day to waste indoors," Vivienne interjected, looping her arm through Tess's and giving Muriel a meaningful stare before hauling Tess down the path before them.

Lord Traneford offered Muriel his arm. "I was quite grateful to receive Lord Draycott's invitation, especially when I learned you would be in attendance."

Muriel worried her bottom lip as she accepted his arm. "Lord Traneford, we have always been honest with one another."

"Oh dear." Traneford's smile paused with his stride. "Are you about to tell me I have failed in my wooing of you?"

She released her hold on him, folding her hands before her skirts. "You have proved your honorable character to me in more ways than one. I'm afraid we lack . . . how shall I say this?"

"We lack a spark between us?" Traneford supplied, his smile knowing.

She exhaled in a rush. "You feel it too? I have not wounded you?"

"Mayhap my pride. I have found duty and love rarely align." He glanced up the road to where Vivienne and Tess were getting too far ahead. "I need funds and you need a title. I had hoped our friendship would be an added boon." He chuckled. "You wouldn't happen to know of any wealthy single ladies, would you?"

"Actually, I know two." Muriel grinned, extending her hand. "To being matchmakers?"

"To friendship and matchmaking." He clasped her hand and wrapped it about his arm, sighing.

Chapter Seventeen

WHAT EXACTLY DOES ONE DO for a house party? Erik rolled out of his bed and flipped the latch to the window of the master bedroom, seeking the fresh night air to clear his mind after a long first dinner with his guests. Being shut indoors had never suited him, not when he had spent most of his life with his boots on the deck of the *Twilight Treader*. He hadn't been in this room since he was a small boy, and he wondered if this room would ever truly feel like his own. The rich mahogany paneling did bring him comfort, as it reminded him of being aboard ship. That was where the familiarity ceased. The four-poster bed and its heavy burgundy curtains were too luxurious to coax him into a deep sleep, and after hours of tossing and turning, he was beginning to consider bringing a hammock into his room. He rested his palm on the cool, wavy glass of the window, looking out onto the lake below, the moonlight reflecting in its still surface.

As a child, he had been frightened to swim in the lake, recalling stories of knights placing water beasts in the depths to protect castles in times of siege. It took several reassurances from his uncle before he gathered the courage to row to the other side and, eventually, swim in its murky waters. It wasn't as pleasant as the creek. However, it made for a quick way of cooling off after a long ride in the summer. *Perhaps boating today will keep my guests occupied? Surely the ladies in the party will have no objection.*

After years without hosting a house party, the castle felt near to bursting, even though not even a quarter of the rooms were in use. The staff were exhausted and so was he, yet the work had only just begun. He had next to nothing planned for the house party, so a day of boating was about as good as he could come up with at this hour.

He was tired—exhausted from years of the chase, years of fighting for king and country. As was his habit when he was unable to sleep, he reached for his father's worn Bible and flipped it open to the ribbon-marked page—the last chapter his father had read before he died, Psalm 103.

> *Bless the LORD, O my soul, and forget not all his benefits:*
> *Who forgiveth all thine iniquities; who healeth all thy diseases;*
> *Who redeemeth thy life from destruction; who crowneth thee*
>   *with lovingkindness and tender mercies;*
> *Who satisfieth thy mouth with good things; so that thy youth is*
>   *renewed like the eagle's.*

He bowed his head. *Lord, I am at my wit's end. I have tried again and again to capture Requin, resulting in so much destruction in the name of the Crown. And now that I have inherited the responsibilities of Draybridge village, would You have me surrender my first call, after everything I've sacrificed in my pursuit of Requin, and allow Adams to take on the mantle? Please, reveal to me Your will.*

The clock on the mantel above his now-dwindling fire chimed thrice. He sighed. Sleep was not within reach tonight. He tugged his linen shirt over his shoulders and didn't bother tucking it into his pantaloons as he shuffled down to the kitchen to rummage. His mind was always sharper with a loaf of bread in hand, and hopefully, with his belly full, sleep would at last claim him.

His bare feet padded on the stones as he traveled down the familiar steps to the kitchen, when he heard a memorable croaking tune as pots and pans rattled and a kettle hissed atop the stove. He rounded the corner to find the door open to the massive kitchen and Muriel with her hands deep in a mixing bowl, her hair arranged in a loose braid that cascaded past her waist. She was singing a jaunty sea shanty, her feet tapping as her thumping of the flour added to the beat.

He stomped his feet in time and joined the familiar song. She whirled around, her hands covered in flour, her cheeks tinting at being caught singing such a tune.

He finished the line, grinning. "Of course you would find my kitchen."

She brushed a lock from her face, leaving a trace of pasty flour on her blooming cheek. "I found it my first night here, and asked the cook's permission to create some confections and baked goods for tomorrow. She said as long as I kept out of her way, I could. Your kitchen is impeccable by the way." She bit her lip as if becoming aware of the flour coating the countertops. "Or was before I began baking. I figured I would clean it before the cook awoke and discovered my messy nature." She returned to working the dough. "I hope you don't mind my liberty in helping myself to these ingredients."

"On the contrary, I was hoping not to be forced to rummage for my food. You are an answer to prayer." *In more ways than one.* He moved over to where she was busy kneading the dough. "And thank you for your praise regarding my kitchen. It is none of my doing, as it has been updated every decade or so by whichever lord was in residence. I have yet to add any improvements to the estate." He nodded to her working the dough. "You make it look easy, though I know from my one attempt at baking aboard ship that it is far from easy."

"I could teach you." She grinned at him, the teasing lilt in her voice daring him.

Why not? He rolled up his sleeves, appreciating her covert glance to his corded forearms as he unwrapped his wrist, dropping the linens in the waste bin before scrubbing his hands, the action only causing a mild twinge in his wrist. "Where do I begin?"

She blinked up at him. "You are serious?"

"Always, Miss Beau."

She cleared her throat and gestured to the mound of dough atop the counter. "Shall we begin with some light kneading? I am making those scones you enjoyed so much."

He sank his fists into the dough, the texture surprising as it moved through his knuckles. He flopped over the dough and pounded it with his good fist as he had seen Cook do in his childhood.

"You mustn't overwork the dough," she instructed, moving closer to him. "Instead of pounding, try folding it like this." She reached around him and grasped his hands in hers and moved his hands as her own, demonstrating how to fold without even looking around his shoulder, as if the movement was so ingrained in her, she could have performed it blindfolded.

When she moved away, he purposefully botched folding the dough and thumped it with his fists for good measure.

"We will have to throw it out, Erik, if you aren't more careful," she scolded with a laugh and moved to take over the dough, inadvertently stepping between his arms.

He dared to lean closer to enjoy her heavenly scent of vanilla and sweetness as she demonstrated the proper technique. "Ahh, I see how it is done now. Do you trust me to attempt it once more?"

"I think that is enough folding," she replied, oblivious to his dazed state as she handed him a small drinking glass. "Dip the rim in flour and use it to cut the scones into circles and then *gently* fold the remaining dough again to one inch high, as I showed you, cutting and reshaping the dough until there is none left." She whirled away from him and set to chopping fruit with a precise and experienced hand.

He set to his task and was doing a poor job, he suspected, but she did not say another word. *Is she offended I've taken the liberty of being with her unattended?* He glanced over his shoulder to the petite Miss Beau, who had her back to him, intent on her dicing. He left his station to watch her, admiring her skill. She glanced up from her work and jumped at his proximity, her knife slipping and slicing her finger.

"Muriel! I'm so sorry." He snatched up a rag and wrapped it around her injured finger, applying pressure to staunch the bleeding, calling himself all kinds of fool for inadvertently scaring her while she wielded a knife.

She wobbled, her skin paling. "Oh no."

"Muriel?" *Surely, she isn't going to faint?*

"Ever since I was a girl, the sight of blood made me weak," she murmured, her head lolling.

He wrapped his arms about her and held her close as he lowered her to the stones, keeping her back against his chest. "Deep breaths, Muriel." He shifted her slightly to one side and lifted her chin, directing her gaze. "Don't look at the blood. Focus on me and take deep breaths."

※

Focus on him? She hardly dared, but even knowing the blood was there was too much. Since she refused to faint . . . She slowly lifted her lashes and met his gaze, sinking, falling ever so much more for this gentleman—a nobleman who would never be hers. She closed her eyes against him, but that did not distract her from the raw power of his arms. "So what brought you down to the kitchen, Lord Draycott?"

"You mean besides my hunger, Miss Beau? Your enchanting sea shanty."

She heard his teasing smile even as her eyes were still closed. "It is hardly ever only hunger that makes a body traipse through the corridors at night against the chill and haunting shadows. For me, I never feel more like myself than when I am elbow deep in flour, and I needed to find my peace once more after refusing Lord Traneford's suit."

She felt him stiffen. As the blood was likely still flowing, she kept her eyes firmly shut.

"You did? Why?"

"We were better suited as friends. Now, no more avoiding my question." She dared to open one eye and found him staring so intently at her that she jerked back, but, as she was wrapped in his arms, she managed to smash his lip with her head.

He grunted.

"Oh, Erik!" She reached into her apron pocket and withdrew a surprisingly clean rag. Twisting around in his arms, she dabbed at his lip. "Look at the pair of us on the kitchen pavers—each injured."

He chuckled. "I should wear a suit of armor every time I am near you, Miss Beau, if only for my own protection."

"You didn't answer my question."

He sighed and checked her finger, then reapplied pressure at once. It wasn't done bleeding yet. "If you must know, the party has my stomach in more knots than the first time I boarded an enemy vessel as captain."

"How is boarding a vessel less terrifying than a house party?" She shook her head at his exaggeration and allowed herself to settle against him once more. "I would imagine it takes a raw courage that most do not possess."

He paused as if weighing his words. "Courage is needed, indeed, and skill. But those are not always enough. On my vessel, there is rarely ever a need to use our weapons. It is more about a show of weapons to convince the enemy to surrender."

"Well, I am pleased by that." Her brows furrowed. "I've never heard of another naval captain whose story matches your own."

"I'm one of the fortunate ones." He chuckled. "Well, until I decided to host a house party."

She giggled. "Are you having regrets already about protecting me here?"

His mirth faded at once, his dark eyes burning into her. "Never."

She dared a peek at her finger and groaned. "Tell me something quickly. What house party did you attend that made you dislike them so much?"

"I've never actually attended one myself as I've been at sea for so long . . . I hardly know what is expected of me as the host."

She turned her head to look up at him, taking comfort in the steady rise and fall of his broad chest against her back. "How long did you say you have been captain?"

"Five years."

"That's right." She nodded, squinting at the ceiling.

"You are calculating my age?"

"Well, yes. I've been wondering, as your tales lead one to think you are much older, but your form doesn't bespeak of an older gentleman."

At his grin, she at once realized her forwardness. *Will I never keep my mouth shut?*

He chuckled. "I am eight and twenty."

"Eight and twenty? And you have never attended a house party?" She scooted away from him, though remained seated to avoid bashing her head should she faint. "Well, Providence is smiling upon you, because I have spent the past seven summers at Tess Hale's family estate and know how to guide you."

His eyes brightened. "Truly?"

"Truly." She held out her finger to him and closed her eyes. "Is it still bleeding?"

He pulled the rag back before removing it completely. "It's finished. I'd best wrap it so it doesn't open again while you work." He reached for his shirt and tore off the hem. Her eyes widened at the flash of his muscled, contoured abdomen. She at once dropped her gaze as he wrapped her finger ever so gently.

"I'm certain the cook keeps cloths for cuts in here somewhere. You needn't have ripped your shirt for me."

"It's only a shirt. Your finger is infinitely more valuable to me." He lifted her now-wrapped finger. "There. You would make a fine sailor, Miss Beau, with your stomach of steel."

"Very droll, Captain Draycott. Now, let's begin making a list of ideas for entertaining your guests, and you can tell me what suits your fancy." She allowed him to assist her to standing, then withdrew her hand. Finding scraps of paper atop the cook's desk in the corner, she removed a sheet, along with the inkwell and quill, to the counter. "From what I've seen of your grounds, I'd say an exploration is a must, as well as riding, of course. I noticed you have an excellent library. Perhaps readings after the evening meal for the elder ones in our set while one of the more accomplished ladies can play the pianoforte for dancing? Tess is quite proficient." She lifted her hand, palm out. "But, before you ask it of me, I do not play nor read aloud, I'm afraid." She ran the feather quill under her nose, thinking.

He nodded. "Perhaps you can sing?"

She snagged a roll and hurled it at him, which he caught and sank his teeth into with a chuckle. "No one hears my voice, good sir."

"Except me—twice. And I find that it grows on a person, much like barnacles on a hull."

She rolled her eyes and returned to the list. "Any suggestions of your own?"

"Boating on the lake? There are some fine rowboats available and even some fishing poles, as it is kept well stocked, or we might even host it at the river for a change of scenery. There is excellent fishing to be had there as well."

"Perfect! And what if we hold a competition for the most fish caught?"

"Yes! And for an added layer of fun, the winner should be given a prize."

She jotted it down, and she knew he was observing her writing. Her cheeks heated, hoping he had not noticed that her penmanship was not as refined as that of most young ladies. *Who am I trying to fool? It's hardly legible.* She rested her hand over it, knowing she was smudging the ink, but having him study her writing was unbearable. "And if it rains, what other indoor activity would you suggest?"

"You teach everyone how to bake something."

She stared at him. "I hardly think the nobility will deem it entertainment to soil their hands. Can you imagine Elena willingly participating?"

"They will if we place the best product as the centerpiece for the evening meal, honoring the amateur baker."

Her heart warmed at his kindness. It would be wonderful to be seen as something other than the uncultured country girl. And she knew her friends would adore seeing her thrive in her element, especially in front of the gentleman who had stolen her heart. "Very well. I shall add that to the list too."

It was nearing five of the clock by the time Muriel crept back into her chambers with a light heart and full spirit. Erik had sought out her advice. He had even suggested an activity she excelled at as she had nothing to offer for the musical night.

She flopped on her bed and gazed at the canopy above and sighed. This fortune hunter business may have been the best thing to ever happen to her.

Chapter Eighteen

"THE GOAL IS SIMPLE—TO create an edible cake. The team who creates the finest cake will have it set in the place of honor on the table as the centerpiece for the entirety of tonight's evening meal and be the sole dessert for everyone," Muriel explained as she strode about the great kitchen, her hands folded behind her apron strings. Rain had begun that morning and, as it was not letting up, Erik's idea for boating was pushed to another day. Despite the necessity for another activity to fill their idle hours, the group of lords and ladies seemed quite unsure of this baking competition.

Erik stepped beside her. "And, to help you all get to know our party better, Miss Beau and I have divided the guests into partners."

"I claim Miss Beau!" Lord Traneford called.

Muriel laughed along with the group. "I shall not be participating other than to demonstrate the task and answer your questions. But be aware that I will only answer three questions per team. After you use all three, you are on your own for the remainder of the game, so choose your questions wisely."

"To see who is your partner, please see the list on the counter and find a baking station along the table. Miss Beau has already set out your ingredients," Erik instructed.

Murmurs of excitement filled the kitchen as the guests split into their groups, Elena pausing to whisper to Muriel, "I'm paired with Lord Traneford . . . but I need to form a bond with Lord Sullivan—"

"Trust me. I know what I am about." Muriel patted her arm. "Just be your most charming self with him and see what happens. I doubt you will be disappointed."

Elena shrugged on an apron as Tess marched by. "Very well. I hope whatever you are planning is worth the effort of being my most charming self."

Tess snorted and joined Lord Sullivan as Elena sent her a scowl.

Like Erik predicted, the lords and ladies found the task quite novel, and, as expected, Tess was all business while Lord Sullivan attempted to flirt with her. Muriel noticed Elena noticing, but Lord Traneford was keeping her well entertained. As she had hoped, Lord Traneford quite enjoyed Elena's quick wit and charm. She wouldn't be surprised if Elena decided to drop Sullivan in favor of a more devoted beau after seeing Sullivan blatantly flirt with Tess.

"Miss Beau, I find I have a question, and since I have no partner to assist me, I insist on having six questions," Erik called from his station, flour already flecking his ivory waistcoat as he rolled up his linen sleeves.

"No fair!" Lord Traneford shouted, Elena giggling as his distraction caused his spoon to slip in the bowl and send a shower of flour up his nose.

Muriel joined Erik's station, at once thrusting her hand before his mixture. "Consider this a hint. I wouldn't add those eggs directly onto your freshly melted butter."

"No?" He paused in the cracking of the shell, the egg white dripping onto the scarred wood table.

"The hot butter will cook the eggs, and you will be left with yellow flecks in your cake that are rubbery in nature."

"That counts as a question," Elena interjected.

"Huzzah!" Traneford seconded.

The rest of the afternoon passed quickly. While the cakes baked, the lords and ladies attempted to follow Muriel's detailed instructions for making sugar flowers and icing, which led to even more laughter over their sad attempts to recreate Muriel's simplest designs. Some were so distracted in making their sugar flowers that they forgot their cakes in the oven and overbaked them, while others underbaked them so much that when they went to flip their cooled creations, the cakes broke apart.

Lord Traneford crossed his arms over his chest, shaking his head over Elena's attempts to salvage the ruined cake. "I must say, I have a newfound respect for bakers." His eyes met Muriel's for a moment before his attention returned to Elena.

Muriel's cheeks tinted at his praise. She moved along the row of remaining bakers to Tess and Lord Sullivan, Lady Ingram and Widow Whelan, and Erik, whose cake was certainly the worst of the bunch. She giggled over the darlingness of Erik's curl falling onto his flour-streaked forehead as he attempted to layer the cakes without waiting for them to cool properly.

"Miss Beau, the top cake appears to be gliding off the bottom one!" Erik cried, holding them together with both hands.

"I believe that is due to your missing a step. Never fear. If the cake itself tastes good, there is no reason it cannot yet win." She scraped a piece of cake caught in the bottom of his tin and, sucking it off her finger, nodded. "Not too bad, sir. You are in the running yet."

She moved toward Tess and Sullivan's station and was astonished to find a nice little cake being iced by Tess.

"No need to tell us that we won because I know we did." Lord Sullivan grinned, rubbing his hands together.

"Best not boast before she tastes it, Sullivan," Tess grumbled and concentrated on a troubled area of the icing, attempting to cover it up with impressive chocolate curls.

Knowing it was best to leave Tess be when she was focusing on winning, Muriel approached Elena as Lord Traneford departed their station to fetch them refreshments from the table in the corner of the room that Erik had thoughtfully requested.

"I cannot believe it that not one, but two viscounts are vying for my hand, and I have you to thank for it. I hardly know which is more handsome." Elena squealed, seizing Muriel's hands. She pressed a kiss to

Muriel's cheek, drawing Tess's and Vivienne's wide-eyed alarm. "And I already have a thank-you planned that is worthy of your kindness." *Oh dear.*

It had been three days since the threat, and with Muriel safely seated at his breakfast table surrounded by guests whom he was beginning to consider friends, Erik allowed himself to relax over his last cup of coffee as the dishes were cleared away by the footmen.

"I believe it is time for the drawing, eh, Draycott?" Sir Alexander called out, the table cheering in anticipation of the day's festivities.

"Fetch the bowl please, Cedric." Erik nodded to the first footman, who departed and returned moments later with a crystal bowl containing the names of ladies on slips of paper. Each gentleman would draw the name of the lady who would join him for the curricle ride to the riverside picnic today. Erik reached into the bowl first, his fingers itching for the paper with Muriel's name. He had instructed the staff to keep the slip of paper with her name in the ice box until the last possible moment in hopes that the chilled paper would find its way into his palm . . . but all the papers felt the same. He fought back a scowl. He unfolded the paper. "Miss Vivienne, it seems we are to be partners." He inclined his head to her, even as his gaze flicked to Muriel, who was still enjoying a sticky bun.

Lord Sullivan drew next. "Ah, it seems my partner is the lovely Miss Beau."

He watched as Elena's ears burned. She kept her smile steady while Muriel choked on her bun, leaning into Tess's patting her on the back. Erik did not know the viscount well, but when he saw Sullivan near Muriel yesterday, she seemed more than uncomfortable. He should have spoken up or rigged the drawing himself to ensure he had her name. Lord Traneford paired with Tess, who at once asked of his skill in driving, assuring him of her own. That left Elena and her mother without a gentleman free to escort them and having to join Sir Alexander and Lady Ingram in the barouche.

"Excuse me, my lord. We have another guest," Trumbull called from the doorway, his shoulders stiff, as if warding off the uninvited person on the other side. "He says he is here at the behest of Miss Whelan."

All cast curious glances at Miss Whelan, who merely grinned in expectation.

"Please, fetch him inside." Erik rose along with the rest of the gentlemen in the party as the ladies eagerly craned their necks to see who would be joining them.

The butler gritted his teeth into the most pleasant expression he could apparently muster. "May I present Baron Deverell, Miss Whelan's cousin."

Erik's jaw dropped, and if Muriel had been choking before, she was near death now, judging from the sounds of Tess's whacking her on the back.

Baron Deverell strode into the room and bowed. "My lord, pardon my intrusion. I was coming to retrieve my cousin and aunt after your house party ended and made much better time than I had anticipated."

"Yes, I'd say so, being days ahead of schedule." Erik nodded to him, leaving his seat to offer Baron Deverell his hand. "If Miss Whelan is not keen to leave us just yet, did you make accommodations?"

"I've taken a room at the village inn but thought it would be offensive not to call to pay my respects." Deverell smiled.

Erik motioned a footman forward to set another cup at the table. As much as he detested extending an invitation to the gentleman Muriel had once claimed to love, he was unwilling to ignore what polite society would dictate he do with so many eyes upon him. He cleared his throat. "Nonsense, Baron. You must stay on at the castle for the rest of the entertainment, including the ball tomorrow night."

Chapter Nineteen

OSMUND DEVERELL IS TO JOIN our party? Muriel's hand trembled as she reached for her crystal glass of water. Tess and Vivienne sent her compassionate, discreet smiles while Elena was . . . beaming at her? She stole a second glance at the woman. *The little minx knew he was coming. I'd bet my best bonnet she sent for him after the viscount's attentiveness to me this week, despite my obvious disdain for the man. So much for our alliance.*

"I see you are all about to set off on a lark, judging from the line of curricles, gigs, and carriages outside." His voice sparkled, and she did not doubt his enthusiastic smile was blazing down the breakfast table, enchanting every member of their party as the men took their seats.

She kept her eyes firmly on the sticky bun that had lost all appeal. *Lord, how am I to survive this blow? Will I never outrun the shame of a single reckless deed? I had hoped Erik would somehow forget and forgive me for it, but with the man in his house reminding Erik at every turn of my folly? Erik will never wish for me to be his wife.*

"You must join us for our outing! Do say he may join." Elena directed her plea to Erik.

"I wouldn't think of denying it. Another vehicle shall be ordered." With a nod, Erik signaled to a footman, who disappeared at once.

"We have already drawn the names. There weren't enough gentlemen for all of us ladies to have a partner, so your timing is quite fortuitous," Elena cooed. "Perhaps, as you are my cousin, we should consider switching our pairings?"

"Excellent idea," Erik interjected, looking to Muriel as if he were planning on rescuing her.

But Elena wasn't finished. She looked at Muriel. "Viscount Sullivan and I shall ride together, leaving your old friend free to ride with you." Elena folded her hands around her teacup, her eyes dancing.

Erik stiffened, no doubt at her audacity in taking charge of his house party.

Muriel fought against the urge to flee the room as all turned to her.

"Miss Beau," Deverell said, "it is delightful to see you again and looking so well. I would be honored with such an arrangement, if you would allow it?" He bowed his head to her.

She forced herself to meet his gaze, the full force of the weeks between them fading, and all that remained was the raw memory of his sound rejection and her abject humiliation in the Chilham assembly hall.

"Will you join me, Miss Beau?" he queried once more.

She had waited too long. She had to say yes, no matter how much she wished to escape. *Was this how he had felt on the dance floor? Forced to offer a positive response when all he wished was to flee?* But, no. She was unwilling to believe he had felt nothing for her back then. He had said things—led her to believe he enjoyed her company. She offered him a light smile. "Of course, Baron."

"It's settled then." Elena clapped.

Erik rose and the guests hurried from their chairs, eager for the ride ahead.

Deverell slowly crossed the room and held the back of her chair. Her skin prickled at his nearness, her stomach twisting at this nightmare come true. Baron Deverell was being forced to be with her by circumstances and not by choice. She nodded her thanks to him and followed the guests as they filed out the front door to the line of buggies awaiting them. Another conveyance pulled from the carriage house as the staff distributed the ladies' and gentlemen's hats and wraps.

She stood stiffly away from Deverell, but close enough to acknowledge they were riding together. In truth, she felt as if she could melt into the earth. She glanced sideways and started at Elena's nearness.

Elena towed her aside. "What do you think of my surprise?"

"This is how you thank someone?" Muriel snorted. "I'd hate to see how you handle someone you feel slighted you."

Elena's trilling laughter drew Deverell's eye. She touched Muriel's arm and whispered, "Trust me, my dear Muriel. I have things well in hand."

"I trusted you once and in doing so, I ended up here," Muriel muttered under her breath as Elena sauntered away and possessively threaded her hand through Viscount Sullivan's arm.

A curricle approached and parked before Muriel and Deverell. She swallowed back a sigh. *Lord, let me bear this, and let me not make matters worse for both of us.* She looked up at the narrow seat perched above the pair of giant wheels and cringed. There would be no pressing herself to one side to avoid all contact with him. With the brisk pace required to reach their destination in time for all the day's games and a luncheon, she would need to be firmly planted beside him if she wished to avoid being tossed out and trampled. She never particularly enjoyed curricle races, but she had pretended to when the baron had called on her so many months ago. She could hardly cry off now without revealing the depth of her former infatuation with him.

Baron Deverell offered her his hand. She braced herself, placed her hand in his, and climbed as confidently as Tess might, cringing as she accidentally flashed an ankle before the baron, praying he did not think she did so on purpose. He hoisted himself beside her, and she at once felt the old familiarity return. They had ridden so often in his curricle about Kent that if she closed her eyes, she could easily imagine this was one of dozens of rides she had enjoyed with a man who had become such a dear friend after that wretched day in Dover with her former fiancé.

As the men guided their horses to the road, Deverell lingered until they were the last in position before following the troupe at a brisk trot. She dared a glance to her companion, finding the baron's jaw clenched, a sure sign of his discomfort. If someone were to begin speaking, it needed to be her.

"How is your family, Baron?"

"In good health, I assure you," he responded stiffly. She would not fault him, as the whole situation was difficult and of her making. "And your family?"

"You would know better than I, as you have come from Kent yourself. It has been too long since I've been home."

He chuckled. "Indeed. I'm happy to report they are well. Declan is growing quickly. I saw him briefly during my last business meeting with your father."

Declan. The ache in her chest roared to life. She had tried not to dwell upon missing his infant months. That had been the hardest element of leaving home, her dear brothers. She cleared the emotion from her throat and, without thinking, continued, "And Miss Fox? Have you settled a date for your upcoming nuptials?" *Why?* her mind screamed at her. Why did she feel the need to speak of such things? *You might have asked about his mother. His business. Anything but Miss Fox, you bottlehead!*

His brows shot up to the brim of his hat, his grip slacking on the ribbons before he flicked his hat back to see her more fully. "Have you not heard? She is married."

Muriel's stomach dropped with a bump in the road, and she gasped. "What? To another? But Miss Fox was so devoted to you."

"Apparently not as much as she led me or society to believe. She was using me to conceal her true motives. She was secretly engaged to a soldier, and the moment he returned from duty, which was about a week after your departure, she absconded with him to Gretna Green, where they wed before the blacksmith's anvil. It was quite the talk of the county. I am surprised your family did not alert you in their letters." He snapped the reins, bringing their curricle closer to the final carriage in the group.

She knew why they had not alerted her. They'd likely feared Muriel would abandon her opportunity in London and return home to fall at his feet once more—a ridiculous notion, but one she deserved after the way she had behaved. Is that why her friends hadn't told her either? She glanced toward Vivienne, clinging onto Erik's arm to avoid being shaken out of the curricle as she chatted, her cheeks pink from the sharp wind rolling over the hill. "I'm sorry your courtship did not advance as you intended, Baron."

He frowned. "Must you keep calling me Baron? I feel as if you do not think of our time together at all."

She twisted in her seat to see if he was in cruel jest. "How could you even consider I do not think on it?" *It has been pressing on my every breath, and it is only by the greatest amount of prayer I can put it from my mind.*

He frowned. "To begin, you did not seem pleased to see me."

"A fact you deduced how?" She crossed her arms, but at once uncrossed them to grip the side of the curricle.

"You would not even meet my gaze when I entered the breakfast room, which was most disheartening. Why do you think I came for my cousin days before I was required?"

"Because your horse was swifter afoot than you gave him credit for, along with the fair weather that led to good roads?"

He met her gaze, the earnestness in it startling her. "I came to see you, Muriel."

She focused on her lap, twisting her gloves in her hands. Why was he acting as if their parting had not wrenched her heart in two? As if he had not rejected her soundly? "And why, pray tell, did you wish to see me?"

"After Miss Fox departed with her new husband, I was free to explore our relationship once more. I have not forgotten your request." He pulled back on the reins, dropping them far behind the last carriage in the tight line. "In fact, it is something I think about every time I open my eyes. It is my greatest regret that the choices I made led to your unhappiness and to your departure to London. I know how much you love Chilham and how much pain you must have been in to leave it and your family in pursuit of the unknown."

Her cheeks burned. "My unhappiness was my own doing. I wish you would forget my forwardness. I do not know what came over me that day. I fiercely regret my boldness."

"Do you?" He rested his hand with the fist of ribbons on his knee and tossed his beaver hat into the curricle well, taking her in as if he couldn't keep himself from her another moment. "Because, you see, I do not regret your display of affection. I only regret I was not free to answer favorably at the time." He nodded to Erik, who was looking over his shoulder at them, no doubt wondering what was keeping them. "I heard the earl has been most attentive. Do you have an understanding with him?"

Was he asking if she were free? And if so, why? Deverell had had his chance with her. If he were telling the truth in that he felt honor bound to wed Miss Fox and had not accepted her proposal because of it, perhaps there was hope for redemption in the greatest way possible? Was this what Elena had meant in trusting her? She followed his study of Erik, and her infatuation for the baron seemed childish in light of how well she knew this captain nobleman who only wished to be her friend and yet protected her with a fierceness that spoke of much more.

"Has he spoken of his intentions toward you?" he repeated.

"No. We do not have an understanding. He is not interested in me in that manner."

"Not interested in you, eh?" He chuckled, flicking the reins. "Then why, Miss Beau, is the earl constantly checking over his shoulder to see if I have returned to our place in line?"

He's worried for me. She reminded her heart that Erik had taken her in because of his friendship with her guardians and the lurking danger of a fortune hunter. "He's simply being a concerned host. Perhaps you should catch up to the rest of the party to save what little reputation I have managed to salvage."

Deverell grinned. "Only if you return to calling me Osmund."

"Very well, Osmund."

He slapped the reins, passing the Ingrams, Elena's curricle, Tess's, and drew alongside the earl and Vivienne. Vivienne's eyes widened as she sent Muriel a smile, silently asking if she were well. However, with Erik directly beside her friend, Muriel was incapable of disclosing anything. She smiled tightly and waved as they raced past.

Deverell released a whoop and sent his horse into a full gallop, assuming the lead position. With a cry, she held onto her bonnet and the side of the curricle, praying she didn't tumble out and get trampled by the earl's horse, which would indeed prove the most tragic ending to her desperate tale.

Chapter Twenty

THIS WAS PAINFUL. WATCHING MURIEL and the baron ride past his and Vivienne's curricle, Erik gritted his teeth at the prospect of seeing her reunite with the man she had professed to love mere weeks ago. But, at least this way, he didn't have to keep glancing over his shoulder to ensure her safety. Five miles to the riverside and back had sounded marvelous to him at the time of planning. However, he supposed in his mind he always had Miss Beau at his side, the baron nowhere near her, or her thoughts—much less beside her for so long.

But his time without Muriel had not been all torture. Vivienne proved a wealth of information in regard to Muriel. She never ceased her chatting from the moment she assumed her seat. Apparently, she had known Muriel since her school days in the village, and they had been friends for nearly all their lives.

"I was fortunate, really," Vivienne continued. "After my father's passing, I was brought up in my stepbrother's household just outside the village of Chilham. He, like most gentlemen, had little wish to spend a pound of their inheritance on his mother's other family, but, as it turned out, I met one of my dearest friends because of attending the village school instead of having my own private tutor."

"Where did you meet Miss Hale?" he asked, curious about Muriel's other dearest friend, who seemed as peculiar in society as Muriel.

"At finishing school. That was the one thing my father ensured I had enough funds for upon his death. When Muriel's mother married,

Muriel was sent to the small finishing school I was attending—against my stepbrother's wife's wishes, I might add." She chuckled. "Tess was another 'wildling,' as the teacher often called Muriel. Even if Muriel was rather unpolished, she has always been kindhearted, brilliant, and generous to a fault."

"I have seen this to be true. Nothing makes her happier than to bring a smile to someone who needs it, usually in the form of a baked good." He snapped the reins, attempting to close some of the distance between his and the baron's curricle.

"She needs someone who will love her for it and not attempt to mold her into what he thinks a proper lady should be." She pressed her lips into a thin line, scowling at the couple before them. "Too much change for her could prove detrimental to her sweet spirit."

They crested the hill, and he was thankful to spy tents dotting the riverside, where boating, picnics, and games awaited them. He fought back a sigh of relief. He had enjoyed his time with Vivienne, but his being fought to be beside Muriel. He shouldn't give in to his need to be near her. Heaven help him, the urge was impossible. The groomsman awaiting them secured the horses as Erik dismounted the curricle and reached up for Vivienne.

"Thank you, my lord." She smiled up at him as her feet touched the grass. "Now that I understand your intentions toward my friend, let's see what we can do to keep Muriel from falling under the baron's spell once more."

He jerked his head back. "I beg your pardon?"

"You spent the entirety of the journey here asking leading questions that referred to her, and, from what I have gathered from your character, I'd much prefer her to accept your hand than that man's." She shook her head. "There has always been something lurking behind his expressions that I could never quite put my finger on. Despite his winning nature, I do not trust him."

Erik gritted his teeth. *Neither do I.* But dare he trust this young lady with his secret, growing admiration for Muriel? If Vivienne was anything like Muriel, he had little choice in the matter if her mind was made up.

☙

Baron Deverell grinned as he hopped down from the curricle and lifted his hand to Muriel. She accepted his help. Unlike the old days, when she couldn't get enough time with him and every inadvertent brush of her hand against his sent her to perspiring profusely, she found her heartbeat accelerated at the approach of Erik. He looked impossibly dashing in his striking cutaway coat of burgundy, matching neckcloth, and ivory pantaloons. The curricle ride had set his bonny curls to even greater heights, while her hair was no doubt as wild as Grandfather's sheep.

"Miss Beau!" Erik showed no signs of his trot over in his breathing, his eyes bright as they met hers. "How was the drive? I trust you enjoyed the countryside?"

She glanced sideways to Deverell. "The conversation was interesting, and the country I found enthralling—such splendid meadows and graceful trees. With such views as these, it may hold some temptation over the sea for you?"

"I receive only the compliment of 'interesting' while the country is 'enthralling'?" Deverell thumped his fist over his heart. "My lady, you wound me most egregiously."

Muriel released a strained laugh, glancing over to Erik at the man's obvious flirtation.

Erik's smile did not falter in the slightest as he bowed to her. "Miss Beau, will you assist me as you promised?"

Her heart stumbled. Ah, yes, the promise. Of course that was all. He needed her assistance and nothing more. He certainly did not view Deverell as a rival. Well, if she had no other bachelors in the running to save her reputation, she needed to flirt in return and secure her family's standing in society. Swallowing her disappointment, she looked to

Deverell. She had believed that she loved him once. She might again. "Shall we? I need to oversee the finishing touches, and then perhaps we can begin the festivities with one of the entertainments we have arranged for today."

Deverell's shoulders rolled back, and she spied the confidence of old returning to his features at being invited to stay by her side. "I would be delighted. Lead the way, Lord Draycott."

On the baron's arm, she followed the earl toward the sprinkling of tents beside the ambling river, where servants circulated on the bank, tempting guests with silver trays of punch and small iced sponges. Ordinarily, she would be tasting them straightaway, but her heavy heart did not even race at the sight.

Erik paused to speak with a footman, gesturing for Muriel to join him as Sir Alexander called to the baron.

Erik touched her elbow. "Miss Beau, the servants are having complications with the finish line of the boat race. Something about the flags I had draped overhead falling into the water. Will you join me in rowing down to the end to help secure them?"

"I thought the point of drawing names was to have a partner of the day?" the baron interjected with a grin that did not quite reach his eyes.

Erik scowled. "And as you were never supposed to be in the drawing in the first place, I do not think you will mind sparing her, as she has already promised to aid me in today's festivities."

Deverell's neck reddened along with his ears. "Of course. As you have been such a gracious host, I shall release Miss Beau to your care."

Muriel rested her hand in Erik's, allowing him to guide her to the short dock that appeared to be a few decades old, and sent Deverell an apologetic smile over her shoulder. No matter how she felt about Deverell now, Erik shouldn't have embarrassed him. "That was unkind, Erik."

"The man was overstepping. I won't have him stealing you away for the entirety of the day simply because he feels he has a prior claim to you." Erik hopped into the rowboat, his stance confident and true. He lifted his hands to her, and she attempted to hop in as he did, sending the boat to listing dangerously to the left. He laughed as she fumbled, his hands steadying her waist, his feet stabilizing the vessel. "We meet like this once more."

She laughed and lowered herself to the rear bench seat and reached for the oar to steady herself, for, unlike their entrance to Vauxhall, all knew them here. To be caught in such an intimate fashion would not do.

"Do you wish to help me row, or do you prefer to sit?"

She rolled back her shoulders. "I'll row."

His brows rose at this, and he took the seat opposite her. "Have you done it before?"

"Your wrist is only just out of its wrappings. I'd hate for you to reinjure it." *Even though it would mean you must stay in England near me.* "Besides, how hard could it be?" She grinned.

He settled in his seat across from her, his eyes bright. "Not too difficult."

She pressed her feet against the hull and, dropping the blades into the river, she pushed the oars away from her, sending the boat into the dock instead of forward.

"Almost," Erik gently corrected, wrapping his strong hands atop hers, guiding her hands to the end of the oars, and turning the vessel so that the stern pointed away from the riverbank. "Your blades should be moving toward the stern, which will pull us in the direction we need to go."

She nodded, too breathless from his touch to say much of anything. He didn't remove his hold and, instead, rowed with her, his calloused hands caressing hers with each pull, gently correcting her movements until they reached the row of colorful flags drifting in the gentle current.

Erik fetched them up, draping the dripping flags over the side of the boat. "Do you think you can direct us to the edge of the bank?"

Muriel laughed. "My arms are quite strong, but rowing has used muscles I did not know I possessed. Please, take charge."

Erik's deep laughter filled the air as he expertly maneuvered the rowboat to the bank and lifted the string of flags, pulling it taut so that it hung over the river, and fastened it to an overhead branch. The wind sent the little triangles to fluttering and sprinkling droplets on them both, when she spied something on the flags that had not draped into the water.

"Erik?"

His mirth fell away at her tone. "What is it?"

"Row us to the opposite end. There is something painted on the flags."

Frowning, he guided the boat to the other side. On each flag there was scrawled a letter.

"C-E-D-E." Muriel read. "What on earth does this mean? 'Cede' what? The game?"

Erik paled and murmured, "My ship." He turned to her. "Muriel, you are not safe away from the castle."

"What do you mean? What do I have to do with you giving up your ship?" She shook her head. "This is most likely a lark one of the guests is having, regarding the boat race." She rested her hand on his arm. "Surely, there is nowhere safer in all of England than Draycott Castle by your side."

Erik stared at her. "You truly believe that?"

"I have felt it since the moment you rescued me from an inebriated Lord Traneford on the dance floor."

He dropped his gaze to the oars, adjusting his hold on them as he cleared his throat.

"I've done it again, haven't I?" She laughed, her cheeks warming. "I've grown too comfortable in your presence, my lord. Please, do not worry on my behalf. Inquire of the guests which pulled such a jest."

"I shall," he fairly growled as he turned the boat, cutting through the water faster than she had known was possible for one man.

Chapter Twenty-One

LORD DEVERELL PANTED AS HE dragged their boat onto the bank. "Well, Miss Beau, I hope taking third place did not lower your opinion of me."

Muriel smiled at him and grasped his hand, leaping to shore. "On the contrary, a man who can gracefully accept defeat is to be admired."

"Spoken like a person who lost," Vivienne teased. Under Erik's expert rowing, her vessel tied for first with Lord Sullivan and Elena.

Tess lugged her boat to shore, glaring at Traneford, not caring that her hem dragged in the water. "We would have won if *someone* had not been so prideful in not allowing a lady to row until we were stuck in the reeds."

Elena threaded her arm through Muriel's. "This outing with Lord Sullivan has proven to be most confusing. He is attentive but doesn't seem as genuine as Lord Traneford."

"Knowing Traneford, I think that would be true. I do not know Sullivan as well. It might be unfair for me to judge him before I have properly ascertained his character," Muriel replied. "But I do think you are better matched with Viscount Traneford." At Tess's and Vivienne's concerned glances, Muriel sent them a smile and allowed Elena to lead her to the tent hosting the next event. "Don't you agree?"

"I may. Viscount Sullivan has a dangerous air about him that I find most pleasing." She whipped out her fan, lifting her delicate locks with the frantic flapping. "I am most eager to partner with him in the flower arrangement competition, but will you vow to stay near us? It would hardly be proper for us to be caught too far from the group in search of the perfect blossom for our arrangement . . . no matter how much I may secretly desire to be alone with him. You know better than most about the high cost of breeching etiquette."

Muriel bit her lip at how the rules of polite society hadn't even crossed her mind when she was baking with Erik and when he tended to her wound with her in his arms, her head resting against his broad chest. She vividly recalled the brush of his fingertips as he handled her cut with such care. "I do. I'll stay near you both."

"Perfect. Now, if you will excuse me, I must see to my beaus," she whispered and whisked away to where the lords stood conversing.

Muriel wove through the stations in the tent, ensuring each had a crystal vase and a pair of scissors for the arranging contest in which the ladies would be allowed only to verbally instruct the men on their placement of the blooms.

"How did you manage to get on her good side?" Vivienne whispered as she and Tess met Muriel in the tent, tugging on her silk ribbons to reform the perfect bow beneath her chin.

"Did you put something in her drink to weaken her defenses?" Tess teased and popped a tart into her mouth.

Muriel realigned a pair of scissors atop the cloth and filled them in on the good deed that had launched her tumultuous friendship with Elena. She had just finished the tale when Erik clapped his hands.

"Ladies and gentlemen, please find your partners from the drive. We will have a quarter of an hour to select the perfect blooms, and then the gentlemen will begin arranging. For those who do not have gentlemen partners, I'm afraid you will have to abstain from this event."

Widow Whelan lifted her plate of treats. "Which is no trial, my dear lord. Please, enjoy without any concern for those of us watching."

Lord Deverell joined Muriel, bearing the scissors and offering her his hand. "My lady, shall we?"

She accepted his hand. It still felt strange to be near him again, to feel this companionship between them. The rest of the party spread over the nearby hills, gathering wildflowers as Muriel guided Deverell behind Elena and Sullivan along the riverside.

She tore a handful of tiny yellow wildflowers at their base. "I must confess, Osmund, I do not have much experience with flower arranging—besides the edible ones on my cakes."

"As you may recall, I am most proficient in collecting wildflowers," Deverell returned, his voice low as he snipped a cluster of yellow daffodils growing near the bank.

Her heart skipped in remembering that first bouquet of white snowdrops he had collected for her on their first ride home from Dover in his attempt to cheer her up. "I do. You were very kind when I needed it most. I don't know what I would have done if you hadn't happened upon me."

He bent and cut away a sprig of violet-colored blooms. "I pray you will think on that instead of the way we parted." He stayed on bended knee, lifting the flowers to her. "It is my deepest wish we remember what we were before the misunderstanding that led to our parting. I have missed our conversations."

Muriel accepted the blossoms, his fingers caressing hers. "I have as well, Osmund."

"Then let's put the matter behind us and be friends once more?"

She tugged him to standing with a smile. "I would like nothing more." At Elena's squealing over a flower, she shielded her eyes from the sun and pointed down the bank to where Elena was kneeling. "You best collect whatever she found, lest we are put out of the running for first!"

"Your wish is my command, my lady." With a grin, he trotted over to claim one for their vase.

Muriel spied a sprig of pink blossoms a few paces away that sparked her memory. She rubbed her chin, trying to recall if this particular wildflower was edible. After several stomach aches, she knew better than to test it on herself. Sighing, she added the bloom to the bouquet. Muriel nearly jumped at the brush of a gentleman's hand on hers.

"Viscount Sullivan!" She sidestepped away, thinking it was merely an accident. Viscount Sullivan relocated with her, his gaze locking on hers. She glanced to Elena and Deverell, who had moved farther away in pursuit of another cluster of flowers. "Is there something you needed? Or perhaps Miss Whelan requires?"

"There is something you may help me with."

"Oh?" She attempted to keep relief from her voice as she took another stride away from him, lest Elena mistake their interlude for something more than it was—an awkward exchange.

He selected a purple flower that she knew for certain was edible. "I heard tell that you are quite a wealthy woman."

"Yes?"

"I thought you were merely a poor relation of the Ingrams." He twirled the stem of the bloom. "But when I received the earl's invitation, I inquired of our mutual friends and found I have you to thank for it . . . which led to my discovery of your fortune."

"I believe it is actually Sir Alexander and Lady Ingram whom you have to thank," she murmured. *Does he think I managed to secure an invitation for him in order to have him court me?*

"Of course." He grinned, offering the flower for Muriel's bouquet. "That is the way of polite society."

"To accept it would be cheating, my lord. We may only use the blossoms from our team."

"There is no need to play the coy, innocent maid, Miss Beau, not when I heard from my valet that you were seen in the kitchen the other night in the earl's arms."

She gasped. "It was nothing like that, I assure you. I was merely giving him a lesson on baking, and I cut my finger and was in a faint—"

He gently took her injured hand in his, pressing a kiss atop the bandage before she jerked her hand away. "Well, if you do not wish for Miss Whelan's reputation as well as your own to be tainted by gossip, I suggest you give me a private lesson like you gave the earl."

"How dare you?" She straightened to her full height. "Remember yourself, Viscount."

"Miss Beau?" Deverell strode across the field toward them, his gaze flashing from the viscount's expression to her flushed cheeks. "Is something amiss?"

Sullivan grinned at her as if daring her to speak out against him.

Elena called out to the viscount, her eyes narrowing on Muriel in a fashion she knew all too well. By the look on her face, their truce was on dangerous ground. But at the moment, Muriel was too vexed to care. *How dare that cad insult me?* Her fingers itched for something to strike him with, and for the first time she understood why Tess carried a weapon. She despised this feeling of helplessness.

She turned a smile up to Deverell. "Would you mind escorting me back to the tent? I believe we have enough for our arrangement."

Deverell glared at the smirking Sullivan, the baron's fists curling inward. But at her gentle touch, he allowed her to lead him away.

"What did the man say to you?" Deverell demanded, his voice growing huskier with each word. "Did he harm you? Insult you?"

She shook her head. She could never admit to being alone with Erik, no matter how innocent it had been. "Let's just say that he is not a gentleman, and I shall be warning Elena against the man's wanting character."

"I'll thrash him." Deverell turned on his heel, ready to confront the man.

"Please. I can handle it." Muriel rested a staying hand on his chest, drawing the eyes of returning guests with their bundles of flowers. She sensed rather than saw Erik's confusion. She kept her gaze on Deverell, praying he would release the matter, lest he make matters worse.

He frowned. "Very well. However, if he bothers you again, I will not stand down a second time."

Guy Mayfield rang a silver bell, calling out, "Ladies and gentlemen, return to your stations and let the arranging begin!"

Chapter Twenty-Two

"THAT SHIMMERING OLIVE GOWN DOES wonders for your complexion." Tess stepped back as the three friends admired their reflections in the floor-length gilded looking glass. "Your suitors will not be able to keep themselves from your side."

"I will not make the mistake of assuming I have *any* suitors again." Muriel fidgeted with an unruly curl framing her face. "I will only allow myself to assume a gentleman's feelings after he proposes—even then I doubt my judgment given my previous fiancés."

Vivienne wrapped her arm about Muriel's shoulders, careful not to crush the delicate sleeves. "This time is vastly different. Deverell has made no secret that he is attempting to win your hand, Muriel. By the end of the ball, word will have spread to the neighboring families, which we all know will lead to news reaching Kent of Deverell's intentions toward you, along with Lord Draycott's attention."

"I fear you are right." Muriel readjusted one of the diamond pins sprinkled throughout her coiffure. While it might be all well and good to wear a crown out in the country, it would be unseemly to don anything other than diamond pins and feathers with actual royalty about and wearing their coronets passed down from generation to generation, not simply purchased at Garrard's on Regent Street.

Vivienne frowned. "You *fear* I am right? Is not a proposal from Deverell what you seek? I know we discussed your feelings for Lord Draycott when we first arrived, but that was before the baron appeared."

"We all know how smitten she was with Baron Deverell only weeks ago." Tess snorted. "Vacillating so after a proposal—"

"Is reprehensible. Nonetheless, the whole point of this drastic change of scenery was to find a brilliant match," Muriel interjected.

"To be honest, he is not my first choice in a husband for you after all that you have endured, but even I cannot argue his actions in following you across the counties would not only redeem your breach of etiquette but make you a part of one of the most romantic tales people have ever encountered. His proposal would confirm he did indeed find himself too entrenched with Miss Fox to accept Muriel's original proposal, and now that he is unencumbered, he wishes for nothing more than to secure her hand." Vivienne shook her head. "And yet, I must ask, what of your earl? Have your feelings progressed? Has he spoken to you?"

Muriel turned away from the looking glass and moved to the window, staring out onto the moonlit garden beyond the castle's lake. "From what I can tell, Erik only wishes for friendship, and, as I have learned so harshly in the past, I will not under any circumstances allow myself to speak out of turn again. If Lord Draycott wished for anything more, he would have spoken." She folded her hands at her waist. "I must be stronger than I was this spring."

"I too supposed Lord Draycott would have spoken out by now," Vivienne admitted, scowling.

At the chime of the clock atop the mantelpiece sounding the tenth hour, the women started and snatched up their gloves in a flurry of satin and feathers, making haste down to the banqueting hall. The servants had transformed the austere, masculine hall into a fairy garden. On the ancient wheel chandelier, ivy was woven around the wheel and spokes with purple blooms that dripped over the rim, creating the illusion of streamers. All about the room, there were flower arrangements, including the ones the gentlemen had made yesterday, bringing the very meadow indoors. Along the walls, there were long linen-draped tables with a veritable feast upon them that the guests could enjoy at any time. The violins were already playing, and the country gentry stood in the reception line flowing from the foyer that led out to the first courtyard, awaiting admittance as they greeted their host.

Her breath caught at the broad shoulders of Erik in his ebony dress coat. He cut a fine figure and looked every bit the earl. As if sensing her gaze, Erik turned and spotted her, his full lips parting into a broad grin.

Vivienne squeezed her arm. Of course, she would see the interaction. "See. He does care for you," she whispered through her smile. "I know you must have something concrete, but my heart would break to see you marry the wrong gentleman when Lord Draycott simply needs time to step forward."

Muriel clutched the neck of her fan. "I do not have the luxury of time."

At the butler's signal for the next guest, Erik returned his focus to the couple at hand. Though she thought he did so with a sigh, judging from the slight rise and fall of his shoulders before he turned to his guests with his brilliant smile. The absence of his attention left her colder than she had been only moments before.

"Miss Beau, you are a vision." Baron Deverell bowed to them at the bottom of the stairs, lifting his hand to her. "Would you do me the great honor of granting me the opening dance?"

She had hoped to open the ball with Erik. As he had never asked her, she could hardly argue such a thing. "The honor would be mine, Baron Deverell." *You can do this. You can love Deverell again.*

※

"We were thrilled to receive your invitation, Lord Draycott. Honestly, with you away at sea for so long, we were beginning to think the castle was in danger of having to be sold off. It would have been a pity to allow it to fall out of the family after being the Draycotts' seat for centuries," Lady Pomphrey commented, motioning to the lady behind her. "You remember my daughter, Lady Cecilia? I believe you may have met her in London at the Hughlots' ball?"

Erik bowed to the slender lady before him, whom he vaguely recalled. There had been so many ladies clamoring for his attention that night, which was quite disorienting after years of hardly interacting with any women. "Of course. Very happy to see you again, Lady Cecilia."

"Yes. It was rather a trek from our vast estate, but as she's our only unattached child remaining, we considered it could be worth the drive." She eyed Erik with a frankness that took him aback. "Perhaps you would like to open the dancing with her?"

Erik's mouth felt dry. How did he confess he wished to ask another? He should have secured Muriel's answer last night. But, as Lady Cecilia was the first young lady whose mother was bold enough to ask, he bowed to her and extended his hand. "If the lady agrees?"

Lady Cecilia turned crimson but placed her hand in his as Erik nodded his greeting to the guests behind in the line. Trumbull at once took charge as Erik escorted Lady Cecilia to the ballroom for the opening minuet, taking their place at the top of the set. The ladies and gentlemen quickly found their places behind him, Muriel directly to Lady Cecilia's left in her brilliant gown.

"You must forgive my mother. She is always attempting to arrange a good match for me," Lady Cecilia whispered as their palms touched. "I believe I shall forever be uncomfortable at dances until I am married, for I shall always be wondering what scheme she has up her sleeve."

Erik laughed, garnering Muriel's attention. He knew if he glanced her way, he would forget the figures of the dance. "I understand the feeling."

"I'd imagine it is all new to you, though, with your being able to escape society for so many years aboard your vessel. I quite envy you."

"Oh?"

"To have such freedom is truly marvelous."

"Yes, but to remain untethered for so long can have adverse effects." He dared a glimpse toward Muriel, who was laughing on the arm of Deverell.

Her eyes widened. "Such as?"

Such as now possessing the fear of marrying and having a family because I have a dangerous position that could cost my loved ones their lives. The flags fluttering above the river with their painted warning still wrenched his gut. He had foolishly hoped his retreat to the country was enough for Requin to forget his threat . . . however, years of experience should have taught him that revenge never forgets. "Such as attending country dances, Lady Cecilia."

She laughed as the music ended and he escorted her from the floor, leaving her in the care of her mother so that he might speak to Muriel. However, every time he had nearly reached Muriel through the crowd, the baron was always there, sweeping her away to taste some delicacy, or join a dance, or a neighbor would approach Erik and pull him into a long-winded conversation. It was positively maddening. After seeing her dance and laugh with Deverell, he was finding he could not withstand his need to speak to her—to make an offer for her hand, despite his instinct to withdraw in order to protect her after the last warning.

Perhaps he did stand a chance. After all, he possessed everything she wished for when she started out on this journey to find a husband. Although, she had never flirted with him. Was he not wealthy enough to gain her attention? But, knowing her character, he knew Muriel was not as shallow as society believed her. She was the sort of woman he wanted at his side through life. He needed someone strong, who would be independent enough to remain at home alone for months on end while he served the Crown. Perhaps if he offered her something more than Deverell could, she would be open to his request. What might she say if he purchased the bakery in Draybridge for her to run as she wished? She had said it herself. What other gentleman would be amenable to his wife working when she should be playing the fine lady? He did not care what she did, as long as she placed her hand in his . . . forever.

꧁

"Miss Beau." Viscount Sullivan bowed to her. "I find I am at a loss in this sea of guests, and you are my anchor."

Muriel glanced over her shoulder to see if Elena was nearby. "There are certainly more guests than I thought would attend tonight. Though, I suppose a new earl garners much interest, far and wide."

"As well as near." He winked.

She frowned. "I beg your pardon?"

"We all see how he looks at you, Miss Beau, and we both know of your evening of baking with him." He reached for her hand, his drink sloshing in his other hand. "You have yet to give me my lesson, you tart little coquette."

She snatched her hand back, curling it into a fist. "You are drunk."

"And you are just a light-heeled kitchen wench dressed in gilded feathers who shouldn't be putting on airs." He threw back his drink and tossed the glass into the arms of a passing footman.

"How dare you? A lady is a lady because of her character, not her birth."

"Spoken like a true kitchen wench."

She ached to slap him, but knowing such an action would reflect poorly on herself, she bolted from him and escaped onto the stone balcony for some much-needed air. She would earn Elena's ire, no doubt, but she could not allow Elena to bind herself with such a wretch as Viscount Sullivan when he was not committed to the woman he was pursuing even in the earliest stages of that pursuit. He was a man without honor to say such things to her, and she would see to it that Elena knew what kind of so-called gentleman she was seeing before it was too late to retrench.

Baron Deverell may have done the same to her only weeks ago in his vacillation between her and Miss Fox, yet she truly did not think he meant it in ill spirit. He had only protected himself from a known jilt. She knew the man's character . . . or at least she thought she knew Deverell's character. Still the Miss Fox chapter in their relationship was disconcerting, even though he had been the model of a smitten gentleman since. *Lord, what do I do? I know You have forgiven me for my moment of weakness. Father said to evaluate the man on his character and not his title. You know my circumstance, and You know the baron's. Let me not misjudge him the way I was judged. Guide me, Lord.*

"I find you alone at last." Erik's voice embraced her from behind.

She whirled about, her heart skittering, the flickering torches lighting the balcony casting his handsome face in shadows. "Erik, you managed to slip away? What will your guests think?"

He chuckled, drawing nearer to her. "Well, I wished to ask you for the first dance."

Her brows lifted as the strains of the fourth dance could be heard already. "Why didn't you?"

He shrugged and leaned on the railing beside her. "It never seemed like the right time before the ball, and then, before I knew it, I was escorting a Lady Cecilia." He rotated his wrist, rubbing where the bandage had been for so long.

"How exactly did you injure your wrist anyway?" She leaned against the railing as well, lifting her gaze to the stars above. "You never told me."

"I wished to tell you—many times."

"An intrigue?" She twirled around to face him. "Pray, do not keep me in suspense, Erik." But, at the serious light upon his expression, her mirth faded. "What happened?"

He cleared his throat. "There are things you do not know about me. That many people do not know—"

"The reel is about to begin, Miss Beau," Baron Deverell called from the French doors, extending his hand to her. At her hesitancy, he smiled. "You promised. Will you break my heart over a dance?"

Blast. She looked back to Erik, who nodded his farewell, ending their confusing conversation. He once again had not promised anything, but there had been promise in his eyes, his touch—the words unspoken. She shook her head. She could not allow herself to be drawn into the unspoken again. She needed a man who was not hesitant about her or her future.

Deverell swung her onto the floor. "Do you recognize the melody?"

Her eyes widened. How had she failed to notice? "It's the song that was playing when I proposed to you."

"And I was loath to reject you then. Now this song gives me the opportunity and the honor to repay your kind act." He paused in the center, the chandelier's candles dancing overhead as he knelt on the banqueting hall's stone floor.

"Baron?" She gasped. *He is going to propose! He is going to propose.* Her stomach twisted. She should say yes. She *needed* to say yes. The crowd paused, encircling them, those in the house party smiling behind their fans and whispering to one another. Her eyes found Erik on the outskirts of the crowd, and she was shocked to find him scowling in a manner that sent chills down her spine. In that moment, he was very much the dangerous sea captain and not at all the distinguished gentleman earl. *Surely, he must care.* But at the very next skip of her heart, she remembered he'd had every chance to declare himself.

"My dearest Miss Beau. Not long ago, I was given a glimpse into heaven when you spoke to me. I was a fool for waiting this long, and I pray you will not take my foolishness as a reflection of my feelings for you. They are as strong as they were the day I met you, and I am kneeling before you now, a man who has longed for no other. Will you do me the honor of becoming my wife?"

The crowd of dancers had paused by now, along with the orchestra. She swallowed. She did not wish for him to think her vacillating, but to make such a choice now? After such a confusing conversation with the man she loved with all of her being? Surely, it would be wrong to accept one man when another filled her every thought—her every breath.

She bestowed upon him her most charming smile, dipping her head in modesty. "I am honored, Baron, and because I hold you in such high regard, I will take up your request in prayer and let you know of my answer upon the morrow."

His grin faltered slightly as he rose, extending his hand to her and escorting her from the floor.

"I want you to know I would never attempt to humiliate you by my hesitation as an act of cruelty," she whispered, clutching his arm. "It is only that I truly need to bring this matter before God. I will not act rashly a second time."

His gaze softened. "Then I shall pray for a favorable outcome."

Chapter Twenty-Three

ERIK TOSSED IN HIS BED for the hundredth time. Every time he closed his eyes, the image of the baron on bended knee before Muriel was there. The memory nearly strangled him. When she did not accept him at once, his heart had soared. What was holding her back? He didn't dare hope he was the reason for her hesitation. From what Vivienne had told him and from what Miss Whelan had revealed that day in the abbey, Muriel had been madly in love with the man. Could she really have changed her mind so quickly after meeting him? He turned over. *You did. You were completely against the idea of a wife and a family, and yet she turned everything on its head, rearranging your carefully laid plans in a matter of weeks.*

The drawn bed curtains were suffocating him. He threw off the covers and padded in his bare feet to the windows, looking over the lake to the sky, where hints of a new day were beginning. What was the point of sleeping with such a proposal haunting him and dawn so near? He needed to be out of doors—to stretch his limbs and clear his mind. Perhaps a baked good and a walk would do the trick until breakfast. His stomach rumbled, and, tossing a simple linen shirt over his head and tucking it into his pantaloons, he tugged on his boots, threw his greatcoat over his arm, and lit a candle. He strode down the hall toward the kitchen, letting memory guide him more than the weak flicker of the flame.

At the high-pitched warbling coming from behind the door, he paused with his hand on the wood planks, slowly pushing it ajar to silently view the scene he knew would be there—his dear Muriel. "We must stop meeting like this, my lady baker."

She started and nearly dropped her wooden bowl and stirring spoon to the floor. Prepared for her reaction, Erik darted across the stones and caught them from her, setting them on the counter. Judging from the mounds of baked goods, she had been in here all night.

"Did you never retire, Ariel?"

She smiled softly at the sobriquet and pressed her hands to her back, arching. Her full apron revealed the puffed sleeves of her costly evening gown. "I had a lot of thinking to do. Cook wouldn't allow me to use the kitchen until after the last guest was in bed, and by then I had a full list of items I wished to bake. I only intended on baking my first choice, a meat pie, but one thought led to another and then . . ." She waved to the basket of colorful macarons, trio of perfectly iced cakes, a dozen loaves of bread, breakfast rolls, and muffins. "My thoughts ran away with me."

"I'm guessing this baking storm is in regard to Baron Deverell's proposal?"

She wiped her fingers on her apron, giving a sharp nod.

Sensing she wasn't ready to discuss it, he motioned to the mound of food. "Must be a difficult decision, because I doubt we will eat a third of all these baked goods."

"I discovered that after I finished this last batch of muffins." She dipped her head, her cheeks reddening. "I'll pay for the ingredients. I only needed to think, and to think, I need to work—to feel useful once more."

"Think nothing of it." He reached for a golden macaron and popped it in his mouth, the lemon flavor bursting through at once. His mouth twisted at the tartness.

"Is it that bad?" She reached for one and took a tentative bite.

"I was only expecting vanilla, not lemon. It's delicious." He took a second golden macaron to demonstrate his enjoyment of the treat. "I have a better idea than this food going to waste. The drawbridge should be open now, and I was about to take my morning constitutional. What if you join me in taking a few basketfuls down to the church? I know the vicar's wife brings baskets to the war widows in the area. I am certain she will be ecstatic to have your fine foods to deliver, even if it is not on her usual delivery day."

She clasped her hands to her chest. "What a lovely idea, Erik."

"Perhaps we can depart after you change?"

She gasped, glancing down at her dress as if aware of it for the first time. "Yes, of course." She opened a door to what appeared to be a dry pantry and withdrew some baskets. "I found these while I was rummaging. Would you mind filling them while I slip into my walking gown?"

"Of course." He set aside his coat. The packing was more meticulous a process than he had thought, and after several attempts to pack the two largest cakes without damaging them, he decided at last to leave the large cakes for the house party to enjoy over luncheon instead of risking their demise by transferring them into a basket.

Muriel panted as she reached the kitchen door, dressed in a white muslin confection with a pink-rose-embroidered emerald spencer that brought out her lovely coloring, with a matching pink poke bonnet. "All finished?"

"I managed to get as much as I can in four baskets." Erik slipped on his coat. "I hope you are carrying the one with the cake. I fear if it is left in my care, I might harm those delightful sugar rosettes you created."

"Of course. I've been carrying cakes since I was a girl." She hefted two baskets off the table without so much as a grunt at the weight. She was quite the strong little thing.

Erik reached for the remaining baskets and followed her out the side door that released them into the first courtyard, where a scullery maid was approaching with her coal buckets in either grip. She skirted away from them, concealing her surprise before shifting her gaze away, only nodding at Muriel's "good morning."

Crossing over the drawbridge, he delighted in Muriel's expression as she lifted a wonder-filled gaze to the rosy light streaking through dawn's clouds.

"What a glorious morning," she murmured as birds greeted them from the trees lining the winding road that led into town. "How I've missed this."

"What do you miss?"

"Strolling into the village in the early light. Back home, I ambled down every morning to bake for a few hours before my assistant took charge for the day." She shook her head. "I only hope that I do not return home to find the bakery devoid of customers . . . she tends to put her own mark on my time-tested recipes."

"Quite enterprising of you," Erik said, instead of addressing the fact that if she indeed wed as she planned, she would most likely have to sell her beloved bakery in Kent.

She shrugged. "I enjoy it, and it does pay for itself as well as my assistant's wage and my pin money."

"You don't have access to your stepfather's funds?"

"He supplies me most generously with a dress allowance and has promised a vast dowry. Otherwise, I would still be as poor as the day he met my mother. Oh!" She halted and clasped his arm, lips parted in astonishment at the appearance of a doe and her fawn at the edge of the forest. She lowered her baskets, watching until the pair disappeared into the shadows, then bent and gripped the handles once more. "I know it is a silly dream to hold onto my childhood bakery. It reminds me of a simpler time, when my father was alive. I am quite grateful for my lot in life, but it is trying for me to surrender my passion for baking. Even all these years later, you can see the transition into polite society has been rather difficult. I can only hope that one day my husband will see my baking as a boon and not something to shame him."

Any man would consider himself most fortunate to have you as a bride, baking skills or no. Erik cleared his throat. "Would the baron appreciate your baking?"

She released a shaky laugh. "You are speaking, of course, of his proposal? I suppose everyone will be speaking of it today."

"It was quite the apogee of the evening for the country gentry. Everyone was speaking of it—even going as far as to inquire of me if the wedding would be hosted at the castle as he used it as the milieu of his renewed courtship and proposal."

"It's people talking that got me into this mess in the first place." She shook her head, grunting. "That and my own stubborn romantic heart."

"You have not made up your mind to accept him, then? Even though you, forgive me for bringing this up, proposed to him only weeks ago?"

"I have not." She lifted her wide eyes to him. "Why do you think I was baking all night? But, to answer your first question, I would no doubt be forbidden to ever set foot in a kitchen again with him as my husband. He is kind, but as he is only the first baron in his family, he is determined to be quite proper for all his days, and that is where I know I would prove to be a thorn in his side. He is handsome enough to win the hand of a noblewoman. Obviously, I am not titled, and it could prove challenging for him one day to accept my oddities should my funds ever deplete."

"I understand how you feel. I know that one day, when my work ends, I'll have a difficult time adjusting . . ." He rolled his shoulder, subconsciously checking his wound along with his wrist. Both were healed, but still not as strong as he'd like them to be. "But hopefully that day is far into the future, despite the suggestions I have received to retire and accept my new duties as Earl of Draycott."

"And what is it exactly that you do?" She lifted a single brow. "At the ball, you hinted at something more than just being an officer serving the Crown."

He cleared his throat, suddenly unsure of what to do. "Is being a captain not exciting enough?"

"Yes, but that is what you say to people to explain everything away." She motioned to his arm. "I know there is something more to the story of how you were injured."

"Oh?" He grinned. He was quite good at covering his tracks after years of practice. Did she really have something on him?

"You have this sense of urgency and confidence when it comes to your work. You are not merely a sea captain." She rested her hand on his arm, her baskets in the crook of her elbow. "I have a feeling you do much more. But I will not press you into sharing your secret before you are ready if you have changed your mind since the ball last night."

"And what is it that you think I do?"

She blinked. "Why, you are a spy, of course."

"Am I?"

"What else explains your tendency to draw away from me? Or the fact that you are the best man to keep me safe after the threat? And, speaking of the threat, why would I suddenly receive a threat now when I have been an heiress for years?" She shook her head. "No, I am quite certain it is due to our friendship."

Dare he confide in her? If he were to ask her to become his wife, he needed to tell her, to let her know all that she was agreeing to in marrying him . . . that he was not simply an earl. "And is friendship all you seek with me?"

Her cheeks flamed and she dipped her head. "It is all you have offered me, and, as Deverell has offered me his hand, I must see you only as a friend if I am to accept him."

He halted in his tracks, his heart racing faster than the first time he boarded a vessel. He set down his baskets and then hers, drawing her hands into his. "Before I can offer you more, I need to tell you something about my work."

Her breath caught. "More than friendship?"

He slowly nodded, the action obliterating the wall between his heart and hers. "I have not spoken of this outside of my colleagues. It is paramount it stays between us."

Her eyes widened. "Of course. You know my darkest secrets and have kept them well. I would do the same for you, even if it proved my undoing."

He searched her eyes and found not only honesty but complete adoration mirrored there. *First the confession and then, God willing, the proposal.*

Chapter Twenty-Four

KEEPING HER EXCITEMENT TO HERSELF had never been more impera-tive. She pressed her lips into a firm line against her demand that he first explain what he meant by his suggestion of "more." He hefted the baskets, and she, following suit, kept her eyes on the road leading into the sleepy village of Draybridge. The stone church stood at the bottom of the hill, with the vicarage directly behind it. She slowed her steps, hoping he wouldn't notice too much. There was no way on the Lord's green earth she was going to allow them to reach the village until he had explained himself. Thoroughly.

"I have been at sea for many a year. As you know, I started as a cabin boy aboard Captain Ingram's vessel."

At his long pause, she prompted, "He was captain of a merchant ves-sel, the *Twilight Lady*. Yes? I read about it."

"Of a sort . . ." He cleared his throat. "She was a merchant ship, most of the time. But not all the time. The records do not necessarily carry the full history . . . nor the true name of the vessel. I was not long under his leadership before I learned he carried a letter of marque from the Crown."

"A privateer?" If she hadn't been holding two baskets full of baked goods, her hand would have flown to her throat. "Is that how Sir Alex-ander gained his fortune and knighthood?" And as soon as the question was released, her next thought was to wonder if it was how Erik had made his fortune as well before being named the earl. *But why would he need to pursue a fortune if he was heir to a title and a castle?*

"Aye. When we were about to reach port in England, he would lower me over the stern to paint *Lady* over *Treader*." The true ship's name held such weight to it that the baskets tottered in her hold. He set aside his and grasped hers, setting them beside the road. He gently took hold of her arms and led her to the shade of a beech tree. "Ariel?"

"The *Twilight Treader*?" She fanned herself with her hand, a memory flickering to life. A news sheet with a sketch of the famed privateering vessel. "Then Sir Alexander was prone to—to—" She clamped back a moan. She could hardly release her question, but she had to know. "Was he prone to violent boardings? Or did he inherit the vessel as you did?"

"Not all privateers are like pirates," he answered slowly. "And during those days I think Ingram sometimes wanted out of the privateering game. He wanted to be a merchant, plain and simple. Nonetheless, he was a privateer."

"Was he violent?"

"I was but a lad and was kept below decks during the boardings." He swallowed. "On more than one occasion, I was put to work scrubbing blood from the decks."

She pressed her hand to her mouth. "Dear Lord in heaven. And you call this man your mentor? Your friend? As does my stepfather? Does my stepfather know that he was dealing with the captain of the infamous *Twilight Treader*?"

"I doubt your stepfather knows of Ingram's past." Erik rested his hand on her shoulder, offering her his strength. "But Sir Alexander was my first captain and a man who was like a father to me when I had none. As you know, I worked for him as his cabin boy from the age of eight to sixteen, when my uncle summoned me home to learn under him. Captain Ingram continued privateering sporadically until the war began two years later. Rather than join the Royal Navy, he executed his service to the Crown by making himself into the most effective privateer in British history. By this time, I longed to return to sea, and as Ingram was now further legitimized by the war, my uncle agreed at last to allow me to return. However, my uncle did not know of the man's privateering . . . no one outside of Ingram's inner circle knew the truth.

"I became second-in-command aboard Captain Ingram's vessel in the throes of the battle with France. Our mission was to peacefully board as many French merchant ships as we encountered to help blockade the flow of goods between France and its allies. I worked alongside Ingram for five years, attempting to minimize any violence, until he was injured in the line of duty by a masked smuggler. He was knighted for his services. Ingram named me his successor to his vessel and his name at the age of three and twenty."

She swallowed. "You are the captain of a privateering vessel?"

"Yes."

"You mentioned inheriting his name. What name?" she whispered, her heart fearing the answer. If the *Twilight Treader* was under Erik's command . . .

"Captain Warrick."

No. Her heart stuttered. "Captain Warrick? He is known for his brutality!" She took a step back, unable to make sense of the man before her and the reputation of Warrick.

He lifted his hand to cease her panic. "I understand how it sounds. Under my leadership, there has not been a single death related to boarding. I was further recruited by the Crown to specifically chase down weapons smugglers who were thought to be passing messages back and forth between French sympathizers and Napoleon himself. These messages were discovered quite by chance. After seizing a ship two years ago, I opened a crate taken from the enemy vessel and found a message hidden inside a brick of tea leaves. I've caught quite a few of the messengers and their letters since then, but never the leader. Only recently did I discover his nom de guerre, Requin. I even boarded the very ship he was on and realized he was the same man who had injured Captain Ingram. We battled." He gestured to his arm. "I was injured, and he escaped."

"Then you saw the smuggler! Perhaps someone might create a sketch of Requin and send it to every port in England. Baron Deverell might be able to help you distribute them or be on the lookout for Requin. He frequents many ports as the owner of a merchant fleet, which I'm sure you know."

"I didn't see his face. Requin was masked. He did not become the leader through carelessness." He swallowed. "There's more."

"Oh?"

"The reason I was so adamant about protecting you was . . ."

Because you love me? "Yes?" she prompted, her heart pounding out of her chest.

"Was because I received a threat against you from Requin himself . . . multiple threats actually."

She paused to collect herself. "So I *was* correct that you were the reason. But why would Requin threaten me?"

"One of his many spies must have followed me and spotted us together. In my desire to befriend you, Requin's spies decided to use you as the leverage they needed to force me to permanently set aside my mission to take Requin and his shiver down."

Trying not to focus on his comment of befriending her, she asked, "His shiver?"

"*Requin* is French for "shark," and a shiver is a group of sharks." He grasped her hands in his.

She swayed and his arms at once wrapped about her. "And the warning on the flags? Will you heed it, Erik?"

"I could not live with myself if something happened to you on my account. I brought you here to keep you safe, and in saving you, I lost myself forever. Even if Requin had not requested I cede my position as Warrick, I would have done so still if it meant protecting you."

She closed her eyes against the spinning.

"I know most in society despise our kind because privateering is essentially legalized piracy. I vow to you, I have never killed anyone in the pursuit of fame or fortune, which is why Sir Alexander wishes to have me replaced. He thinks I am weakening the name of Warrick because I refuse to follow his advice and his example. I beg of you to tell me that you do not despise me for being a privateer."

She ached to lift her hand to his cheek, to reassure him that she felt nothing but the deepest respect for him. "I'd never—"

"Miss Beau, what a wonder I should find you during my morning constitutional." Baron Deverell gripped his beaver hat and trotted up to them, grinning. "I see you have a bounty of baked goods. May I offer my service?"

"Well, Lord Draycott and I—"

He snatched Erik's baskets from the ground. "As your guest, allow me, my lord. Where are you taking these?"

"It's no burden, I assure you." Erik's jaw clenched.

She swallowed back her retort for Deverell to let them be. "We are taking them to the vicarage to donate for the war widows."

Baron Deverell grinned at Erik. "Our Miss Beau has quite the kind heart."

"Indeed." Erik offered her his hand, the question between them weighing in the air.

Chapter Twenty-Five

MURIEL PAUSED OUTSIDE THE BILLIARDS room to gather her courage to speak with Baron Deverell. While Erik had not been able to ask her to be his after his confession, she hoped when next they were alone, he would explain what he meant by "more."

Unfortunately, the moment they returned to the castle, Erik had disappeared on an urgent matter. To avoid being caught alone with the baron, she retired to her room for rest, only to awaken some hours later and find Erik had yet to return. Knowing his secret, she did not question his absence. The knowledge did not keep her from glancing out of the window every few minutes, however, watching for his return and promising herself that if she did see Erik returning, she would wait for him to seek her. She would not give in to her impulse to meet him in the courtyard to confess her love.

She would not make her heart known to Erik until he spoke of love . . . which might lead to her dying an old maid. Perhaps such women were given an unfair representation in novels? She'd spend her days loving her little brothers and then dote upon any nieces or nephews who would follow in a few decades, all while living out her days baking in the village. It truly wasn't a terrible prospect, for marrying a man she didn't love while Erik lived was unthinkable.

"It's happening Friday night."

She paused with her hand on the billiards room door. Friday? Who was Deverell speaking with? She pressed her ear to the door but couldn't hear the mumbled reply.

"Of course not. Do you think I would wait for my dear Muriel's answer if she did suspect? I would have had her in a carriage to Gretna Green last night. It's only a matter of time before she accepts my hand. The lady is as besotted with me as I am with her. I shall press her for a swift wedding, as we need her funds to continue our work."

Another inaudible reply filtered through the door.

"Of course the shipment for France is ready as per your request. Therefore, when I received my cousin's note, I saw no harm in arriving early to secure the girl's hand."

Shipment for France? The fluttering letters—the warning. Her vision blurred. *The spy is Baron Deverell?* Memories washed over her. Things that had not made sense months ago that she had ignored, lost as she had been in a haze of what she'd thought was courtship. Such as when they had viewed his grandmother's cottage by the sea in Dover so long ago to determine whether or not to sell the property. The old shed behind the cottage had seemed like an odd place to store tea shipments when Deverell had a perfectly good warehouse in Dover. When she had peered through the dusty window and spied barrels instead of crates, which was the traditional way to store tea, he had grown uncommonly angry with her questions. At the end of the visit, he had decided to sell the place. Was that because of her discovery? Her vision swam and she stepped back. The floorboards released an alarming creak.

The door flew open and Deverell strode out, keeping the door from swinging wide enough to reveal who he had been speaking with inside. "Miss Beau! Have you been standing there long?"

His strident tone did little to calm her nerves. If everything Erik had told her about this infamous Requin and his crew was true, she was in grave danger. She forced herself to offer him a warm smile, drawing brightness into her voice. "Baron Deverell. I wished to bring you an answer to your proposal."

Her tone must have been convincing, as his hard eyes softened, his features shining. He stepped into the hall and clasped her hands. "Yes?"

She ran her thumb over his hand. "I would be honored to become your bride by summer's end."

"Truly?" At her nod, he swept her into his embrace, his face buried in her neck. "You have made me the happiest of men, my darling Muriel."

She drew back, hoping he did not desire a kiss. "Osmund," she chided gently, her blush genuine from the touch of his lips upon her neck.

"Forgive my boldness." He laughed, carving his fingers through his thick hair. "I am exultant you would choose a mere baron when you could have the Earl of Draycott. Such a pure heart demonstrates the depth of your feelings—a depth that reflects my own."

"Why would you think I would choose him?" She lifted her lashes shyly to him. "Did I propose to him or to you?"

He pressed a kiss atop her hand. "Meet me in the lower gardens in an hour?" He leaned his forehead to hers. "The guests should be departing for the abbey soon, and I wish to kiss you properly without the threat of another guest to break us apart."

She pulled away with a smile, allowing her fingers to linger until the last possible moment as her answer. Rounding the corner, she broke into a run, hiking her skirts to her calves as she climbed the stairs to Erik's quarters. When he did not answer her knock, she stole down the servants' stairs toward the stables, praying the groomsman would know where Erik had gone and when he would return. At the bottom of the stairs, she rammed straight into a familiar broad chest. "Erik!"

"Muriel? Whatever is the matter?" He tucked an envelope into his coat and took her hands in his. "I thought you were going on an expedition to the abbey with the other guests before luncheon?"

She cast a glance over her shoulder, unable to control her shaking. "You were right. The spy is here."

"What?" He gripped her by the arms. "How do you know? Did he hurt—"

Muriel wrung her hands, hardly able to comprehend the turn of events. "I—I was seeking Lord Deverell to inform him that I couldn't marry him."

His hands slid down her arms to gently encompass her hands again. "Truly?"

She nodded. "There's more. Before I could knock at the billiards room, I overheard him discuss his plans for a shipment to France."

Erik's handsome features twisted into a scowl. "*Deverell* is Requin? He does not match the slight frame of the man I faced . . . unless the man I have been chasing all these years used the masked pirate as a scapegoat, keeping himself removed from the sea."

"I'm not certain who Deverell is at the moment." She frowned. "There was another in the room who seemed to be in charge, as he was asking Deverell questions I was unable to hear."

Erik gripped his hands into fists. "Multiple traitors under my own roof? I'm a fool for thinking I could keep you from danger under my care when I cannot even see the danger right before us."

"Spies do not become spies without having the ability to fool even their closest family." She rested her hand on his shoulder and swallowed, pushing out the hardest bit of news. "Deverell caught me listening."

He stiffened. "Did he threaten you?"

"He was angry to find me outside the door. Deverell attempted to hide it as I managed to convince him I was innocent." She worried her bottom lip.

"How did you escape his suspicion?"

"Please do not be cross."

"Muriel . . . what did you do?"

"I couldn't rightly refuse his suit once he caught me at the door. I overheard him say he would spirit me off to Gretna Green if I refused him."

"He said what?" Erik fairly growled.

She held her palm up. "I had to think of everyone's safety in Draycott Castle. I had to prove I was his besotted Chilham lass, and the only way to accomplish that was to . . ."

He took a step back, his stare pained. "Please tell me you did not promise yourself to a traitor?"

"Well, I'm not actually going to marry the baron, but yes. Yes, I accepted his proposal."

He ran a hand over his jaw. "You are not going to marry him?"

"Of course not."

"Good. Because I would like the privilege of marrying you."

Her heart stumbled. "What?"

He tucked a curl behind her ear, his eyes lingering on her lips. "I hold you in the greatest of affection, Muriel Beau. I believe I have been in love with you since the moment I awoke on the kitchen floor to you pressing your ear to my chest."

"You *love* me?" She shook her head and stared up at him. "You, Lord Draycott, love me?"

"With everything that I am and everything I will be." He clutched her hands. "Say something."

She dared to cup his chin and guide his lips closer to hers, pausing a breath away to whisper, "My dearest Captain, do you know how long I have waited to speak of my feelings for you?"

"You return my adoration?" His eyes flashed.

It took everything in her to keep herself from giving in to a kiss. "Most ardently."

"I ache to kiss you. Even in a false engagement with Baron Deverell . . ." He pressed his forehead to hers, his voice dipping into a husky growl. "I wish to wait until you are mine alone, for I am irrevocably yours forever."

Her knees wobbled at the passion in his voice, and she retreated a step to clear her thoughts. "Speaking of kissing once I am free, this is how I shall cry off the wedding. Step one, you will plan an activity that will keep all guests from the house for at least a few hours this very afternoon so I can search his room."

At this suggestion, all tenderness melted, and he crossed his arms, becoming the dangerous privateer. "Absolutely not. It is far too precarious a position in which to put you."

"But, as his fiancée has pulled all sorts of antics in the past, he surely will not find it out of character if I am discovered in his room, setting a gift for him on his pillow."

"The man is dangerous. If he is working for Requin, or, heaven forbid, *is* Requin—"

"You've dedicated your life to aiding the Crown. I can dedicate myself for a few hours."

"That's different. I have trained to be a weapon nearly the entirety of my life." He pressed his lips into a firm line. "You cannot protect yourself."

"I rendered you unconscious the first time we met." She crossed her arms. "I'd say I can defend myself quite well."

"This is not a jest, Muriel. Requin broaches no failure. If he even senses a traitor—"

She intertwined her fingers in his, emboldened by his declaration of love. "I can do this, Erik. You only need to trust me to help you."

He closed the distance between them once more. "I believe you can do anything."

"Now I really wish to kiss you."

His eyes were so full of love and trust that it nearly undid her. She pressed her hands to his solid chest and gently pushed herself away from him and his dizzying scent. "Hopefully I may when my engagement is officially broken."

He sighed. "If you are determined to take on such risk, I shall arrange an outing to keep the house party busy."

"From which, I shall be conveniently ill." She cracked her knuckles. "We are going to need some help. Shall I bring Tess and Vivienne into our small circle? If you agree, I need to fetch them before they leave for the abbey excursion."

Erik ran a hand over his jaw, clearly uneasy.

"If they can protect the secret that I once rent my dress in half from a tree-climbing expedition and was forced to run home in my buntlings and was nearly caught by a herd of gentlemen on a fox hunt as my unmentionables were the same color as the fox, they can protect your secret."

His brows shot up. "While a shocking tale, surely a secret from one's childhood does not match a secret such as this?"

"This was last year." She shuddered. "I knew ordering such a color was outlandish. I thought it amusing and, as no one would ever see them, it was a safe enough color . . . Indeed, it was not."

Erik chuckled at Muriel's scandalous caper. Guiding her to the private library, he tugged the bell cord and instructed the footman to fetch her two best friends, who appeared in only moments with their bonnets already in place for their promenade. Muriel noticed Erik clenching his fists as she explained all to her two dearest friends. She supposed after years of having his secret identity known only to Sir Alexander, it went against his very nature to bring anyone else into his confidence.

"What do you think?" Muriel halted her frantic pacing of the library.

"We will, of course, assist you in any way we can," Vivienne reassured them, though her eyes darted back and forth to Erik in a manner that betrayed her apprehension of him now that she knew of his dangerous occupation.

"I cannot believe you promised your hand to Deverell despite suspecting his true loyalty." Tess scowled, flipping her knife over in her palm. "If that traitor so much as looks at you wrong, Muriel, I will—"

Erik stepped forward, placing a hand on Tess's shoulder. "I appreciate your sentiment and echo it in my heart, but you need to leave him to me, Miss Hale. While you may be able to defend yourself with your skills and the element of surprise, once you lose that surprise, he will overpower you. But, on the score of Muriel's hand in marriage—" Erik looked to Muriel, silently asking her permission to share more. At her slight nod, he continued, "Allow me to settle your mind. As soon as we capture this dangerous spy and this farce of an engagement is over between her and the baron, and as she will not be allowed to take any of the credit for the capture of this dangerous spy, Miss Beau and I will have banns read in church, eclipsing the scandal of her being attached to a traitor's name."

His last words were lost in the cacophony of squeals.

"I *knew* you were special." Vivienne seized his hand in hers, squeezing it.

Tess engulfed Muriel in a hug. "Only a man of great character would do for our dear Muriel."

"Felicitations will have to wait." Muriel disentangled herself from her friend. "For now, we need to formulate a plan that sees me in Deverell's chambers while he is out of the castle." She cleared her throat. "Until then, I need to meet him in the lower gardens. He is expecting me."

Tess reached under her skirt and untied something from her calf, then knelt before Muriel. "If you should need it." And without further ado, she lifted Muriel's skirt, revealing her shapely calf.

Erik whipped his back to them, clearing his throat. "Please do not be tempted to use it unless there is no other option. I would hate for you to be wounded."

Muriel's hand rested on his shoulder, turning him to her. "All will be well. There is no telling how long our meeting will be, otherwise I'd say search his chambers while I keep him entertained."

"Entertained?" He released a growl and shook his head. "I will be watching you from the bushes. We will find a way for you to search his room while *I* keep him busy."

Muriel did not stop to think of the danger as she hurried out into the courtyard and across the drawbridge to the gardens just beyond. If she didn't know Erik was close behind, keeping her safe, the journey in the gardens to meet an enemy spy would have frightened her even more so.

"Muriel." The baron strode out from behind the topiary that led into the maze. He reached for her hand. "Shall we take a turn, my darling?"

"It's highly improper for us to find each other alone in the maze." She glanced over her shoulder, looking for Erik. "Even at midday."

"That's why he brought me, my dear." Lady Ingram glided around the corner.

Her cheeks heated. Did Lady Ingram think less of her for meeting a gentleman alone when she had no idea if there was a chaperone present? *She was the one who taught you about chance meetings . . .*

She grasped Muriel's hands, beaming. "Deverell told me all. I'm so pleased for you two. Such a good match to a gentleman your father will heartily approve." She winked at them. "Now, take your secluded stroll, my dears, I will not be far behind. Though, I may unintentionally turn my back for half a moment if someone wishes to steal a kiss."

Muriel felt the heat spring to her neck. At the baron's taking her arm, she summoned a shy smile, as a woman in love might give.

"Muriel, I was wondering if you'd be willing to wed me sooner rather than later?"

She ran her fingertips over the hedge of hawthorns. "After my scandalous proposal to you, I think that would be best."

He clasped her hands to his chest, pressing a kiss atop her fingers. "I know my title may not be as grand as some who wish to wed you, but I can avow that my pockets are deep. With our fortunes combined, there will be no others in Kent as wealthy as we."

She lifted her gaze. "You would have us settle in Kent?"

He gently clasped her chin, smiling down at her. "Of course, my sweet. I would not separate you from your family. I know how much they mean to you, and I've always longed for a houseful of brothers. Yours shall be mine as well."

She swallowed back the unexpected emotion clouding her throat. "You are too kind, Baron."

"Come now, my dearest. We are engaged, surely you can call me by my Christian name consistently again?"

"Osmund," she amended.

He lifted her chin with his finger, bending low to claim her lips. She had wished to save her first kiss for Erik. There was no way to dodge it when she needed to prove her infatuation and, in turn, protect Erik.

"Deverell!" Erik strode from his place behind the shrubs, unable to keep himself from interfering.

Deverell jerked back, anger flashing in his gaze. "Lord Draycott." He cleared his throat and put a pace between himself and Muriel. "Where did you come from?"

"I came in search of Muriel and heard from one of the servants she was heading toward the maze." He frowned. "Imagine my surprise to find her alone with you. I do not appreciate you absconding with a lady in my house party."

Lady Ingram appeared, rolling her eyes. "They were not alone, I assure you, my lord. I would never allow my charge to sully her reputation with such an indiscretion."

He shifted his stance. "Ah, I beg your pardon, Lady Ingram."

Muriel folded her hands in front of her skirts. "Did you need something, my lord?"

From his inside pocket, he lifted a stack of papers for a play Vivienne had magically supplied from her trunks as if she had been waiting for just such an occasion. "Before setting out for the abbey, Miss Vivienne provided a play for today's entertainment. I was assigning parts when I realized three of our party were missing from the group leaving for the excursion." He flipped through the papers, removed a slim stack, and handed it to the baron. "You have been cast in the role of the male lead, my lord."

Deverell ran a hand over his chin, smothering a weighty sigh. "And the female lead?"

"Goes to our fair Miss Tess Hale."

He frowned. "And our dear Miss Beau?"

Erik flipped through the papers. "It appears Miss Poppy has assigned Miss Beau the role of the tree."

"A tree?" She blinked at him as Baron Deverell snorted in his effort to control his laughter.

"It is a very special tree—a beech tree in fact," Erik assured her. "It is where the two lovers first meet. One might say you are the root of the story."

She rolled her eyes. "Very droll, my lord."

"Miss Vivienne apparently has not forgotten, nor forgiven, your part in last Christmas's tableau," Deverell whispered to Muriel, his eyes dancing with mirth.

Erik tensed, abhorring that Deverell shared such memories with *his* Muriel, especially when he posed such a threat to her and their country. *Patience. He may win the battle, but you shall win the war.*

Chapter Twenty-Six

AFTER MURIEL WHISPERED TO DEVERELL that she felt poorly from inadvertently ingesting strawberries at luncheon, he had at once accepted her claim, which caused Erik's eye to twitch once before he corrected his expression into one of concern for her. She knew it irked Erik that Deverell was aware of her reaction to strawberries. She simply had no time to reassure him. With a convincing clutching of her side as she sped from the garden, where the party was rehearsing, back into the castle, she knew she had played her part well.

She had only been searching for three quarters of an hour, but the sheen of nervous perspiration had grown to an embarrassing level. If Deverell did not believe her ill before, he certainly would now if he happened upon her. She had already propped the letter on his bed for her story in case she was caught by him, one of the maids, or his valet. The note was filled with sweet nothings. On the heels of her anarchic proposal, he would believe her to be capable of practically anything in the name of romance.

She had searched nearly every inch of his chamber and carefully gone through each of his coat pockets to no avail. She plunked her hands on her hips and turned about the room, her gaze alighting on the desk once more. In one of Vivienne's novels, Muriel had read about someone pinning her private letters under the desk. She dropped to her knees and searched under the drawers of the writing desk. *Nothing.*

Sinking back on her heels, she studied the furniture. Her gaze returned to the wardrobe. She crossed the room and lay on her belly, running her hand underneath the piece, squeezing her eyes shut as her fingers grazed cobwebs and scattered piles of dust, when she felt something different altogether. She ran her fingers over the perimeter and, finding a pin, tugged it free. Her hands trembled as she retrieved a small packet . . . in a feminine hand. *Love letters?* Despite their engagement being a farce, she could not help the twinge of betrayal in her gut.

The sound of boots in the hallway had her darting to her feet. Closing her eyes against the cobwebs caught on the packet, she shoved the finding down her bodice, moving to the bed as if in the middle of setting the letter atop the pillow. She had barely gained the bedside when the door opened. On seeing her, Deverell leaned against the threshold, crossing his arms and grinning.

She gasped, her cheeks burning at being caught in such a manner even if it was for Erik's cause. "Osmund! What are you doing here?"

"Miss Beau? I think that is my question." He shoved off the door and into the room, his cutaway coat draped over his arm, silk double-breasted waistcoat taut against his muscled chest. "I find you in the most unusual of places."

"I—uh." She had never before considered how a gentleman might achieve such a physique . . . Was he simply a Corinthian, Requin, or one of his spies?

"Miss Beau?" He chuckled. "You seem rather surprised to see me in my own chamber."

"I was leaving you a note." Her cheeks flamed, sweat trickling from her curls down her neck. "I thought you would still be in the garden and I—I wished to surprise you. To let you know I was thinking of you."

"It is a relief to hear you aren't abandoning me already."

"Wh–what?" She fluttered her hand at her neck, desperate to cool her cheeks.

He closed the door and strode toward her. "Usually notes are left when unhappy news is to be had instead of passed discreetly under the dinner table when there is good."

Her flushed deepened. "You will have to read it to determine that for yourself."

He grasped her trembling hand, and she prayed he did not notice the dirt marring it. "My darling, our engagement must be short, for in finding you here in my room, I see my feelings are returned most heartily." He drew her into his arms, resting his chin atop her head. "As a gentleman, I must not kiss you. Instead, I must bid you farewell." He set her firmly back and guided her to the door, poking his head out into the hallway first. "Your path is clear. I look forward to reading your note."

"If you like it, I may return when you least expect it and leave another." She dipped her head at her shocking reply and hurried away, praying he would not check under the wardrobe before she returned the packet. Safe in her bedroom, she bolted the door. Sinking atop the window seat, she opened the packet, her heart plummeting at finding only notices of shipments, something she had seen a hundred times on her stepfather's desk. Surely if they were affixed to the underside of the wardrobe, they had to be special. She opened her desk and began copying the list, vigilant not to leave out a single detail in case Erik would think it important.

⚜

Where is the man? Erik strode about the terraced garden. He had kept his eye on Deverell for an hour as he practiced his lines for tonight's play. Erik surveyed the refreshment tent. Deverell had been there only moments before, when Lady Ingram had pulled Erik aside. Striding out of sight of the party, he broke into a run for the castle as soon as he was able, imagining Deverell alone with innocent Muriel. Entering through the old guard's turret, Erik raced to the library.

He pushed the settee away from the wall and shoved the tapestry aside. The hidden door looked as it had two decades ago when he'd discovered it—ancient and ominous. The passages had been created from centuries of adding new wings to the castle, and he had spent many a rainy day exploring every inch of them. He jerked open the door and traversed the secret passage, winding with the castle, ducking under cobwebs. He had not used these passages since his boyhood, yet he navigated them with the precious little light streaming in from the cracks in the walls. He paused at the door that, in her room, masqueraded as a bookshelf. He sucked in a breath, praying she was well and, if so, that she would not be offended at his intrusion. He released the lever and slowly let himself inside. "Muriel?"

A book sailed at his head. He ducked, but not fast enough. The volume hit him square in the nose. "Muriel, it's me!"

She gasped, falling back a step and sinking onto the bed. "What on earth are you doing?"

Dabbing his nose with the back of his hand and finding no blood, he closed the bookcase door. "Checking on you. Deverell disappeared, and I couldn't go knocking on your door lest the staff catch me."

She rose and moved to the desk, where papers were scattered about. "Deverell is in his chamber as we speak. He caught me, but he understands me well enough to know I tend to place myself in odd situations."

"Thank God." He sagged against the bookcase. "I must say, you are terrible at spy work with being caught every time you attempt to be clandestine."

"Oh, really?" She withdrew the stack of papers from the desk. "I found these. They appear to be just shipments and coordinates. However, I started making copies in anticipation of returning the originals."

He crossed the room and riffled through them, hope soaring. "They will have to be confirmed, but if these documents are what I think they are, we may have our man. Well done, Muriel."

"Only doing my duty to our country. But what are these papers, exactly?"

"They note the shipments of recent goods, marked as certain dry goods leaving ports all over England."

"Meaning?"

"Requin uses these exact dry goods as his cover for gunpowder and pistol shipments to France."

She paled. "Will these prove Deverell is the spy?"

"Possibly. Though we will not be able to confirm it unless we intercept his next shipment, which is, judging from this manifest, in a week. Unfortunately the port is not marked." He thumped the page with his finger. "If only we had time to finish copying them all before we return them. I cannot risk him discovering their absence after you were in his chambers."

"If I seek him out, do you think you can return them to the bottom of the wardrobe without being seen? Or is it too perilous?"

He laughed. "One does not become a privateer without taking risks."

"Does Deverell's room have a secret entrance?"

"Only your room, my childhood bedroom, and the master chambers have access to the passages, as well as the library and the tunnel that releases in the woods. A former earl and countess wished to whisk away their children at any moment should the castle be attacked."

"Brilliant. Give me five minutes to convince him I am well enough to return to the garden party and then take the passageways, which I will insist on seeing after this is all over." She paused at the doorway and turned to him, a question in her eyes.

"Yes?"

"I'm afraid he might kiss me."

The very thought of the man holding his darling's hand was enough to make Erik wish to revoke the entire plan, but Muriel had asked him to trust her. "If you are chaperoned at all times, you should be safe from his advances."

"I was chaperoned in the garden by Lady Ingram and now that he is engaged to me . . ." She twisted her hands. "I do not know if his gentlemanly resolve will hold much longer."

He frowned. "A fact which plagues me."

"Yes, well, he will take my first kiss if he does."

Erik closed the distance between them. "We must not have that, must we?" He placed his hand at her waist and waited for her to lift her chin to him.

She shook her head, gazing up at him. "It would be piracy."

"How fortuitous I have a license to steal," he whispered in her ear, lingering until she closed her eyes. He lowered his lips to hers, Muriel's sweet kiss sending a thrill through his being. His hands found the small of her back, their kiss deepening—their breath mingling as he stole a second kiss that turned into a third. At last, he broke away, chest heaving.

"My dear Captain. Stealing ships and hearts." She fanned herself with her hand and took a step back.

"My darling Ariel, you are the greatest treasure a man could ever dream of." He bowed, wishing to steal more kisses. Such a thing would have to wait until they were properly one another's. He ducked into the passage, shoving open the door that led to the back of the wardrobe in his chambers. Pushing through his clothes and flinging open the wardrobe doors, he leapt out and landed on the balls of his feet. Soundlessly, he moved to the hallway and then to the baron's room, where he listened for a moment before letting himself inside. Following Muriel's instructions, he lay on his belly and affixed the pin through the exact hole in the packet, so as not to raise suspicion.

He rose, catching a glimpse of a miniature on the man's night table. He lifted it and frowned. It was Muriel. The man truly did have feelings for her to commission such a piece . . . which was, perhaps, even more dangerous for her than if he were simply after her funds. Setting down the miniature, he raced for his chambers.

Having run a comb through his hair and changed his dusty cutaway coat, he rejoined the others in the gardens. He bowed his head to Widow Whelan, Lady Ingram, and Elena, who were all in cluster around Lord Sullivan in the refreshment tent, while Lord Traneford strode arm in arm about the garden with Miss Poppy and Miss Hale, no doubt practicing a scene in the play. Beyond them, Muriel hung on Baron Deverell's arm, her head tilted up to him as if enraptured while walking slowly enough to convince him she was recovering from the strawberries. And by Deverell's adoring smile directed at Muriel, the baron suspected nothing . . . at least not yet.

"Ladies and gentlemen," Baron Deverell called out to the party, his hand resting over Muriel's. "I have the honor of announcing that Miss Beau and I are to be wed in a month's time."

Chapter Twenty-Seven

ERIK STUDIED DEVERELL OVER THE rim of his cup. Since the baron had announced his and Muriel's engagement yesterday in the garden, the party spoke of little else. Lady Ingram had even gone as far as to have the village seamstress call on Muriel to take her measurements to send off to her favorite dressmaker in London. As much as he despised having all consumed by talk of Muriel's romance with the baron, he was confident the distraction kept Deverell from noticing anything was amiss. He only had to keep Deverell and his accomplice in the dark until the party ended on the morrow.

The butler accepted the silver letter tray from a footman and bowed beside Sir Alexander. He broke the seal, his mien betraying nothing as the ladies at the table continued chattering over the coming nuptials.

Erik nodded to the missive. "Is there news?"

Sir Alexander sighed. "I am sorry to break up the party. I just received a note from Lord Deverell's mother. Mrs. Deverell wishes for our presence at once at her London residence."

"Why would Mrs. Deverell wish for us to attend her?" Lady Ingram interjected.

"Apparently, she received your note, Deverell, that you were about to propose to Miss Beau. She had no doubt of Miss Beau's answer and is most eager to meet her future daughter-in-law before Miss Beau returns to Kent," Sir Alexander explained. "And as her guardians during her stay in London, we will, of course, need to be part of the caravan escorting her."

Erik swallowed back his retort that *he* would escort Miss Beau. He knew society would see her as under the Ingrams' and baron's protection, not his. And if Requin was indeed not Deverell, she would be safe enough. But, if the man *was* Requin, Miss Beau had never been in more danger than she was now, and he was helpless to save her. Any action on his part could put her in even more peril.

"And with their departure, I believe we too must attend Eliza, as she is my sister-in-law and will surely welcome help in planning an impromptu celebration of the happy couple's engagement," Widow Whelan said, rising from her chair.

Though the rest of Erik's guests bemoaned the breaking up of the party, with so many leaving early, Lord Sullivan decided to return with them instead of on the morrow.

By half past three of the clock, the entire party was packed and ready. Erik stood beside the Ingrams' carriage as the servants scrambled about, lifting the trunks into the correct carriages for each guest.

Erik grasped Ingram's arm. He had not even been able to tell Sir Alexander of Deverell, and there was no way to do so now without putting Muriel in danger if he was overheard by the wrong person. "You know I do not approve of Muriel leaving—not with the way things are."

"She is now promised to the baron. It is hardly proper for her to remain here under your protection. In fact, I think her engagement to Baron Deverell is even more protection than you are able to offer, given the threat by the river and your ill-advised refusal to cede. Further, Parliament isn't out yet, and we both have our duty to the Crown and House of Lords. It is time we each return to London." Sir Alexander's reply brooked no argument. "If we dally, society would undoubtably gossip about Miss Beau being engaged to one gentleman while another courts her."

Muriel approached on Deverell's arm, resplendent in her traveling pelisse of navy and gold piping.

"I was hoping you would allow me to escort Miss Beau home in my carriage, Lady Ingram?" Deverell bowed his head to Muriel's female protector. "I'm certain the ladies Miss Hale and Miss Poppy would be happy to chaperone as I overheard that they are staying with my bride-to-be in London instead of returning to Chilham."

"Actually"—Elena interjected and looked to the two ladies in question—"my mother and I were hoping to join my cousin with Viscounts Sullivan and Traneford. Miss Hale and Miss Poppy don't mind riding with Sir Alexander and Lady Ingram, do you?"

Six to a carriage? Erik swallowed back his retort. Despite his not liking the arrangement, Muriel would indeed be much safer with two other gentlemen present. He despised seeing her on the enemy's arm, and now, knowing she would be spending the next two hours traveling with the man, he could hardly bear it.

Lady Ingram smiled to Elena and Lord Deverell. "Of course. With so many in our party and our carriage following directly behind, no one could object. Perhaps Widow Whelan will wish to join us to allow a little more room for everyone?"

As if sensing his discomfort, Muriel slipped away from the group under the guise of petting the horses, a secret smile at the corner of her lips as Erik followed her. "I persuaded your maids to pack my trunks with Charlotte, leaving me enough time to bake a few things for your journey to London tomorrow morning," she whispered.

"You are a gift, Miss Beau."

"It is nothing. Consider it a thank-you for hosting us." She squeezed his hand and released him, returning to Deverell's side, bestowing smiles upon him that pained Erik far worse than a rapier through the shoulder.

※

Muriel studied Deverell's striking profile as he gazed out the window. If she weren't in love with Erik and didn't know about Deverell's condemning packet of shipping records, Muriel could have easily allowed herself to bask in the romance of it all. The man whom she had proposed to followed her to Draycott Castle to ask for her hand the moment he was free and was now escorting her back to London to introduce her to his mother. But she was in love with Erik, and she knew too much about Deverell's true character.

The carriage ride passed surprisingly quickly, with Elena taking the lead in questioning the gentlemen until she focused on Deverell's plans for the wedding.

"So, cousin, a little bird told me that you desire a hasty wedding?" Elena turned from Viscount Sullivan and smiled at Muriel, whispering, "Speaking of which, I haven't received any thanks as of yet for my part in orchestrating the romance."

"Did you now?" Lord Traneford interjected, his lip twitching. "Is that the only romance you are interested in orchestrating?"

Elena laughed behind her gloved hand, sending a coquettish smile to each viscount before returning her gaze to Muriel. Despite Muriel's warning about Viscount Sullivan's character, Elena had persisted in allowing both men to court her. Muriel only hoped that Sullivan's wanton ways would be revealed before it was too late.

Deverell grasped his cousin's hand in his. "And I shall be forever grateful for your assistance in making me the happiest of men, Elena."

Muriel supposed, after a fashion, Elena's actions did indeed spur Erik onward into realizing what he wished. No matter the dire circumstances, Elena had indeed done her a favor. "You have my everlasting thanks, Elena."

Deverell turned to Muriel, his eyes bright with appreciation as the carriage halted in front of the Ingrams' residence, and he assisted her to the sidewalk. "This has been by far the shortest trip back to London that I have ever had thanks to your lovely company, and while I am loath to part with you, knowing I shall see you tonight makes it bearable."

That line would have stopped her heart not long ago. Now, it fell like a soufflé taken too soon from the oven. "Pardon?"

He laughed. "I'll see you tonight."

"But it is nearly six of the clock now, and we have no plans—"

"You'll see." He pressed a kiss to her forehead, whispering, "Wear that sapphire evening gown you know I love."

Before she inquired further, he returned to his seat, waving his farewell as the front door burst open. She was at once wrapped in her mother's embrace, the scent of her favorite biscuit, Shrewsbury cake, lingering in her hair. Mother truly must have been flustered to have been in a baking storm. Muriel laughed. "What a wonderful surprise! But, how did you know I was returning to London?"

"Lady Ingram wrote to me, telling me of the Baron's upcoming proposal. I knew you would accept him, of course, so I at once accepted her invitation to come to London and surprise you." Mother pressed her hands on either side of Muriel's face, holding her back to study her. "My dear girl. It is a miracle. I hardly believe your dream of a marriage to Baron Deverell came to fruition."

"Let her inside, my darling." Father laughed from behind them, jostling a far plumper Declan.

With a little cry, Muriel seized the babe from her stepfather's arms, kissing both her parents on the cheeks before pressing a kiss to sweet Declan's button nose as he waved his delightfully pudgy arms in an attempt to get his dimpled fist into his mouth. "It has been too long."

"And we have much to discuss in regard to Baron Deverell's missive. It seems out of turn for the man to propose before seeking my permission," Father replied, holding the door for her and Mother. At his wife's pointed look, he cleared his throat. "But first, we must sample some of those delightful Shrewsbury cakes your mother took the liberty of baking in the Ingrams' kitchen for your arrival. She wouldn't give me even one, as she wished to wait for the lady of the hour."

"If I gave you one, it would ruin the specialness of them," Mother teased, wrapping her arm about Muriel's waist and smiling down at her babe. They ushered her into the parlor, where Grandmother Fletcher perched in her finery, looking down her hook nose at Muriel.

Her stomach sank, and all hope of having a candid conversation with her parents about the situation evaporated.

"I see you have spent your time in London well, Muriel." She frowned as she dusted the crumbs of a biscuit from her fingertips. "But where are your chaperones? Have you disregarded etiquette once more?"

Muriel curtsied. "The Ingrams are just behind me. Good to see you too, Grandmother Fletcher."

The old woman's lips quirked. "Lying isn't becoming on one so young. I know you have no desire to see me. Nonetheless, I had to see for myself that you had indeed landed the baron after all your antics."

Muriel gnawed on her bottom lip. She would have to be careful lest the woman ferret out her true feelings on her so-called engagement. Muriel shifted her attention to her mother. "The baron mentioned something happening tonight. He would not say what, though. Judging from your state of dress, I suspect there is something more than our family reunion occurring this night?" She lifted Declan to her nose, sniffing his hair, but instead of the usual sweet scent, something pungent clung to his thin locks. She twisted her lips.

"Sorry, my dear. Declan has been tossing his accounts left and right these days." Mother lifted him from her and nodded to the maid in the corner. "Would you mind bathing him? I would have, but I didn't wish to miss Muriel's return."

The maid curtsied and removed the little chap, Muriel aching at his absence at once.

"Perhaps you should take the opportunity to bathe as well, Muriel," Grandmother interjected. "Before you dress and soil your fine clothing with the grime of travel."

"And for what occasion exactly am I dressing?"

"For one of the best moments in a young lady's life. The man is obviously smitten with you." Father grasped her hand.

She paled. *Surely, he hasn't arranged a wedding for us?*

"And despite his having to reject you that night and not securing my blessing beforehand, I do respect the man for coming to you the moment he was free. He wrote to his mother of his intentions and had her arrange for a ball tonight at his London residence in your honor."

She nearly sagged in relief that it was not a wedding party, though an engagement ball was hardly any better. "I—I am not certain I am feeling well enough for a ball the moment I return."

"Would I take the trouble to set aside my schedule in Dover only for you to refuse to attend your own engagement ball?" Grandmother Fletcher scoffed, filching another Shrewsbury cake. "Everyone who is anyone will be there, and you will be attending."

"I hear it will be quite the crush." Mother's cheeks heated as if just the thought of it was overwhelming. "Regardless, I agree it is imperative you attend."

"One can take the baker out of the bakery, but it does not make her anything more than a baker." Grandmother rose, leaning heavily on her cane.

Father scowled at her before turning an apologetic smile to Muriel and Mother. "Despite her words, my mother is actually quite excited about the prospect of tying our family tree to nobility."

"Hardly. I was a baron's daughter myself, though you did not receive a subsidiary title." Grandmother sniffed. "The title of baroness is hardly worth the shame your stepdaughter has put our family through these past months. However, her new connections may prove useful for when my grandsons are of marriageable ages . . . something I hope to witness one day." She swept from the room. "Until then, do try your best not to shame us further."

Muriel attempted to blot out her grandmother's harsh words, but as she bathed and dressed, she could not help but believe them to be true. What was she but a baker in a fine gown? She ran her hands down the sapphire creation. Truly, all she ever wished for was to remain a baker with a loving husband of her choosing. If she did not take great care, she would end up with neither. She must tread wisely to see her mission through and be able to wed Erik. Muriel was ever grateful for her lovely elbow-length gloves. The white fabric would keep her damp palms hidden from her step-grandmother.

Bracing herself for the drive with the woman, Muriel withdrew into herself. Her family attempted to drown out the snide remarks for the short ride, but the ordeal left her wishing she had walked the half mile to the party. She straightened her shoulders and stepped into the Deverells' London receiving room in Cavendish Square. The five-storied home was far grander than the Ingrams' residence. Opulent furniture perched about the parquet flooring, and a gilded ceiling overhead boasted a charming fresco that displayed an English shepherdess being serenaded by her lover.

"I can hardly believe it. You will be the lady of this fine house." Mother squeezed her arm as they wove about the press of guests, the reception line slowly parting at the realization that Deverell's bride-to-be was approaching. "I never imagined such grandeur for my darling little Muriel."

She inwardly cringed that her mother was admiring the home as if it were already her daughter's when she had no intention of marrying the man who had purchased the grand house with tainted money.

Deverell spotted her in the crowd, his expression bright. "My darling." He swept her hand into his, pressing a kiss atop it. "I have so many friends I wish to introduce you to before the night is over. We must begin now if we are ever to hope of meeting them all."

Muriel had never felt so beautiful nor so desired as when she met Deverell's guests. His hand never left the small of her back, as if their engagement were not claim enough on her. His attentiveness brought smiles from the guests who pressed near, wishing to be introduced to the baron's heiress fiancée. The room seemed too hot, even for her. Deverell, noticing her flushed state, guided her to the open set of glass French doors, leading her out onto the balcony that overlooked the circle park below. Passersby on the sidewalk craned their necks to observe the merriment within the row of fine residences.

"I see I have overdone it. My apologies, my dearest. In my zeal and eagerness to show you off, I didn't think to fetch you any refreshment." He pressed a kiss to the inside of her wrists, bestowing his most apologetic smile upon her. He leaned toward her—his intention clear.

With the memory of Erik's kiss on her lips, she couldn't allow Deverell to steal one. She swayed.

His hands instantly captured hers. "My darling? Are you unwell?"

She leaned her head on his chest for good measure. "I think I may need to lie down for a few moments. Are there any free chambers upstairs?"

"I'm a bachelor, my dear, there are always free rooms."

"I only thought that with the party . . . some of your friends might be staying with you," she whispered, pressing her hand to her forehead.

"Not a one." He led her through the crowded ballroom to the foot of the stairs. "Any room you desire is yours besides the one for my mother."

"And yours," she whispered, her cheeks heating as she pushed out the request. "Which are those so I may avoid them?"

His gaze burned her skin as he brushed his lips to her hand. "The first on the right. My mother's room is directly across. Go claim a room before anyone, or myself, sees you, else I might forget to keep my kisses chaste."

She wavered at the fourth step, glancing down at him. "I'll return in a quarter of an hour." Waiting for his smoldering gaze to leave her, she hurried up the stairs and down the hallway to the door she knew belonged to him and entered. Unlike his guestroom at the castle, this one was filled with stacks of books, scattered papers, and neckcloths draped over furnishings as if it hadn't been cleaned in many months. The sight was so unexpected she paused. But, rolling her shoulders back, she started to methodically search, wary not to alter the room in any way as she worked. Though even if she did, it was so shambolic she doubted he would notice.

Filtering through a stack of papers, she gasped at the sound of foot-falls outside the door. She released the papers and dropped to her belly, rolling under the skirt of his bed as the door opened with a squeak. Her panting drew a dust ball into her nose, and it took everything in her not to sneeze.

"Did anyone see you follow me up the stairs?" Deverell's breathless whisper made her stomach knot.

"I took the servants' stairs. They were all attending the guests and didn't see me."

Muriel stiffened at the feminine lilt of the voice. *Deverell would bring a woman into his chambers when I am supposedly resting on the same floor?* She shook the thought from her head. It mattered little. She was in fact *not* marrying the man. Instead, she focused on what they were saying.

"I warned you to keep away from him, and now you tell me that a page is missing from the packet I gave you? How did you not notice it before?"

She knew that voice—though it sounded a little less genteel than usual. She dared a peek under the skirt of the bed and slapped her hand over her mouth to keep from gasping aloud at the sight of the lovely Lady Ingram. *She is the one pulling the strings?* She thought of the signature *R* that she had copied over and over from the packet from Deverell's chamber in the castle. She had thought it stood for Requin, but what if it was Lady Ingram's first initial, for Rebecca? Muriel's stomach churned. If her guardian was a spy for Requin, did that mean Sir Alexander was as well? Was he Requin? Since they knew Erik well, they knew exactly how to end him should he come too close to deducing the Ingrams were a part of the ring. *Dear Lord in heaven, protect my beloved.*

"I was rather busy with my engagement to Muriel."

"Because of your distraction with the girl, you grew careless. How do you think he came to have those documents in his possession?"

Deverell crossed his arms. "No. I know where you are going with this. You know I love her, and I refuse—"

"Don't be a fool. Despite my best efforts to keep her affections away from him and direct them toward another, the girl cares for Erik. She stole the packet and delivered it to him. They know too much. You need to end the pair of them before they go blathering to the Crown of their findings," the woman growled.

"I won't allow you to harm her. I'll marry her tonight if that's what it takes."

Lady Ingram crossed the room, pausing a foot from Muriel's hiding place. "Do it. And then I want you to kill Erik."

No! Muriel clenched her fist, desperate to act—to save Erik. No matter the cost.

"Done. But Erik Draycott is rather too high ranking for his death to go unnoticed."

"Then make it an accident so memorable people cannot question the validity."

"We've been gone too long. Let me depart first. Wait three minutes and then you leave," Deverell commanded and closed the door behind him.

Lady Ingram wove about the piles of belongings and lifted a pen-knife from his desk. She ran her fingertip over the dull blade before flipping it in her hand in a practiced manner. "Farewell, my dear Erik. You will be missed."

Chapter Twenty-Eight

FIGHTING TO BREATHE, MURIEL COUNTED to a hundred before sliding out from under the bed, her sapphire gown mottled with dust. She needed to find Erik, even if it meant running into the night alone. Taking the servants' stairs, she wove through the bustling servants' hall to the exit and around to the line of carriages outside. Her gaze rested on the strongest-looking team of horses. With a sigh, she knew she wouldn't be able to get away with taking them. Gazing over the others, she spotted her stepfather's coach.

"What on earth is going on? I arrive late only to find you already leaving?" Tess whispered, snatching Muriel's elbow. Her gaze flowed over the ruined gown. "You found something."

Muriel nodded. "Lady Ingram is a traitor to England."

"What?" Tess gasped. "You are certain?"

"Absolutely. There is no time to explain. I need you to distract everyone from my departure. Lie for me and say I took my parents' carriage and returned to the Ingrams' with an upset stomach. I need to return to Draycott Castle posthaste."

"You cannot protect yourself. Let me go in your stead."

"It would take too long to explain everything. I need you here to watch Lady Ingram until I can ensure Erik is safe. Tell Vivienne and act as my shield while I try to save him."

Tess wrapped her in her arms. "You know we will do anything for you." She tugged off her reticule and handed it to her as well as her wrap. "Use the money if you have need. Save your love, and I will keep an eye on that traitor—both of them."

Muriel climbed into the coach and gave the coachman directions.

"Miss Beau, you know I like you. I cannot simply drive away without knowing how your stepfather and mother will return."

"My mother and stepfather approve of my journey." She forced out the lie. *If they knew, they would approve, as long as I had an army before and behind me.* She gritted her teeth. *Forgive me, Lord.* "Please, trust me and travel as fast as you dare. There will be a hot meal and a bed for you at the end of our journey as well as a generous tip, Roger."

Careening through the city, the coachman took to the countryside, the rolling, moonlit hills causing her stomach to knot for fear Roger would break a wheel in the darkness. Under the carriage wrap, she was falling into a fitful sleep when the crack of gunfire had her dropping to the floor of the carriage.

She spread herself on the floor as the speeding carriage jostled her very teeth. Whoever was shooting at them was far too close. A second shot rent the night. Judging from the bumpiness, the horses were dashing wildly as they evaded danger when the carriage hit a rut. She screamed, flying upward. She seized the leather straps at the roof as she rolled with the carriage, gripping the straps to keep herself from slamming against the opposite wall. The carriage ground to a painful halt, the horses' pitiful nickering sending pangs through her heart. *Dear Lord, let Roger be alive!* She released her vice grip on the strap. Her hands shook as she tested her limbs. Her elbows and knees stung from striking the wall with each turn, but miraculously, she had suffered no further injury. She shoved against the door with her shoulder with all her might to get it to swing outward, wincing as she discovered a cut on her arm. Grasping the side of the carriage, she hefted herself out, her evening gown tearing to her thigh as she scrambled through the opening, wind rippling through her thin garments.

Moonlight cast a veil over the horrid scene before her. One horse flailed in its harness while the other lay motionless. Beyond them, she spotted a lone figure. She raced to Roger's side. The coachman's head listed dangerously to the side. "Roger! Oh, Roger." She pressed her ear to his chest, listening. Her heart eased a hairbreadth at the steady beat and rise and fall of Roger's chest. But her hope faded the moment she spied the blood pouring from his shoulder. The valiant man had so desperately attempted to save her from the gunman. Tears streaking down her cheeks, she ripped the hem of her gown free, pressing it to his wound. He groaned, his lashes fluttering.

"Miss. I—I shot the highwayman's horse out from under him. If he is alive, he won't be far behind. You must fetch h–help."

"I cannot leave you." Her voice shook. The man after them was certainly no highwayman and would end Roger's life without hesitation, but saying such a thing would hardly help the situation.

"You must." He nodded, resting his hand over hers and taking charge of pressing the fabric to his wound. "If you can help me to the edge of the trees, I might be able to hide while you find help. D–Draycott Castle should not be far."

Wrapping her arm about him, she stumbled with him toward the woods in painful slow strides. "Stay with me, Roger. We are almost there," she whispered as his pace decreased. Just as they entered the shadow of the trees, she spotted a man cresting the moonlit hill. She dropped down to the weeds with Roger, resting her palm on the man's back. "He's here."

Roger nodded, his eyes glassy. "You must leave me now. Stay as close to the road as you can manage, miss, without being seen. I heard tell the castle is surrounded by bogs."

She nodded and sprinted along the tree line, her lungs bursting from the effort. She kept her eyes ever on her next step as the vicar's recommended psalm came to mind. *"But the mercy of the LORD is from everlasting to everlasting upon them that fear him."* She pumped her arms. *Lord, renew my strength. Do not let evil triumph. Let me reach Erik before the assassin.*

Erik riffled through the stack of papers on his desk in the castle's library. The moment word had reached him of the engagement ball, he'd enlisted Guy's help, determined to solve the question of Requin's identity as quickly as possible as he attempted to rush through his tasks and writing missives in order to return to London tonight. But it was taking longer than he'd anticipated. He shoved back the copied Deverell papers he had been studying against his ledgers for the better part of an hour.

"My lord." Guy rose from his smaller writing desk. "Might I suggest you retire for the evening? I will continue to study the ledgers and see if I can break the code of Deverell's papers while you rest."

"How can I rest when Muriel is attending an engagement ball? With such a public announcement, it will be difficult for Muriel to break things off without proof of Deverell's being a traitor. Proof that I am having difficulty putting together!"

Guy picked up the ledger. "Fetch us something to eat then. I cannot work on an empty stomach."

"Fine." Erik trotted down to the kitchen, berating himself for sending her to London without himself as a guard. *If only the next shipment was arriving sooner, I'd be able to provide proof and break their engagement before too much damage is done.* He paused in the doorway, imagining Muriel at the counter, kneading dough. The picture calmed him. Ever since he'd met her, the kitchen had transformed to a haven where clarity dwelled alongside Muriel's constant pile of baked goods. A pile that was dwindling rapidly. He sighed and reached for the pie dish, cutlery, and two plates.

The light scuff of a boot against stone caught his ear. Guy and his staff would never approach without announcing their presence. Nonchalantly, he reached for the knife, slicing a piece before whirling around and flinging the blade into the shoulder of the stranger approaching him with a dagger of his own drawn. The man grunted and fell to his knees.

"Who sent you?" Erik growled, kicking the blade from the man's weakened grasp, lest he attempt to throw it.

"*Le Requin* told us to be careful, but Allen there was confident an uppish lord would be easy to take." A second man emerged from the shadows, smile gleaming.

Erik dove and snatched a skillet from the stove, gripping the handle like a broadsword. "What do you want?"

"I came to tie up a loose end. My fearless leader hates loose ends and yet did not wish to end your life, but you know too much."

Why would his leader wish for my safety? Erik stiffened. Deverell would most likely rather him gone, what with his dislike of Erik and Muriel's friendship. *Unless, there is another man behind the scenes who knows me well . . .* Possibilities flitted through his mind, but now was not the time to attempt to discover the second traitor's identity. He had one name, and that was enough at the moment.

The second man drew his blade and lunged. Erik parried, the weight of the pan sending him slightly to the left, so he barely evaded the man's second attack.

Erik swung the pan, catching the rogue across the knuckles. The man grunted at the crunch of bone, but merely switched the weapon into his good hand. Erik's breath grew labored as the unwieldly weight of the pan pulled on the fresh skin at his shoulder and made his wrist ache. He could not fail. Not when he was so close to ending his part in the war. Not when he had only begun his journey through life with Muriel. If he didn't survive, she would no doubt be tied to Deverell for the rest of her days.

He swung again, at last making contact and rendering the man unconscious. Ripping some kitchen rags, Erik fashioned makeshift ropes to secure the man to a chair. He would question him later. As Erik moved to affix the first man, his chuckle made Erik pause. The man called Allen wheezed, holding his hand to the wound, crimson seeping through his shirt. "My superior did not wish to end your life *nor* Miss Beau's, but you both knew too much."

Muriel. "What have you done with her?" He thought of her with Deverell *le Requin* . . . of how she was completely in his power as his fiancée. *He could force her into marriage as easily as kill her off.* But, from what he knew of the man, he did seem to love Muriel. He jerked the rope against Allen's wrists, cutting into the skin. "Answer me."

"Poor girl seemed to think she knew the identity of our leader. She rode nearly all the way here from her engagement party . . . until we shot her coachman and sent her carriage on its head."

His heart stilled. "We? Are there more than just you and your companion?" At the man's hesitation, Erik withdrew the assassin's cutlass from its sheath and turned it in his hand, allowing the flickering of the fireplace to catch on the blade. "Do not make me ask again."

"You do not have the stomach to take a life." Allen spit at his feet.

"Do you not know who I am?" Erik laughed, thrusting the tip of the blade in the kitchen's blazing fireplace, praying the fiend would not call his bluff. "On land I am a lord, but on the sea I go by another name—Captain Warrick."

Allen swallowed as Erik lifted the glowing amber tip. His eyes flickered with fear. "C-Captain Warrick? No one said nothing about Warrick. You are bluffing."

Erik gripped the man by the back of the hair, exposing his throat. "Let's see how well you talk when this touches your throat."

The man jerked, inadvertently touching the blade. He cried out, his eyes widening. "Stop! Stop. Deverell was sent to ensure the girl kept her mouth shut for good."

Erik turned on his heel and raced for his room, strapping on his dependable rapier before running for the stables, shouting for the groomsman. He bridled the horse but did not bother with a saddle as he threw himself atop his mount. Sensing Erik's haste, the horse tossed his head and pawed the ground.

"My—my lord?" His tiger panted, hopping as he thrust his second leg into his striped trousers.

"Rouse the castle! Summon Mr. Mayfield and tell him to follow me with whatever weapon he can lay hand upon. Oh, and there are two men tied up in the kitchen. Send for the law, but guard the men until they are carted off to jail," Erik called over his shoulder, directing his mount to the road, praying with every breath and every pounding hoofbeat that his love was alive and safe.

Chapter Twenty-Nine

MURIEL DUG HER HAND INTO her side and bent over double. She spied the castle at last and, judging from the steady flicker of lamplights and the serene chirping of crickets, there was no obvious danger . . . Still, she was too far away to hear any cries of alarm, much less be heard if she screamed a warning to Erik if he wasn't lying dead in his bed already. She prayed she wasn't too late.

At the crunch of twigs behind her, she pressed herself against a tree trunk, hoping against all odds the man pursuing her hadn't seen her.

He passed on her left, the full moon illuminating Deverell's broad shoulders. With his golden curls freed from their queue and his blade gripped in hand as he strode without fear through the woods, she saw at last the dangerous spy in his countenance. Her chest heaved, but she kept her breathing muffled. She could not be found now, not when Erik was so close and she could save him.

She ran, the laces on her ballroom slippers holding true. She leapt over a fallen log, her long skirt's once-lovely train ripping. She ignored it, pumping her arms even harder. Her side was in agony. The pounding of feet behind her pushed her to keep going.

Deverell snatched her elbow, bringing her to him in a single motion. "No! God, please no!" She screamed, slamming her fists against him as he braced himself for her struggle. She twisted in his arms and rammed her elbow back into his throat, then fled from his momentarily loosened grip, releasing a shriek. The one good thing about being a baker turned heiress was that most people underestimated her strength from hefting sacks of flour her entire life.

"Muriel," he wheezed, holding his hand to his throat, the other gripping his rapier as he reached toward her.

She dodged him and raced through the woods, straying far from the path in her terror. With a thud, she tripped over a cluster of moss-covered fallen stones. *The abbey?* Her stomach dropped. She had gone too far!

"Muriel, my darling," Deverell called, crawling over the stones of what had once been the north wall of the abbey. "Why are you running?"

She pressed herself against the stone wall and slid down, creeping toward the turret, praying it would conceal her long enough for him to move his search elsewhere. Her chest heaved as she watched Deverell examine the area, searching and calling out for her. *Lord, let him not find me. Have I come so far, only to die at the hands of the man I once thought I loved?* Tears pooled in her eyes, and desperation clawed at her chest, when the verses flitted through her heart once more. *"Bless the* LORD, *O my soul . . . Who redeemeth thy life from destruction."* She dipped her head and prayed with all her might, her heart racing yet as Deverell neared her hiding place. *Lord, help me!*

With a grunt, he took to the path that would lead him back toward the castle. She prayed the drawbridge was up, but with her supposedly safe in London, why would Erik have it drawn?

Erik. Gathering her courage, she pushed herself from the turret and bolted through the woods, hoping to cut in front of Deverell and the winding path. All at once, her feet were no longer on solid ground. Gasping, she sank to her waist in a bog, the filth climbing further up her torso with every wild movement to free herself. Having no other choice, she screamed, "Osmund! Osmund, help me! Please!"

"Muriel?" Deverell burst through the trees and into the clearing, terror flashing in his features at the sight of her. He ripped off his coat and, gripping the collar, whipped the hem toward her, slapping it against the surface and flinging the grime onto her face. "Grab hold. I'll slowly pull you out. If we move too quickly, the bog will swallow you all the faster."

She snatched the fine fabric, seizing it with both hands as he eased her toward him. His forehead beaded with sweat from his restraint until at last their fingertips brushed, and, grasping her wrist, he drew her from the bog and into a fierce hug. "My darling. My beautiful, sweet Muriel. Why are you running from me? I would never harm you."

"Surely you jest?" She pushed off from him to meet his gaze, finding concern written across his features. Had she completely lost her wits? Wasn't he the spy?

"I wish your blasted curiosity had stayed quiet this once, Muriel. I cannot bear the thought of losing you." He brushed a lock from her face, his eyes welling as he dipped his head, pressing his forehead against hers. A tear slid down his cheek.

The action was so surprising she did not even attempt to jerk away. "If you are who they say you are, why would you save me?"

"You know why, which is the very reason you called out for me to save you." He lifted her hand to his, kissing it. "Because, despite the fact that I was sent to silence you, I do care for you, and death by suffocation in a bog is too horrible for anyone, especially the woman I have come to love."

Well, that did it. She jerked back with a snort. "As opposed to death by what—a blade?"

"Never. I told you. I love you." He unscrewed his flask, taking a long draft before handing it to her with a little shake, the sloshing contents awakening her fierce thirst.

Satisfied it wasn't poisoned, she accepted the drink. Something tasted too sweet for it to be only water, but since he had drunk so much, she satisfied her rabid thirst. She tossed the empty flask back to him, wiping her lips with the back of her hand, and flung the grit from the bog to the ground. "Thank you. Though, I do not know why you would take pity on me when your mission is to end me."

"I didn't say end." He slowly returned the flask to his pocket, his hand reaching for hers. She did not resist. What could she do at this point, weakened as she was from the fight with the bog? "You have never done me any wrong. I do not wish to return your sweetness with ill. However, I have a duty to Napoleon, and you know too much for my leader to allow you to escape."

The name of England's enemy sent chills down her spine. "You truly work for Napoleon then? This is not some grave misunderstanding?"

He ran his thumb over her hand. "He is destined for greatness. I will not be on the losing side when there is so much to be gained."

"B–but you are a baron. Isn't that enough for you?"

"Not for my children. I am promised a dukedom for my service to France." His eyes sparked. "A kingdom I would willingly share with you if you would look beyond all this and agree to be my wife in earnest. I can save you from my superior if you agree to marry me at Gretna Green at once."

Deverell's misplaced, so-called affection could be her salvation. But run away with him tonight? Marry him? She snatched her hands from his grasp, even though her mind screamed for her to play along. Erik would wish her safe.

"Even when faced with the prospect of having an even greater title and the man you once professed to love over *death*, you would still choose your earl?"

Her stepfather's words flashed through her heart. *Choose a man of character over title.* She swallowed. She doubted, though, that Father would expect her choice to be her undoing. Her stomach twisted with such force, she sank to her knees, gasping for air as if she had been stabbed.

"I knew you would choose him." He sighed, removing the flask once more and giving it a shake. She had drained it. He dropped it in his pocket.

At the roiling in her gut, she fell to her side, groaning. *The sweetness* . . . "Y–you laced the water with stra–straw–strawberries?"

"I made a tea from dried strawberries, along with apples to disguise it." He snatched her hand and pressed a kiss atop it before backing away. "I have never cared for anyone as much as you, Muriel. Consider this a kindness over what my superior asked of me. Once I confirm Erik is dead, I will return for you and help you remember why you fell in love with me, and you will marry me this night."

She cried out as she lifted herself to her elbows, clawing at the earth in an attempt to follow Deverell and save Erik. She had never endured such pains from the berry before. Agony radiated through her body as she tossed her accounts, falling perilously close to the bog once more as darkness edged along her vision. "Erik," she whispered, imagining his strong arms about her as she gave in to the darkness.

Erik knelt beside the injured coachman and pressed his fingers to the man's neck, praying for a pulse. "Praise God." When he'd seen the wreckage and immobile horses, Erik had feared the worst. Muriel was nowhere in sight, which meant she had either been taken or run for help along the tree line. But, if she had, she would have seen him— found him. *Father, protect her.*

"Lord in heaven." Guy Mayfield murmured as he approached on horseback, his jaw slack.

"Guy!" Erik shouted from his place beside the fallen coachman. "I need you to take this man to the doctor. Miss Beau cannot be far from here. If she is free, she would seek help from the castle, as the village is too far at this point."

The injured coachman groaned. "Th–the woods, my lord."

Erik leaned toward him. "She's in the woods?"

He gasped, his eyes glassy. "Man followed on foot. Save the lady, my lord. She is too sweet for this end."

Guy knelt, assessing the man's wounds. "I'll see to him, my lord. Save Miss Beau."

Erik swung up atop his horse and cantered along the tree line, not daring to call for her lest the third man be hidden from view. Spying nothing, he turned his horse and retraced his path, slowing his mount to an infuriating slow gait when something caught his eye. Dismounting, his heart soared at the tiny footprints. He followed her trail into the woods. The path was safe, but the woods held dangers even greater than Requin and his shiver.

He tied his horse to a branch and followed her flight toward the abbey until her prints merged with a second trail. Signs of a struggle were evident from the churned dirt, and that is where he spied the man's boots pointing the opposite direction. There was no second imprint or indication from the indention that he was carrying extra weight.

Muriel was somewhere in these woods alone. When Erik realized the direction, he released a groan, bolting toward the clearing where he knew the bog awaited. Under the light of the moon, a sapphire and silver gown glowed ghostlike. Mindful of the treacherous edge of the bog, he ran to her side. She lay crumpled, covered in muck as if she had crawled from the bog. He scooped her into his arms, the foul stench enveloping them both. He hardly noticed it as her eyelashes fluttered.

"Y–you're in danger," she whispered through chapped lips. "They've sent Deverell to k–kill you."

"Deverell did this to you?"

She nodded. "Lady Ingram ordered your death. He's coming back for me to take me to Gretna Green. We need to hide."

Lady Ingram? Erik did not wait to question how she knew this. He rose with her in his arms and ran for the abbey, pausing only when they were inside the little turret that had sheltered them not long ago, the remains of their fire still visible.

Her teeth began to chatter, her body convulsing. With a moan, she closed her eyes, her head listing back, the moonlight betraying the sallowness of her complexion.

He stripped off his coat and wrapped her in it before gathering kindling.

"Y–you can't light a fire. He'll see."

"You are in shock. I'd rather take my chances in a fight than allow you to catch your death." He struck stones together several times until a spark sprang out and caught the dried leaves. He blew onto the ember, encouraging it to grow.

He scooped Muriel in his arms and, keeping their backs to the stone wall, held her hands toward the flames.

She gasped, eyes wild. "My coachman! Roger isn't . . . he isn't . . . ?"

"No, Mr. Mayfield has him well looked after. I am certain the good doctor will be attending him shortly." At the thought of what might have happened to her in the carriage, he clasped her closer.

"Don't," she gasped, lolling her head away from him.

"Don't what, my darling?"

"Hold me. I'm . . ." Muriel made a feeble effort to push away from him, "truly disgusting."

He laughed, tears filling his eyes. She would be well enough if she was concerned about her scent. She propped one eye open at him in question, keeping her hands extended toward the flames.

He kept vigilant watch as she warmed herself until at last he shifted her in his arms. "I'm sorry, my love. I've been frantic with worry for you. With Deverell still out there, we need to move. Do you think you are able?"

"I feel much better now that I can feel my limbs again."

"Thank God. Once we are safe, I want you to tell me everything you know about Lady Ingram." He lifted her in his arms and rose, kicking out the fire then trotting down the path and ducking beneath a low-lying branch. "I will feel more at ease after I have the doctor visit you, and while you freshen up, I will send for the vicar."

"The vicar?"

"You ran headlong into the night after a man who was not your intended from your own engagement ball. Your reputation will be in even worse tatters than before. You must be married by the end of this adventure, and I can assure you it will not be to Deverell."

"One should not put reputation over a man's life." She coughed, pressing her hand to her stomach. "But, even if you secure a special license, it will take time to be approved."

He spotted his horse munching on some grass alongside the road, a thin branch dangling from the reins. He shook his head over his careless securing of his mount. "Once I make up my mind about something,

I do everything in my power to make it so." He lifted her onto the horse and shoved his hand into his vest pocket. Withdrawing a folded paper, he opened it for her to read. "I had a common license drawn up and received it today. It's valid for a few months yet." He caught the horse's reins.

"You have a common license already?" Her shining eyes met his as he folded the document and placed it back in his vest. "You truly wish to marry me, not out of obligation?"

"I believe the only obligation would be a need to breathe, which I cannot do when I know you are in danger." He mounted up behind her, drawing his arms around her waist and keeping her steady as he kicked the horse into a canter. "If you agree to be my wife, I shall marry you at once and then go after Requin. I have already sent for my ship to meet me at the coast. You will be safe in the castle. I can have my men—"

She shook her head. "No."

He stiffened even as his heart dropped. "No, you don't wish to marry me?"

"No, I do not wish to be left behind in your castle. There are plenty of women who join their husbands aboard their vessels, and I plan on being one of them."

"Yes, but this is not a merchant ship. It's a privateering vessel and the crew, though loyal, aren't the most gentlemanly sort. No, joining me aboard the *Twilight Treader* is out of the question."

"Then so is our marrying so quickly." She twisted around to look at him and pressed her lips into a firm line. "Do you realize that, while you are saving me from certain scandal, you are also taking an enchanting wedding ceremony away from my mother and friends? I think you agreeing to my request is the least you can do after I saved your life, and you were so forward as to secure a common license before even confessing your feelings to me."

He sighed. "Will I ever be able to say no to you?"

"I certainly hope not." She laughed, resting her head on his chest. An owl's screech sent her recoiling into Erik's chest. Like whatever prey the owl had found, she too felt exposed. "Deverell is still out there."

"My groom and steward will have the staff alerted, footmen searching the grounds, and the local lawmen arriving with weapons. The safest place for you at the moment will be the castle."

"Then we best return home, because I'm afraid the strawberries I ingested will not be long in making their grand fifth encore."

Erik guided the horse over the drawbridge into the first courtyard, which was bustling with servants as alarm over the attack on the carriage had spread. Men with torches were already covering the grounds, searching for danger. Erik wished there was a more private entrance to the castle than the courtyard. The cover of darkness did help a little to disguise Muriel's disheveled state from the servants. He led her through the door to the turret that was used for knights and guards hundreds of years ago. It was musty from disuse, but at least he was able to whisk Muriel to her former room without much interference, though word would soon spread of their return. He paused outside her door, eager to fetch the vicar despite the hour but loath to leave her even with the extra men about the castle and grounds. He checked the room. Deverell had not been here.

"Oh no." She pressed her hand to her mouth, shoving him down the hallway. "You need to leave now."

"Muriel, I've seen—"

"I don't care what you've seen. You've not actually *seen* me in this state, and once you have, I'm afraid it may change everything."

"Do you not remember the park after your meeting with Lord Traneford? I doubt—"

"I was behind a tree. Depart at once!" She shoved him again and slammed the door.

It was difficult to ignore the retching emanating from the other side of the door. Erik forced himself to trot down the stairs. He found the housekeeper in the kitchen, her hair in a long braid down her back, helping the cook and maids prepare an impromptu meal for the searchers, and requested her presence for his marriage to Muriel while he had a maid scour the castle's storage for some of his aunt's old gowns. Muriel would want to replace her ruined ballgown.

After dispatching a courier to his ship bearing a message of his arrival time, Erik packed as quickly as he could, praying for Muriel's health to improve so they could leave as soon as the marriage vows were spoken. First the marriage—then formulate a plan to end this mission once and for all . . . starting with Deverell and Lady Ingram.

Chapter Thirty

WITH THE TRIP TO DRAYBRIDGE being a night terror, Muriel was finding it hard to believe she was living one of her fondest daydreams—atop the castle with dawn's light bursting over the forest hills, her love at her side. The gentle breeze ruffled through her locks that she had released from its coiffure to flow to her waist in wild curls adorned only with a crown of flowers. With a full heart, she held her true love's hand. She admired Erik's strong jawline that was shadowed with a fresh beard and promised faithfulness in sickness and in health. She was so happy that she managed to set aside the ache brought by the absence of her family and friends, along with the fear of Deverell and the Ingrams still roaming free.

Erik had certainly passed the sickness part before any vows had been spoken. He would be a good, true spouse to her and she to him. As the vicar declared them to be husband and wife, she gazed up to her strong husband, confident in his love for her. She was so lost in his presence that the vicar and the servants around her faded, and there was only Erik and the glorious sunrise illuminating his strength and devotion.

She unfastened her gold necklace and slid off her father's gold wedding band. Tears filled her eyes as she guided it onto Erik's little finger. Her fathers would be proud of the man she had chosen to be by her side forever.

Erik lifted her hands to his lips, kissing each. He retrieved a stunning gold ring with an emerald surrounded by a halo of diamonds and slipped it on her finger. Before she could properly admire it, he gently tugged her to him. She slid her hands up his arms and behind his neck, drawing him toward her. He needed no encouragement. One hand found the small of her back, his left sliding to her nape as he bent, his lips claiming hers. His kiss deepened as if he had been storing every word left unsaid, every chaste touch, and every passionate gaze for this moment.

Her fingers twined in his hair as she answered his kiss in a fashion that left them both eager for another. At the cough that turned into a hack from the vicar, Erik broke their kiss at last, leaving her flushed and breathless. His roguish grin sent heat speeding through her. He sighed and pressed his forehead to hers as if he wished for the moment to last as much as she. But time was not on their side.

"I fully intend to continue that kiss tonight," he whispered into her ear. He winked before turning to collect the signed certificate that proclaimed to the world they were legally husband and wife.

He extended his arm to her and led her down the winding stairs to the awaiting coach with his two trunks tied to the back. Even though they had not had much time to discuss it, Erik still hadn't mentioned where they would be spending their first night together, but she was too dazed from the rapid turn of events to much care where they were going as long as she was with him.

"To the port," he called to his coachman.

Well, that answers that question. She cleared her throat. "Would you mind if we stop at one of the shops first?" She gestured to his aunt's gown that his housekeeper and maids had quickly altered for her. There had been precious little they could do to hide the low neckline besides adding a lace shawl to cover her décolletage. "I know time is of the essence with capturing Deverell and Lady Ingram, but I'm hardly presentable in this gown, and if we are to be surrounded by your men—"

He nodded and redirected the coachman to Draybridge's only dress shop. Unfortunately, the sign to Mrs. Wilson's Dress Shop was of course flipped to proclaim the shop closed. Erik, not to be deterred, sent the footman to wake the seamstress on behalf of the new countess.

"I'm thrilled you have graced my shop, Miss Beau—I mean Countess Draycott. So much has changed in so little time," the shop owner prattled as she opened the door. "I can hardly believe we have a new countess at last. What can I do for you?"

"I don't have much time, but I need a little bit of everything, Mrs. Wilson." Muriel smiled, gesturing to her gown as she perused the few ready-made items the seamstress had in stock, setting aside anything that caught her fancy.

Mrs. Wilson clicked her tongue and moved about the store, selecting a few ready-made gowns and, after a nod from Muriel to each, setting them on the counter. "If you wouldn't mind waiting for a couple of hours, we could have the dresses tailored for you and sent to the castle."

"I'm afraid we do not possess the time. But if you will add thread, needles, and scissors to the order, I can manage."

The dressmaker eyed her doubtfully. "Truly, Countess, I can have them ready in two hours. There is no need for you to tailor them yourself."

"Normally I would wait, but my husband and I are departing Draybridge at once." The dearness of the word *husband* bathed her heart. She glanced over her shoulder to the window where Erik stood with his back to the shop, speaking to Draybridge's baker on the opposite side of the street. Her stomach rumbled in anticipation of the baked goods Erik was surely purchasing to break their fast.

"Your husband!" Mrs. Wilson giggled. "So romantic. Yes, if you were married so quickly and quietly, I can understand your wish for being away." She followed Muriel's gaze to the unmentionables and nightgowns. The seamstress selected the frilliest of nightgowns with the loveliest lace and added them to the pile.

Muriel selected an emerald gown with a higher neckline and changed as quickly as possible, for every moment she lingered, Deverell and Lady Ingram got farther away from them. She knew from Erik's increased pacing on the other side of the shop's windows that she was taking too long. She settled her bill and hurried out of the store, the seamstress and the footman carrying five boxes between them to the coach. "I'm sorry it took me a quarter of an hour. I had to get a few things." At the stack piled on the seat, her cheeks heated further. He would think her a glutton, but a lady had needs.

"I should have thought of it and arranged for it while you were freshening up this morning." He pressed a kiss to her hand and helped her inside, settling beside her. "I know it was not the wedding you wished for. After this is all over, we will host a ball at the castle that will be spoken of for years to come."

"My lord! Your box."

Erik leaned out the window, retrieved a box from the baker, who was huffing from his trot across the street, and nodded his thanks to the man. He handed the box to Muriel. "But, to celebrate with my countess, I have purchased some cakes and savory pies for our wedding breakfast to eat on the way."

"Such a thoughtful husband you are." She smiled up at him and stole a kiss on his cheek, relishing their first quiet moments alone, despite the urgency.

"None of that now," he whispered, gently taking her face betwixt his hands, kissing her softly. "From now on, I expect you to kiss me properly. Every time."

She set aside the box, closed the distance between them, and kissed him until he growled and kissed the base of her neck. Her limbs weakened. With a trembling laugh, she scooted away from him—pleased at his protest and smoldering gaze that he had been as affected as she. But, now was not the time for such kisses. She retrieved the box and popped it open with a sigh of delight.

Baked goods consumed and remains set aside, she rested her head on his shoulder, comforted in his strength that they had done the right thing in wedding quickly. Her letters, in which she confirmed her marriage to her parents and friends, would reach London and Chilham in a few hours by courier. She prayed her parents would be happy for her . . . even though eloping was hardly the way to silence the society matrons. She closed her eyes against the scathing reports she was certain were already circulating in London's parlors regarding her disappearance from her own engagement party. *That doesn't matter. What matters is that we are both safe and wed.* She studied the emerald with the diamonds surrounding it.

"Do you like it?"

"Like? No. I adore it. What's the story behind it?" She curled her legs beneath her and leaned into his chest, holding out her ring to admire it.

"It belonged to the first Countess of Draycott." He traced the gem with his fingertip. "And, as much as I wish to stay this way with you, we are about to reach the port. Are you ready to talk about last night and what you learned about Lady Ingram's involvement? We need to make our plan."

"It all started when I snuck into the baron's bedroom." Muriel rushed through her scandalous tale, recalling as many details as she could that might benefit him, and all too soon, she heard the gulls as they approached the port of Southend-on-Sea where his ship stood, majestic in the lapping waters. The British flag's colors warmed her heart as it flapped jauntily above the dock, which bustled with sailors loading and unloading ships. At the stern, she spied the name *Twilight Lady*. Unlike the rest of the ships in the harbor, it looked as fresh as the day the ship was christened.

"Erik," she whispered. "What about your beard? Don't you usually grow it out more?"

"It will have to suffice." Erik hopped out and lifted his hands to her, keeping his hand at her elbow the moment her feet touched the ground, already vigilant in the open.

The salty wind tore at her skirts, and she had to slap a hand on her bonnet to save it from toppling as they rushed across the plank and boarded the ship.

"Captain Warrick." The man she guessed was second-in-command bowed to her husband. "Welcome back, sir."

"Adams." He returned the bow with a dip of his head and gently pulled Muriel forward, his gaze emphasizing the importance of her not forgetting his name. "Allow me to introduce you to my wife, Mrs. Warrick."

Mrs. Warrick? Her heart stuttered. She had only been thinking of herself as an earl's wife up until now with the threat on Erik's life and all, but the wife of his famed privateer alternate identity? The address left her rather breathless. *Will Father forgive me for marrying a privateer?* She bit her lip. *Well, he did say to marry a man of character, not just title, and Erik is the best sort of man.*

"Any word, Adams?" Erik accepted a sheet of paper from the young man.

"After we received your message regarding the identity of Requin's man, Deverell, and the lady spy, we sent scouts across London and to all of their estates. The pair of them have disappeared, Captain Warrick." Adams frowned, crossing his arms over his broad chest.

"You mentioned estates. Have you checked his cottage in Dover?" Muriel interjected.

The men looked to her.

"Why would we check there, Mrs. Warrick?" Adams asked, his tone kind but confused. "He doesn't have any holdings there, and we checked his warehouse."

"There is a chance he simply kept it not in his name, or under his other identity, but in his maternal grandmother's name. Perhaps if we find him, we will find Lady Ingram as well."

"That's brilliant. Do you remember where it is?" Erik asked.

"Oh yes. It is by the sea and quite the darling little place." Her cheeks flamed at the shocking admission. It had been another time, another place, when she had been infatuated with him. In Erik's care, she'd come to know true love. "After our drive to Dover, he mentioned he might wish to keep it, as it reminded him of where they came from as their title is relatively new, but that was the very reason his mother wished for him to sell it."

Erik nodded, his jaw clenching for half a second, betraying his ire at her knowledge of this and, no doubt, how she had come to that knowledge. "Very well. Set sail for Dover, Adams."

"Captain, I respectfully disagree." He nodded to Muriel, pressing his lips in an apologetic smile. "I have a man in Dover. Neither Deverell nor his men have been seen."

"Yes, but Mrs. Warrick knows the man in question. If there is a chance he is hiding out in his family's cottage, we need to follow through."

"Captain, I—"

Erik took a step toward him, narrowing his gaze. "Do *not* forget who is captain here, Adams."

Adams swallowed and ducked his head. "Yes, sir. I beg your pardon, sir." He turned on his heel and relayed the orders.

Erik grasped Muriel's elbow and guided her to the captain's cabin.

She paused with him outside the door, whispering, "I must apologize. I didn't mean to cause any contention between you and Adams, and I know how it must have made you feel to know that I knew—"

He drew her inside and closed the door. He pressed his lips to hers. "It matters not. I won."

She looked up at him. "But Deverell and Lady Ingram are not behind bars."

"You are mine and I am yours. Deverell has lost his hold on you forever."

Her stomach growled, ruining their perfect moment.

He ran his hand over the back of his neck. "In my zeal to keep you safe from Requin and his informants, I've neglected to provide more than just our breakfast. You are going to have to allow me to make it up to you once this business is concluded." He strode to the door. "I'll find something and bring you a tray. We should be arriving in Dover by this evening."

She took in the captain's cabin for the first time. Located at the stern of the ship, there was a bay window with a marvelous view of the dock as the ship sailed away, the workers and passengers milling about growing smaller and smaller as the sea overtook the distance. She imagined what it would be like to awaken to the sea each morning, for with this capture, he would surely be awarded another letter of marque to finish the job. She tsked over the sturdy, serviceable bedclothes in faded navy. Perhaps a shop in Dover would have something she could purchase straightaway while she ordered the fine cloth a man of Erik's station should have to dress his bed. She ran her fingers over the richly carved, stained paneled walls and burgundy curtains, smiling at the masculinity of it all. She couldn't, or rather shouldn't, change too much at once. A spot of color here or there would certainly add a much-needed touch of femininity.

A light tap sounded at the door, and Erik appeared with a heavy-laden tray piled with tea, a loaf of freshly baked bread, cheese, and fruits. He set the repast on the table that she discovered was bolted into the floor. At a quick perusal, it appeared all the furniture was bolted down besides the two chairs. She twisted her hands. She would hate to discover why that was the case. As a captain's wife, she needed to keep her fears to herself. Such a thing as a fear of storms would not do in convincing Erik that she was a worthy cabinmate. She smiled up at him. "Thank you, my husband."

He grinned at the name. "Normally we would not have fresh fruit after we leave the port, but unlike most voyages, we will reach our destination within hours. So, if you decide sailing isn't for you, you will not have to endure it for long, wife."

"Surely you do not think me so weak as to surrender so quickly?" She laughed and reached for the knife to slice the bread, the sawing of the hardened sourdough crust grating her ears.

Erik grimaced and acquired the knife from her. "You might, as our cook is less than proficient with the oven." He tore off the corner of the loaf and handed it to her before taking a piece for himself and snagging a slice of cheese. "I must see to my duties. Enjoy your luncheon, wife. I would suggest dunking your bread into the hot tea first. More than one sailor has chipped his tooth on Cook's fine bread."

She popped the fruit into her mouth, sweetening her lips before pressing a kiss to his cheek.

He crossed his arms, shaking his head. "My dear Mrs. Warrick, what did we just discuss about kissing?"

"How about you remind me, Captain Warrick?" She looked up at him through her lashes.

He reminded her. Thoroughly.

Goodness. Breathless, she smoothed back her hair. She would never grow used to kissing him whenever she pleased. "Have a good morning, husband."

She returned to the table, knocking the bread on the wooden surface. *It could be the cornerstone of a house.* She dusted off her hands. Well, she may not be of any use to anyone aboard the vessel, but she could certainly bake. Perhaps that would be the key for allowing her to set sail with Erik wherever his mission took him. After eating what she was able, she donned her most modest spencer and slipped out of the room. She nodded to any sailors in passing and searched until she found the ship's kitchen. The room was so cramped she wondered how a chef might produce a meal for a small family, much less a crew. A rotund man in a disgusting mottled apron perched atop an overturned barrel at the corner of the room. He was peeling a mound of potatoes as a young man beside him, in an equally revolting apron, washed them in filthy water before chopping them and plunking them into a pot of boiling water one by one. She inwardly grimaced at the sludge such a technique would produce.

The cook, spying her at last, scrambled to his feet and nodded to her. "You must be the captain's bride." He inclined his head. "Can I be of help to you, Mrs. Warrick?"

"Actually . . ." She examined the kitchen. It was in sore need of a good deep cleaning. Her focus landed on the stove, which was old and smaller than she had hoped. She had made do with less in a pinch. "I was hoping to help you."

He blinked. "Pardon?"

She nodded to the stove. "Would you mind if I tried baking something for the captain's table and crew?"

He grimaced, gesturing to his pile of potatoes he'd yet to peel. "I don't really have the time to teach you, Mrs. Warrick. I cannot be late with the crew's meal. They get mighty crabbed if I am."

She folded her hands before her skirts. "Allow me to give it a go this once, and if you abhor my baking, I promise I will never set foot in your kitchen again. I thought to start off with some simple rolls."

He sighed. "Seeing that you are my captain's wife, I can't rightly say no, as I have the ingredients."

Grinning, she rolled up the sleeves of her spencer and set to work, praying they would rise in time. After successfully baking enough rolls for the crew, the captain's table, and some for the cook to sample, she set to work on a simple cake. Every bride needed a wedding cake, but as she lacked enough time for icing and decorating, she decided upon the simplest of chocolate cakes dusted in powdered sugar.

As she carefully carried the finished cake to the cabin to await Erik's return from his duties, she caught her reflection in a small looking glass hanging above his desk and gritted her teeth at her unsightly hair. From the heat of the kitchen and a few hours of ocean air, her curls had turned positively feral. She reached for her brush to make herself presentable, longing not for the first time for her pretty pink muslin, or at least something more formfitting than the gown from the shop in Draybridge. She withdrew the delicate silk shawl and wrapped it about her shoulders for a bit of color. At the sound of boots outside the door, she assumed her seat at the table, arranging her hair just so as Erik stepped inside, looking dashing in his captain's coat.

His chocolate eyes widened at the sight of her hair down, flicking to the cake atop the table and back to her hair.

She twisted the lock hanging to her waist before her. "I know it is quite tempestuous. If you give me a moment, I can pin it up."

"I like it down." He reached out and twined a lock in his fingers. "It reminds me of the first time we met . . . when your braid flowed past your waist."

"I made you something."

His gaze lingered on her before he sat at the table as she sliced him a piece and waited for him to sample it before having her own.

"Divine. You are a wonder." He finished off the slice in an impressive five bites. "I'd love to linger, but I thought you'd like to see the coast.

We are approaching, and I remember you saying how you wished to see the cliffs of Dover from the sea—"

She squealed and shoved back the chair, grasping his hand as she ran for the door.

"What about the cake?"

"I'll make another!"

Chapter Thirty-One

As Erik studied the approaching white cliffs that rose from the angry waves crashing against the wall, he found himself wondering where in Dover his darling Muriel had spent lambing seasons on her grandfather's sheep farm. Judging from her awestruck reaction to the white cliffs as she sidled up next to him, the farm had been on the other side of Dover. She had promised to show him all after their adventure— from her grandfather's farm to her favorite girlhood haunts around the seaside town . . . but first, she had to take him to Deverell's cottage.

He had thought that when the time came to capture Requin, it would feel different—more fulfilling. In setting sail this morning, for the first time in his life, Erik didn't feel the exhilaration of setting sail for the next adventure. Instead, he felt a sense of urgency to conclude the mission in excellence so he could begin a new chapter with his bride. He rested his chin atop her wild curls and smiled. *Thank You, Lord, for this unanticipated blessing. Thank You for this new calling to be a husband, a leader in the village of Draybridge, and mayhap a father.*

Muriel pointed out a regal mansion perched in the hills beyond the cliffs. "That's my step-grandmother's home."

"Grandmother Fletcher? You never mentioned she lives in Dover and so close to the sea at that."

"Oddly enough, she actually enjoys sea bathing. On the other side of that cliff, there is a sturdy path chiseled out that winds down to a cove where I would spend most of my required visits with her after my mother's marriage. As much as I loved the sea, I would have been much happier working on my grandfather's farm on the northwest side of Dover than taking the waters with Grandmother Fletcher." She shivered from the wind breaking over the waves beneath the hull. "If it isn't too cold, I think sea bathing would be quite invigorating after this ordeal is behind us."

His arm encircled her waist, and he tucked her in front of him, wrapping his arms about her to keep her warm as they enjoyed the stunning view. As he breathed in her hair, which had grown even wilder since departing the cabin, he once again reminded himself that not only were they *not* alone, this was certainly not their wedding trip with his crew about.

First, they had spies to capture. And from what Muriel had told him of Lady Ingram on their carriage ride to the port, he feared who else might be behind the plot to see Napoleon in power—mayhap even Sir Alexander, though that made little sense. Erik had spent years at the captain's side, and he had known nothing but complete devotion to the Crown from the man. Sir Alexander had nearly died for his country while Lady Ingram was aboard the *Twilight Treader*. Surely she would not put the man she loved in danger for her cause? Would she? *She ordered my death when she knew me since my childhood . . . She is capable of anything.*

Within the hour, they weighed anchor. Erik climbed down the rope ladder into the skiff before aiding his new bride. He chuckled at her cloak whipping about her and flowing above her shoulders as if trying to return up the ladder and into the ship. "It seems your wardrobe doesn't wish to row ashore, and I can't say your visage says much differently. Are you afraid?"

"I feel I have been away for years after only a season with you. I'm not certain word of my change of fiancés has reached all in the village, and I am certain no one has heard of our marriage." She sank down beside him on the cold bench seat and snuggled into his shoulder, shivering. "What if the gossips inadvertently warn Deverell that I have returned? What if I am endangering the mission by selfishly coming with you?"

"I am glad I did not leave you behind. I would have worried every moment we were apart that Deverell had tricked me into leaving you, or that Lady Ingram would find a way to harm you." He wrapped his arm around her, leaning into her as his hand found hers. "As for your reputation, we have done nothing to be ashamed of."

"You mean besides our hasty marriage?"

"We had a common license, which actually takes some planning."

"Which there is nothing common about. I've scarcely heard of but one among my acquaintance."

"Common licenses are not as scandalous as special licenses, as they do take time to acquire, though not as much as a church wedding license. Take comfort in the fact that we have been nothing but the picture of propriety." But, at her heating neck, he knew she was thinking of their stolen kiss in her bedroom. A stolen kiss sounded quite nice. He settled for pressing his lips to her knuckles, ignoring the grins from the sailors rowing the boat to shore.

Muriel held her head high and her shoulders back as she ascended to the dock, her husband's reassuring hand at the small of her back, guiding her through the crowd of dockworkers as she led him toward the village stables.

She could have sent someone to her step-grandmother's estate for a carriage, but time was of the essence, and she ordered two mounts. As they were all the stablemaster had, it was decided a company of the strongest privateers would follow as soon as they procured a carriage from the Fletcher estate per Muriel's hastily scrawled note.

Muriel guided her horse to the road at a brisk pace with Erik at her side. She longed to kick her mount into a gallop, yet knowing to do so would raise an alarm, she settled for a trot through the town, waving and smiling in passing to any of her acquaintances, promising to explain her unexpected appearance soon. On the road leading to the white cliffs, she tossed her leg over the saddle horn and kicked her mount into a gallop, racing against the sun's descent. Despite her fear of losing control of the horse, she loved the freedom of the wind whipping through her hair with her husband by her side, only slowing when they reached the bottom of the hill that hid them from the view of any occupants of the cottage by the sea. She reined in her mount, signaling with her fist for Erik to do the same. She nodded to the horizon. "There's smoke coming from the chimney. Someone is home."

He scowled. "And you are certain it is usually vacant?"

"If he indeed kept it, he only ever used it when he was in port . . ." She worried her bottom lip. "Which I now believe means that he only used it when he was relaying messages to and from France through his tea trade. And remember, he did say something about tonight when he was in the billiards room, even if the log we found did not reflect it."

Erik guided his horse in front of hers. "I need you to stay here."

"But—"

He lifted his hand to her. "I cannot concentrate if you are in danger, which will put not only me in harm's way, but the mission as well."

She frowned. "True."

"So you agree you will stay here?"

Her horse shifted from hoof to hoof as if sensing her eagerness to join Erik. "Very well."

He turned his horse to stand alongside hers and pressed a deep kiss to her lips. "Time to put away a traitor." He kicked his mount and surged ahead, dismounting just before the crest of the hill.

She slid off her horse and stretched her legs and back, watching him until he disappeared. She at once grew eager for any sound from over the hill. She groaned and ripped up a clump of grass and handed it to her mount, petting his mane as he crunched the grass as loudly as if it were a carrot. "Why do I make promises when I know it will be nearly impossible to keep them?"

※

Shadows veiled Erik as he withdrew his double-barreled pistol, pressing himself against the cottage wall as he dodged the light streaming through the two front windows. He glanced back down the hill to ensure she was still hidden away and following her word. He shook his head. His wife may be stubborn, but she was not reckless.

"You failed me again." A woman's voice brought him to a halt beneath a broken windowpane.

Erik's neck bristled. He *knew* that voice. He slowly rose, daring to peek over the sill. His heart dropped at the sight of Lady Ingram sitting before the hearth in a rocking chair, scowling at Deverell, who was kneeling to stoke the fire. Erik sank down. He'd never doubted Muriel, though part of him had hoped there had been a misunderstanding. He'd admired Lady Ingram since he was a child—had thought her the most lovely lady alive.

"I poisoned her."

Lady Ingram snorted. "You gave the girl a stomach ailment. I knew you held her in affection, but to display such weakness in the face of Napoleon's rise to power? He will not be so forgiving of your taking such a risk with his campaign."

"I was going to retrieve her after I confirmed the earl's death, but the grounds were crawling with his people. When I returned for her, she had already escaped."

Erik squinted in the deepening twilight, trying to make out the shed Muriel had mentioned. He needed to advance before he lost his advantage. He'd just shifted his stance, when a metallic click at his ear rooted him to the ground.

"Looks like we have caught ourselves an earl." Deverell chuckled from the window, his pistol aimed through the missing pane.

"Dash it all." Lady Ingram darted through the front door, raised her dagger, and smashed the butt of it into Erik's skull.

♛

Erik blinked, the room coming into focus. He was tied to a chair. Lady Ingram was speaking with Deverell as he paced the room.

"Finally." Lady Ingram crossed the room to him, tugging his gag free. "If you call for help, I'll gut you where you sit."

"Why? Why would you betray your country?" he croaked, finding his throat impossibly dry from being gagged. "Your husband? Or is he part of Requin's ring as well?"

She ran her finger down his jaw in a maternal fashion. "I wish you would have stayed away. Why did you have to become so involved? I made certain to stab you in the shoulder to keep you safe, you foolish boy."

"You?" His jaw dropped, recalling the slight man from the ship . . . but it hadn't been a man at all. "*You* stabbed me?"

She chuckled. "It is maddening how you men think you are the only ones capable of expert swordsmanship. Yes, I wounded you when I could have easily ended your life."

He glared at her. "You were a spy long before I took over the *Twilight Treader* and the name of Warrick, weren't you?"

She shrugged, flipping the dagger from hand to hand. "My father was the original Warrick, the most fearsome pirate to roam the seas before he was offered a letter of marque from the king himself. Although my father may have bent the rules more often than not, the Crown made an exception for the man who brought in three times as many prize ships, thwarting their attempts to aid the American colonies in their revolution—a fact that my French mother abhorred. But I was in awe of my father at the time. He taught me the skill of the rapier, and it was my dearest wish to follow in his footsteps. He should have named his daughter, the one who sailed with him since birth, as his successor. Women pirate captains were not unheard of. But no. He wished to keep his name alive through a *man*, so, when he was ready to retire, he gave his name to my sailor."

"Sir Alexander? He was a sailor for your father?"

She laughed. "He wasn't even a high-ranking sailor. But I loved him. So my father allowed him to take over the family business with me safely in the background just like my mother. My husband decided to take the *Twilight Treader* in a new direction. And when the war with France began, my husband was much too trusting of me, a woman of French descent. Well, I learned my mother had not sat idly by all those years after all, and she brought me into her secret world of spies, where Requin was born."

"Your mother is Requin?" Erik's mind spun. "I thought she was dead."

"Since you will not be making it out of here alive, I suppose it won't hurt to tell you. Yes, she was the original Requin." She smirked. "She was our washerwoman in Grosvenor Square until she passed the month before you became captain. While my father, the original Warrick, would not allow me to inherit his kingdom on the sea, my mother laid the groundwork for me to assume the identity of Requin upon her death."

No wonder Requin had always evaded Sir Alexander during his time as Captain Warrick . . . Requin was Lady Ingram's aged mother, who was always in London but in the background, never to be seen by Sir Alexander. Posing as a servant—the perfect way for her to gather information—to remain unseen.

"I would pass my mother notes in my laundry containing any information my husband confided in me over the course of our marriage. When Napoleon became Emperor of France a decade ago, Requin began sending the missives through her web of spies to Napoleon himself. Napoleon was quite grateful for our loyalty and even went as far as to invite us to his palace."

Erik's jaw slacked. "And yet your mother chose to remain a washerwoman."

"Her devotion to our emperor knew no bounds." She sighed. "But her sudden death flustered me. I asked too many questions about Alexander's work, and he began to grow suspicious that I had changed my loyalties. I feared I would be compromised. So I fed my husband that French ship to make him a knight, and, for good measure, I made certain he broke his leg in the skirmish, ending all our days on the sea. It was difficult for me to leave the sea, but it was better than being caught and fitted for the noose."

Erik frowned. "And when I took over?"

She shrugged. "That was when my reign began in earnest. You were entirely too trusting, as we had known each other since you were a cabin boy. Thus, I hosted you every moment I was able. You would tell your old captain all the details, and when I plied my husband with enough drink to loosen his lips, I too became privy to that information. It was relatively easy to continue to assist Napoleon's cause. However, I grew tired of you ruining my father's legacy and started to sow the seeds of doubt in Alexander's mind about your competency as captain of the *Twilight Treader*."

"You were behind everything." His chest heaved as pieces shifted and formed a whole picture. "You were pushing for Adams to take over, weren't you?"

She laughed and squatted by the fire, letting her knife be licked by the flames. "Well, my father did want it to stay in the family. I discovered he had an illegitimate daughter and she had borne a son. I found him working aboard a merchant ship. By then you had long been captain, so I convinced Alexander to champion Adams as your second-in-command. It was only a matter of timing to begin my campaign for Alexander to change his loyalties to my nephew. We decided not to tell you of his relation to me, and I made Adams swear to remain silent on the matter, lest the identity of the true Warrick became known."

"Adams may be strong willed, but he is no traitor," Erik growled.

She whipped away from the fire and pointed the amber blade at Erik, smiling at his instinctive flinch. "Not *yet*. By the time I win Adams this position, he will kneel before me and do whatever I bid. Napoleon will reward us generously for aiding him in England's defeat."

"And Deverell? How did you bring him into the secret circle of Requin?"

Lady Ingram smiled up at Deverell. "His ambition led him to me, and he became the son I never had." She narrowed her gaze at Erik.

"Unlike you, who grew too proud to listen to my dear husband's advice, which was, in reality, my advice. Unfortunately, it's time for you to step down as Captain Warrick and into a grave. I will allow you the courtesy of choosing your demise, bullet or drowning?"

"I vote bullet." Deverell aimed his pistol at Erik's temple. "With you out of the way, Muriel will remember her love for me once more."

Chapter Thirty-Two

"Shouldn't he be back by now?" Muriel paced the road, craning her neck to look up the hill yet again. But it was growing so dark that she didn't think she could spot him even if he were riding down to her. She cracked her knuckles and continued pacing. "Three quarters of an hour is far too long for anything good to have happened. Wouldn't you agree, Brutus?" She held out another fistful of grass. The horse eyed her warily, chomping on the grass. "I'll take that as a yes."

Dropping the reins, she patted the gelding's neck, requesting he wait for her before she scampered up the hill to the cottage. She crouched behind the bushes and squinted in the moonlight. Through the illuminated window, she spotted three forms, one of whom was affixed to a chair before the fireplace with a gun pressed to his temple.

Erik. She fought the urge to scream. She whipped about, searching in vain hope of finding a weapon, her gaze landing on the shed. Deverell had once told her that's where he stored his extra-special blends of tea, and she had believed him. But what if his extra-special tea was something else entirely? Bending as low as her skirts allowed, she bolted for the shed. The door was locked, but the window slid open. Muriel hiked her skirts to her thighs and hoisted herself through the opening, scrambling, her knees banging against the frame before she finally flopped hands-first inside, collapsing over a barrel. She groaned as she shoved herself to standing. It was one of dozens. Each barrel was carefully stenciled with the name of an exotic tea that Deverell had spent his life curating. Not for the first time, she wondered, *Why would he ship bricks of tea in barrels? Wouldn't a crate be better?*

She glanced about for something to open the barrels and found a crowbar planted in the packed earth beneath the window. If she hadn't landed on the barrel, it would have impaled her. *What nincompoop stores a crowbar thus?*

She grasped the crowbar, tugged it free from the earth, and wrenched open the nearest lid, finding blocks of tea. She dug through the first layer, grimacing as she dumped the precious bricks on the floor, until she reached the second layer, which was blocked by a cylinder of wood, black powder clinging to the edges. She attempted to pry it open with her fingertips, but it appeared to have been glued in place. Seeing no other recourse, she lifted the crowbar overhead like an axe and, closing her eyes, she smashed it onto the wood, splintering it. The scent of sulfur wafted to her, making her gag against the stench of rotten eggs. She flung aside the debris and gasped at the sight of gunpowder, which brought another round of gagging. Digging out her handkerchief, she covered her nose and surveyed the shed. If the rest of the barrels were full of gunpowder, there was enough in here to blow up a palace. *What is Deverell up to?* Here she'd thought all he was doing was passing messages back and forth in his bricks of tea, but this, this was something else entirely. *Either he is supplying the enemy with gunpowder, or there is a plot to blow up something to aid Napoleon's cause.* She pried open a second barrel, smashing another cylinder layer to find more gunpowder.

As much as she wished to look through all the barrels, what she needed was a weapon to help rescue Erik. She squinted in the dark for something useful and spied what she needed lining the back wall, nearly concealed behind the barrels. Gathering her skirts, she carefully crawled over the barrels to find rows upon rows of what she instantly recognized as double-barreled flintlock pistols, along with stores of ammunition. She eased one from the rack on the wall and attempted to load it as Vivienne had taught her during her bout of hands-on research for a novel about an English lady and a Frenchman who secretly worked for England. But the pistol was already loaded and ready to shoot. A quick check proved the rest were loaded as well. The hair stood up on the back of her neck.

She was standing in a powder keg that was primed to go off if she so much as dropped a pistol. *Why on earth would Deverell keep these loaded?* Her hands shook as a plan formed in her mind. She was a terrible shot, but she only needed the traitors to think the house was under attack. She needn't aim anywhere near Erik if they believed her and surrendered peacefully.

Taking the smallest barrel of gunpowder, she rolled it out of the shed a good distance and smashed a hole in the barrier layer. She sprawled on the ground, waiting to be found out. Nothing. Scrambling to her feet, she drew a line of gunpowder along the cliffs to the cottage's woodpile, which, once ignited, would illuminate the coast and sound the alarm. With her arms loaded with guns, she painstakingly raced back and forth to the overgrown rose garden just outside the cottage until all thirty weapons were ready and piled in wait. *This is madness! This is madness!* her footsteps seemed to chant. "You are a baker, not a heroine," she moaned to herself.

Knowing from experience her shooting was just as poor if her eyes were open or closed, she whispered another prayer that she wouldn't shoot herself in her attempt to save the man she loved. "God help us all." She aimed for the cottage roofline, closed her eyes, and pulled the trigger.

⚜

A bullet shattered the vase atop the mantel. Erik rocked his chair to the left and threw himself to the stone floor along with the rest of the occupants as a series of bullets pelleted the room.

After the tenth shot, a husky masculine voice shouted, "We have you surrounded. Release Captain Warrick or die with him."

Lady Ingram's eyes widened, her fear plain. "Surrounded?" Lady Ingram hissed to Deverell. "Where are the guns you are storing? We need to fight our way out of here."

Five shots fired in rapid succession, smashing the china dishes in the open cupboard, the blue and white shards flying across the room. Erik winced as a shard dug into his lower back.

"In the shed. I was loading them before you arrived to ensure all were working properly before shipping them to the troops," Deverell explained, ducking as another round of bullets planted themselves in the mantel.

"What? That is madness."

"It is my first time smuggling guns. Besides, seagulls have always annoyed me and make wonderful targets."

Lady Ingram growled. "Loaded guns in the same place where you store the gunpowder? What were you thinking?"

"We are running out of patience," the man outside shouted again. Erik still did not recognize the voice.

"Obviously, the loaded guns were not supposed to stay there! I didn't know it was you approaching in the carriage, and I did not want to be discovered with an arsenal. I panicked." Deverell grunted and rose to his knees, shouting through the jagged gap in the window, "Cease your firing. Would you kill your own in your pursuit of Requin?"

"Our captain knew the risks. The privateer is a hero and is ready to die for his country. Are you ready to die for Napoleon? I doubt he will even hear of your passing, much less mourn it."

Five more shots fired, Lady Ingram screaming as one found its mark in her calf. "Deverell!"

Deverell scowled, drawing his pistol as he crawled to her and pressed his handkerchief to her wound. "What say you? Are we so weak as to surrender it all now, Lady Requin? When we are so close to ending this war?"

"My man outside is right. You would die for Napoleon?" Erik panted, shaking the shards of glass from his coat, save the one embedded. "We can work out a story. Say you were forced via blackmail. If you report your mother was the famous French spy—"

"You would have me turn on my own blood? A woman who should be lauded a heroine? No. I would rather die than turn on my Requin.

She recognized my talent. She made me who I am today." She pressed the cloth to her leg, panting. "We will call their bluff and use Draycott for leverage. Use him as our shield and get us out of here, Deverell. I guarantee you they will not shoot their own."

Deverell looked between Erik and Lady Ingram, hesitating. "I say blackmail is best."

She narrowed her gaze at him. "I may be injured, but I am still Requin. I say we use him."

Five more shots. "Last chance. Surrender now, or you all die."

Lady Ingram nodded to Erik. "Answer your sailor."

Whoever it was, it wasn't his sailor. He nodded and Deverell untied him. "This is Captain Warrick. They agree!" he shouted. "Hold your fire. I'm coming out now."

Lady Ingram gripped a pistol, thrusting it in his back. "Do not test me, Erik. As much as I loved you, one wrong move, and I'll put a bullet in your pretty head myself."

🐚

Muriel pried open her eyes, keeping her place behind the rose bushes as her finger trembled on the trigger. She had only five shots left. She cleared her voice and reached inside for the voice she used to tell her brothers stories of such absurdity that they wouldn't sleep for nights on end. "Captain Warrick, tie them up and come forward."

"I don't think so," Lady Ingram returned, backing to the cliff where Muriel knew there was a path that led down to the sea, where they no doubt had a boat docked.

It was all lost unless she proved she had the upper hand. *Where are those blasted privateers? The traitors are getting too far away!* Three paces more and they would be on the cliff path and away with her love. They might even shove him to his death. With shaking hands, she aimed her gun at the line of powder. *Lord, please, please, please don't let me wound anyone.* She blasted the gun to the line, igniting it and exploding the barrel and the firewood into an inferno.

Lady Ingram shrieked, falling to her knees and releasing her hold on Erik, who bolted toward Muriel's hiding place. Deverell recovered quickly and pursued on Erik's heels, rapier drawn. With a shriek, Muriel aimed and sent dirt flying at Deverell's feet. Aiming a second time, she shot, the bullet striking Deverell's foot. Screaming, the baron collapsed as Erik secured the traitor's rapier and pistol. Muriel drew a deep breath, preparing to stand, when a carriage sounded on the road below her. The crew leapt out of the carriage, surrounding Lady Ingram and Deverell.

Shoulders sagging in relief, she grabbed a fresh pistol and emerged from the bushes.

"Muriel?" Deverell gasped, spitting the dirt from his mouth as he was jerked to standing on his good foot by Warrick's men. "How could you do this to me? You loved me once. I was going to marry you."

Erik strode to her side and wrapped her in his arms and, ignoring the sharp pain radiating from his lower back, kissed her until she bent backward. When he broke away at last, he turned to Deverell. "And because you let her live, I will return the favor." He nodded to his guards. "Toss him in the brig."

"Horatio! My sweet nephew, save me!" Lady Ingram cried, reaching out to Adams with bloodied fingers as crewmen seized her.

Erik tensed, reaching for the pistol in Muriel's grip. Adams did not notice as he strode to Lady Ingram's side.

Adams halted a pace away and just stared at the woman. "Aunt Rebecca? I hardly believed it when I read that you were the lady spy. I prayed it was a mistake."

"Command your men to release me."

His shoulders slumped. "Even if I could, I would not. You are a traitor."

Anger flooded her features. "Horatio Adams, would you allow your own aunt to hang? After all I've done for you. You were nothing before I found you—before I gave you the position of second-in-command."

"You are beyond my help, madam." Adams swiped his sleeve over his eyes. "You are no aunt of mine. Lock her in the brig with Deverell." He strode to Erik and grimaced at the shard sticking out from his back. "Captain, let's get you to the ship's doctor."

Chapter Thirty-Three

STANDING BEFORE HER PARENTS, ERIK held Muriel's hand in the library of Draycott Castle as sounds of merriment from their marriage ball flowed through the heavy mahogany door.

"No one outside of the inner circle will ever know the truth of your daughter's daring rescue of me and the capture of one of the most notorious smugglers in the war against Napoleon. But the Prince Regent himself has written to thank her for her service."

"The Prince Regent?" Father's hands trembled as he accepted the letter from Erik.

"Such bravery." Mother held a handkerchief to her eyes. "And such danger. I expect you to take better care of my daughter in the future."

"I intend to." He looked at Muriel. "Even though I was offered another contract from the Prince Regent after this capture, I have decided that I will not be accepting it. I planned on returning *Twilight Treader* to a merchant vessel only, but Sir Alexander was so distraught over his wife's betrayal that he secured the letter of marque himself. He will be Warrick once more and attempt to alleviate some of the damage Lady Ingram caused. With my bride at my side, I intend to focus on Draybridge village and my holdings here."

"Thank the good Lord," Mother murmured.

Mr. Fletcher grasped her hand. "Indeed. The life of a privateer is not what I wish for my only daughter. There is such a thing as too much adventure."

"Agreed." Erik chuckled. "And to keep my new bride from becoming excessively bored, I have purchased the bakery in the village for her to manage as a wedding present."

Muriel gasped as she threw herself into his arms, knocking him back a good six inches. "Truly? The owner did not mind?"

"I paid him a small fortune. He will live out the rest of his days in luxury along the coast, nearer to his only child and his grandchildren."

"I have married the best of men." She pecked his lips even though she wished to kiss him properly. *Oh why not? That is our rule after all.*

Father shifted, clearing his throat at Muriel's display of affection.

"As heroic as your tale has been, we had best allow the countess to return to her duties, lest word circulate she is not fit for the job," Mother interjected, rising with Muriel's stepfather.

Given the dazed grin he was sporting, Erik didn't seem to mind her kisses.

"You are quite right, Mother." Muriel straightened her tiara and, on the arm of her husband, strolled out into the crowd of well-wishers, many of whom were the gentry and friends from Chilham who were staying in the castle for a weeklong house party.

"Everything is stunning, Muriel!" Elena grasped her hands. "Who could have imagined such an ending to our dear house party—you married to the earl and me betrothed to Lord Traneford! For my part in your romance, you must host my wedding at Draycott Castle to properly thank me."

Before Muriel could respond, Elena was swept away by Lord Traneford to dance the Scottish reel and another couple approached, offering Muriel and Erik their felicitations.

The ostentatious wedding reception party was grand enough to silence even the worst of England's gossips, but she could take no credit. Vivienne and Tess had kept her away from any and all planning. They declared that as a new bride, Muriel needed to enjoy these fleeting first days of wedlock with Erik, tucked away in their own wing of the castle. She had happily obliged on the condition that she bake the cakes and pastries for the party.

After an hour of exchanging niceties, Muriel grasped her punch glass and escaped out to the torchlit balcony, joining Vivienne and Tess in their own private celebration. "So, ladies, what do you intend to do for the whole of the summer now that the London season has concluded?" Muriel rested her palms on the rail, breathing in the delightfully cool air.

Vivienne sighed. "I'm afraid my stepbrother's wife is ready for me to return to oversee her saucy bantlings." She shuddered and sipped from her glass.

"You mean your nephews?" Tess giggled, nudging her, even though they all knew what tyrants the little boys were, as they took after their mother and father's treatment of their poor relation.

She shrugged. "Upon their arrival home, they expect me to return at once and teach the children while their tutor is on holiday for the summer."

Muriel grimaced. "Perhaps I can have Erik busy your brother and his family in London for you?"

Her eyes widened with hope. "That would be marvelous. It would give me the time I need to finish this next novel. My public is clamoring for more, and between all the excitement here and my family arranging my life for me, it has been difficult to find a quiet moment to write the novel I've been aching to since discovering your husband's profession."

Muriel scowled. "You cannot possibly pen a privateer novel."

"And why not? I have the best source available to me, and besides, I write under a nom de plume." She pressed her lips into a fake pout. "You wouldn't ask your dearest friend to ignore such a wealth of muse when she has been sorely in need of inspiration? Especially when she is so close to making her living from her writing?" She sighed. "Can you imagine my life away from my stepbrother's family?"

Muriel rubbed her forehead. "You may ask Erik. I cannot promise you that he will agree to disclose much, given the delicate nature of the matter."

"And what about you, Tess?" Vivienne asked. "Any plans?"

"With my father constantly away in Scotland, what plans could I have? I shall follow along with whatever you two have in mind. I have no aunts to host me, or cousins to squire me about town, and I refuse to hire a companion just to satiate polite society's expectations of an heiress on her own."

Muriel snorted. "I'm not so certain I would thwart polite society after my series of misadventures."

"Well, I'm not planning on proposing to anyone . . . especially one who turned out to be a traitor to his country and gunpowder supplier to the French."

Muriel frowned. "Will I never be free from that shame?"

Tess grinned. "Society will forget, thanks to your marriage, but *we* never will. We shall always have it in our reticule to pull out whenever we have a need to tease you, should your countess head grow too big for your crown."

"But that shall never happen, given your sweet nature." Vivienne patted Muriel's hand. "We must not keep you from the party much longer, Countess. It is time for you to find your earl and have that dance."

Muriel could not keep her smile from spreading when Erik spotted her across the ballroom floor. His entire countenance altered when he was aware of her presence, as if he couldn't wait to be near her. Her handsome husband excused himself from his conversation and wove through the guests to greet her, his hand at once finding the small of her back in such a familiar fashion it sent shivers down her spine.

"Where did you disappear to?" he whispered into her hair with a discreet kiss to her ear.

"Vivienne and Tess."

He nodded in understanding, as he had become accustomed to seeing them flock together.

The doors to the ballroom burst open, the butler announcing, "Ladies and gentlemen, His Royal Highness, the Prince Regent."

☙

His wife's pulse quickened as her grip on his hand tightened in the most alarming fashion. "You've met him before, my love. He thought you were quite charming."

"I know I've met him, Erik, but I'm supposed to be the hostess, and as this is my first formal evening, I have yet to discover what to do and not do."

"Don't propose to anyone," Erik whispered.

She rolled her eyes. "Very droll and seeing as I am wed to you, I won't be doing any such thing in the near future."

"Just be yourself, my darling, and he will find you perfectly delightful."

"Wonderful advice if being myself did not usually render me in the most unpleasant of situations," she muttered.

"I'd hardly say hosting the Prince Regent at your wedding ball is an unpleasant situation," he teased, loving watching the purse of her lips.

The Prince Regent strode into the room amid a wave of curtsies and bows as he passed, nodding to his subjects as he came to stand before Erik and Muriel. Erik bowed as his wife dipped into a flawless curtsy.

"Earl and Countess of Draycott." The Prince Regent inclined his head and grasped Muriel's hand, waiting for her to rise to her full height before leaning forward and whispering, "I have much to thank you for, Countess. The people of England will never know the depth of your service, but I intend on honoring you *both* for your heroic act." He released her and clasped Erik's hand before turning to the whispering crowd. "For services rendered in Lord Draycott's time at sea, I hereby introduce the *Duke* and *Duchess* of Draycott."

Muriel fumbled, and if Erik's hand had not caught her waist, she would have sunk to the ground in a faint. His chest pounded in the same panic. He had only just grown accustomed to being called an earl . . . but a duke? He managed to set aside his shock and accept the cheers with a bow as he thanked the Prince Regent most heartily, his arm still around his bride as she collected herself.

"I—I do not know how to thank you." Muriel rested her hand on Erik's chest as if drawing strength from him.

"You've already thanked me enough with your heroic act, Your Grace. Now, if you'll excuse me, I hear that you bake the finest cake in all the land, and I must claim my piece to see for myself. Who knows, if it is as delicious as they say, I may need to have you bake my birthday cake come August." The Prince Regent winked and moved into the throng of guests, all clamoring for his attention in the wake of his grand announcement.

Vivienne and Tess joined their side, Mr. and Mrs. Fletcher close behind.

Mrs. Fletcher grasped her daughter's arm. "Was that because of . . . ?"

Erik nodded. "You have an extraordinary daughter, and I'm honored to call her my duchess."

"The Duchess of Draycott Castle." Muriel rested her head against his shoulder. "Who would have ever imagined this for the earl who wanted nothing more than to sail upon the high seas and the simple baker from Chilham seeking her happily ever after."

Epilogue

THE WEDDING CELEBRATION BALL WAS grander than she had ever expected, especially with the Prince Regent in attendance. But strolling into the village at dawn with her husband at her side for a morning of baking, she could not imagine a more beautiful, romantic setting. She threaded her arm through his. "Are you certain you wish to spend your first day as duke with me in the bakery?"

He grinned down at her. "As long as you don't accidentally knock me out with a rolling pin and a tin of flour, yes. Nothing is equal to your baking, my duchess, and I pray you will never stop providing me with such delights." He tilted her chin upward to press a kiss upon her lips. "Now, remember, you promised me a quiche Lorraine for breakfast and then Shrewsbury cakes to take home with our meat pies."

She laughed and caught his hand in hers, pressing a kiss atop it. "I won't forget."

The village was slowly waking. Some villagers stumbled to a halt at the sight of their duke and duchess, especially with Muriel wearing an apron, but most villagers simply nodded to them in passing, as all had chores to occupy their attention at this hour. She reached into her apron's pocket and retrieved the skeleton key and unlocked the shop door. The jingling of the copper bell overhead sent excitement flooding through her veins. Her shop in Chilham was serviceable, but this bakery was a thing of beauty with the marble counters that Erik had ordered installed and the beautiful pale pink silk wall coverings. He had transformed the simple bakery into a confection itself. It would be a pleasure to fill up the new display case and the pretty white shelves behind the counter.

Erik caught her about the waist and twirled her over the brick pavers of the shopfront. "Is it pleasing?" He gently rested her on her feet.

"You have transformed it. I am certain the villagers and any guests touring the region will be pleasantly surprised to find such luxury this far from London. I am beyond happy." Muriel wound her arms about his neck, admiring his broad shoulders and raw strength, basking in the love shining through his dark eyes. "I never thought such joy might belong to me. For years, I saw friends whisked away to happy marriages, with babies soon filling their arms. I have never felt such longing before."

"One day we will have children filling the castle. Would five be to your liking?"

She grinned up at him. "I was hoping for a baker's dozen."

He drew her deeper into his arms, pressing his lips to hers that held the promise for more. "Then a baker's dozen it shall be. I thought when my time at sea ended, my life's adventures would be concluded, but it seems as if our adventures are only just beginning, my duchess."

"Indeed, my duke." She rested her head upon Erik's chest, the blessings of the Lord filling her being. "The Lord has taken my folly and redeemed it, turning it into a crown of lovingkindness and such tender mercies that I could never have imagined. And I cannot wait to see what the Lord has in store for us next."

Author's Note

DEAR READER,

Thank you so much for joining me for my very first Regency romance in the Best Laid Plans series! I hope you have enjoyed this story as much as I loved writing it.

I have to admit, as a writer, taking the leap back in time from the American Gilded Age to Regency England was rather terrifying, but also a grand, challenging adventure with a fantastic excuse to make my husband watch all the delightful Jane Austenesque films and to collect the most delightful research books for the time period.

As with all my novels, I attempted to stay as close to historical details as possible, but I decided to create the fictional village of Draybridge for our dear earl. Using research and Regency-era maps, I endeavored to create a village that truly felt like it could have existed. As for the places Muriel visits in England, most of them are real. Vauxhall Gardens was a pleasure garden created in the 1700s. For the purposes of this story, I did open the gardens a month before their usual June opening because it was just too priceless of a gem not to include. As for the Montagu House Museum, the original home of the British Museum, it did indeed require written application for tickets. Unlike in my story, they usually limited the number of visitors to ten people per hour. I had Requin break the system for the day in order to leave the warning note undetected. If you are curious to see the places Muriel visits for yourself, check out my Pinterest board for any pictures I collected in my online research at Pinterest.com/grace_hitchcock.

While Baron Osmund Deverell is a fictional character, the war between France and England was rife with spies and plots against the Prince Regent and England. I took my inspiration from some of those conflicts. As for Captain Erik Draycott's occupation, while not as popular as it had been, privateering was indeed used in the war against Napoleon. In times of need, merchant vessels were outfitted with wooden guns and fake cannons in shows of strength to encourage peaceful surrenders of French vessels. This allowed for the privateers to make the most money in their prizes, which, once captured, were brought to port and heavily taxed. However, the captured ships had to have a reasonable level of proof of being a supplier to the enemy to warrant capture. If privateers did not report a prize in full or wrongfully attacked innocent ships, they were considered no better than pirates. They would have their licenses revoked and be sentenced to death. As you can imagine, it was a different sort of fighting, which led me to think that Erik would indeed wish to keep his identity as a privateer separate from society's knowledge. And the idea of a legendary legacy pirate was born.

If you enjoyed the novel, please take a moment to leave a review on your favorite bookish website. If you want more updates on where I am in the writing process, behind-the-scenes news, and exclusive giveaways, join my newsletter list on GraceHitchcock.com.

Stay tuned for Vivienne Poppy's journey to love in the second book of the series! Happy reading, friends!

Acknowledgments

It has been a joy and an honor to write these novels for my readers and Kregel Publications, a dream publisher whom I have long admired.

To my heartthrob of a husband, Dakota, it took years for us to find one another in the world, but angels sang the moment I first beheld you. Thank you for being my love, my dearest friend, and constant inspiration.

To my sweet babies on earth and in Jesus's arms, I love you with all my heart and am so proud of you.

To my family: Dad, Mama, Charlie, Molly, Sam, Natalie, Eli, and nephews, thank you for always being so supportive of my writing.

To the team at Kregel, my acquisitions editor, and senior editor, thank you for all your hard work in bringing Muriel's story to further life! You are amazing, and I am thrilled to be a Kregel author!

To my agent, Tamela Hancock Murray, thank you for your dedication in helping me build my writing career and for your constant encouragement.

To the reader, thank you for reading Muriel Beau's story. I hope you enjoyed my first ever Regency romance novel.

And to the Lord, thank You for being with me through every doubt, for being my place of confidence, for guiding me, and loving me through every rocky moment. You are my joy and forever love!

Secret Recipe for Muriel's Scones

My mama and I love to bake together, and in our pursuit of the perfect scones, we created the following secret recipe that has been a sensation at parties for the past decade. It makes about 24–30 scones. Enjoy!

4 cups all-purpose flour
1 cup granulated sugar
2 teaspoons baking powder
½ teaspoon baking soda
¼ teaspoon salt
¼ teaspoon cream of tartar
2 teaspoons pure vanilla extract
1 cup sour cream
½ cup melted butter
1 egg
1–1½ cups dried cherries

Preheat the oven to 375°.

After combining and stirring all dry ingredients, form a hole in the flour mixture and fill it in with the remaining ingredients, only mixing in the egg after the butter is cooled enough not to cook the egg.

Using your hands, gently mix together the ingredients, being careful to mesh the melted butter into the mix. If the dough feels dry, add more softened butter (1 tablespoon at a time).

Flour the counter before rolling and *folding* the dough.

- Tip: The secret to perfect scones is the mixing process of folding. Be careful NOT to knead the dough, as it will overwork the scones and cause them not to rise.

Fold three to four times and then roll the dough for cutting.

Select a cup or cookie cutter with the desired diameter (preferably 2–2½ inches).

Refold and roll remaining dough to finish cutting.

Place scones on greased cookie sheet about 2 inches apart. Bake for 13 to 18 minutes or until the tops of the scones become a very light golden color.

While scones are baking, prepare the Lemon Glaze.

2 cups powdered sugar
1 teaspoon lemon extract
2 tablespoons lemon juice
1 teaspoon water

Combine in a small bowl and stir vigorously with a whisk or fork until the mixture reaches a smooth, thick consistency.

Allow scones to cool for five minutes, then use a spoon to apply the glaze to the top of each scone, and enjoy!

More Tips

- The dried cherries can be substituted with dried cranberries, apricots, or blueberries.
- For extra sweetness, add ½ cup white chocolate chips.
- Unbaked scones can be frozen, but baking time will be longer if not thawed.

About the Author

GRACE HITCHCOCK IS THE AWARD-WINNING author of multiple historical novels and novellas, including the Aprons & Veils series. She holds a master's in creative writing and a bachelor of arts in English with a minor in history. Grace lives on the Northshore of New Orleans, with her husband, sons, and daughter in a cottage that is always filled with the sounds of sweet little footsteps running at full speed. When not writing or chasing babies, she's baking something delightful and can usually be found with a book clutched in her fist.